KATE'S WORLD

MIKE—The husband who walks out on her one day and never comes back. His note reads: "It's too lonely living with you. I'm really sorry."

BELINDA—The bitter, defiant daughter Kate's in danger of losing on her way to the top.

CHUCK—The sex god who uses her to beat a morals charge and rebuild his career... by offering her something resembling passion.

WOMEN TODAY—The deliciously all-knowing women's magazine that has all the answers... for everyone but Kate.

"Sex, violence, sex, gossip, sex, drama. The book's gorgeous."

Cindy Adams' column "Cindy Says"

IN PLACE
OF
LOVE

Aviva Hellman

BANTAM BOOKS · TORONTO · NEW YORK · LONDON

This low-priced Bantam Book
has been completely reset in a type face
designed for easy reading, and was printed
from new plates. It contains the complete
text of the original hard-cover edition.
NOT ONE WORD HAS BEEN OMITTED.

IN PLACE OF LOVE

A Bantam Book/published by arrangement with
G. P. Putnam's Sons

PRINTING HISTORY
Putnam edition published January 1978
Bantam edition/July 1979

ISBN 0-553-12046-8

Published simultaneously in the United States and Canada

PRINTED IN THE UNITED STATES OF AMERICA

To Norma Lee Clark,
my friend and agent

1

Kate climbed the stairs slowly. She had worked the night shift at the Dayton *Chronicle* and the fatigue that set in after the final edition was put to bed had caught up with her. She paused as she reached the landing before last and transferred her huge tote bag from one arm to the other. The hall was dimly lit and as Kate looked up the stairs leading to her apartment they appeared steep and uninviting. The stifling heat of the day could still be felt in the darkened stairway and the odor of rotting wood mingling with the humidity made Kate feel ill. Vaguely she realized she had not eaten all day, but she was sure Mike would have something ready for her. She took a deep breath and started up the last flight of stairs.

Slowly the sound of a child crying hysterically

pierced her tired brain. It took a minute for her to realize where the sound was coming from, and then she leaped up the stairs two at a time, dropping her bag as she ran. Kate was now aware that she had been hearing Belinda crying since she opened the vestibule door downstairs. Reaching her door, she turned the knob and to her horror found it locked. She rattled the handle furiously and the tiled nameplate Mike had nailed to the door came crashing down. She looked down, dazed, and saw the tile had broken in two. Her name, printed in bold black letters, was visible on one part and MICHAEL CAMERON on the other. She started to bang on the door with her fists.

"Mike," she yelled frantically, oblivious to the lateness of the hour. "For Christ sake, Mike, open the door."

Her shouting succeeded in silencing the child for a brief moment, only to have her resume crying with fuller force, now gasping, now moaning.

"Mike, Mike, what the hell is going on in there?" She placed her ear to the door. Except for the sobbing child there was no other sound.

"Lady, will you lower your voice? It's nearly three in the morning."

Kate looked down at a man who was standing on the landing below. She also caught sight of her bag, some of its contents spilled out on the stairs.

"It's my baby," she said, "and the door's locked."

"It's been going on like that for hours," the man said furiously. "Any decent woman would have been home—"

"Oh, shut up," Kate screamed as she ran down the steps and started searching through the things on the stairs and in her bag for her key.

"It's got to be here," she kept mumbling, "it's got to be here." She found it in a small change purse and charged back up the stairs. As she fumbled with the lock the crying stopped suddenly and Kate went cold with fear.

"Elie," she whispered in horror. "No, God, no, not again." She became paralyzed as her mind flashed back to the time when she was thirteen years old and her younger sister, Elie, was crying in much the same way. It had been a hot night, just as it was now, her mother was out, and

2

she could not quiet her sister down. Elie had been burning up with fever and squirmed with pain every time Kate tried to touch her. When she finally reached the doctor on the phone, Elie had suddenly stopped crying and Kate remembered screaming to the doctor that her sister was dead. The memory of the ambulance siren ripped through her now as she pushed her apartment door open and rushed through the darkened room to her daughter's crib.

Kate felt the baby's head. It was damp from writhing and crying but the brow was cool. With relief she picked up the child, who moaned weakly and started to sob again. The sound almost relieved Kate. Holding Belinda close to her and murmuring sounds of quiet reassurance, she walked over and switched on the light. The room, as she looked around, was as she had left it in the morning except that the sofa was closed. There were several soiled diapers around the crib and a half-empty nursing bottle of milk Belinda had obviously not finished was standing on the bureau.

Placing Belinda carefully on the sofa bed, Kate took a fresh diaper and smoothed away the perspiration from the baby's face. The room was hot, as hot as the halls outside, and she realized that all the windows were shut. It was all too bewildering. Mike never locked their door and on a hot night like this he would have opened the windows, especially at this late hour, with the hope of getting some cooler air into the tiny apartment.

She was undressing the baby when she heard someone come in and shut the door. She was sure it was Mike and the anger she now allowed to surface was in her face as she turned and saw Mrs. Simms, the wife of the building superintendent, holding Kate's tote bag.

"I heard Mike leave about an hour ago," Mrs. Simms said quietly, "and I was sure he would be right back. Then Belinda started crying and I came up but the door was locked." The woman spoke with embarrassment, which bewildered Kate.

It was at that moment that she noticed the envelope propped up against her wedding picture on the desk. Mrs. Simms must have seen it the minute she walked in. Both women knew what the note contained.

"You poor child," Mrs. Simms said.

There is nothing poor about me, Kate wanted to scream, but controlled her impulse. The phrase infuriated her. She hated to be referred to as a poor child. They had said it about her when her father died, leaving her, at the age of twelve, fatherless and her mother penniless. They had said it again when her sister contracted meningitis a year later and she sat with her mother in the hospital waiting to hear if Elie would live or die. And the phrase was always on the faces of the ladies when she delivered the clothes her mother altered for the women of Dayton. They would pay her for the alteration and then give her a small tip, which screamed the phrase louder than words.

"I'll be all right, Mrs. Simms," she said coldly, then, remembering she would need the woman's help for the next few days, she managed a brief smile. "You were sweet to be concerned. I can't imagine what got into Mike to lock the door." She bit her lip and looked again at the envelope. Obviously he had locked the door because he was not intending to come back. The broken tile outside the door loomed before her eyes. It was all too idiotically symbolic. Her name broken away from Mike's and a locked door. She was alone again, separate, apart, and the locked door seemed to state that a brief, almost happy time of her life, the only time when she seemed to be part of something, part of a unit, was over.

Walking over to the desk, she picked up the envelope and, without opening it, turned to Mrs. Simms.

"I'm on early shift tomorrow, Mrs. Simms. Could you help me out with Belinda until I can make some other arrangements? I'll be home no later than four, maybe even earlier."

The woman nodded, came close to Kate, and squeezed her arm. "I'll be here at seven-thirty in the morning." Just before she left she turned and after a brief pause said, "Honey, shouldn't you be calling your mom?"

Kate lowered her eyes and didn't answer. She knew she would have to call her mother, but she didn't want to think about that now. When she heard the door close she tore open the envelope. It was in Mike's usual childish scribble and was obviously written in panic.

Sorry, Katie, I just couldn't take it another minute.
It's too lonely living with you. I'm really sorry.
Mike

The words "too lonely living with you" leaped off
the page and she felt a sharp pain shoot through her. The
idea that Mike had been lonely living with her stunned
her. She had been lonely all her life. Like a nearsighted
child who sees the world as a blur and assumes, until the
first pair of glasses, that everyone sees a blurred world,
Kate thought her deep inner loneliness was the normal
state, felt by everyone. Everyone she knew seemed lonely:
her mother, Elie, people she worked with, and certainly
Mike. He seemed to her the loneliest person she had ever
met. An orphan, growing up in foster homes, finally
running away at sixteen and shifting for himself, Mike
had no one at all. Surely that was one of the attractions
between them. Her own loneliness had abated when she
married Mike, and she assumed she had filled the void in
his life. It was shattering for her to realize that her
presence was a cause of further loneliness.

Still holding the letter, she sat down and looked at
her wedding picture, taken just after the justice of the
peace had pronounced them man and wife. She examined
the picture carefully. She had been three months
pregnant, but it didn't show. Twenty years old and
wearing the same white dress she had worn at her
high-school graduation, she looked much younger. The
dress was the only party dress she had ever owned and she
had worn it only twice. She hated party dresses. They
made her feel conspicuous. She didn't have the figure for
them, being small and flat-chested and slightly hippy. But
more than that, every article of clothing she had was made
for her by her mother and had "homemade" written all
over it. The garments were well made but never quite
right, basically skirts and blouses made over from drab
hand-me-down outfits given to her mother by her elderly
customers. Aside from being limited in style, there was
always the problem of color. Her mother saw them as
practical, whereas Kate craved bright colors and prints.

"I can't spend my days over a sink, washing and

5

ironing fresh clothes for you every day" was her mother's answer. Kate would look over at Elie, always dressed in lovely pastel shades, which enhanced her fresh blond prettiness, and she hated and envied her. Then she would feel ashamed. Elie was crippled and she was well. Elie was a baby and she, at thirteen, was expected to understand.

Kate looked at the picture more closely. It was not just her clothes. Her hair was straight and mousy-colored, her nose too long, her lips too thin. Her eyes, which were large, didn't appear as an important feature. With a nose operation, she thought furiously, a proper hairstyle, clothes bought in a store or boutique, a professional makeup artist, she would be striking. Someday, somehow, she would make enough money to have them. She would be lovely and admired, and dress in floating, light-colored silks and chiffons. Even now, sitting alone in the dimly lit room, deserted by her husband and solely responsible for a baby, she was determined that day would come.

Her eyes wandered over to Mike's face in the photograph. He was tall and lanky, handsome, and was grinning happily. She was sure Mike had loved her then. His arm was holding her with a pride of possession. For a brief moment she felt like crying. It was not that she really loved Mike, and had certainly never imagined herself growing old with him. But she was simply not ready to face the world alone again.

She first saw Mike when she went to work as a part-time file clerk at the Dayton *Chronicle*. He was a cub reporter, working out of the sports department. He affected all the manners of an old-time Damon Runyon or Ring Lardner character, wearing the trench coat with collar sloppily raised in the back. His clothes were sporty and properly mismatched, giving him the air of assurance that she later discovered was really a pathetic cover for weakness and insecurity. He never seemed to notice her, but she was aware of him, and whenever he passed she would feel herself blush with excitement.

She was seventeen when she got the job at the paper through Mr. Patterson, her English teacher and adviser, whose wife, Edna, was food editor. Without the job she couldn't have finished high school, for her father's meager insurance policy and the pathetically small Social Security check her mother got were hardly enough to cover their expenses and Elie's exorbitant medical bills. Small as Kate's salary on the paper was, it enabled her to graduate. She maintained a grueling schedule, her time divided among her schoolwork, writing editorials for the school newspaper, and working as a file clerk. It was a difficult year, but she didn't mind. In spite of everything, she looked on her life at that point as a time of preparation. The feeling never left her that she was grooming herself for a different life.

When Kate graduated, Edna Patterson succeeded in getting her a full-time job as secretary in the women's-news department. Soon after that, Mike stopped to chat at her desk and invited her to lunch. It quickly became a routine. For the first time, she minded not being free to go out on dates and resented having to rush home after work to help care for Elie, run errands for her mother, and help with household chores. Mike, sensing her frustration, began dropping by her house in the evenings with pizza or ice cream and would regale them all with funny stories. These evenings were important to Kate. The ice cream was a treat for Elie, and her mother's laughter touched Kate deeply.

The relationship with Mike took a serious turn the day she went to his apartment with him instead of going to lunch. She knew they were going to make love and the thought excited and thrilled her. Her anticipation, as they climbed to his fourth-floor walk-up, surprised her. She was considered a prude by everyone who knew her and she would blush furiously at the hint of an off-color joke.

Kate picked up her wedding picture and, holding it close, turned to look at the room. This was the room where she first went to bed with Mike. She smiled wistfully. That day, with the sun streaming in, the messy, unmade sofa, clothes strewn everywhere, she had thought it glamorous. Remembering herself trying to clean up the spot of virginal blood still made her blush. Mike had gone to get a glass of water. Kate, still hurting from the lovemaking, stood up and was looking around for her clothes when she spotted the stain on the couch. She ran into the tiny bathroom, dampened a towel, and was on her knees frantically scrubbing away at the spot when Mike came back.

"You idiot." He laughed good-naturedly. "I'll leave it there always to remind me that I was the first guy in your life." He then leaned over and drew her up, holding her thin, naked body to his. The desire she felt for him was greater than anything else she had ever known. He pushed her back on the sofa and made love to her again.

"You're skinny all right, Katie, but you sure are warm and you sure feel good." He ran his fingers over her tiny breasts, along her flat stomach until he reached her pubic hair. His searching fingers were moist from lovemaking and she felt the full thrill of being truly desired.

Mike had taught her to love her body and appreciate the pleasure she could derive from it. She was still fully aware of her physical imperfections, but now, when no one was looking, she experimented with makeup and different hairdos.

At the paper she was given new duties. She was sent out to cover stories that dealt with the social life of Dayton, debutante parties, garden parties, bridge parties. But most important, she was now assigned to answer letters written to the advice column. The promotion meant more money, but Kate would have taken the job even if it hadn't. She found the letters fascinating. The problems described by the women who wrote were not unlike her own. When a letter arrived that she could not relate to directly, she succeeded in conjuring up the feelings of the writer and giving compassionate and sincere advice. The new work, along with Mike as a constant companion, made her life seem pleasant. In any event, it was not displeasing, for now, she would say to herself ... for now.

Then she got pregnant. Her mother sensed it before she did.

"You look pinched today, Kate," her mother said one morning at breakfast, "and you haven't eaten a thing, not last night or this morning."

8

Kate felt sick to her stomach but assumed it was something she had eaten the day before.

"It's nothing, Mom. Just an upset stomach."

"It's your stomach all right," Mrs. Johnson said sarcastically.

Kate got up from the table and left the house without a word. When she didn't get her period that month she went to the doctor. His congratulations, when the result of the test was in, were lost on her. She felt panicky and helpless. She did not want children, not yet, and she was sure Mike would be equally unhappy. An abortion was the only solution. The problem was to find the money. She had no savings. Every penny she earned went to her mother except for pocket money her mother gave her. She was sure Mike had none. He had no relatives and few friends. His salary was all he had in the world.

"Pregnant?" Mike said with delight when she told him. "Hey, that's great, Katie." They were lying on the sofa and Mike was puzzled by her reluctance to undress.

"Mike, being pregnant is one thing, but after a while there's a creature that has to be cared for, fed, clothed...."

"I bet being pregnant will make you develop a bosom," Mike said, ignoring her remarks as he started unbuttoning her blouse.

Kate smiled in spite of herself.

"What will we call her?" Mike asked, pulling her skirt down, leaving her only in her panties as she started unzipping his trousers.

"Will it be a girl?"

"Yeah, it'll be a girl," he said with assurance as he caressed her back. As always, she felt the pit of her stomach contract with excitement. Sex with Mike never ceased to thrill her.

"We'll have to get married," she heard Mike say as he pressed himself into her. She didn't reply. The pleasure of having him make love to her made it impossible for her to answer. The only thought she had as she felt herself reaching a climax was that she and Mike would live together and their time would not be relegated to lunch hours and brief moments before she rushed home from work.

Her mother took the news badly.

"Kate," she said with suppressed fury, "you can't possibly have a baby. You've got to have an abortion."

"Mother!" Kate was horrified. "An abortion? What a hell of a way to react to your daughter's pregnancy."

"We're too poor to have such high moral standards and too poor to have a bastar—"

"For Christ's sake, Mother, this is 1958. Morality has nothing to do with it," Kate interrupted angrily. "I want this baby."

She spoke vehemently and was amazed at herself. Her own first thought had been abortion, yet hearing her mother say it infuriated her. "As for being too poor, Mike and I are going to be married and I'm going to have this baby."

"You can't afford it." Her mother was now screaming with anger. "You need money to have a baby and raise it properly."

"Money." Kate's anger matched her mother's. "Money is all you ever think about. It's you and Elie you're really thinking of, isn't it? You're not thinking of me or the baby, you're just worried about the money I won't be contributing to the house. You've never cared about me or what I want. It's always you and Elie."

Mrs. Johnson turned her back on Kate and said no more.

Kate was instantly ashamed. She wished she could take back her words. She went to her mother and touched her tentatively on the shoulder. Physical contact between them was rare and awkward.

"I'm sorry for what I said, Mom. You know I'll always take care of you and Elie. Mike makes a decent salary. I'll take what I need to care for the baby and give you the rest."

Well, it hadn't worked out that way. Soon after they were married Mike was fired. Belinda was born in the ward of St. Francis Hospital and even though Mike visited her constantly, everyone assumed she was just another girl who had got herself in trouble, as most of the rest in the ward were.

All magic went out of her life after Belinda arrived. Her passionate need for Mike disappeared. If anything, he began to annoy her with his constant desire for her. His attentiveness now seemed like possessiveness and sniveling dependence. Both attitudes infuriated Kate. She discovered he had wanted the baby to ward off his feelings of not belonging to anyone or having anyone belong to him. For Kate the baby was a constant source of concern. She looked exactly like Elie, and although it pleased Kate to have this beautiful child, the idea that something might happen to her, as it had to Elie, never left her. Her mother rarely came to visit and Kate could not depend on her to baby-sit. On the few occasions when Mrs. Johnson did succeed in finding someone to sit with Elie, which was necessary, since Elie could not climb the stairs, the visits ended in disagreements and hurt feelings.

"Mama, Mama." Belinda's voice made Kate turn and look at her daughter. Quickly she walked over to her, picked her up, and hugged her tightly. As the child's arms circled her neck, Kate felt a surge of maternal love. For the first time since Belinda was born, two years ago, Kate experienced a complete, unselfish feeling toward her child.

Holding her daughter close, Kate felt the tears stream down her face. Mike had wanted this child as insurance against loneliness, yet he had left her. It didn't matter, she now had Belinda and she would always be hers, always.

2

Kate moved back to her mother's house. It was considered a lower-middle-class neighborhood when she was young, but over the years it had further deteriorated, and Kate resolved that it would be only a temporary arrangement.

Mrs. Johnson accepted her daughter's return and took the baby off her hands without recriminations, which was a great relief. Elie, who now moved around with greater ease in spite of the brace on her leg, was the greatest beneficiary of the new setup. She and Belinda looked like sisters and the baby became the constant companion of the crippled girl.

In spite of the drabness and poverty of her life, Kate, relieved from the daily worry of caring for Belinda, threw herself into her job with new ferocity and determination. Money and furthering her career were uppermost in her mind.

She arrived at the office early and left late. She was determined to learn every aspect of the workings of the paper. She had time on her side and she was using every minute with good purpose. She decided to take over the women's page. She got the social column with ease, then the decorating and fashion columns, followed by the beauty column, and, finally, Edna Patterson's job. When the woman was fired, Kate feigned surprise. She dismissed her guilt with the thought that it was better for the paper and that the woman had underestimated her competition and that was her mistake. With each additional responsibility, Kate's paycheck grew. Still she did not let up from the backbreaking schedule she had set for herself.

The managing editor was fully aware of what Kate was doing but did not complain as long as she was an economic asset to the paper. He presented this fact to his superiors as his personal achievement.

Her work load was so enormous that one day he suggested she stop bothering with the letters in the advice column. It was a menial job and one of the new girls could do it, he said, but to Kate these letters were her bible. She gained valuable insights from those letters, and they provided a most reliable education about her readers. She would take them home and read and reread them. She began to separate them into categories—age groups, work groups, social groups. These were then cross-indexed into types of problems—love, sex, work, appearance. Each letter was important, each one answered personally. The problems the girls and women wrote about were real and far more serious and lasting than the headlines of the Dayton *Chronicle*. The thing that never ceased to amaze her was her readers' gratitude for her replies. She, Kate Johnson, was actually helping some faceless, sad, and lonely creature. It gave her a strange sense of power.

The idea for a book took shape gradually in her mind. Why shouldn't she try to help even more women,

women outside the range of her advice column? She tentatively began writing down some of her ideas and the book seemed to take off by itself. She knew it was not clever; in fact, it was the kind of simple, homely advice that would seem unnecessary to state, but she knew better. All those letters begging for help had to mean that it *was* necessary. She wrote it in the first person, making it clear that she had incorporated all their problems into her own life experience. The knowledge that she was no different from others, the ability to face up to the fact that everyone was cut basically from the same mold, gave her writing the direct appeal of simplicity and a down-to-earth quality.

Belinda was ten when Kate received word from her agent that the book had been accepted for publication. She had become a minor celebrity at the *Chronicle*, respected by some, admired by others, despised by those whom she had eliminated, and adored by all the women readers. She continued to use her maiden name professionally, and knew her by-line meant sales for the paper. It was this knowledge that gave her the courage to demand a decent advance from the publisher.

The day the advance arrived, Kate went to see a plastic surgeon.

Her mother was shocked.

"Plastic surgery?" She gasped when Kate told her she would be gone for several days. "What on earth got into you, Kate?"

Kate looked at her mother for a long time. Although she had grown old and was by now wrinkled, Mrs. Johnson's perfect features, inherited by both Elie and Belinda, were still there, and Kate had to fight not to word her long-harbored jealousy.

When she was a child she always waited for the day her father would suddenly see her as the beautiful child she knew he wanted. She knew she was not beautiful, just as she knew her mother was. When he came home from work, her father would hug her warmly, but his eyes lit up when her mother came into the room. There was a romantic magic about her parents when they were together, and young as she was, she knew she was excluded. She wanted to be taken into that magic circle, but her mother seemed to resent every moment Kate spent with her father, and Kate couldn't understand what caused these feelings. Her child's mind decided that if she were pretty, her mommy wouldn't be mad at her. These feelings were vague, undefined, until one night it was spelled out for her.

Kate had come home from school with a drawing and a short story she had done for her father. The minute he walked in, she ran to him and presented them proudly. Her father was delighted and swung her up and held her close. Kate wanted the moment to last forever. Her father was all hers at that instant.

"Time for bed, Kate." Her mother's voice was sharp.

"Let her stay up awhile tonight." Her father still held her.

"I've had a terrible day"—her mother sounded cross—"I'm exhausted."

Kate's father carried her to her room and kissed her good night. She lay in the darkness, tears running down her cheeks. Suddenly she heard her parents talking.

"You're so impatient with her," her father was saying. "She's very young, you know. Be patient." He seemed to be pleading.

"She's so awkward and thin, like a little old woman," her mother answered angrily.

"She's not as beautiful as you are, my dear," her father answered, "but she's clever and very sweet." He sounded sad. "Give her time."

"Am I beautiful?" Kate heard her mother ask, and a long silence followed.

Kate crept out of bed and looked into her parents' room. Her father was holding her mother close, kissing her. Her mother's eyes were closed and she seemed more ethereal than ever. Her long blond hair was loose, her neck as she lifted her face to her husband was long and white, her hands, caressing his hair, were graceful.

Elie's birth was a further blow to Kate. Elie looked exactly like her mother and was everything Kate was not. She was a most beautiful baby, with blond hair and delicate, cherubic features, and Kate knew she could not compete with both her mother and sister. She could see her father's pride in Elie grow. He never ignored Kate, but there was a special look of adoration on his face when he looked at the baby. Even his gifts reflected his attitude. Elie's were soft and cuddly, the beautiful doll, the furry stuffed animal, the little music box with a dancing ballerina on top. Kate's were useful and practical, the book, the pencils and crayons, the blackboard.

Her father, an accountant by profession, was a singularly well-read and informed man. Kate set out to win his attention—his love, praise, and pride—with the grades she brought home from school. She began to think she had succeeded when his sudden death put an end to that dream. Instead a deep void appeared and Kate embarked on a long waiting period for someone or something else to fill it.

Her mother took the death badly. She shriveled up with unhappiness and grew thin and haggard. The flowing blond hair turned dull, the sparkling light, always there when her husband was around, was gone. She became garrulous and miserly. When Elie contracted meningitis, Mrs. Johnson seemed to retire from the world of the living completely. She spent her time caring for Elie, rarely leaving the house, and became completely dependent on Kate, as though Kate were the master of the house. She seemed oblivious of the fact that Kate was a child herself.

In spite of the tragedy around her, Kate's dreams were not dampened. If anything, the misery strengthened her determination to achieve a position in life that would enable her to escape this physical and emotional poverty.

Now, as her mother waited for an explanation, Kate knew it was too late to burden her mother with all the unhappiness she had created for her first daughter. She simply said, "Mother, the cards I was dealt at birth got me this far, but I need some help to get further."

"Why, Kate Johnson, I never knew you were that superficial." She said it lightly, but turned her eyes away, as though embarrassed.

"Well, now you know."

16

"Will that really make the difference?" Mrs. Johnson looked up at her daughter. She had always believed her feelings about Kate had been well hidden. Now she was not so sure.

"Mom," Kate said quietly, "I'm not complaining, believe me. I know I'm doing well here in Dayton, but damn it, there is a whole world out there . . . and I want it. Beauty, that thing you call superficial, is something that might help me get it. I don't know how far I can make it work, but there are ways of improving what I do have, and by God, I'm going to give it a try."

She had her nose fixed, and when the bandages were finally off, she studied herself in a mirror.

"I'm still no ravishing beauty," she said to the mirror, "but it's a good beginning."

In the years since she'd given birth to Belinda, her figure had developed a bit, and now that she was able to afford better clothes, she had learned how to cover the obvious defects. She had ample time to practice what she preached in her columns, and by the time she came to her first meeting with her publishers in Chicago she could not help but be pleased at the surprised faces of the editors in the room.

"Now," she said with authority after acknowledging the introductions, "let's talk about the promotion of the book."

A loud laugh made her turn around. A tall, heavy-set man wearing huge black-rimmed glasses stood in the doorway, smoking a cigar.

"I'm Jason Reid," the man said as he walked over to her, his hand outstretched. "I'm the publisher and I must say I didn't expect the author to be so very attractive and self-assured. Logically, you should have been a mousy, middle-aged woman in space shoes, who pours out all her frustrations onto paper." He paused. "And I really can't say I'm displeased." He pulled up a chair. "All right, what about the promotion?"

Some of Kate's bravado evaporated. Jason Reid was a name she had heard, as had everyone else at the *Chronicle*, but as far as she knew, no one there had ever seen him. He owned the paper, which was one of the minor papers in his publishing empire. Had she given it any thought, she would have realized that he probably owned publishing houses as well. Aside from being overwhelmed by the meeting, Kate was also aware that she had used material in her book that, if anyone wanted to split hairs, belonged to the *Chronicle*. This thought made her even more wary. Could that have been the reason for Jason Reid's being in the room?

She looked at him and felt reassured. He didn't look like a petty man.

Slowly she began mapping out her ideas for the promotion campaign. She was to cover all the radio stations and television interview shows according to a convenient travel schedule. She was to be booked into every women's club in every town she was to visit. She would stand in various bookstores, department stores, and dime stores, where she would greet prospective buyers and autograph her book.

"I want to make money on this book, Mr. Reid," she said, finishing her dissertation. Then, smiling self-consciously, she lowered her voice. "I don't know that I have another book in me, so I want to make the most of this one."

Jason Reid watched her with admiration. He calculated she must be about thirty, and he was aware she had been at the *Chronicle* for a long time.

He was well into his fifties. Born to wealth, he had multiplied it many times over through the purchase of a string of newspapers, magazines, publishing houses, and, finally, real estate. He loved his work, loved his power, admired power in others, and liked few individual people. He had a few men friends, lots of mistresses, but no women friends. He couldn't be bothered with the flirtations, the small talk, the little niceties he knew women expected of him. He worked long into the night and knew that no one woman could match his zeal and ambition.

Now, watching this thin young woman, who had obviously mapped out a campaign to promote herself into the world of the known, he could not help but find her both attractive and stimulating. She certainly succeeded in piquing his interest. Mentally he undressed her and realized she was not too exciting physically. He shook his head, annoyed at himself. She was young and obviously inexperienced.

"And who, if I may ask, is going to bankroll this venture?" he asked, knowing he was being unnecessarily cruel.

"Why, isn't that in the contract?" Kate asked in surprise.

"You must learn to read the small print, too, my dear. Yes, there is a provision for promotion, but nothing that would begin to finance your plan."

The disappointment on her face irritated him. "And besides, what happens to your job at the *Chronicle*?"

Kate's eyes took on a glazed look. Jason wondered if she would begin to cry. He stood up.

"So you now have something to think about, Miss Johnson, don't you?"

"It's not really very complicated," Kate answered evenly. "I'll simply continue to write my columns and send them in. You will advance me the money which the contract gives toward the promotion of the book, and then, if it sells, as I'm sure it will, I don't think either of us will be the loser."

Jason felt himself grow angry. He hated to be talked to as an equal by his employees, but he had to admit the girl had guts.

"Now I have something to think about, don't I?" he said mockingly. He turned around and left the room.

Everyone spoke at once. The editor who'd worked on the book, her agent, the promotion gal, and two other girls whose jobs were never explained to Kate.

"Well, you certainly blew it," the editor was saying. "Hell, Reid will no more go through with this deal..."

The agent was nearly in tears and yelled that there was a signed contract and they had no right to renege.

"Big deal. Reid will pay off the advance without batting an eyelash and give you back the damn book."

"We'll sue," the agent said, "and we'll win."

Kate watched everyone haggling and finally stood up.

"I'll bet you Jason Reid buys the book and buys my idea for promotion. So why don't you all stop yelling and start working."

She returned to Dayton that night, and by the time she arrived home her self-confidence had disappeared. She didn't know where she had found the courage to talk to Jason Reid that way, nor did she know why she had the gall to think that he would phone her and apologize for his uncalled-for pettiness. But she did think so.

She and Belinda were having their bedtime chat when her mother called her to the phone.

"It's a Mr. Reid," her mother said.

"Tell him I'm saying good night to my daughter, and if he'll leave a number, I'll call him back."

Her mother came into Belinda's room a few minutes later with a bewildered look on her face.

"Who was that pompous, dreadful man?"

"What happened?" Kate was now amused.

"He refused to be put off, got very angry, and finally said he expected you for breakfast at the office at seven-thirty. Sharp."

It worked, Kate thought triumphantly. All the years of struggling to become a person in her own right, all the years of teaching herself discipline, all the years of setting her goals and sticking by her decisions, had paid off. Not even Jason Reid could stand in her way.

3

Kate awoke early. She looked over at the illuminated clock-radio and saw that it was five-fifteen. She slipped out of bed quietly so as not to wake Belinda, tiptoed out of the room and down to the kitchen to have some coffee. Passing the room that her mother shared with Elie, Kate quietly shut their door. She had a great deal to think about and she didn't want her mother to come down just yet.

She put on the coffee, made some toast, and sat down to plan her day. Automatically she took her vitamin pill and gulped it down with the first sip of coffee. She felt strongly about physical fitness and to her way of thinking, vitamins were important.

What to wear was the first problem. Since becoming the main writer on all aspects of a woman's life within the radius covered by the *Chronicle*, she had learned a lot about clothes, makeup, decorating, flower arranging, and how to give a tea party, but she herself was not an instinctively chic person. She didn't have the figure for flamboyant clothes, and she still could not afford the finer designer clothes. She had often been courted by various stores to buy her clothes at their wholesale price and to have her hair dyed, cut, trimmed, or styled by the newest "rage" in town, but she never did. She was simply not willing to be obligated to these people.

She went through her wardrobe in her mind. When she saw Jason Reid yesterday she had been wearing a skirt, a man-tailored shirt, simple pumps, and a sweater. The thought came to her that she could wear her new suit, but she dismissed it. She was not sure it really became her, and she wasn't yet completely comfortable in it. Suddenly she smiled. How often had she been asked by a faceless letter writer, "I've got the most important date of my life, what should I wear?" or "The job that I want is there, but I've got to knock their eyes out and I'm only five feet tall. What do I wear?" Her stock answer was, "Be sure you wear something you are truly secure in. Don't let the clothes wear you, you wear them. Don't, for heaven's sake, burden this important occasion with concern as to how you look in the new outfit. Put on something you *know* fits you. That way you will have more time to concentrate on your goal."

The problem of what to wear was now solved. She would put on a shirtwaist dress that showed off her tiny waist and disguised her rather unflattering lower part, wear her highest heels, since Jason Reid was immensely tall and she didn't want to feel cowed by his height. Also, she had good legs and in high heels they showed off best.

As she was putting on her makeup she took extra care with the false eyelashes she had learned to wear, brushed her hair back so it fell loosely around her shoulders, and, picking up her shoulder-strap bag, stood back and surveyed herself in the mirror.

"Kate, I have to admit you look real smashing," her mother said with pleasure. "That surgeon you went to did a fine job and you were right to do it."

Kate's eyes glistened with pleasure. Her mother had

22

always been the realist in the family and a compliment from her was important and rare. Not once since the nose operation had she made a comment.

Kate hugged her mother warmly. "Wish me luck. Mr. Jason C. Reid should not be kept waiting."

She arrived at the office at seven-fifteen. The skeleton crew of the night shift was getting ready to leave.

"Is Mr. Reid around?" she asked the night editor, who was yawning with boredom.

"No one around here yet."

"But I have an appointment with him at seven-thirty," she said, and it occurred to her that she was the butt of some mean little joke.

"Well, he's probably still up in the penthouse."

Of course, she thought, Jason Reid maintained an apartment on the top floor of the *Chronicle* building. It was never used by anyone else but him, and somehow she had forgotten about it.

She got back into the elevator and pressed the button for the penthouse floor, and the elevator shot up and came to a halt in front of a massive oak door, entirely different from any other door in the building. It also did not open automatically. She was still wondering what to do when Jason Reid opened the door and smiled at her.

"Good, you're punctual."

She entered the large living room and was immediately impressed by its enormity, austerity, and masculinity. Mentally she made notes of several decorating nuances, which she filed away for future columns.

"Come in and sit down, Miss Johnson."

She sat down in a brown suede chair, and the luxury of the fabric was intoxicating.

"Coffee, toast, eggs?"

"Just coffee, thank you."

A butler appeared from nowhere and took the order. Jason Reid ordered a huge breakfast.

"Now, Miss Johnson, I must tell you that I read your book last night."

She was about to make a sarcastic remark but decided against it. She simply smiled and looked interested.

He watched her face change expression and knew

that she caught the phrase "last night." When he had met her in Chicago he had indicated that he had read the book. The truth was that he had read a reader's report and was neither impressed nor unimpressed by it. The reader and the editor felt that it had merit and he usually went along with their decisions, especially since it was a relatively inexpensive paperback. But then he met her, had been impressed by her manner and the cool way she stood up for herself and her book. When he decided to come to Dayton, as was his habit when something there caught his fancy, he started to delve deeper into Miss Kate Johnson. He took the manuscript with him and read it quickly on the plane before landing in Dayton. On arriving at the *Chronicle*, he invited the editor in chief to come up and bring everything he had on Kate Johnson.

"What's up, Mr. Reid?" The editor seemed nervous. Kate was good at what she did and she certainly had succeeded in running the women's pages well and was an economic asset to the paper, but she had also made quite a few enemies and now he wondered if someone had stabbed little Kate Johnson in the back.

Jason Reid leafed through the numerous pages in front of him.

"She's done all of this on her own?" he said, marveling. "No assistance, no plagiarism, all alone?"

"Yes, Mr. Reid." The editor didn't know whether to be proud of Kate or not. The word "plagiarism" worried him. "She's a very hard worker, more like a workaholic, and very ambitious, very thorough. And besides all her regular work she also answers the lovelorn column. It's become one of our most valuable columns." He shrugged his shoulders. "If she deserves any credit, it's for those damn letters. Boy, they come in by the droves. Why, I gotta tell you, Mr. Reid, I don't even know where she gets the time to answer that drivel, but it doesn't seem to affect her other work. . . . I guess she does it at home." He paused, since Jason didn't seem to be listening. He seemed engrossed in the answers to the readers. "I'll say another thing, Mr. Reid. We have a segment of readers who would never be buying the *Chronicle* if it weren't for those letters. It's a younger group, women mainly, from all over

Ohio and even out of state. And advertising has gone up, too."

A workaholic, Jason mused, that's what people said about him. "Tell me more about her," he said brusquely. His mind was already made up. This woman was obviously into a readership that he wanted for *Women Today*. The magazine was dying and he was anxious to save it. He had given himself until the end of the year to find an editor in chief for it. Kate Johnson seemed to have the formula he was looking for. He tried to conjure up her appearance but found it difficult. All he could really remember was that she had a youthful brittleness about her mixed with an insecurity that made her seem vulnerable. That was good. He could cope with the insecurity, he liked the vulnerability, he could use the brittleness, and he could certainly use the youth.

He turned his attention to the man who was relating facts about Kate. He made some notes and then, thanking him, he walked with him to the elevator.

"Is anything wrong?" the editor asked.

"Not really. As a matter of fact, I think I should compliment you on having the guts to keep her. Most people in your position would have found it uncomfortable having someone like that around. They're the kind who, given a chance, will wipe out anyone who stands in their way." He smiled. "Even to the point of biting the hand that feeds them, and in this case it could have been you."

The editor blanched and Jason nearly laughed as the elevator arrived.

Now, as he watched her, he couldn't resist baiting her further.

"It will sell, all right. I agree with that. Did you write it yourself?"

He could see the anger quiver through her whole body, but she stifled it and merely nodded politely.

"Tell me about yourself," he said abruptly. He was annoyed by her lack of reaction.

"I'm sure you know most of what there is to know, Mr. Reid. I've worked at the paper for almost thirteen years, starting as a file clerk. I believe everyone is pleased with my work, and I enjoy it thoroughly."

"You're married, I believe, to a Michael Cameron?"

"Divorced." Now she was really annoyed. He obviously knew everything there was to know about her, so why was he playing this game?

"Children?"

"One."

"Girl, boy?"

"Girl."

"Do you have a lover?"

"Is it relevant to what we are going to discuss?"

"Maybe. Are you frigid?"

She smiled. There was no answer that would have been appropriate; besides, she was not sure she could control her rage.

"You feel you are very bright, don't you?"

"I get by."

"Well, you're not really, you know." He smiled pleasantly. "You push too hard. Granted, you've chased every female out of the *Chronicle*, but you did it with a clumsy hand and made enemies. That's not clever."

"Mr. Reid," Kate said quietly, although she was beginning to lose ground and she knew it, "I don't think there have been any complaints about my columns. As for being, shall we say, disliked by some of the ladies who have been pushed out, to use your phrase, they obviously were dispensable, wouldn't you say?"

At that point a table was wheeled in by the butler and Kate watched Jason Reid sit down and eat every morsel of food with a relish that was completely overwhelming.

"I enjoy food," he said as he wiped his mouth and then lit a huge cigar.

Kate was wondering what this meeting was for and was becoming increasingly uncomfortable. The man was being obnoxious and yet she realized that there was something enormously attractive about him. He was, without doubt, an ugly man. His features were enormous, his face weather-beaten, his eyes large and practically black behind the enormous black-framed glasses, yet she found him physically attractive. The thought upset her.

"And you think you can carry off that promotion idea you set forth yesterday, do you?"

"Yes, I do."

"You've appeared on many radio and television interview shows I gather, and you feel comfortable doing them?"

She did not flinch, but she knew that he had set her up and that she was trapped. She had appeared on few radio programs and had categorically refused to appear on television. With all her outward security, she was enormously shy, and this monster had guessed it.

"Yes, Miss Johnson, did you, do you, will you?"

She could not answer.

"You conceited little bitch," Jason roared. "You're scared shitless and you know it. Making that grand plan to travel and have me finance it when you might very well, probably would, fall flat on your face the first time that microphone is put in front of you or that camera is pointed at you."

"I can do it," Kate said through clenched teeth. "I can do it and I will do it. If you won't finance it, I'll withdraw the book." She stood up. "I believe this meeting is over, wouldn't you say?"

"Oh, sit down, sit down and relax." He smiled suddenly and it was a warm smile. "I'll say one thing for you . . . you've got guts, that's for sure. As for withdrawing the book, no need, other than the fact that you can't. But if you're going to do this promotion and if I'm going to bankroll it, you'll have to do some pretty fast learning on all levels."

"Learning what?"

"Well, we'll start with how to dress, how to fix your hair, how to answer questions when you're up against interviewers who are going to smash your little book to smithereens because the reviewer is a lady who hates your guts because you're young and she's old, when you're faced with celebrities whom you may have dreamed about meeting someday but who will be treating you as an equal and you'll have to behave like one, and when you've graduated, and it will be a crash program, you'll have to pay me back."

"Pay you back?" She had been listening carefully

and the insults that he had flung at her—criticizing her clothes, her hair, her manner, her demeanor, all the things she was sure she had mastered and that gave her the confidence to be where she was—did not escape her, but the last phrase threw her completely.

"How?" Suddenly she felt herself blush. Did he mean that she would have to sleep with him? The thought was not unappealing, but his phrase was degrading.

"Relax, relax." Jason Reid watched the redness cover her face and it amused him. "It's not that little body of yours that I'm talking about. I'm talking about business. I want you to come to New York after we've done this promotional tour and I want you to become editor in chief of one of my magazines, *Women Today*. It's on the verge of bankruptcy because it is not what today's market calls for. I could close it down and I wouldn't even feel the loss, but I love that magazine. Somehow that's the one I care about and I'm damned if I know why. Your little book is what that magazine should be talking about."

Kate felt faint. Editor in chief of *Women Today*. She had set her goals high, but never that high.

"So we'll leave for New York in the morning and we'll put you through a crash course on how to come off best on the tour, and then we'll go from there."

"Tomorrow?"

"The book is coming out in December. This is the end of August. You've got to start that tour several weeks before publication so that we have a good advance notice on it. And, believe me, you've got a lot to learn."

"I have a child...."

"So?"

"Well, I'll need a place for her to live in New York, I'll have to find help to care for—"

"I'm not hiring the family, Kate, I'm hiring you."

But he said it with a gentleness that surprised both of them. Something about her was suddenly tremendously appealing to him. Thin, not particularly attractive, not too well put together, although the effort was obvious. The nose job was fair, but the lashes were not the best. He took in all the flaws, and yet he actually desired her.

She was staring at him and he knew that what he was feeling was being fully reciprocated. Walking over to where she sat, he raised her to her feet. She was tiny. As he put his arms around her he felt her body tremble ever so slightly. He kissed her hair and lifted her face to his.

"Come on, Kate. You come to New York. Trust me. I've been around a long time, and I feel who you are, I know who you are. I know things about you you don't know yourself. I'm going to make you *somebody*, Kate."

4

Nothing she had anticipated in her wildest dreams matched the luxury she encountered as she entered Jason Reid's private plane. It was decorated much like the apartment he had in the *Chronicle* building, but having it reproduced on an airplane was unbelievable.

The Japanese butler she had seen at her first breakfast with Jason Reid was there to greet her, lead her to a comfortable armchair, and help her with the seat belt. She looked around for Jason.

"Mr. Reid will be out shortly," the butler said, as if reading her mind.

At that moment Jason appeared from the back of the plane, smiled at her, seated himself in another armchair, took out some papers from a briefcase on the coffee table, and began to read, making notes as he went from one sheet to the next.

Kate leaned back in her seat and looked out the window. It was raining lightly and she wondered what Belinda was doing. The past few days were a muddle in her mind and now she found herself trying to sort out exactly what had happened.

Jason Reid had given her one week to straighten things out in Dayton. He hadn't told anyone at the paper what was in store for her. The managing editor was simply told that Miss Johnson would be gone for several weeks and would probably be back by Christmas. She wrote columns for the next eight weeks, got a mother's helper for Belinda, and arranged for a bank loan to carry her through the period she would be gone. She hadn't dared ask Jason about money, feeling that too much was at stake to bring up the subject. She figured her salary would continue while she was gone, but obviously there would be a gap between the time she left the *Chronicle* and the first paycheck from *Women Today*.

"Kate." She heard Reid's voice and turned to look at him. "There's a stack of magazines in the cabinet beside your chair. I suggest you start doing some homework."

Obediently Kate opened the cabinet and found it full of copies of *Women Today*, as well as many other popular magazines. She started to skim through the latter.

"I would suggest you familiarize yourself with *Women Today*," Jason said impatiently.

"Mr. Reid, I've bought and read every copy of *Women Today* that came out in the last twelve months." She took a deep breath. "And the reason I've only read the issues of the past twelve months and not others is that I couldn't get my hands on them in Dayton. I have written to *Women Today* and asked them to get me back issues. I hope they will be waiting for me when I arrive in New York."

Jason Reid smiled and the wrinkles in his face deepened and finally the smile turned into laughter. "Little Katie Johnson of Dayton, Ohio, you are the one."

At that point the roar of the plane's engine before

31

takeoff sounded, and Kate paled. She had not flown much, had gone to several conventions in the Midwest and once to California, but this was different. On the other flights she was one of a crowd and it gave her a sense of confidence. Now she was alone with Jason and a butler, who was nowhere in sight.

"Give me your hand." Jason interrupted her thoughts.

She stretched out her hand and he enveloped it in his own. A surge of confidence shot through her, along with a definite excitement not unlike the feelings she had when she first went to bed with Mike.

"Thank you, Mr. Reid," she said when she felt she could trust her voice.

He did not let go of her hand, but he was again absorbed in the papers he was reading.

Kate closed her eyes. She thought briefly of Mike for the first time since the day he walked out on her. Over the years, she had developed the ability to blot out the memory of bad experiences. Once something was over she cut it out of her mind, her heart, her soul, as though it had never been. Until this moment Mike had been obliterated from her conscious mind. She had slept with only two men since Mike left, but neither evoked his image. One affair was a short-lived flirtation with an assistant manager of a department store that advertised in the *Chronicle*. She had met him at the annual Christmas party the paper gave, and they had both been slightly tipsy at the time. He was not particularly attractive—she recalled that his suit did not fit properly. When she commented on the fact that the sleeves were too short, he had taken the jacket off and thrown it into one of the wastepaper baskets. She'd left the party with him and they had slept together in a downtown motel. He had called her several times after that and although flattered by his attention, she hadn't wanted to see him again. Her other experience was with the head waiter of a restaurant not far from her office. He was Italian, elegant, attentive, and since she always took people to lunch there when the office was footing the bill, they became very friendly. When he asked her to have a drink with him one day after work, she agreed and the affair got under way. He was married, but that didn't bother Kate. She enjoyed his attentions, and he obviously enjoyed her as a bed partner—a simple fulfilling of each other's needs. No one knew of this affair, which suited them both. It ended when he left Dayton. There were no regrets. But Jason Reid was different. Emotions too long dormant were suddenly coming to life. It had not happened when he took her in his arms that morning in his apartment. Then he was her employer, a steppingstone to a brighter future, not a man, and certainly not a potential lover. She smiled. Well, he was very much a man at this moment, an attractive man, a man who was capable of stirring a strong reaction in her. It took all her strength not to press his fingers, not to indicate her newly discovered feelings.

"Okay, Katie." Jason's voice startled her and her eyes flew open. "We'll be landing in New York shortly. You've never been there, have you." It was more of a statement than a question. "So I've arranged for you to stay at the Regency Hotel. We keep an apartment there for visiting executives. Obviously, all your expenses will be paid."

"I've got money," Kate protested.

"Hang on to it," he said sternly. "A lady named Dee Dee Smith will be taking charge of you for the next few weeks. You will listen to her, you will follow her advice, and when she is through with you, we'll go from there."

Kate withdrew her hand from his. There was a patronizing tone in his voice that she resented.

"Take charge of me? Give me advice?" She spoke quietly, but the rage was evident. "What exactly are we talking about, Mr. Reid?"

"I'll spell it out, Katie, but to start with don't pull tempers on me." His voice was cold and he took out a cigar and lit it. "I'm going to transform you from a little hick newspaper girl who wrote a book into a top-notch journalist, author, and editor. Your clothes, your hair, your makeup, they all need redoing. Bows and ribbons in your hair just don't work. If you're going to take charge of one of my magazines, you're going to look the part. You are right for it inside, that's why I'm offering it to you, but the cover needs some remodeling."

Kate instinctively put her hand to the ribbon she

had tied in her hair and felt her face grow red with embarrassment.

"Now, Dee Dee is the fashion editor of *Women Today*, and a damn great gal. She is the only one who is aware of where you are heading and will know what I want."

Is she his mistress, Kate wondered, and the feeling of envy was stifling.

"Tell me, Mr. Reid," Kate said tentatively, "when I take over as editor, do I keep the staff there now, or do I have a free rein in hiring and firing?"

"You'll have a free rein, Katie, but I trust your judgment will be tempered with good horse sense."

She felt foolish and wondered if her thoughts had been that obvious.

"Incidentally," Jason was saying, "the galleys of your book are to be ready within a week. I've made some revisions and I'd like you to look at them. I took some corn out and put a lot more sex in, but basically it's still your book. I've also had an illustrator work on the cover. You're to proofread them and I want the book ready to go by Christmas. As I see it, with hard work you should be able to go on the promotion tour four weeks before Christmas. You'll spend Christmas in New York, where I've gotten you on the big shows—Johnny Carson, Dick Cavett, and Merv Griffin—the *Today* show, and several radio shows. Between Christmas and New Year's we'll book you into several key bookstores and department stores in New York for personal sales and autographing and right after New Year's we'll get down to the meeting with my board of directors."

Christmas away from Belinda and her mother! That was the one thought that struck and held, so that she didn't react to the last phrase immediately. It took a few seconds to seep through.

"Board of directors?" she echoed. "Why do I have to meet with the board of directors?"

"They have to meet you and give their okay. So you'd better impress them."

"And if I don't?"

"You will."

The captain's voice announcing the pending arrival

34

at La Guardia Airport came through the intercom. Kate wanted to say something else, but Jason again took her hand and held it as the plane landed and she found herself unable to speak.

The limousine dropped her off in front of the Regency Hotel. The doorman helped her out and took her bag.

"I'll call you," Jason said pleasantly, and the car moved down Park Avenue.

"This way, miss," the doorman said, and Kate, completely dazed, followed him into the magnificent lobby. She looked around with pretended nonchalance, trying to suppress the terror she now felt. What was she doing here? Who was Jason Reid? What was it he expected of her? And above all, why her? She wanted everything he spoke about; she had never stopped dreaming of coming to New York, doing all the things he described, but she had never thought it out completely, and certainly in her wildest dreams she had never seen herself doing it alone.

"Mr. Reid has checked you in, Miss Johnson, so if you'll just follow me." A pleasant man had taken hold of her elbow. "I'm John Sloan, the assistant manager, and Mr. Reid asked me to look after you."

As the elevator shot up to the sixteenth floor Kate wondered if she had to tip this elegant man. The thought preoccupied her. She tried to remember how the situation was resolved in some motion picture in which the star was escorted by the manager to her room.

The problem never arose. He escorted her to her door, took her hand and kissed it lightly, and was gone.

Kate found herself in a huge living room. A maid came out of what Kate assumed was the bedroom and smiled warmly at her. "I've unpacked your clothes, Miss Johnson, and if there is anything you need, just dial the housekeeper and we'll take care of it for you."

Left alone, Kate walked around the room. There were flowers in several vases, fruit and chocolate on the coffee table, and a large pile of magazines neatly placed on the floor near the desk, which stood in the corner of the room next to large French doors. She walked over and looked at the magazines. They were all copies of *Women Today*, issues dating back several years. Alongside was the dummy of the next issue. She had never worked with a magazine dummy before and as she started leafing through it a new panic struck her. Where the hell did she get the nerve to accept Jason Reid's offer, with her limited newspaper experience?

Quickly she moved away from the desk and opened the French doors. A long, narrow terrace ran along the length of the living room. The September chill struck her. It felt good. Stepping out, she looked down at the large, expansive avenue below. Cars were streaming by rapidly, their lights dancing cheerfully in the near darkness of the early evening. The people she saw rushing about looked like little ants crawling along, now bumping into each other, now running, now stopping. Kate felt relief at being far above the crowd, but the knowledge that she would have to enter that rushing melee, fight them, conquer them in order to survive, made her nervous. She looked up at the darkened sky. No stars were visible and the air felt moist and heavy. Quickly she walked into the living room and closed the door. The room was almost completely dark except for the desk lamp, which threw off a warm yellow glow. She found a light switch and as the cleverly concealed indirect lighting came on, Kate was again struck by the beauty of the decor.

As she walked into the large bedroom her feelings of helplessness, of being misplaced and abandoned, grew. The four-poster bed was massive and in excellent taste. She wondered if all the other rooms in this hotel were furnished as lavishly. Opening the armoire, she noticed the texture of the wood and realized that this was probably an authentic Louis XVI piece. Her few clothes were neatly hung in the closet and she wondered what the maid thought when she saw the inexpensive wardrobe, which contrasted so poorly with the wealth around it.

Did people really live like this, she wondered. She remembered that she had protested when Jason said her expenses would be paid. She realized now that her miserable five hundred dollars would hardly cover a week in this hotel. She wanted this world and fiercely resolved that she would have it. But suddenly, for no apparent reason, her eyes filled with tears. She wanted to be back in Dayton, wanted to be with Belinda, her mother, and Elie, in a world she felt safe and confident in. At this hour, back home, she would have been on the bus going home for supper. Belinda would be playing with Elie. She would look up and run to her with bubbling joy and full of stories about her day.

She flung herself on the immense bed, sobbing uncontrollably, and gradually, between exhaustion and tears, fell asleep.

When she woke up she felt cold and totally confused. She looked at her watch. It was midnight, and she was fully dressed. Gradually her mind oriented itself. She sat up and noticed a light on her telephone. She called the operator, who told her the light meant there was a message for her. A Miss Dee Dee Smith had left word that she would be over the next day at ten o'clock for breakfast. Kate hung up, amused at the idea of having breakfast at ten in the morning. That was half a day's work shot to hell, as far as she was concerned.

Though still exhausted, she felt calmer. She undressed, showered, and put on her bathrobe. Sleep now was out of the question. She went into the living room, took an apple, and settled down in the corner of the couch with the stack of old issues of *Women Today*.

It was six o'clock in the morning when she finally went to bed. By then she had put together a completely new format for *Women Today*.

She had paid special attention to Dee Dee Smith's fashion pages. They were superbly done, the copy good, but too sophisticated, the clothes too rich for Kate Johnson from Dayton, Ohio.

5

Kate was dressed and waiting when the desk announced that Miss Smith was on her way up.

She had tried to visualize what the woman would look like, but was totally unprepared for Dee Dee. She was tall, about five feet ten, Kate estimated. She had blond hair piled casually into a French knot with side curls carelessly caressing her cheeks, barely hiding the huge gold loop earrings. She was a mélange of beige and camel's hair. When she smiled, the perfect white teeth seemed to gleam against her suntanned face. The eyes were amber-colored and serious.

"Hi, Kate." Dee Dee extended her hand. The handshake was firm, the palm cool and dry. She spoke in a low, well-modulated voice, and Kate felt uncomfortable as the woman's eyes took her in.

"Hello, Dee Dee," Kate said calmly, although her heart was pounding furiously. "Do sit down and I'll order breakfast."

"I've ordered it already," Dee Dee said casually as she sauntered over to an armchair and flung herself into it. Kate stiffened at the presumption and felt her lips grow tight.

"I hope you ordered only one breakfast." She tried to smile. "You see, I had mine around seven-thirty this morning."

"Seven-thirty?" Dee Dee exclaimed. "Is there such an hour?" She laughed pleasantly. "It matters not. J.C. can easily afford two breakfasts."

Jacey? Kate thought for a moment and then realized the woman was referring to Jason Reid. It was without doubt a most unsuitable nickname for someone like Reid. She wondered again if they were lovers, and the feeling of envy that had swept over her on the plane returned, now reinforced.

"I'll be right back, Dee Dee," Kate said slowly, and walked stiffly from the room. She knew she was being rude, but she had to regain her composure. Gorgeous as Dee Dee was, talented as she obviously was, Reid had chosen her, Kate Johnson from Dayton, Ohio, to be the editor of *Women Today*. Dee Dee would be working for *her*. She had to hang on to that thought.

Deirdre Smith watched Kate leave the room and felt annoyed. The thought that this woman would be her boss was almost too ridiculous to contemplate. Jason couldn't be serious, she decided. He was too good a businessman, too brilliant an editor himself, to allow someone so unsophisticated, so unpolished, to take over *Women Today*.

Dee Dee had been a top fashion model in the early fifties and although her modeling days were over, age having nudged her out of the running, she still looked the part. The perfect bone structure remained, and she had never lost the stance or the flair. She still slid along rather than walked, her shoulders slightly stooped, her stomach flat. She did not merely wear clothes, she paraded them as if still in a fashion show. But unlike many other models of her day, she was bright, knew fashion, and used her fashion sense. She made the transition from model to fashion editor without trouble. She could take the most inexpensive outfit and by the time she was through with it any reader could identify with the garment.

She had been married when she was at the top of her profession to a second-rate fashion photographer, and supported him until he found a new career as a motion-picture producer. When Hollywood summoned him, he assumed Dee Dee would go with him. She fought it, then agreed to try it. The marriage hit the rocks shortly after she arrived. Douglas Smith began courting the voluptuous young starlets he was directing. "I want a woman, not a clothes hanger," he once told her. It was a terrible blow to her. What had once been her greatest asset had now become her curse. She stayed a while longer, and this was her big mistake. She watched his annoyance with her grow to downright distaste. By the time she returned to New York she had become an insecure, neurotic lady in her late thirties, lacking the energy to buck the modeling field she had once ruled, and which she felt was all she really knew. A long period of intense analysis with a reputable doctor made it possible for her to understand and accept what really happened. Slowly, as though recovering from a severe illness, she was able to resume a new and productive life. She went to work for a top fashion photographer as a coordinator, and it was from that vantage point that she began to pity the girls who depended on their appearance alone for their success. Writing about fashion began to make more sense. There, at least, she felt she could be a guide to the young women who wanted to improve themselves, get ahead, use their external appearance to enhance their positions in life, unlike most of the models she worked with, who cultivated nothing but their physical beauty.

She never remarried. In fact, as time went by she grew to fear men and instead turned her energies to working for causes. She was one of the original founders of the women's-liberation movement and devoted much of her free time expounding on the subject, working for it, writing about it.

She met Jason Reid when she got involved in trying to put out a newsletter about women's liberation. Their relationship quickly developed into a convenient love affair. He was the one who urged her to take on the fashion department of *Women Today*.

She had burst out laughing. "It's a trashy rag, J.C."

He was furious, which surprised her. Their relationship had been an easy one. Neither was interested in marriage, and after the first few weeks of pretended euphoria, which in spite of her liberated manner Dee Dee needed to justify the affair to herself, they never really touched each other to the point of rage or any other emotion, for that matter. Jason was a superb lover, tender yet aggressive, and fully conscious of a woman's needs.

"Jason C. Reid, why, I do declare, such passion over one little magazine?"

His expression did not change, but his tone was quieter. "I don't know why, Dee Dee, there's something about it that always gets to me." He laughed self-consciously. "Must be a hang-up from my childhood. My mother always had it around the house. I remember looking through it and marveling at the beautiful pictures. It all happened so long ago, but I still remember it. Mind you, it was before I could even read, so I couldn't pass judgment on the contents."

"But now that you know how to read, have you looked at it recently?" she asked. "It's not even old-fashioned, it's simply undiluted garbage." In all the time she had known him he had never once referred to his youth, certainly not to his childhood.

"I agree, and I have every intention of finding a new format for it. It needs a drastic revision and hiring you for fashion editor would be the first step."

"Why don't you let me run the magazine?" Dee Dee was excited at the thought. "Not just the fashion but the whole works. Let me redo it for the new woman today, as I see her, as everyone should see her."

"I'm not the crusading type," Jason answered, and his manner cooled. "I'm in the money-making business, Dee Dee. A women's-liberation magazine does not quite fit into my plans for *Women Today*." She took the job and he did give her a free hand. She enjoyed being fashion editor but never gave up the hope that Jason would someday ask her to become editor in chief. When he called her from Dayton and told her about Kate Johnson, she wrote her letter of resignation but then cooled down enough to put it aside and wait. Her curiosity about Kate got the better of her.

Now that she had seen her she was glad that she hadn't sent the letter. This mousy, drab little number wouldn't last a month, she said to herself with glee. She couldn't even remember what Kate looked like, now that she was out of the room, much less what she was wearing. The thought that Jason was having an affair with Kate never crossed her mind. Dee Dee knew that Jason slept with many women, but it didn't bother her. Her attitude toward sex was similar to a man's. Sex was in no way a prelude to a lasting, binding relationship. Her affair with Jason was fully satisfying to her. He obviously needed many women, and that was fine with her.

Kate returned to the room. She had washed her face with cold water and put on fresh makeup, adding a bow to her hair as if in defiance. She had felt the need to hang on to her own identity, her own being, her own style. As Kate poured her coffee she knew she would never be able to compete with the stunning creature casually eating her breakfast. She glanced at the breakfast table and exclaimed, "Is that all you're going to eat?" There was an empty orange-juice glass, two thin slices of melba toast, and coffee on the table.

"I really shouldn't drink the juice," Dee Dee purred, "it's so fattening, but what the hell, we've got a long day ahead of us and I won't eat again till dinner."

"Okay, where do we go from here?" Kate asked as she sipped her coffee.

"Where did J.C. meet you, Kate?" Dee Dee asked suddenly.

"He's publishing a book of mine."

"Oh, you wrote a book? What's it about?"

"Women, girls, working girls, working women, how to get along in this world when you don't have everything handed to you on a plate."

"Tell me more, Kate, tell me more." Dee Dee was

trying not to smile. This tacky-looking woman had the gall to give advice! It was too much.

"I'll give you an autographed copy when it comes out, Dee Dee," Kate said pleasantly, "but for now, I understand that you are to guide me into becoming a..." She faltered, not knowing how to phrase the painful fact.

"Dream-boat model for the ladies you're guiding into happiness?"

Kate bit her lip. "Dee Dee, let's not fence. Mr. Reid said you would help with my clothes, my makeup, my hair, and whatever.... I obviously need help if I'm to make any sort of splash on the various interview shows that are scheduled for me." She avoided mentioning the editorial job at *Women Today*. Jason had told her that Dee Dee knew, but still Kate did not want to broach the subject.

They spent the next week going from designer to designer. The head makeup man at Revlon worked on her makeup, the finest hairstylist at Vidal Sassoon was assigned to come up with a hairstyle and several wigs, and the designers started sending over their wares for inspection.

"Pink and paisley are out," Dee Dee kept mumbling every time Kate reached for her own choices.

"Why?" Kate asked innocently. "I like them."

"You're in the big league now, not the little homebody from Detroit," Dee Dee snapped.

"Dayton!" Kate snapped back.

It was finally decided that Courrèges was the most obvious designer for her. The tent shape was right, Dee Dee explained patiently. "It covers the hips, and with a padded bra—small padding, mind you, just to give it a shape—it works best for you."

Kate's first weeks were exhausting. Dee Dee kept her to a demanding schedule of appointments with the hairdresser, facials, makeup artists, shopping, and fittings. She called Belinda and her mother every few days, and her longing for them grew.

"Mommy, you will be home for Christmas, won't you, Mommy?"

"Sure, baby," Kate kept reassuring the child, although she suspected that it would not really work out.

"Kate, don't muff your big chance," her mother said reassuringly when Belinda handed the receiver over. "Don't worry about Belinda or me, we're going to be fine. This is your chance. You've earned it."

Jason was never around during those weeks. Her loneliness was hardly bearable, but she knew that this was a crash course she was taking and it was important.

The galleys arrived ten days after she arrived, and when Kate saw them she was furious. Some of her thoughts and ideas had been deleted and replaced by not-too-subtle sex advice. Her impulse was to call Jason and refuse to go along with the changes, but as she thought it over she realized he was completely right. In the final analysis, her readers were desperate to discover who they were as women, sexually as well as emotionally and intellectually. She had never delved too deeply into the sexual aspects of these women's lives, but obviously they wanted miracle solutions to how to get along with their men.

Her most difficult problem was how to get along with the very demanding Dee Dee. Kate was getting bored with having to look like a fashion plate every minute of the day.

"Dee Dee," she said one morning while they were having coffee, "I'm not a fashion model. I wish I were but the fact is I'm not. My readers aren't, either. They mostly look like me, they sound like me, they think as I do, that's where my audience is."

"But don't they want something more glamorous?" Dee Dee said sarcastically. It was the first time she had heard Kate voice an opinion other than approval or disapproval of an outfit she was trying on. In spite of the complete disarray in the corner of the room where Kate worked, Dee Dee was convinced that the woman didn't have a brain in her head.

"Sure they do"—Kate smiled tolerantly—"but they also want to fit into a mold. Their instinct is to be part of the crowd. I'm trying to help them know who they are. They know me, they can identify with me, whereas you are something they might envy, envy as they would a mannequin in a shop window."

She did not mean to insult her, and the phrase slipped out inadvertently. She saw Dee Dee flustered for the first time. She was about to apologize but decided against it. She had meant every word she said.

"You see, Dee Dee, I believe that is why Mr. Reid chose me to run *Women Today*."

She walked over and picked up a dummy she had started to prepare for the new *Women Today*. On the cover she had a beautiful girl, wearing a stock-tie shirt. The tie, however, was loosened and the curves of the girl's breasts could be seen. Her hair was long and fell loosely around her shoulders. On close inspection, however, one saw that the girl, although beautiful, was not beyond reach of any girl's daydream. Kate handed the picture to Dee Dee.

"What are you trying to do, compete with *Playboy* or *Esquire*?" Dee Dee asked as she stared at the picture.

"Look carefully," Kate suggested. "She's not naked, she's pretty, no doubt, but above all she's human. She's got breasts, a backside, a waist. She's got flesh on her. A man would want her." She paused. "I can relate to her. I know I'll never look like her, but she could come from Dayton or Muncie or Hoboken."

There was a deep silence as Dee Dee continued to stare at the picture.

"Where do you come from, Dee Dee?"

"I was born right here in New York."

"Have you ever traveled to my part of the country?"

"I lived on the Coast for several years."

"That's my point," Kate said with satisfaction. "That's why you don't really understand what I'm talking about."

"Would you like me to resign right now?" Dee Dee asked seriously. "Surely my fashion pages must turn you off."

"I wish you wouldn't," Kate said sincerely. "I think you're great. Mind you, I'll ask for a different approach. I'll ask you to look at me and understand that I am the reader and I can't afford Courrèges or Blass or Donald

Brooks." She spoke more vehemently than she meant to, but it was the first time that she had voiced her thoughts about *Women Today* and she felt better for it.

Dee Dee looked at Kate for a long time. "Okay, that's the fashion part of the magazine. What about the other drivel they have there now?" She picked up an old copy and began reading out loud the blurbs on the cover. By the time she was halfway through, both women were laughing.

"It all goes," Kate said emphatically. "Instead we write about love, work, sex, self-analysis, how to behave on a date, how to order in a restaurant, how to make out with a man you want, masturbation, menstruation, menopause, seduction, being seduced, seducing, food, wine"—she caught her breath—"everything that can make life bearable, if not enjoyable." She was talking too much, but she didn't care. "I want to create a magazine for women who are trying to make it on their own. . . . I'll give them choices. Sure, I know it all has to start from inside, from the gut, but I want them to be aware they have a gut to work from, that they *have* a choice. Maybe I can make it easier for them than it was for me. I worked like a dog to get what I wanted. I've been working since I was seventeen, with no one to guide me, but I set my goals and went at them. The book is proof of that." She stopped and looked expectantly at Dee Dee. "What do you think?"

"Honestly?" she asked, and without waiting for an answer continued. "I hate it, but you obviously know what you're talking about."

"Why do you hate it?"

"It's too cutsie-poo for me and the idea of telling shop girls and stenographers which fork to use and where to put perfume bores me." She paused briefly. "Have you spoken to J.C. about your ideas?"

"No."

"Do you think he'll let you get away with it?"

"Free rein is what he promised me."

"Well, I'll tell you, Kate, as far as the fashion end of it goes, I'm willing to give it a try. The question is, will anyone else?"

"They'll have to," Kate said, although her conviction wavered. She knew she still had to convince Jason.

6

The young man sent over by Vidal Sassoon moved away and looked at Kate, who was sitting in front of her dressing-table mirror.

"Miss Johnson, it looks terrif. You should always wear your hair that way."

Kate was staring at herself. The wig was beautiful and she had to admit it suited her. She was fully made up, false eyelashes and all, all done to perfection.

"Ben"—she smiled at the young hairdresser—"I'm a working girl, not a debutante or a society lady. This is fine for evening, for a party, but not for the day-to-day life-style I lead."

Ben looked at the room and wondered what she did. She was obviously being kept by someone, but looking at her, he could not quite understand why a rich man would choose her.

"Not to worry. I'll create something special for daytime. Where are you going tonight?" he asked bluntly.

Kate looked at him in surprise. He was a slightly built blond young man, quite attractive, obviously a homosexual. She liked him and did not really mind the rudeness of his question.

"Believe it or not, I'm going to a party in my honor. My book came out a few days ago and the publisher, Jason Reid, has invited the elite of the literary world, as he calls them, to meet me."

"What book?"

She picked up a copy from the night table and handed it to him.

"No!" Ben exclaimed, obviously impressed. "You didn't write this!" He looked at the luscious girl on the cover and wondered if the torrid phrases that the book advertised could possibly have come from this woman, who looked as though she would blush if you said the word "orgasm" out loud. In spite of his compliments to her, she certainly did not look like a sexpot who could have had the experiences the book purportedly talked about.

"Can I have this copy?" he asked.

"I'll even autograph it for you."

As she signed her name on the inside cover she smiled to herself. The assurance with which she did it testified to the poise she had gained in the past months.

It had all fallen into place on the promotional tour. The day before she left, Jason suddenly came by, unannounced. Like a benevolent father, he spent several hours tutoring her on behavior.

"No talk about anything but the book and its contents. Is that clear? They will try to pull you into controversial subjects such as politics, medicine, foreign affairs, psychoanalysis, child rearing, you name it. But you are to stick to the one subject and that is your women, the plain, nice, unnice, ambitious, young, old, frustrated, oversexed, undersexed women. You speak only about

them. If the question is in any way out of your range, hang
the question, talk about what you came to talk about.
Look pleasant and smile and go back to the book. The
interviewers are no fools. They'll get the message."

"But I do have opinions..."

"Oh, crap, Katie, of course you have opinions, but
your opinion on how to settle the Berlin crisis is not going
to sell this book. You can discuss your opinions with me
when you get back, but not in an interview."

"Will I see you while I'm on tour?" she asked, aware
that it was the first time she had injected a personal note
into their conversation. She had been busy while in New
York and had done a great deal of work on the format of
Women Today, but she had also been terribly lonely. It
was a loneliness similar to what she had felt before
meeting Mike. Since Belinda was born she had not felt
this awful gnawing pain of being cut off from everyone,
simply because she had not actually been alone till now.

Jason got up and walked toward her. "It's been a
hell of a visit to New York, hasn't it, Katie?" he said
gently.

She looked up at him and felt the tears ready to
spring to her eyes. Quickly she got up, wanting to rush out
of the room before they came. She was barefoot and since
she was not expecting anyone, she was dressed in an old
terry-cloth robe she had brought from Dayton. Jason
caught her arm as she passed.

"You'll be okay, Katie. I promise. I'm staking a
great deal on you and I'm never wrong."

She turned and smiled up at him. "Sure, I'll be
okay."

He leaned down and kissed her forehead. Again, as
in Dayton, when he first met her for breakfast, he
wondered about his feelings for this strange woman. He
was sure there was a hard core of determination in her and
he was waiting for it to show. He had been very conscious
of her being in the city for the past few weeks, aware of
everything that had happened to her, but he knew that she
had to conquer the city on her own. Dee Dee was
probably a dose too strong to throw at someone as

inexperienced as Kate, but he figured that if she could stand up to Dee Dee, she could stand up to the rest of the vultures she would meet at *Women Today.*

"Here," he said, releasing her, "my card with my private number on it. Call me while you're on tour if you want to talk."

Kate looked at the card and started to laugh. "*J.C.* Reid?"

"What's so funny? That's my name, Jason Cornelius Reid."

"It's a relief, that's all." She couldn't explain about Dee Dee and "Jacey." She pocketed the card. "And I will call."

Kate set off on the promotional tour fully equipped. She knew her lines, she knew her theme, she looked better than she had ever looked in her life. As she entered the part of the country she knew, she switched to some of the old outfits she had brought along in spite of Dee Dee. The expensive designer clothes were fine for the East Coast and Los Angeles and the bigger cities along the way, but she felt she knew the women like herself best, knew what they would accept and what they would not.

As much as she had looked forward to it, Dayton turned out to be the worst part of the tour. Although she was a local celebrity and her mother and Elie were thrilled by her success, Belinda was weepy and cantankerous. When Kate had to leave, the child became hysterical, and if it hadn't been for her mother's soothing words of encouragement, Kate would have been miserable the rest of the tour. As it was, she made a point of calling Belinda every night and started sending small presents to her from all over the country to try to make it up to her.

The success of the tour was reflected in the growing sales figures. The book was going into a second printing when Jason called her in Los Angeles to confirm what she already knew, and she felt a security she had never known before. *Women Today* would be a breeze, she decided. She also decided she was going to have an affair with Jason Reid.

50

The ringing of the phone brought her abruptly back to the present.

"Answer it, Ben," she said with authority, and was amazed at herself. Ben did as he was told without hesitation.

"A Miss Smith is downstairs waiting and wants to know if you need help."

"No," Kate said dryly, "tell her to wait."

Slipping into brown silk pumps, Kate stood erect and stared at herself. Dee Dee was right, she looked superb. The heavy brown silk Empire-style dress was tucked gently under her bosom with a beige lace sash woven into the fabric, ending in a long, streaming flow down the front. The slightly A-line of the long skirt falling stiffly to the floor made her look taller and majestic. The wide boat neckline gave her a long and graceful neck. She picked up the brown velvet cape trimmed with feathers at the neck and hem, took the small brown beaded bag, and smiled at Ben.

"Will you escort me?"

"My pleasure, Miss Johnson. My pleasure," he said with enthusiasm.

Her self-assurance faded as she stepped into the waiting car and saw Dee Dee in the corner, wrapped in a luscious wild fur. Kate didn't even know what it was, except that it was beige, and as always, even seated, Dee Dee dominated.

"You look great, Kate," Dee Dee said sincerely.

Kate smiled to cover her confusion. "I feel like Eliza Doolittle," she confessed, and sat down next to the gloriously beautiful Dee Dee, trying desperately to regain the feelings of assurance she had felt when still up in her room.

"Well, I'm not Rex Harrison, so relax," Dee Dee quipped as the car headed down the avenue.

Jason Reid lived in a town house in the East Thirties. As always, Kate felt a sense of anticipation at seeing Jason. Since leaving Dayton, she had grown accustomed to being entertained in grand rooms and elegant houses. In most of the cities she had visited she had stayed at the company's hotel suites, each one decorated with the finest antiques and in extraordinary taste. Still, the sight that greeted her when the butler opened the door to Jason's town house took her breath away. She was still marveling at the height of the ceilings when Jason appeared. At the sight of him she forgot her awe. She felt herself blush and tried to restrain herself from reaching out to touch him.

"Dee Dee," he said, embracing her with obvious affection, "you are magnificent, as always." Dee Dee kissed Jason on the cheek, and Kate knew without a doubt that they were lovers. She also wondered if she could compete with someone as bright and beautiful as Dee Dee.

"And, Kate," Jason said, turning to her, "you look lovely." He helped her with her cape and as his hand brushed her shoulder she tried not to show any emotion.

As Jason led them into the living room Kate froze at the sight of the people, all turned expectantly toward her.

"Ladies and gentlemen," Jason said loudly, "our guest of honor."

Everyone applauded politely and moved toward her. She shook hands endlessly and listened attentively to every name. Two names struck her. Allyson Fenster and Hank Storm. The former was the temporary editor in charge of the magazine; the latter was the managing editor. She had seen their names numerous times when leafing through the back issues of *Women Today*. So, she thought, these two and Dee Dee were the skeleton crew that she would have to cope with when she took over.

Allyson was a woman in her mid-fifties. She had been with the Jason Reid empire for a long time and knew everything there was to know about the mechanics of running a magazine, but she lacked the flair Jason wanted. She knew he was looking for someone but she kept hoping he would not find anyone and that she would get the job. When Jason had invited her to come to a New Year's Eve party to meet his new discovery, she had first been ill with disappointment, then furious. But now she felt reassured and not a little bewildered. This could not possibly be the great new discovery. She could not decide if she was relieved or upset. Obviously it would never work. She would simply sit on the sidelines and wait until Miss Kate Johnson buckled under the responsibility.

Kate felt nervous as she shook hands with Allyson, who was extremely attractive in a brittle sort of way. Her dark hair was drawn back into a tight bun that gave her face a hard look. Her eyes, as she appraised Kate, were light blue and almost transparent.

"Kate." The woman repeated her name as she turned to a man who was standing beside her. "I want you to meet my husband, Cliff Fenster."

Kate looked over at a tall, heavy-set man who was obviously a drinker. She had seen too many at the *Chronicle* not to recognize one. As he smiled at Kate she could smell the liquor on his breath. She also caught the look of concern and tenderness that transformed Allyson's face as she made the introduction. At that moment her eyes were not cold and hard; instead they seemed to shower love on this overgrown drunk. Kate made a mental note for future reference. The woman was obviously too old for the job of editor, and having an alcoholic for a husband was too much of a distraction.

She turned her attention to Hank Storm and his wife. They looked like the classic picture of the well-to-do, well-bred, attractive couple in their late fifties who have few cares in the world. Jean Storm smiled warmly at Kate and squeezed her arm while whispering, "Good luck." Hank Storm was tall, extremely attractive, and very easygoing in manner. He was about Jason's age, and Kate assumed they had been friends for many years. His greeting to Kate was warm and pleasant. Instinctively Kate knew she would depend on him when she went to *Women Today*. As if reading her thoughts, he winked at her. "See you," he said as he and his wife sauntered away.

Except for Cliff's becoming a little boisterous and Allyson's having to take him home, the evening was uneventful. Kate was never left alone. Everyone was complimentary about the book and predictions were made that it would hit the best-seller list and stay on it for a long time. To the question "How did you happen to write it?" or such comments as "How timely and clever of you, when women's liberation is just around the corner," Kate simply smiled.

Just after midnight, after everyone toasted the coming of the new year, the place began to empty out. Suddenly Kate found herself alone in the room and heard Jason in the hall saying good night to Dee Dee.

"You don't mind being dropped off by my chauffeur?" he was saying.

"I'm a liberated woman, have you forgotten?" Dee Dee answered, and Kate for some reason felt embarrassed. There was a moment of whispering that followed the statement and Dee Dee's contemptuous laughter. The front door slammed and Jason was back in the room.

"Let's go up and have a nightcap," he said, and held out his hand to her.

As they entered his study, Kate saw that the room was identical to one he had in Dayton and on the plane. The familiar surroundings broke her tension and she relaxed. Jason was standing close to her. She put her head on his chest and, without looking at him, whispered, "Please make love to me."

He lifted her off her feet and carried her toward the bedroom, kissing her and murmuring her name.

Kate didn't remember undressing. Her only clear recollection was feeling Jason's naked body beside her, his touching her, caressing her, kissing her, and, finally, thrusting himself into her. Her body seemed to melt into his and all the pent-up emotion stored inside since meeting him exploded. Her mind was a blank as her body enjoyed his knowledgeable hands and the intensity of her own response. Her only thought was that she wished the experience could go on forever.

In the early hours of the morning, lying beside him in his darkened bedroom, Kate evaluated her feelings. He was a magnificent lover, and she hoped there would be more, many more nights like last night. At the same time she was very much aware of the absence of that state she had only read about—being in love. There was no wild, swooning passion of feeling for him. And she was equally sure he was not in love with her. She needed him and for some reason he needed her. Was it only for the magazine? For him? For her? Was she paying for all he had done for her? Hardly. He had the pick of the most beautiful women in New York or anywhere else. No, there was a bond between them. It was a fair trade. She would make his magazine a success, he would make her a success, and he would be proved right for having chosen her.

Jason was still fast asleep as she climbed out of bed and went into the bathroom. She was surprised to find her clothes and wig on the bathroom floor. She could have sworn she had not been in the bathroom the night before, but obviously she must have undressed there. She looked at herself in the mirrors that lined the walls from floor to ceiling. Her hair was messy, but Ben had been careful when putting on the wig, so the line of her own hairdo was still there. She examined herself carefully and was not displeased with what she saw. She was no Dee Dee Smith, but it was she, not Dee Dee, who had been made love to by Jason Reid.

She was taking her shower when she heard Jason come into the bathroom. Opening the door to the stall shower, he watched her for a moment, then he pulled her wet body to him and carried her back into the bedroom.

When she next woke she felt dazed. Her mouth was dry and for a moment she didn't know where she was, then she saw Jason in his dressing gown, sipping a drink, and the events of the night came back to her.

"What time is it, Jason?" she asked.

"I wondered when you'd cut out the Mr. Reid bit." He smiled warmly at her.

"Well, I figured that sexual intercourse is as good an introduction as any, wouldn't you say?" She smiled back at him. Then, looking around, she asked, "Never mind what time it is, what day is it?"

"It's New Year's Day, Kate, and it's now six o'clock in the evening."

Oh, my God, Kate thought, and I promised to call

Belinda at midnight. "Jason, may I use the phone please?" she said, trying to hide her apprehension.

"It's right beside the bed," he answered, and tactfully left the room. Her life in Dayton was hers and he wanted no part of it.

The disappointment in Belinda's voice was heart-rending. "But you promised, Mommy, you promised," the child wailed uncontrollably.

"Sweetheart, I'm sorry and it won't happen again," Kate said, trying to quiet the child down. "Mommy had something she had to do." The words were hollow. What was she doing, she wondered. What was she trading to get ahead? She had used Belinda as a shield against her loneliness and now she was abandoning her, without a fight.

When she hung up, she jumped out of bed, picked up a robe that was at the foot of the bed, and ran into the next room. Jason was absorbed in some papers and Kate walked over to him.

"I don't think I can do it," she said quietly.

"Do what?" He looked up at her through his thick-rimmed glasses.

"I can't give up my child."

"Yes, you can," he answered coldly.

"I won't, though."

"Well, if that's your decision, and you think it's final, I can assure you there will be two grateful ladies, if nothing else," he answered sarcastically.

"You mean Dee Dee and Allyson?"

"For starters."

"And you won't let me bring her to New York?"

"Won't let?" He raised his brows in surprise. "You can bring her to New York, but think of what's in store for her here while you're climbing the ladder which I've conveniently set up for you." Then as an afterthought, "And I hate having ladies who are constantly looking for baby-sitters."

"But she's alone out there."

"Alone? In Dayton with your mother and I believe you have a sister, don't you?"

"Yes."

"Well, then, how alone can she be? She'll be a hell of a lot more alone here in New York." He paused and pulled her into his lap. She nestled there, placing her head against the velvet lapel. "Katie, careers such as I have planned for you and which you have have planned for yourself have to paid for. Nothing, but nothing, can interfere with that one goal you set for yourself. Not children, not family, not friends, nothing." He spoke quietly, but the words were serious. She felt him kiss her head and knew that everything he said was true... and familiar to her. She had often thought these things herself and had written letters in the *Chronicle* to her readers saying much the same thing, though couched in platitudes, since she knew that few of them had the ambition she had or would do what she was now agreeing to do. She felt Jason reach into her robe and touch her breast. The desire for him of the night before returned.

"It's the woman who seduces the man, Jason," she whispered as she looked up at him. "Didn't you know that?"

"That's one I'll never believe." He kissed her.

They made love again and both knew that Kate had sealed the bargain. Belinda, she thought, was, in fact, better off with her grandmother until the time came when she could afford to bring her to the city.

7

There was an air of anticipation at the offices of *Women Today* the morning that Kate Johnson was to arrive for her first meeting with the staff. Speculations were running rampant. Jane Caulson, the story editor, who had been with the magazine just a short while, was nervous. She had quit her job at another magazine to come to *Women Today*, fully aware that the magazine was in bad shape. She was in her late thirties and believed she could inject some life into the articles, which were aimed at a dwindling readership. She was constantly overruled by every one of the old guard, and in order to hang on to her job, she began to copy the same style that was killing the circulation. Married, with two children, she wrote about the young marrieds, bringing up children, suburbia, the high cost of living, things she hoped would draw the attention of her own age group, but to no avail. Now that a new and, from what she had heard, young woman was coming into the top job, she hoped there would be a chance for her to explain her line of thinking.

Maggie Pearson, the food editor, was indifferent to the change. She had been with the magazine for some fifteen years, brought up her family on the recipes that she tried out on her brood of six children and then wrote into funny, amusing articles for the readers of *Women Today*. Her husband, John, was still writing the great American novel. Money was certainly a problem to her family, but they were a close-knit clan, and if she were forced to leave she was sure she could manage. If anything, she was rather pleased that some young blood was coming into the magazine. Her two teenaged daughters were a constant reminder to her that a new world was growing up and that *Women Today* was simply not reaching them.

Joe Parkins, the art director, was furious at the change and the manner in which it was being done. "They're treating us like children who were about to meet their new headmistress." Joe had sniffed around and heard through the grapevine that Kate Johnson was a simple, homely, totally unchic woman and the idea that she would give him orders appalled him.

"I'll resign the first time she gives me an order," he announced as they were all sitting in Hank Storm's office, waiting. "Has anyone actually seen her?"

"I saw her on a television interview show a few weeks ago," Joyce McGuire, the beauty editor, announced.

"And?"

"For the birds, my friends, for the birds. Not a brain in her head, quite simple-looking, almost unattractive, and she was dressed like the cat dragged her in."

"Really?" Dee Dee had been listening but not reacting. Now her ears perked up. "What was she wearing?"

"Well, it was hard to tell, she was sitting down, but from what I could see she was a cloud of paisley and chartreuse, with a ribbon bow of the same paisley in the back of her hair. It was ghastly, my dear, ghastly."

"Where was this, anyway?" Dee Dee sounded nonchalant. She had seen Kate on one of the bigger shows in New York over the Christmas holiday and had thought she looked superb and handled herself well, although she was obviously nervous and quite shy. But she had certainly got her points across about the book.

"I was out visiting my mother in Kentucky," Joyce answered. "And I repeat, she's not very bright. She kept evading questions and going on and on about that piece of crap she wrote. It was too embarrassing."

"Has anyone read her book?" Dee Dee asked.

They had all read it and were quick to admit it. The consensus was that it was garbage, badly written, almost indecent, and although there must be a market for it, somewhere, certainly they were not it.

"My daughters loved it," Maggie Pearson said quietly. "They thought it was great. And I'll tell you something else, most of their friends loved it."

"She won't last a day," Joyce McGuire announced with conviction. "And if she does, she'd better not interfere with my department. If there is one thing I know, it's the beauty field, and no one, but no one who looks like that is going to tell me what to do. If she does, I'll speak to Hank about it."

"You don't say. Speak to Hank Storm?" Dee Dee said mockingly.

"What is that supposed to mean?" Joyce was ready to pounce. "We're good friends and he knows my background and how valuable I am to *Women Today*."

At that moment Tony Umberto, the production manager, came in. Everyone looked surprised. He was the oldest employee of *Women Today*, had been with it since its inception, but he was never invited to the inner circle of editorial meetings. He was carrying a pile of magazines under his arm and placed them carefully on Hank's desk.

"Hi, everybody," he said self-consciously. "Miss Johnson asked me to be present at this first meeting."

"Have you seen her?" Joe asked suspiciously.

Tony nodded, went to sit in the back of the room,

and took out his pipe, pretending to be occupied with cleaning and lighting it.

"Well, what's she like?" Joe demanded. Tony continued to clean his pipe, ignoring the question. He had not only seen Kate but had spent the last two weeks in her company. The minute Kate knew that she had the job, she had called Tony and asked him to come to her hotel suite.

Originally from Tulsa, Oklahoma, Tony Umberto had been in New York many years, most of them spent with *Women Today*. He had been heartbroken as he watched the circulation of the magazine go down, and was more aware than most how badly the magazine was hurting. He could not understand how the readers of the day could not appreciate the serialized stories, why the pictures and articles were no longer read by millions as they had been in the past. Advertisers were leaving them in droves, and it pained him to see the magazine dwindle in size from month to month.

He was completely taken aback when he walked into Kate's living room. She was too young to understand, he decided, too young to run *Women Today*. Yet, in spite of his reaction, he liked her on sight.

"Tony," she said as she took him by the arm and led him toward a seat, "I need your help, and I hope you will bear with me." She had a direct way of talking and he loved her Midwestern twang. He believed the phonies at *Women Today*, with their pretended Boston or British accents, were probably responsible for the demise of his beloved magazine.

"Anything I can do, Miss Johnson, I will."

"Please call me Kate," she said pleasantly. "Now, let's get right down to business." She sat down across from him and looked directly at him. "For starters, I know nothing about running a magazine." She saw him blanch and she smiled. "But I'm going to learn, and learn quickly. What I want from you is guidance about the mechanics. You see, I want the first issue with the new format to come out for Memorial Day. This is the middle of January and I expect to be ready to go with a whole new approach by then."

The rest of his meeting with her, and the many meetings that followed, had been spent with her showing him how she wanted the magazine to look, the new look of the models who would be shown, the new approach to copy. At first he was shocked at her ideas, found them distasteful, but even so he could not disagree with her. It certainly was a new approach, almost crude, but still it never went overboard or became in any way vulgar. Certainly he knew he would not object to his own daughter reading it.

Tony helped her put together several rough but nearly complete issues, demonstrating what she envisioned for the magazine. Now Tony was curious to see how the staff would react to Kate, fearful they would not take kindly to her or her ideas for *Women Today*.

Kate's confidence was at a peak as she walked into the office building of *Women Today*. She knew exactly what she wanted to achieve and how to go about getting it. Tony had been of enormous help and so had her newfound friend, Ben. The young hairdresser was now always around helping her in every way. His knowledge of what was going on in the city was staggering. If he did not have the information firsthand he knew someone who did. Ben's suggestions were invaluable and in many cases saved her unnecessary worries. It was Ben who suggested she hire a personal secretary before actually starting her work at the magazine.

Kate broached the subject to Jason, who had the personnel manager of Reid Publications send over several girls to be interviewed. Although they all tried to look bright and sophisticated, Kate could sense their nervousness and even awe. It would be the opportunity of a lifetime for any of them to come to work as personal secretary to the future editor in chief of a glamour magazine. Kate could not help but be amused by their credentials. Each had majored in English literature and had graduated from a fine college; each reported working during the summer for her father's or uncle's business. Their typing skills were meager, none could take shorthand. Kate saw them as overindulged and inexperienced children who would be totally inadequate for the job. She was coming to the conclusion that Jason had been right when he suggested she take one of the older and more experienced secretaries from *Women Today*. Then Carol Butler walked in. The minute she saw her, Kate knew she had found the right girl.

Carol ambled in, her long legs moving her torso with ease, hips pushed forward, shoulders slightly stooped, head held high. She was not beautiful but she carried herself as though she were. Her ash-blond hair, parted on the side, fell loosely to her shoulders; her clear hazel eyes slanted upward and her mouth, devoid of makeup, was full and sensuous. Her skin, almost transparent, gave her a look of delicate porcelain. She was dressed in mushroom-colored suede pants, a tuxedo-style coat made of the same fabric. The soft man-tailored silk shirt matched the lining of the coat. The bag slung over her shoulder and the gloves she carried were pigskin. In contrast to all the other girls who were interviewed, Carol walked directly over to where Kate was sitting and put her hand out. Her handshake was firm.

"I'm Carol Butler, Miss Johnson," she said.

As she looked around for a seat Kate could think of only one word that adequately described the young woman—thoroughbred.

"Tell me about yourself, Carol," Kate said as she had to all the others who had been in before.

"I was born in London because my father's work made it necessary for my parents to be there. I lived there until I was three, when we came back to New York. I've been here ever since. I graduated from the Nightingale School and spent one year at Bennington, where I thought of majoring in journalism."

"Why did you leave?"

"I didn't feel it was giving me what I wanted."

"How old are you?"

"Twenty-two."

"What have you done since leaving Bennington?"

"I joined the Peace Corps and spent some time in

Africa. Contracted some disease out there and had to come back. I was sick for quite a while and that's when I took a course in typing and shorthand, which I hate but do quite well." She smiled for the first time. Her teeth were straight and very white. "So when I heard about this job I thought I'd apply. Actually, I'm very well qualified for it," she added without modesty. "Incidentally, I took the test the personnel office gave." Kate was amused. None of the other applicants had.

"Have you done any writing?" Kate asked, and wondered about her question. She had purposely not asked any of the others if they could write, certain that each would have been enthusiastic about the prospect of writing for *Women Today*.

"Is that a requirement?" the young woman asked, and for the first time since Carol had come into the room there seemed to be a crack in her self-assurance.

"No ..." Kate hesitated, then, more forcefully, said, "No, it isn't." Kate stood up. "Well, as far as I'm concerned you have the job."

"Then there won't be any writing on the job?" Carol asked as she too stood up and gathered up her belongings.

"Not really," Kate said, and again was aware of a certain discomfort in the young woman's expression. She tried to figure out if the look was relief or disappointment. Suddenly for no reason Kate regretted having hired Carol. The girl was too sure of herself, too aggressive, too pretty. She could have kicked herself for being so impulsive. Carol Butler had traveled with her family, lived in Europe. . . . But who was she? Who was her father? What did he do? Kate felt she should have asked more questions but knew it was too late. She had already committed herself.

Carol interrupted her thoughts. "When would you like me to start?"

"Well, until I move into the offices of *Women Today* I'll be working out of here. I would like you to be available for several hours every day when I've finished with the production manager. There are all sorts of errands that have to be run and thoughts I'd like typed out for my presentation to the board. I'm afraid it won't really be a nine-to-five job ever, but certainly for starters it will be even worse." Kate looked closely at the girl, almost hoping she'd now turn down the job. "It's Thursday, so suppose you come here on Monday around noon."

"It sounds fine to me," Carol said as she started toward the door.

"You won't mind the hours?" Kate called after her.

"No problem." Carol turned around and smiled a pleasant but cool smile. "Any date that's worth its salt can hold off till later." And she was gone.

Carol proved to be a gem. She was the epitome of the New York-bred animal. Kate never ceased to be amazed at her facility, her assurance, her ability to pick up a phone and handle without fuss the most unusual request that Kate might make. She seemed to know everyone and, young as she was, succeeded in commanding respect from all who came into contact with her. Still, she kept a professional distance, never became personal. By the time Kate went to meet her future staff she realized that despite all their working hours together, she knew little about Carol Butler except that she was bright, wealthy, and evidently quite popular.

Hank and Allyson were waiting for Kate at the elevator as she stepped into the reception room of *Women Today*, and escorted her into Hank's office. As they entered, a silence fell over the room. Tony looked up, his reveries interrupted. She's awfully small, he thought, but she sure can handle herself. Hank suggested she sit behind the desk but Kate pulled a chair over and seated herself in front of the desk. Clasping her hands in her lap, she smiled at everyone in the room. She knew something about each and every one of them. Tony had described them well.

Kate had prepared a speech, but now, looking at the faces around her, she chose a simpler approach. "As you know, I'm Kate Johnson and I shall be taking over as editor in chief at *Women Today*. My feelings are that a complete change of format is the only way to save this magazine. I sincerely hope that all of you will stay and help me in my efforts."

"When you say change of format," Joe Parkins said,

plunging right in, "can you explain what you mean?"

"You're Joe Parkins, the art director, right?" She smiled sweetly, although the man was repulsive to her. He was pretending an aggressiveness he obviously did not feel.

"Well, I could start with your outlook and presentation of the magazine as a whole." She looked directly at him. "It's simply all wrong," she said candidly. "I'm looking for youth, hope, and carefreeness in every page. What you have now is lovely but"—she paused, knowing that the next phrase would be shattering—"it's old-fashioned."

Joe exploded. "You've got to be kidding. What I've succeeded in getting into this rag, and it is just that, is some class. Elegance for the special people who still do live in this country." He was fuming and spluttering, his thoughts racing ahead of his ability to word them. "Long after the fads which these sick kids of today are looking for are dead, the expensive, beautiful classic look I've shown in *Women Today* will be as alive as it was twenty-five years ago and will still be twenty-five years from now."

"You're probably right," Kate said carefully, "but I think we should be more fluid and move with the times. When your look comes back, I'm sure we'll be aware of it and return to it. For the moment the money is in the hands of a different group. Those sick kids you refer to are the ones who have their hands on the purse strings. Just look at the statistics."

"Statistics be hanged," Joe replied in anger. "What you're doing will hammer the final nail in the coffin and push this dying rag right into the grave."

He looked around and realized that no one was going to back him. "I've got too much of a reputation to agree to be a party to the death of *Women Today*."

"That's too bad," Kate said pleasantly, "but I certainly do see your point. I think you should stick to your convictions. For all I know, you may very well be right and I would hate to have you go down with me, if I do, in fact, misread the new trend."

He stood up and looked confused. Although he had actually resigned, he had just been fired. He had no choice but to leave. With a grand gesture that belied his real feelings, he nodded to Kate and walked toward the door. His hand was on the doorknob but he hesitated. He could not believe that this little idiot would let him walk out. The room was completely silent. "You're all goddamned fools," he said, and walked out.

"Well," Hank said, trying to ease the tension in the room, "I think we've heard two rather conflicting points of view about the future of *Women Today*. I believe the floor is now open for another discussion."

Maggie Pearson started to laugh quietly. "The old world and the new have collided, and as far as I can see, the new world has come out the winner." She turned to Kate. "I'm Maggie Pearson, and I'm cook, dishwasher, et cetera, at *Women Today*. And if you'll have an old bag like me, I'll stick around. I live with six creators of the new fads, and it will be a pleasure to participate in this new venture."

"Thank you, Maggie," Kate said. She was relieved that Joe Parkins had walked out. His layouts were dragging everything in a direction that was totally different from what she envisioned. Yet the idea that she was now left without an art director made her uneasy.

Dee Dee was watching Kate. For an insecure person Kate was holding her own quite well. She was annoyed that Kate was not dressed in one of her more attractive new outfits, but assumed that she probably felt more comfortable in what she was wearing and she could not really fault her for that. Dee Dee knew quite a bit about layouts, but she refused to admit it at that point. Let her stew, she thought.

"We'll manage for a while without an art director," Tony said from the back of the room. "We have almost a complete layout for the next two issues and we'll wing it on the others until you find someone else."

Everyone now nodded his consent.

"How are we going to do the switchover?" Jane Caulson asked. "I mean, how long before the unveiling of the new *Women Today?*" She liked Kate. She thought Kate looked like a down-to-earth person and Jane found her youth refreshing.

"You're Jane Caulson, aren't you?" Kate looked at the woman who was talking. She had disliked every one of Jane's articles, but the woman was obviously being helpful and she dared not push her out for now.

"Well, I'm aiming for the Memorial Day issue. As for routines—I would like to establish a day in the week which would be devoted to an open discussion about ideas and direction. I know what I'm looking for, but input from all of you will be a great help."

She had discussed this idea with Jason, and although he saw its merits, he felt it was unlikely that the staff now on the magazine would come up with anything new. Kate had disagreed.

"Thursday seems like a good day," she continued. "We'll meet at four in the afternoon and spend a couple of hours just having a bull session. As a matter of fact, why don't you all write up ideas that you would like to see developed and we can discuss them openly at that time."

"Four o'clock is not a very good hour for me," Jane said haltingly. "I have to catch the five-twelve train to Larchmont." She was embarrassed, but it couldn't be helped. "I have two kids, a husband, and they have to be fed."

This was exactly what Kate did not want. An editor with two kids and dinner to prepare. "Is three o'clock better?" she asked.

Everyone nodded.

Allyson was watching with great amusement. Joe Parkins had been right. They were all sitting around as if in a schoolroom, listening to their new headmistress. Jason had goofed, she decided; this will never work out.

"Any comments about the beauty pages?" Joyce suddenly asked.

"Not offhand," Kate answered. She had hated the woman on sight but tried to hide her feelings. "I'm sure you'll fall into the swing of the new makeup which the kids are into now, or the no-makeup look they really go for."

"What's this with kids?" Joyce kept her voice in check. "This is a magazine for women. The name of it is *Women Today*, or haven't you noticed?" She smiled to cover the bitchiness of the remark. "What I mean is, we *are* still going to write for women, aren't we?"

"Of course." Kate's voice became icy. "*Young* women. I'm aiming for the eighteen- to thirty-five-year-old market. Young unmarried women, whose look is a much younger one than that of the generation before. My mother at thirty-five was old, while a thirty- to thirty-five-year-old today is young. I think you're right, though, and we should stop using the word 'kids.' I do mean young women. And I know that most young women today are far more conscious of their skin, their bodies, their inner and their outer appearance. It's all easier and lighter. The no-makeup look is probably more made up than ever before, but that's what the look is, and our hook to get to them is to show them how to achieve it."

Joyce bit her lip. She had been a beauty editor a long time and resented being told her own business by this newcomer, whose manner seemed even condescending. Obviously her original impression had been wrong, for Kate was a much cooler cat than she had thought. The fact that she allowed Joe to walk out without so much as a word to stop him proved it. Well, Joyce had no intention of leaving. She could wait it out. This new situation couldn't last. She looked at Hank, who was doodling with a pencil and seemed completely at ease. It disturbed her.

"Well, I believe this has been a good meeting," Hank said as the silence deepened in the room. "I'm certainly pleased to have Kate with us. I have great faith in her and I know Mr. Reid has, too." Then, turning to Kate, he said, "Welcome. You know you have my complete support. I believe everyone here feels the same way and will do everything possible to help you achieve a new *Women Today*."

"Yes, Kate," Allyson said, aware that she had kept silent too long. "We're all rooting for you." She stood up. Everyone else followed suit, and as each walked over to shake Kate's hand, Kate felt uncomfortable. Given a choice, she would have fired everyone except Tony, Hank and Maggie. They seemed to be the only ones who were on her side. It was ironic to think that they were probably the oldest people there.

Left alone with Hank, Kate relaxed.

"Well, that wasn't too bad," Hank said as he lit his pipe. "Joe is an ass, always was, so in a way it's good riddance."

"Can we manage without him until I find someone?"

"Oh, yeah. Tony is good, and Allyson is a real pro. She'll resent it, but she's one of the loyal ones, a real company man, she'll go down with the ship, if need be."

"You think we'll go down?"

"We're almost at the bottom now, Kate, so there isn't very far to go. And as they say, when you're that far down, there's only one way to go and that's up." He smiled encouragingly. "Don't look so glum. You were great, and J.C. believes in you."

"Jason Cornelius or Jesus Christ?" Kate asked, a smile spreading slowly across her face.

"In this organization they're one and the same, or haven't you noticed?"

8

Kate was exhausted. She was determined to put out a completely new magazine for the Memorial Day issue, but as the days rushed by, realities she had not foreseen arose.

"You cannot afford to insult good writers who have been with us for years by simply not publishing what they were commissioned to do," Jason explained carefully. They were sitting in his study, waiting for his driver to come and pick her up. "Besides, you have to test out the format slowly. Small doses at first until you feel out what should replace what."

"But the cover will be totally different," she said defiantly. "You promised me that."

"Have you found a new art director yet?"

71

Kate hesitated. She had found someone, and she was determined to have her, but knew she could not afford the enormous salary the girl was asking. Kate had seen Betsy Jorgensen's layouts in several magazines but had never met her. Betsy was the art director of an ad agency and there was a quality she succeeded in getting into her pictures of the men and women she photographed, especially the women, a sensuality that leaped from the page, even when advertising nothing more than a tea bag. Kate had called and tried to set up a meeting, but Betsy was not interested in meetings. She asked what Kate wanted. When she heard Kate's proposal she asked for an outrageous salary and the conversation had ended with "Take it or leave it." Kate was furious but not deterred. She was sure that if she could meet with the girl she could persuade her to come down in price. She had made several efforts, with no luck, when she found out that Ben knew her well.

Kate and Ben had become good friends. He came regularly to do her hair and give her a massage at her new small apartment. Once accepted by the board, Kate had gone on salary and Jason had made no bones about the fact that she was now on her own financially. Ben had found her the apartment on Fifty-seventh Street just off Eighth Avenue, with a sort of Old World charm of its own despite its tacky location. Built at the turn of the century, the building had a courtyard with some wispy, tired-looking trees and several drooping sun-thirsty flowers. Jason had been furious. He considered it inelegant and in a bad neighborhood, not befitting her new position. Although her salary was nearly double what she had been earning on the *Chronicle*, Kate now had two households to support. Once out of the Regency and having to pay for everything—food, clothing, makeup, minimal household utilities—she was not quite sure how she would manage. Because Jason raged, she half expected him to offer to pay for a better apartment, but he never did. Nor did he ever come to see her apartment, but when she moved in he sent her a priceless crystal vase and an antique Bergère chair, both totally out of place amid the Salvation Army furniture Ben had helped her find. Small as the place was, Kate loved it. She had never had her own apartment.

The night she learned Ben knew Betsy, he had come to the apartment to give her her weekly massage.

"You're tense as hell, Kate," he said as he rubbed her back. She was naked, lying on the massage table that had been Ben's housewarming gift, and, as always, she marveled at her own immodesty where Ben was concerned. She had never known a homosexual and found in him a perfect friend.

"Turn around," he ordered. As she lay on her back he began to massage her thighs. "God, you're skinny," he said with exasperation. Then, unexpectedly, she felt his hand rest between her legs, and she opened her eyes.

"Why, Ben, I do believe you're making a blatant pass." She laughed self-consciously. He had massaged her so often, and never once had he even hinted that he was aware of her as a woman.

"Oh, I swing both ways, Kate. Didn't you know?"

She didn't answer but closed her eyes again. Her affair with Jason was sporadic. He would call in the evening and send the car around for her, almost like a royal summons. Soon, however, she realized that there were too many evenings when he was in meetings or, worse, with other women. Jealousy, which she had always felt to be a sign of weakness, burned inside her. She hated the thought of another woman in his bed and was ashamed of her feelings, but she could not dismiss them.

"Let's screw," Ben said suddenly, and Kate opened her eyes and looked directly at him.

"Why not," she said, knowing that she was being childish, taking revenge on Jason, who would never know of this little affair and probably wouldn't care if he did find out.

They walked to the bed, and Ben undressed quickly. Kate, watching him, was surprised to see the size of his sex organ.

"You're as tight as a closed clam," he said softly as he pushed himself into her, "and it feels heavenly. Almost as good as a tight ass."

"Ben, you're vulgar." Kate laughed.

Jason was a good lover, but in no way could he compare with Ben, who seemed to know exactly where every button was and how to push it. He kept plunging himself into her and she felt herself reach a climax, but still he would not stop.

"Come again," he kept whispering, "and again, and again."

Vaguely she heard the phone ring and knew instinctively that it was Jason. She had no intention of answering it. He knew she was at home, that she never went out, for she had no real friends in the city, and usually brought work home. Would he come pounding at the door, she wondered. The thought of Jason coming into her apartment and finding her being made love to by another man was an irresistible fantasy. It would be wonderful revenge for the pain he was causing her.

The phone continued to ring. Suddenly it occurred to her that it might be her mother, that something might have happened to Belinda.

"Ben, I've got to answer the phone," she gasped, trying to push him away.

"Go right ahead," he answered as he went on making love to her. "I'm having a ball, and you can talk all you want." He picked up the phone from the night table beside the bed and handed it to her.

"Kate, is that you?" Jason's voice came booming through.

"Yes-e-ss," she answered, trying to control the breathlessness in her voice.

"Are you all right?" Jason asked after a moment.

"Sure, I'm fine, Jason."

"What took you so long to answer the phone?"

"Ben is giving me a massage," she answered, trying to suppress her laughter.

"I want you to come over."

"Not tonight, Jason," Kate said firmly, now pushing Ben away forcefully, chiding him with her eyes and whispering with her hand over the mouthpiece of the phone, "Hold it a second." Then, back into the phone,

"Jason, there are several things I've got to do and it's awfully late."

"As you wish," Jason said, and the phone went dead.

Kate panicked immediately. "Ben, I've got to go."

"You just said you weren't going."

"He's furious."

"Big deal."

"No, it's important, Ben. I'm trying to get my hands on an art director, Betsy Jorgensen, and the salary she wants is astronomical."

"Betsy?" Ben exclaimed. "The bitch. Where does she come off asking for a huge salary. She's richer than Rockefeller."

"Do you know her?"

"Sure, she's one of my clients."

"What's she like? I've never seen her, just talked to her over the phone. She speaks with an accent."

"She's from Sweden."

Ben, starting to dress, threw her the towel. She caught it and started wiping herself.

"She's a beauty, a real beauty. Very well educated...Switzerland, England, and that crap. She sure doesn't need the money."

"Could you arrange for us to meet? She won't even see me, since she thinks that *Women Today* is a rag, that we're all square, and I can't seem to convince her that I'm changing the format."

"Well...I guess so...sure," he said, but he sounded hesitant.

"You're holding something back," Kate said as she went into the shower, leaving the door open so she could hear Ben's answer.

"No, no, it's all right. I'll call her in the morning."

"How old is she?"

"About twenty-five or so, but she doesn't look it, there's something quite ageless about her. She'll look the same when she's fifty-five."

"Does she like what she's doing now?"

"Hates it," Ben replied, "and that's why I don't

understand your not being able to get her away from it. You're sure you want her?" he asked as she came out of the bathroom and started dressing.

"Of course I am. Why? Is there some problem you're not telling me?" Ben assured her there was nothing, but she felt uneasy.

Now, sitting in Jason's study, she was uncomfortable on several levels. Jason did not try to make love to her. On the contrary, he was still furious with her for having dared to refuse his command over the phone. He started right off with a lecture about the way money is spent on a magazine.

"There are obligations that must be met. We have advertisers who won't buy what we're now planning to put on the stand. Granted there are not that many anymore, but one of the jobs you will have will be to convince *new* advertisers that the new format will reach women who never dreamed of buying *Women Today* before."

"Well, that's why the cover on the Memorial Day issue has got to be really smashing and *different*."

"Okay. But Joe is gone, and as far as I can see, you haven't really found anyone else."

"Oh, I have," Kate answered quickly. "It's just that she's asking for so much money I don't think the budget will carry her."

"Who is she?"

"Betsy Jorgensen," Kate answered. "Do you know her?"

"No, I don't think I do. Who's she with now?"

"Blain and Borg."

"Well, she's certainly at the top. Has she had any magazine experience?"

"No."

"Oh, come on, Kate, you've got no experience and now you're trying to drag in another newcomer?"

"But that's the whole idea, Jason. I want people who will come to the magazine without years of hang-ups. The whole mood has to be fresh. I've seen her work, and she's exactly what I want. We've got to get a different look for the girls who are going to model for *Women Today*. Something girls can identify with, not those six-foot toothpicks we always use. But real girls, wearing real clothes."

"What's she asking?"

"Twenty-five thousand."

"Offer her twenty thousand with a good expense account and a promise of a raise after a year if she works out."

There was a knock at the door. Jason and Kate both stood up. "You did the right thing by coming over after all, Kate. You can fuck around all you want, but not on my time, which is every time I want you to come over here."

Kate blushed and didn't answer.

He walked over to his desk. Picking up a batch of papers, he handed them to her. "I like every one of the ideas in here. I've also written the blurbs for several of them." He smiled, and for a moment he looked like a benevolent old headmaster, complimenting a child on a good grade. "You've really caught on quickly. The sexy stuff is good, and you'll note that I've corrected some misconceptions you have about men-women relationships, especially when it comes to affairs." He led her to the door. "I'm going to be away for a week. I'll call you when I get back."

She froze. "You mean you won't be here? What happens if I need you...for something to do with the magazine?" she added, furious with herself.

"Hank will take care of you, I promise."

"I think you'd better at least call, in case something comes up," she said, trying to be businesslike.

"I won't need to, Katie, you'll be just fine."

He opened the door for her, to reveal a vision in white fox, eyes cold at being kept waiting, who stalked past into the living room without a word, twitching provocatively in her skintight sheath.

Kate headed for the elevator after a "Good night" she could hardly force through her clenched teeth. She felt so helpless, so betrayed, she could feel the nausea rising in her throat.

When she arrived back at her apartment it was nearly one in the morning, and the phone was ringing as she entered. It was Ben.

"Listen, Kate, I bumped into Betsy when I left you, and she's with me now. Can we come over?"

Kate wanted to go to bed, but she decided to get it over with.

They arrived in a few minutes. After a brief introduction Ben excused himself and left.

Kate looked at Betsy and wondered how to begin. The girl gave her no encouragement. She stared back, cold and definitely unfriendly. Her hair was naturally blond and she wore it parted in the center and pulled back tightly into a bun. Her eyes were green and enormous, her skin very white and devoid of makeup. She wasn't tall, and her body was like an hourglass, full-bosomed and full-hipped with a tiny waist. She wore blue jeans and a man's tailored shirt and sneakers. Around her neck was a thin silver chain with a large silver bean-shaped ornament dangling from it. In spite of tiny diamonds winking from her pierced earlobes, there was an uncompromising severity about her that put Kate off but oddly attracted her, too.

"I love your work," Kate started, then stopped. She had already told her this over the phone. "I want you to come and work for me." This direct, simple statement gave Kate courage. It was the first time she had used it. It sounded good and reminded her who she was. "I'm sure Ben told you about what I'm planning for *Women Today*. Here"—she picked up several sheets that Jason had given her—"I think this will show you where we're heading."

Betsy took the sheets, glanced at them casually, and handed them back. "It will probably sell," she said without emotion.

"Please come and help me," Kate said sincerely. "I think your work is super, and you're ideal for this whole concept."

"I will for twenty-five thousand, but Ben tells me you won't pay that."

"I'll give you eighteen thousand to start with, another two in six months, and we'll scale it up after a year. You'll have a good expense account and a pretty free hand in the art department."

She'd instinctively said eighteen. Kate was frugal even when the money was not hers. Besides, she was determined to bring the magazine in at a price that would be attractive to the management.

"I'll let you know," Betsy said simply, and stood up to leave.

"When?"

"In the morning. I'll call you."

When Betsy was gone Kate tried to think rationally about this strange, cold girl. Something about her made Kate uneasy: her hostility, her sensuality, her knowing eyes... Wherever had Ben met her anyway at that ungodly hour? She wondered if he was sleeping with her, too. Did he make it a habit to sleep with other clients? The thought angered her. She remembered Betsy's indifferent reaction to the new format. Hardly flattering, in fact, downright insulting. I won't hire her, she decided furiously. Who the hell does she think she is anyway? But even as her rage mounted she knew that if Betsy agreed to the salary, she would hire her.

As Betsy hailed a cab she thought about Kate Johnson. Ben's description, as always, was uncannily, if cattily, accurate. Plain Jane from someplace out there in the great wide spaces, very unchic but very determined. She would succeed with the magazine, of that Betsy was sure. She would also give her a free hand in choosing her models and would be, at least at first, totally dependent on her. As the cab stopped at her Beekman Place apartment she realized that her mind was already made up. She would take the job.

"You have a visitor, Miss Jorgensen," the doorman said respectfully.

As Betsy entered her apartment she saw Suzanne lounging on the sofa, having a drink.

She walked over, leaned down to cup the beautiful black face tenderly in her hands, and kissed her passionately. Without a word they walked into the bedroom.

9

Joyce McGuire was furious. When she arrived at her office she found on her desk her own copy, corrected, edited, and rewritten, all in that revolting style Kate Johnson insisted on putting into every phrase that appeared in the magazine. She couldn't do anything with the issues that were already set, but the September issue was in preparation, and it seemed that Kate was doing her damndest to induce Joyce to quit.

Picking up the papers, she stalked into Kate's office without knocking. Kate was talking with Hank Storm. They both looked up with astonishment.

"Hank, do me a favor and leave us alone," Joyce said through clenched teeth.

"Don't go, Hank," Kate said evenly, though her lips

thinned with anger. "Joyce, you may sit and wait until we are finished, otherwise I'll call you when I am free."

"I'll wait," Joyce said, and threw herself defiantly into an armchair.

She listened as the two talked about several personnel changes, budgets, and ad-agency campaigns. Hank was listening attentively, and Joyce wondered if they were having an affair. Kate was certainly not his usual type, she thought sneeringly, but then Hank was not known for his discrimination. He was so easygoing that he probably thought he was doing this mealymouthed clod a favor.

"She's all yours, Joyce." Hank smiled as he gathered up his papers. "And please don't leave any scars."

Hank was barely out of the room before Joyce jumped up and threw her papers on Kate's desk.

"What the hell do you mean by messing up my copy this way? What I've forgotten about beauty editing you won't ever learn."

Kate gathered the papers as they flew across the desk and landed in her lap. She made a great play of straightening the papers precisely while she tried to get her rage in check.

"Joyce, I've taken over the magazine, not just as editor in chief but also in concept. I tried to make that clear the first time we met. I grant that you know a lot more about beauty editing than I do, but I think you've been writing for a certain type of woman too long, and the readers I'm trying to reach are different." She looked directly at the older woman, who was glaring at her. "How old are you, Joyce?" she asked without warning.

"I beg your pardon?" Joyce's voice rose and her face went white. "What the hell has that to do with it?"

"A great deal." Kate began to enjoy the conversation. She had taken the lead and knew it. She smiled. "That was rude, you're right. So let me rephrase it. How long have you been with *Women Today?*"

"Too long to have some complete unknown from the sticks come in and start telling me how to do my work."

"Oh, heavens." Kate assumed an innocent look. "I wouldn't dream of telling you how to do your work, if you worked for some other magazine, some other editor. But you see, *my* readers are not really interested in how to get the gray out of their hair or how to look"—she shuffled through the papers, found the page she was looking for, and read aloud—"'when hubby comes home from the office.'" She looked up again. "My readers, most of them, don't have a 'hubby.'" She emphasized the last word with a slight sarcasm.

The two women stared at each other. She wants me to quit, Joyce thought. She's trying to save that damn severance pay she'd have to give me if she fires me.

"I'm not going to quit," Joyce said quietly.

"That's entirely up to you." Kate picked up the pages and put them down near the edge of her desk, forcing the older woman to come over and pick them up. "And incidentally, I won't have any more plugs for companies that do not advertise with us and I won't allow any more misrepresentation about products."

Joyce exploded again. "What the hell is that supposed to mean?"

"I noticed that you've mentioned one makeup company several times that I've never even heard of. I looked for the stuff in drugstores and department stores. I finally found it in a drugstore and tried it. My skin broke out in a rash."

"So?" Joyce became flustered. She had been receiving a hefty kickback from the obscure drug firm in New Jersey for the plugs she had given them. "As for your getting a rash, if you read the label you'd see that there is always the phrase that states that 'nine out of ten women...' You must be the tenth." And then, with undisguised malice, "Maybe the New York air disagrees with you and not the makeup."

Kate simply smiled. "Okay, Joyce, is there anything else?"

"You're not pushing me out, Kate. I've been here too long and know too much for someone as inexperienced as you to come along and sign my death warrant."

"Know too much?" Kate caught the phrase. "Blackmail?"

"Why don't you ask Hank Storm about it?"

"Meaning?"

"We've been having an affair for quite a while and I bet the board of directors would not really care for that sort of publicity to break. Certainly dear little Jeannie up in Greenwich wouldn't like it."

"She might love it." Kate hid her annoyance. She didn't really care if Joyce broke the news. She couldn't imagine anyone really caring. It would, at most, make a pathetic item in one of the columns, and if *Women Today* got a plug it would be free publicity.

Joyce walked over to the phone and picked it up.

Kate reached over, took the phone from her, and quietly replaced it. "Wash your dirty laundry in your own office. And even though I hate people who use the office phone for personal calls, I'll treat you to this one." She stood up. "Now, if you don't mind, I'm busy." She was angry and disgusted.

When Joyce walked out, Kate dialed Hank and asked him to come in. He came in a few moments later, grinning broadly.

"She really took you through the mill, didn't she?"

"Will Jean mind?"

"Jean mind? You've got to be kidding. We probably have the most open marriage this side of the Mason-Dixon line."

This time Kate became flustered, and Hank laughed good-naturedly.

"Honey, your attempts at being broad-minded don't really fool me. But you'll learn. For whatever it's worth, you're putting on a good show and with time you'll even get to believe in what you're saying." He paused briefly. "Don't worry. I think you'll have her letter of resignation on your desk within a couple of hours. She won't call Jeannie. She was shooting from the hip, hoping you represented management and that you would panic."

Kate looked at Hank with new interest. "Open marriage?" she said in wonder. "And it works?"

Hank walked over and kissed her on the cheek. "Stick with us big boys and you'll learn lots and so will your little readers." He walked to the door and paused. "Kate, listen, try to remember to wear gloves when you fight. Not that you didn't handle the situation, but you're making enemies and we live in a small world."

Kate smiled absently. An article about open marriages was forming in her mind. Not from the wife's point of view or the husband's, but from the point of view of the girl who finds herself sleeping with someone's husband and how she can handle it with greater dignity than Joyce had.

The phone rang and she heard Jason's voice. He'd been gone for two weeks and she'd missed him terribly.

"We'll have dinner at my place tonight," he said, and his voice was strange and distant.

"Are you angry with me?" she asked, immediately frightened by his manner.

"No, but you're jumping too quickly and we've got to straighten some things out."

When she hung up the phone a longing for Belinda came over her. She was about to dial Dayton when the door opened and Jane Caulson walked in. As always, she looked frazzled and unnerved. The expression of bewilderment never left her face these days.

"Kate, I simply don't understand what point of view you want me to apply to this article." She handed Kate a sheet of paper. Kate glanced at it quickly. Again, it was all wrong.

"Jane," Kate said, suppressing her irritation and trying to remember Hank's and Jason's warnings, in spite of having been through this so many times with Jane, "we're not interested in how the children are treated in school. I don't give a damn if they do or do not get spanked. We're talking about being the second wife to a man with children. How those children affect their relationship in the home. Let their mother worry about what happens in school or let her buy *Red Book*. I'm sure someone there is coping with it."

"But you have a child yourself, Kate, don't you?"

Jane said tentatively. "Wouldn't you worry if your ex-husband's wife—"

"My child would still be my problem, not hers. I want that piece directed toward how the child affects her feelings about her husband and his about her, not how she feels about corporal punishment."

Jane looked as bewildered as ever and Kate felt sorry for her. She knew Jane was really trying, but she also knew Jane would never be right for the new *Women Today*.

"Look, Jane, what I want are articles about things we've discussed at our weekly meetings. God knows there are plenty of ideas kicked around there to give you a clue to what I'm looking for. Get some young writers. Talk to them about our ideas and I'm sure they'll catch on. As a matter of fact, why don't you talk to Linda Wilson? She's really very bright."

Kate said the last name lightly, hoping Jane didn't yet realize that Linda was her replacement, if Jane ever became discouraged enough to throw in the towel...

"She's really good, isn't she?" Jane asked pleasantly, but her eyes betrayed a sadness. "Where did you find her?"

"She was recommended by Jason Reid," Kate lied. "Now, Jane, be an angel and let's try again."

Jane left looking more frazzled than ever. Kate's conscience about Jane was very bad. She liked Jane and felt sorry for her, but, in truth, she couldn't wait for her to leave the magazine. She had even asked Jason if he could transfer Jane to one of his other magazines.

"Forget it, Kate. In this organization, once you're out you're out, period."

There was a cruelty in his statement. She had seen it in him before in various situations and it always bothered her. Especially since she envied it in a way; at least she envied his lack of guilt about it.

Thank God he's on my side, she thought.

She thought it again now as she watched Jane leave, then she rang for Linda to come in. While waiting, she decided she'd better call Dayton. She knew she couldn't put off any longer breaking the news that she wouldn't be able to come for the weekend as she had promised. She had done this too often. But she was very busy and hardly had time to miss Belinda. She was worried about her. When Kate first came to New York, Belinda had been weepy and angry, demanding and reproachful on the phone; now she was pleasant but remote. The child had not reacted one way or the other to Kate's promise that she would visit Dayton this weekend.

"We'll have a wonderful time, honey," Kate had said, trying to sound gay and enthusiastic. The response had been cool, almost condescending.

"Sure, Mother, we'll have a ball."

Being called Mother instead of Mommy disturbed Kate, but she could not tell anyone about it, nor could she explain why it bothered her. Belinda was growing up and Mommy was a rather childish way to refer to one's mother.

Kate knew Belinda would be disappointed and that it would make things even more difficult when she could finally get home, but there was no help for it.

When her mother answered she told her the trip would have to be canceled but that she would make it for the long Labor Day weekend for sure.

"Well, if you can't, you can't, but at least call Belinda more often, Kate. She misses you terribly." There was a slight pause. "And to tell you the truth, so do Elie and I."

"Did you get my last check?"

"Yes, I sure did." She sounded better for a moment. "We're managing fine."

"Good," Kate said, relieved. She was having a very hard time with money these days, trying to live on her earnings and send her mother money every month. Her book advance had been spent long ago, on her nose operation and expenses since leaving Dayton. But she was sure things would be better after her first year with Reid Publications, when her salary increase would come through, and she expected her first royalty check about the same time.

Although relieved that she had gotten this difficult phone call over with, she still felt guilty and disturbed about Belinda. She wanted to fly out there right now but knew it would be impossible. There was simply too much work to do: endless books and magazines to read, meetings with advertisers, dinners with publishers, play openings that Jason insisted she attend. She didn't enjoy any of these affairs. She always felt like the outsider and hated the looks of half recognition she got when she was introduced. It wasn't too bad when Jason was with her, but he wasn't often available. Sometimes she had to ask Dee Dee to go with her, but she knew Dee Dee always went reluctantly and made Kate feel more miserable than ever. Dee Dee had such assurance, such poise, and she knew everybody. Occasionally Allyson would come along, always bringing Cliff. She, too, seemed to know everyone, and was treated with a deference that was almost humiliating to Kate.

She leaned back in her chair. She had a year in which to succeed or fail. She would save as much as she could, she decided, in case something went wrong. Then she angrily dismissed the thought. Nothing would go wrong. Somehow she would make it.

At that moment Linda walked in. Kate smiled at her and started to feel better. She always felt better when Linda was around.

Linda Wilson was a thirty-two-year-old woman who looked no more than sixteen. Kate had come across some articles she had sent in to *Women Today* in a pile of unsolicited material. One piece in particular, called "It's All There for the Grabbing," was written with passion but still had humor and an almost touching naiveté. She wrote to Linda and asked her to lunch.

Linda arrived at the Palm Court of the Plaza Hotel promptly and from the moment Kate saw her she liked her. There was something very clean cut about her. She was dressed in a simple brown skirt, white shirt with a sweater thrown over her shoulders. Espadrilles and a straw bag completed the outfit. She had short brown hair worn straight to the earlobes and a glowing, soap-and-water-scrubbed skin. She wore no makeup, yet her coloring was extraordinary, with enormous, deep grayish-blue eyes. Her nose was small and straight and her smile captivating. Kate found herself thinking of Belinda. Although Kate was sure Linda was close to her own age, she felt more like her mother. Kate stared at her almost rudely as they shook hands.

"Is my face smudged or something?" Linda laughed, and Kate relaxed.

"Forgive me. It's just that I don't ever remember being so taken by anyone at first sight," Kate admitted candidly, and was surprised at herself. Her inability to communicate on a friendly basis with anyone on her staff or with anyone else, for that matter, was becoming a problem she was only too aware of. "Tell me who you are."

"What a sweet thing to say and what a lovely way to ask about me." Linda smiled again. "Who am I? Well, I'm Linda Wilson and until recently I was Sister Louise in a convent in Quebec. I went there when I was fourteen and was there for eighteen years. I loved every moment of those years, but something pulled me away and when the tug-of-war became unbearable I decided to leave. Mother Marie was very understanding. I came to New York to look for a new life. I've got eighteen years to catch up with, and as I said in one of my articles, it's all there waiting."

"You're thirty-two?" Kate asked, unable to think of anything else to say. Her mind was racing. Linda was exactly what she wanted for her story editor. "You look like a child."

"I feel like a child . . . most of the time."

"Will you come to work for me?"

A faint blush of excitement colored Linda's face as she caught her breath. "Work for you?" She repeated Kate's question. "I'd love it, but doing what?"

"Well, frankly I want you as my story editor."

"Story editor! I don't really know if I could—"

"Oh, you can do it, all right," Kate interrupted. "I'm

not hiring you because of your previous experience. I'm hiring you because of a quality I'm looking for, which you have." She smiled reassuringly. "I'd help you at first and I'd assign Carol Butler to you. She's my secretary and she'd fill you in on the nitty-gritty things you have to know about working for the magazine."

"But don't you need your secretary?"

"She's too good to be just a secretary. She's very young, but she certainly caught on to what a magazine is all about." .

"How old is she?"

"Twenty-two," Kate answered, and regretted mentioning Carol's name. Although Carol was an excellent secretary, Kate never felt comfortable with her. Now, sitting opposite Linda Wilson, Kate could not help but recall how different the interview with Carol had been when she'd hired her while still at the Regency Hotel.

"Why don't you give her the job you're offering me?" Linda interrupted Kate's thoughts in her uncanny way, which was enormously perceptive and yet totally naive.

"She's not ready for the job yet." The last word slipped out and it took Kate by surprise. Briefly it occurred to her that she was afraid of Carol but dismissed the thought and, looking directly at Linda, she repeated her offer.

"Well, if you think I can do it, I'd love it. When do I start?"

"You can start on Monday, but at first you'll be working as my assistant. I've got a story editor now who is awfully nice but hasn't the vaguest idea what I want from her. I'm giving her every opportunity but I think that soon now she'll realize the job is just not for her." She looked at Linda seriously. "And in a way it will all be for the best. It will give you a chance to work with Carol and get to know her."

"All right," Linda said slowly, and picked up her cup and sipped the coffee slowly. A look of pleasure mingled with sadness appeared on her face, which Kate could not fathom.

"Don't you want to know how much we pay, working conditions, and all that?"

"I'm sure you're very fair and if at any point I feel that I can't afford to work for you, I'll tell you." She smiled warmly. "You see, my expenses are practically nil. I'm living with the most delicious man and he supports me as I've never been supported before."

Kate felt a twinge of envy. "Tell me about him." She felt foolish as soon as the words were out.

"He's a minister and I met him one day when I was walking through Harlem—"

"You *walked* through Harlem?" Kate asked, horrified.

"Well, I had only been in New York a few days and I was walking through Central Park and I came out on One Hundred and Tenth Street and then I saw this church and, let's face it, you don't spend a lifetime going to church every day and then pass by a church on a Sunday without being drawn in." She looked ethereal. "So... I went in and heard this marvelous sermon being given by this gorgeous, saintly man. When the service was over I simply went up to him." She shook her head and her soft brown hair moved as though a soft breeze were blowing especially for her. "And that was that. We've been living together ever since."

"Do you live in Harlem?" Kate asked in astonishment. The story was bizarre and, for Kate, frightening. She had few opinions about the racial problems in the country, had never known any black people personally.

"No, we live on Central Park West, up in the Nineties, and we're gloriously happy. He's a widower and has several children who are grown up and really great kids. The whole thing is heavenly." Suddenly she stopped and a serious expression came over her face. "You don't mind my living with a black man, do you? Because if you do we'll forget the job idea. I won't quite understand, but I won't mind. I'll just put it out of my head as something nice that could have been but wasn't."

"Can you start the job next Monday?"

"I'll be there. What time?"

"I get there at eight, but don't mind me, you come in around nine."

"I'll be there at eight."

They finished their lunch, and it was very pleasant for Kate, but the feeling of being completely alone in the world began to grow in her.

10

When Linda said good-bye to Kate, her smile was broad and joyful. When she turned away from the hotel, her smile disappeared. She walked quickly into Central Park and only when the noise of the traffic, the sight of the rushing crowds on the plaza, faded did she relax.

She had not lied to Kate about her black minister. John Gappet was a man of the church but not in the completely orthodox or accepted manner. He was a faith healer some of the time but a Muslim all the time. She had met him in Harlem on a rainy Sunday when she had wandered around the city aimlessly. When she saw a crowd gathered outside a church she was instinctively drawn to it. It was raining and many of the people had umbrellas, so she was unaware that the whole crowd was black. John Gappet was standing on a small platform and was preaching. He was very tall and handsome. His dark skin was glistening with the raindrops, his eyes were coal-black, and his hair was completely gray. He was dressed in black, a white collar contrasting vividly with the rest of his appearance. She tried to concentrate on what he was saying, but she could not quite follow his words, since he seemed to catch sight of her and his eyes were staring at her with a rage and disdain that sent a chill through her. Suddenly everyone turned and was staring at her. Their eyes were strangely accusatory, and the people edged away from her, leaving her standing alone. They seemed menacing as she heard the preacher heaping words of abuse on her. Her thoughts as she lowered her head were frighteningly familiar. "A whore, a white piece of trash," she heard the preacher say condemningly. "A sinful white devil sent to spy." The words poured over her and the voice was now not the voice of a preacher but her father's.

"She's a little whore," her father was saying to her mother. "And she lies, a sinful liar who will rot in hell."

Linda was twelve years old when she sat, pained and bruised, in the corner of their one-room apartment in Quebec. Her three brothers and two sisters, all younger than she, were huddled in another corner of the room and her mother was lying on her bed, coughing incessantly into a handkerchief. Without looking, Linda knew the handkerchief was bloodstained and would be one of several that she would have to wash out later in the day.

"Jacques," her mother said feebly, "what have you done?"

"I did not do anything to her," Jacques Wilssiné shouted. "Do you think me a pervert, a freak who would rape his own child?"

Linda had gone to the shed in the backyard for firewood. Her father was there cutting logs into stove lengths, a jug of cheap wine beside him. As always, he was drunk. She was scared of him when he was drunk. She crept in quietly, hoping not to attract his attention.

The events that followed were vague in her mind.

94

Suddenly he lunged at her, ripped her underpants off, and threw her to the ground. She felt nothing as she watched with terror the man who was her father roughly push her legs apart as he thrust his body between them. His face, as his body came close to hers and moved away in quick, jerky motions, was distorted. Suddenly he made a strange sound and she felt his bulk roll over and he lay beside her, panting. Linda scrambled up and stumbled to the door.

"Mama," she whimpered. "Mama." Before she reached the door, her father grabbed her from behind and she felt the blows of his hand on her face, her head, and her back. She cowered, protecting herself as best she could. He finally tired and turned away for his wine bottle. She ran back to the house and rushed into the bathroom. When she came out she found it difficult to walk. Her mother looked at Linda with concern.

"What happened?" she asked in a whisper.

"Papa hurt me," Linda said simply.

It was at that moment that her father walked in and began the tirade of abuse.

"You are a monster, Jacques." Her mother's voice was low but the revulsion she felt for her husband was clear. She lifted herself from her bed and with a strength Linda had never seen in her mother before ordered him out of the house.

That was one of the last times Linda spent with her family. Within days all her sisters and brothers were sent to an adoption home. She, being the oldest, stayed to nurse her mother. Her father had run away to the north and many years later Linda heard that he was living with an Indian woman who had given him several children.

Her mother lived for two more years, and Linda took care of her and attended the Convent of the Sacred Sisters School. When her mother died she entered the convent and spent the next eighteen years as a devout sister. The memory of the scene in the shed faded and became a dim nightmare Linda finally succeeded in blocking out completely until the Sunday when she stood in Harlem and heard a stranger saying what her father had said so many years before.

Linda did not know how long she stood in the rain that Sunday. All she knew was that the preacher was right in what he was saying about her, as her father must have been right. She had provoked her father simply by being, as she was now provoking these people who were standing around her. The minister felt her guilt. She deserved to be an outcast.

"What are you doing here?" A voice was speaking to her and Linda looked up. She was alone, all the people had gone, and she was staring into the eyes of the minister.

"Who sent you here?" His voice was cold and angry. "We don't like white people butting into our religious services."

She could not answer. She simply stared at him. As he turned from her in disgust and started walking away Linda found her voice.

"May I come with you?" she asked.

He turned and looked at her. A small smile appeared on his face. Then, as he turned again and started walking away, he motioned with his hand that she should follow.

He lived in a basement apartment on Central Park West and Ninety-seventh Street. It was spotlessly clean, and there were many rooms.

Her room in the apartment was not unlike her room at the convent. Her duties were also similar. She cleaned and cooked for John and his followers and although no one ever molested her in any way, they seemed to derive great pleasure out of ordering "the piece of white trash" around. John Gappet was nice to her and often she saw him watching with a look verging on pity.

"You've got to start earning your keep," he said one day when she was alone with him in the kitchen. Her first reaction was that she was earning her keep by doing all the work, but she dared not voice her thoughts. It was the first time that he actually directed a conversation to her, and she felt strangely pleased.

"Come sit and talk to me," he said quietly. "Who are you?" he asked when she sat down opposite him at the large kitchen table.

"I'm Canadian by birth. I've been a nun for many years and have recently come to New York."

"Don't you have any family or friends in the city who may wonder where you are?"

She shook her head.

"You really just happened to come by that Sunday, then," he said musingly.

She nodded and looked directly at him. She felt just as she did the day she knew that she would have to leave the convent. Her physical needs, her desires to be held by human arms, hear a human voice speak to her of love and dreams and hopes, had become all too obvious.

"Now I understand those stories you write," he said gently.

She blushed, and a flash of rage that she rarely allowed to surface rose to her throat. Since leaving the convent, she had begun to write about a life she felt she wanted and was sure most women did, as well. Her stories were written almost in the form of a diary.

"They were private," she said in a whisper.

"Not when you live in this house. Here we know everything about each other."

"I know nothing about you."

"Of course not, you are not one of us. You have no way of understanding who we are, what we think, what we feel, what we dream about."

"But you're wrong," she protested. "People all want the same things. It's just that they try different ways to get them. What you and your people want is no different from what I want."

"You're white."

"I'm not color-blind, but my need for acceptance is not really different from yours."

"A pointless conversation," he said, and the conversation ended abruptly.

She was about to leave the room when she heard him say, "I think you should start sending those written ideas of yours to some magazines."

And she did. She went on living with the fanatical religious group, taking their abuse, which she did not mind so long as John Gappet was around to protect her. She knew he was protecting her. He became the father she never had.

When Kate Johnson called, Linda was surprised and fearful. She had never been to the Plaza Hotel and her greatest concern was that she had no appropriate clothes. When she spoke to John Gappet about it, he gave her money to buy something to wear with the understanding that she would pay it back. She had never been to a shop in New York and was totally unprepared for the quantities of clothing that hung from the racks in Alexander's. The salesgirls were very aggressive and the fitting rooms were crowded with too many other women trying on clothes. She ended up buying a simple brown skirt and a white blouse. A brown sweater completed the outfit.

"You look well," John Gappet said as she was preparing to leave.

She was in her room standing in front of the small mirror that did not afford her the privilege of seeing herself fully. Shyly she looked at the black man. He was standing in the doorway and she felt an overwhelming passion for him. She bit her lip to control the impulse to reach out and touch him. She lowered her eyes but not before he saw her feelings.

"It won't be, Linda," he said, and he sounded angry. "You will have to find your pleasures with men of your own color."

"Why?" she asked in a whisper. "My feelings are color-blind."

"You will leave here the day you find a job," he said soberly. "I should really ask you to leave now, but you may stay here until you get a job," he said, and walked away.

Well, she had a job, but she did not have a home or a place to go to. She thought of lying to John about getting the job but knew she would not.

She did not know how long she had walked when she saw that she was at the exit at 106th Street and Central Park West. It was almost five o'clock in the evening. She had not prepared dinner but she couldn't bear to go back to the apartment yet.

She walked over to Broadway and went into a bar. It was noisy and no one paid much attention to her. She sat down and ordered a glass of wine. She looked at the men and women standing around, talking, laughing, their faces animated by the warmth of the room and the sense of being part of the crowd. She was outside looking in. The urge to be a part of the crowd, to be included in their conversation, to laugh and cry with them, to know them and touch them, was overwhelming.

When she arrived back at the apartment it was midnight. Everyone had gone to bed except a student named Dali, who had recently come to live in the house. He was very young and quite handsome. He was reading a book in the kitchen and had several notebooks strewn around the table.

"Where have you been?" he asked, and his tone was condescending.

"Out," she answered simply as she went to the refrigerator and took out a container of milk. Her head was throbbing and she remembered that she had not eaten since lunchtime.

"That's not good enough," Dali said angrily.

She poured the milk and started to drink it when his hand reached out and slapped her. The glass crashed to the floor. She was on her knees in a minute trying to pick up the shattered pieces when she looked up and saw him coming toward her. She felt a thrill of fear...and excitement.

John Gappet found them on the floor, her new skirt ripped, her blouse open, Dali still on top of her. In a swift motion the older man yanked Dali to his feet and hit him. The blows were furious and finally John Gappet moved away and in a breathless voice ordered him to leave the apartment.

Linda picked herself up and ran to her room. Vicious as the attack had been, she knew that she had experienced pleasure. It was sinful to feel as she did, but she knew she could not escape the fact that for a brief moment she felt as though she were part of another human being. She was sitting on the bed, still dazed, when John walked in.

"You will have to leave in the morning," John said quietly.

"It was not completely his fault," Linda said quickly. "I must have provoked him in some way."

"Yes, I'm sure of that, although you are truly unaware of what you are doing."

That night she moved to the YWCA.

11

The Memorial Day issue was on the stand. Kate stood at a distance from the newsstand around the corner from her office and looked at the pile of *Women Today*. Several women walked over and bought it. A couple of men picked it up, looked at the cover. One of them paid for it and walked away. The other smiled and put it back. Kate walked over and picked up a copy and handed the money to the news vendor.

"How's it going?" she asked.

"*Women Today?*" He looked at her, then at the remaining copies. "Well, I've sold more of 'em today than ever before. I bet I'll be out of them by the end of the week, which will be the first time."

"It's a nice cover," she said, looking at the girl who

was smiling up with a sexy, inviting look. Betsy was working out superbly, and had brought with her a brilliant young photographer. Already Kate was planning on approaching him with a contract.

"Yah, it's a good-looking piece of ass," the news vendor was saying. "Anyway, from what I understand they've got a new editor up there and word has it she's a bitch and a sex maniac, so I expect the magazine is going to take a different turn." He picked up another magazine and looked at the vulgar picture on the cover. "It sure is better than this, so it'll sell, all right. Of course, the little housewife biddies are going to cancel subscriptions, that's for sure, but they'll pick up the office girls and like that."

Kate smiled inwardly. From your mouth to God's ear, she thought as she turned away. As for being a bitch and a sex maniac, well, Joyce's little digs in various gossip columns had only done her good after all.

There had been a big fight with the board of directors when she finally showed them the cover and several of the articles she wanted in her first issue.

Jason was there when she arrived at the meeting. A few uncorrected galleys were lying on the long table and the seven board members, whom she had met before, were sitting as though waiting to be immortalized on canvas.

"Miss Johnson," Thomas Grand, who was around sixty-five years old, said with suppressed fury. "We were all aware that you were aiming at a new concept, trying to attract a reader that we have either lost or never had. But this"—he pushed the galley over to her—"this is going to backfire and we'll lose all the women who are now subscribing to *Women Today*."

Kate looked at Jason and was quick to realize that he would not say a word to help her. He was fully aware of what she was going through, had helped write and edit some of the articles, had written all the thinly disguised and sexually titillating blurbs on the cover, and yet she knew with a certainty that astounded her that he would not come to her aid.

"Mr. Grand," Kate said slowly, "I don't really think

it's a catastrophe if some subscribers cancel their subscriptions. I believe that quite a few of them will stick it out for the duration of their subscription. We've kept all the serialized stories intact and we have a lot of the old stuff still in there. But I believe that subscriptions, what with postal rates going up, are a drain on us. What I'm aiming for is newsstand sales. I intend to pique the interest of a younger crowd of readers who will wait for *Women Today* to come out on the stand and run to get it the minute it's out. I believe we could do better by putting subscription money into advertising, letting everyone know that we are changing the format."

Another member of the board looked at the girl on the cover. "I'll admit she's more covered up than some of the others, but I know my wife would not want it around the house. It's too provocative."

"Andrew, put it down and stop ogling the cover," John Davon said. Everyone laughed politely as Andrew Sloan put the page down quickly.

"I'll agree to go along with a few of the articles you have there, but I want that revolting article about one-night love affairs cut, and I want you to reshoot the pictures of how to make a bedroom more appealing. There is no reason for the man to be shown half naked and the girl draped in a white towel while they're making the bed."

As the meeting went on, Kate found her first issue being ripped apart. Each member had an objection to one thing or another, and she knew that she did not have enough ammunition to fight them at this early stage. She kept throwing desperate glances at Jason, who sat at the head of the table with a small smile on his face.

"Well," he said finally when everyone had had his say, "I believe we now have a new cover for the June issue, a goodly part of the old format, and a couple of glimpses as to what Kate wants to do." He smiled pleasantly at Kate. "I think it will be wise to let it go on the stands as we decided here today and wait for the public's reaction."

The meeting was over and Kate felt completely defeated.

"How could you?" she said quietly when Jason took her to lunch at 21. They were sitting upstairs and although she had been to the restaurant only once before, she was too upset to be impressed. "How could you throw me to the dogs that way and not say a word? You know damn well you had a hand in just about every article and picture in that first issue and you sat there making me the patsy." She caught her breath. "That was vicious of you."

He took her hand in his. "Katie, my girl, you were superb. You handled the old goats marvelously and I was very proud of that subscription routine you threw at them. Damn clever."

"But, Jason, what I've got now is a hodgepodge of old garbage and a couple of titillating articles. God, our publicity campaign promised the readers a revolution and we're giving them a watered-down kindergarten fight."

"That's the only way to do it," Jason said soberly. "Of course I knew it would happen. Frankly, I would have loved to have it as planned, but I'm a practical man. Let's wait and see the reaction to the first issue. That will be the best way to prove the point. Let's see how many subscribers cancel and see reader reaction to the couple of new articles. We'll go from there." He picked up the menu. "Now let's eat. I'm starved." As always, that signaled the end of the conversation as far as he was concerned.

Now the issue was on the stand and the waiting began.

Within a week the results began to trickle in. The number of cancellations was small compared to the mail received praising the new attempts at revamping the book.

"Thank God you're back," several letters from old readers of the Dayton *Chronicle* stated. "Where have you been?" and "Good luck, we love you," said others. But most impressive was the actual sale at the newsstands. By the end of the first week there was a clamor for more issues from the vendors. It was the first time in many years that the orders exceeded the number of copies printed.

The board of directors quickly approved more of Kate's ideas for the following issues and except for the fact that she did not have a beauty editor, everything was going smoothly.

Allyson agreed to do the beauty pages. Although what she produced was not exactly what Kate had in mind, Allyson was a pro and took all of Kate's suggestions with good grace. Still, Kate did not trust Allyson and dealt carefully with her. She was obviously Jason's ace in the hole if Kate failed. And Kate knew that Allyson's pleasantness masked the hope that Kate would not pull it off. However, in spite of her resentment, Kate dreaded the idea that Allyson might leave her. She was a superb editor and was enormously loyal to Jason and the Reid empire. But Cliff was Allyson's nemesis, and Kate was sure that as long as he was around Allyson probably could not afford to quit.

12

The heat wave hit New York in the middle of June and now as August was drawing to a close it seemed the heat would never let up. *Women Today* was doing well but not so well as Kate had hoped. Jason had been away since the beginning of July and although Hank spent a good part of his time going with her to solicit advertising, she felt they were not hitting the right note. Hank knew most of the heads of the advertising agencies but was not forceful enough with them and tended to lose the thread of each meeting. Kate felt totally isolated and longed for Jason's return so that she could discuss with him the advertising situation as well as the developing outlook of *Women Today*. Her days were filled to capacity, and when she was not obligated to be somewhere in the evening in connection with the magazine, she worked at home, going over every nuance of what would be appearing in forthcoming issues. She had been in New York one full year, yet she felt isolated and alone, with no one to talk to.

It was late Friday afternoon and most of the staff and other employees had left early, hoping to beat the Labor Day weekend rush. A hush had fallen over the office.

The room was air conditioned, yet Kate felt warm and irritable. She was working too hard, sleeping very little, eating not at all, and the turmoil was seething inside. What it was specifically she did not know. Everything was going well. She had a staff of editors she was proud of. Jane had finally left and Linda was properly entrenched as story editor. She was superb at what she did and because of her open manner and happy disposition, she succeeded in cooling tempers around her. Carol was now working solely with Linda and proved to be excellent at it. They worked well together; Linda's incredible naiveté, plus her intuitive ability to lend the right note of down-to-earth thinking, was a perfect balance for Carol's East Coast sophistication. Together they succeeded in making each article, each story, come to life for *Women Today* in exactly the manner Kate had hoped for. The two women were very different but had become quite close and maintained a social relationship outside the office. Carol clearly adored Linda and at the weekly meetings discussed her thoughts about future articles as though she had prepared them for Linda rather than for Kate. At first Kate resented this, but since it worked so well for the magazine, she grew to accept it. Dee Dee and Betsy were constantly at each other's throats but that, too, was tolerable. Each was in total charge of her department and Kate had grown accustomed to having one battle royal a month as the layout was being prepared. They had opposite points of view as to how things should be shown, but Betsy's obvious, almost vulgar suggestiveness in many of her pictures gave the magazine the flair that Kate wanted and she was not about to step on Betsy's toes.

Anyway, after pouting or threatening to quit if she did not get her way, Betsy always gave in. Although pictures of her in the society pages and magazines showed her surrounded by well-known bachelors, motion-picture stars, or known sports figures, Kate somehow suspected that Betsy was a lesbian.

She had asked Ben about it once when they were in bed, but he looked at her blankly and said he didn't know.

"Why do you ask?" he asked nonchalantly.

"Oh, I don't know. She seems to thrive on breasts and vaginas whenever she's involved in picture taking."

"Have you ever been to bed with a lesbian?" Ben asked suddenly.

"No!" Kate answered, and wondered at her overreaction to the suggestion.

"Don't blow my head off, Kate," Ben said quietly. "It's really very exciting, you know."

She didn't answer but moved slightly, hoping Ben would get absorbed in making love to her and forget the conversation. The idea of being made love to by a woman had flashed through her mind on occasion, but she always turned the thought off immediately.

"If you change your mind, just let me know," Ben said as he began kissing her thighs while his fingers searched deep in her and she felt, as always, the pleasure of having Ben make love to her in that fashion.

The conversation convinced her that Betsy was indeed a lesbian, and Kate began to look at her differently. Dee Dee had once said angrily that Betsy would get them all in trouble someday and Kate wondered if that's what she'd meant. Homosexuality was no longer a shameful, secretive thing, and many homosexuals were exceptionally creative and talented. Yet, unfortunately, Betsy was rather stupid. She contributed few clever ideas and suggestions to the regular Thursday editorial meetings. Kate always listened to Betsy's ideas, but later, when she and Jason discussed the meeting, she laughed at how childish Betsy really was.

Kate was almost dozing off when Allyson walked in

108

to say good night. Seeing Kate stretched out on her couch, Allyson went over to her.

"Tired?" she asked pleasantly.

"Exhausted," Kate admitted as she stood up quickly and straightened out her skirt. She walked over to her desk and started sifting through her papers. Then, turning around, she looked at Allyson. "Would you stay awhile and talk?"

Allyson pulled up a chair. "Sure," she said, and Kate noted that she was extremely cordial.

Kate did not have anything in particular to discuss, but she wanted to talk to someone.

"Allyson, I need help," she said, her back to the woman.

There was no response.

"Dee Dee and Betsy," she began.

"Oh, don't worry about them," Allyson said. "They're simply worlds apart. What with Dee Dee's women's-lib feelings and Betsy, who is . . ." She stopped. "Well, you know Betsy's needs."

Kate was about to ask about Betsy's needs but decided against it.

She turned around and walked over and sat down opposite Allyson. "Okay, I have a problem with Hank," she said slowly. It seemed as good a subject as any. "Mind you, I adore him and he's a great managing editor, but he's quite hopeless when it comes to the advertising people. He knows them too intimately and he gets sidetracked with college-football stories that they all seem to share from years back." She shrugged helplessly. "I've never been to college. Tell me, did any of them study or did they just play football?"

Allyson smiled. "They never opened a book, nor did Hank."

"Then it's all a waste of time?"

"The way Hank wants to do it, yes. The people you have to talk to are just a notch below the president of the company," Allyson said patiently. "Kate, you're so green at this racket that if I didn't see a magazine emerging with my own eyes, I wouldn't have believed you could do it."

Kate stiffened. It had been a mistake to confide in Allyson, and she knew Jason would be furious if he found out. But she was desperately in need of someone to talk to.

"Don't worry, Kate," Allyson said pleasantly. "You're tired and Jason is away. Don't worry," she repeated, as if to say "I'll keep your secret."

Kate felt embarrassed but was grateful for the kind words.

"Okay, what do I do?" she finally asked.

"You call up the people you want to see directly. Get the names from the manual of advertisers. They're usually the second down the line from the president. Call them directly, take them to lunch, take an adman from Jason's staff with you if you need help, and sell, sell, sell. You've got enough ammunition by now. You're heading a selling book and it looks better every day, so go to it." With that Allyson got up.

"Anything else?"

Kate wished there was something else to talk about but nothing came to mind. Everyone had left the city for the long weekend and although Kate was looking forward to going to Dayton the next morning, she did not want to go home just yet. Allyson looked at her watch.

"Kate, I've got to go. My old man and I are going to Hank's for the weekend." Her voice softened as she mentioned her husband. "Weren't you invited?"

"Oh, yes," Kate answered quickly, and could have kicked herself for having chosen to discuss Hank today of all days. "But I'm going to Dayton in the morning to see my daughter. It's been a hell of a long time since I've spent any time with her, and this will really be my last chance this year. I've got a tough schedule right through New Year's."

"That's one thing I'll never understand," Allyson said quietly. "How the hell does one leave one's kid for a job? I couldn't leave Cliff for a day and you go without seeing your daughter for long stretches of time."

"You don't like me, do you, Allyson?"

"Not particularly," Allyson answered candidly.

110

"You're not really a lovable creature, you know, Kate."
She smiled a thin little smile.

There was a brief silence and Allyson looked at her watch again. "I really do have to run. Cliff gets worried when I'm late. I'll see you Tuesday." And she was gone.

When the door closed after Allyson, Kate sank down in her chair and felt numb. Lovable? She mulled over the word. Who the hell was lovable? Certainly Allyson was not. Nor was Dee Dee or Betsy or Jason. Hank probably was, but he was so ineffectual. So was Linda. But would she want to be Linda? That poor, tortured young woman. Kate did not really know what was going on in her life, but she had a suspicion that the great black minister had disappeared and was replaced by too many transient men. As she listened to Linda at their Thursday sessions, discussing the needs, desires, suggestions for better relationships with men, it seemed to Kate that an awful lot of living was being done by Linda and none of it was really making for happiness. Yes, Linda was lovable, but Kate would not change places with her. Maggie Pearson was lovable. But at what price? Living on the fringe, raising six kids with an untalented husband whom she had to support. Still, Kate resented Allyson's comment about her not being lovable. It was cruel and unnecessary.

The clock on her desk indicated that it was past seven. Allyson had rushed off to see her old man. Drunk, weak, dependent, he was there waiting for Allyson. No one was waiting for Kate. No old man, no young man. Nobody.

Tony stuck his head through the door as Kate was gathering her papers and putting them in her briefcase. "I'm going now," he said.

"Sure, Tony." She looked up. "How's it going?" She could not resist the question.

"I'm embarrassed at what we're showing and writing about, Kate, but damn it, it's selling and nobody argues with success."

Kate smiled. "How's the family?"

"Swell, and yours?" he asked. "How's your little girl?"

"She's fine," Kate answered, and sighed. "I miss her."

"Sure you do, Kate, sure you do." He waved his hand and was gone.

Kate's apartment was not air conditioned and she was tempted to stay at the office and do her work, but she knew the building closed around eight and decided not to ask that it be kept open for her.

She returned home, settled down with a drink, and tried to relax. She was still tense and upset, and did not want to be alone. Yet she had few friends outside her office staff, and now she felt deserted. She desperately wished Jason were around.

She missed him to the point where it hurt. He had become indispensable to her. They would meet every Friday, have dinner, look over the suggestions for new articles, discuss layouts, promotions, and future plans for the magazine. She would spend the night with him and they would have a luxurious breakfast the next morning. Often, sitting across from him, surrounded by the wealth and comfort of his home, she would be tempted to tell him of her feelings of fear, loneliness, her concern for the future. She never dared. He was giving her more than he gave any other human being, of that she was sure.

Her only other companion was Ben, who seemed to be available whenever she needed him. She had begun to take him to social affairs she attended, finding him more pleasant than Dee Dee or Allyson. He was attractive, extremely well dressed, poised, and very well spoken. Yet she would have been mortified if anyone suspected that she was having an affair with him. She enjoyed his lovemaking but it also disturbed her. Ben was a pervert, and it was precisely his perversions that appealed to her. There was something drastically wrong, though, when she considered that in all the time in New York she had come up with only a homosexual and a sixty-year-old man who, she began to suspect, was not really interested in sex but, rather, in the companionship she offered and in her work on his magazine.

Unwilling to continue with these painful thoughts, she picked up the phone and called Ben. There was no answer. She tried to think of someone else she could call. Dee Dee had gone to some women's-liberation convention, Linda had gone to East Hampton with Carol, and Maggie was out on the Island with her six children. That left Betsy. But with her new insight into the girl, Kate was frightened of her. Of course there were the two junior editors. Lovely Marrianne Tyler, a Phi Beta Kappa from Bryn Mawr, was all of twenty-three and came from the South. One of the first blacks to graduate with such high honors from one of the Seven Sisters colleges, she looked like a princess who had come up from the sea in the West Indies. She was small, graceful, bright, and talented and was without question a strong asset to *Women Today*. Her suggestions for articles were always right. She was a good barometer of what a single girl in New York felt, did, and thought. Being black only made her more interesting. She succeeded in using every facet of who she was, where she came from, what was happening in the country as a whole in terms of youth, white or black, and enjoyed life to the fullest. Her counterpart was twenty-six-year-old Stephanie Banks from California. A graduate of Stanford, she had much the same approach to life as Marrianne but was more of a radical. Kate had not quite figured out Stephanie's life-style but found her good to have around.

Even as her thoughts passed over the people on her staff, Kate knew she would not call any of them. She had always kept herself apart, although she knew that with the possible exception of Dee Dee and Betsy, any one of them would have been flattered by her call.

Sighing deeply, Kate picked up her briefcase, took out the work she had brought home, and settled into the wing chair she had bought on sale the week before. Hovering at the edge of her brain was the coming reunion with Belinda, and Kate felt comforted. She did have Belinda.

13

Kate didn't know what woke her up. She was still in her chair, the papers in her lap, but the room was completely dark. The lights had been on, she remembered, and she felt frozen with panic. She dared not move. There was someone in the room, she was sure of it. As her eyes adjusted to the dark she looked around without moving. Nothing. Still she did not move. Suddenly she sensed movement behind her chair, coming from the open window that led to the fire escape. A tiny clicking sound made her shift her eyes toward the digital-clock radio that stood on the dresser across from the chair. It was three o'clock in the morning. She kept her eyes glued to the clock. The seconds digits kept racing along and her fear mounted. When the clock read 3:01, she reached quickly for the lamp switch beside the chair.

Suddenly she felt a hand reach out and cover her mouth, stifling the scream that rose in her throat. Then the figure of a man appeared before her, one hand still covering her mouth and a bright knife blade flashing in the other.

"I wouldn't do that," the man said in a flat voice with no inflection. His hand mashed her lips painfully against her teeth and covered her nostrils, so that she could barely breathe.

The hand holding the knife came close to her throat and he released the hold over her mouth.

"Just don't scream," the man said, and if she hadn't been petrified, she would have sworn the man was pleading.

"What do you want?" she finally whispered. Her eyes were now fully adjusted to the darkness and from the dim reflections that came from the street below, she saw that he was a young blond man, no more than twenty, and his eyes were staring at her vacantly.

"Money," he said simply. "Where is the money?"

She had two hundred dollars in cash in her handbag for the trip to Dayton. It was on top of the clothes in the open suitcase, along with a small radio for Elie, a pearl necklace for her mother, and a gold chain for Belinda.

"I don't have any money," she lied in spite of her terror.

"I'm going to turn on the light," he said, "and believe me, lady, I'll kill you if you move."

The room was suddenly flooded with light and she blinked. He moved around like a cat and came to stand at the open valise. Quickly he put the jewelry in his pocket and his hand reached over to her handbag. She leaped up from the chair and with an adept movement he kicked her in the stomach before she reached him.

"You stupid bitch," he hissed as he grabbed the cord tied around the radio for Elie and tied her hands behind her back. Kate couldn't move, the pain in her stomach was so excruciating. He ripped the sheet from her bed and proceeded to tie her legs and gag her mouth. Once she was helpless, he ransacked the apartment. She moaned as she watched him throw her clothes out of the suitcase and start piling things into it. When he picked up her bag and withdrew the money, she began to kick with her bound legs. Satisfied that he had everything he could carry, he walked over and stood over her. His eyes were truly those of a dead man. He did not seem to see her and he began to kick her in the chest and head until finally she lost consciousness.

The pain was unbearable. When Kate opened her eyes, a strong light blinded her for a minute. She closed her eyes again, trying to remember what was causing the pain. The memory of being kicked came back abruptly and her eyes flew open and scanned the room. It was in a shambles but the man was gone.

Painful as it was, she began to push herself toward her door. She lost consciousness several times, but with great effort she managed to free her hands. She was pulling at the doorknob when she blacked out again.

A cool hand was stroking her brow when she next woke up. She was in her own bed and sitting beside her was a woman whom Kate had never seen before.

"Well, thank God," the woman said softly. "I thought you'd never come around."

"What time is it?" Kate found it painful to move her facial muscles.

"Five A.M."

"Thank God, I can make the plane."

"Going somewhere?" The woman smiled.

"I've got to catch the ten A.M. to Dayton," she said slowly.

"I'm not sure you'll make it," the woman said as she took Kate's wrist and felt for her pulse.

"Who are you?" Kate's mind began to clear and the events of a few hours ago came back to her. "And how did you get here?"

"I'm Janice Barker, your neighbor from upstairs," the woman answered. "I was reading in my bedroom and I heard a thud coming from your floor. When I came down, I found you lying unconscious in your doorway."

"I've never seen you," Kate said, and felt foolish.

She knew no one in the building except the superintendent.

"Well, whoever it was certainly was professional," Janice said, looking around the room. "Now I think we'd better get you to the emergency room of Roosevelt Hospital."

"No," Kate said frantically. "I hate hospitals." She tried to lift herself. "I'll be all right." She fell back on her pillow, unable to sit up.

"You may be hemorrhaging internally or have a couple of broken ribs, which only an X ray could discover."

"I'd have to tell them what happened. It would be in the paper and I'd never make the plane."

"You'll never make the plane anyway. As for reporting the matter"—she shrugged—"I think they'd be relieved if you didn't report anything. One less unsolved statistic. You can give a phony name, and we'll say your husband beat you up and you don't want to prefer charges."

"They'll make me stay there."

"I think I can attend to that," Janice answered with authority.

"Are you a doctor?" Kate looked at the woman again. She was a handsome lady around forty years old. Although seated, she looked tall and erect in her well-cut man-tailored yellow bathrobe. Her auburn hair, pushed back from an extraordinarily high brow and held with a rubber band, reached halfway down her back. She was looking directly at Kate in a serious, almost professional manner.

"You're Kate Johnson from *Women Today*, aren't you?" Janice said, ignoring Kate's question.

Even in pain, Kate could not help but be pleased that this stranger knew who she was. In a relatively short time she had succeeded in becoming somebody in this massive jungle called New York.

"Okay, Kate," Janice continued, "let me get an ambulance and we'll go over to the hospital. It's just down the block."

"Please," Kate pleaded, "no ambulance. Can't we take a taxi?"

"I guess so," Janice answered. "Let me go up and get into some clothes." She stood up to leave.

"Please don't leave me alone," Kate found herself pleading. She had never been afraid before in her life. She wanted Jason. Even Ben would have been a help. Suddenly Belinda came to mind. "I've got to go to Dayton," she said urgently. "My little girl. I rarely get to see her. This is a long weekend, which we've been looking forward to."

"We'll call her and explain," Janice said patiently, but her manner softened. "I'm sure she'll understand."

"Good God," Kate exclaimed as her voice rose and her rib cage began to throb with pain. "Explain that her mother was beaten up by some maniac? She'd be petrified."

"I'll attend to it, if you like. We'll simply say you've got the flu and that it wouldn't be wise for you to travel." Then, walking over to the window, she shut it and locked it, pulling down the shade. "Let me get some clothes on. I'll double-lock the door and I'll only be a minute." At the door she turned. "And don't try to move while I'm out."

Kate ignored the warning. The minute Janice was out of the room she lifted herself up painfully from her bed. Laboriously, crawling slowly, she crossed the room to her clothes on the wing chair. She was perspiring heavily but by the time Janice returned Kate was dressed except for her shoes, which she could not put on.

"You fool," Janice said when she saw Kate sitting on the floor. She helped her on with a pair of thong sandals, brushed her hair out, and with a strength that Kate would not have believed Janice possessed, she lifted Kate and walked her to the elevator. "I've called for a taxi and I've spoken to the night intern at the emergency room. He's expecting us. I told him your name was Susan Jones. You'll have to pay cash, since you can't use any insurance cards or a check under your real name."

The realization that all her money was gone made her forget her pain for a minute. Two hundred dollars gone, probably her wallet with her credit cards, as well. Tears began to stream down her cheeks.

"He took everything," Kate said through her tears.

"You're lucky you're alive, you little fool," Janice said impatiently. "He was probably an addict. I'll take care of paying."

Kate was lying in a small cubicle in the emergency room waiting for the results of the X rays. They had given her a sedative and an injection. Her mind was floating pleasantly. She wanted Jason. She wondered how he would behave. He would be kind and gentle with her, she was sure. She would lie in his large bed, be served her meals, and Jason would be filled with sympathy and concern.

Voices made her come around. "Very well, Dr. Barker, if you say so. She really should stay here for a day or so, but you're the doctor."

Kate closed her eyes as Janice and someone else entered the room. She remembered that Janice had not answered her question when she asked her if she was a doctor. Vaguely she wondered why, but now Janice was beside her bed and Kate opened her eyes.

"Will I live?" She smiled feebly. The medication had dulled the pain almost completely.

"Believe it or not, you will. You've got a couple of chipped ribs, which Dr. Farji will tape up, then we can go home."

Kate shifted her eyes to the young man standing beside Janice. The young Indian intern smiled pleasantly at her.

"You were very lucky, Miss Jones," he said. "As for the ribs, there is little we can do for chipped ribs except strap some tape around your rib cage. That and painkillers will carry you through the next few weeks."

"Weeks?" Kate gasped.

"It's okay," Janice said with authority. "Just relax and let the doctor do his work."

It was eight o'clock in the morning when Kate and Janice arrived back at Kate's apartment. She walked into the bathroom and looked at herself in the mirror. She was deathly pale and her lip was slightly swollen. There was a black-and-blue mark under her left eye and a slight gash on her cheek.

She came back into the living room. Janice was in the kitchenette preparing coffee.

"You'd better get into bed," she told Kate.

"I've got to go to Dayton," Kate said with finality. "There is no way for me to avoid it. My daughter will never understand." She sighed deeply and felt a stab of pain in her chest. "But what do I do about my face? It's too ghastly."

She seated herself at her little dressing table and looked at the quantities of makeup she had accumulated since coming to New York. She tried to remember what the man from Revlon had taught her about shading. She was completely absorbed in trying to cover up the dark bruise under her eye, without much success, when she noticed Janice standing next to her holding a cup of coffee.

"You're really going?" she asked as she placed the cup on the table.

"I'm going, all right. I just don't want Belinda to be frightened when she sees me. She's insecure enough by now without having to live with the idea that her mother is a target for maniacs in New York. Not to mention my mother and sister. I'm their tower of strength." She smiled wryly at herself. She looked like an overly madeup clown by now. "Some tower of strength, eh?"

"All right," Janice said, "drink up your coffee and I'll patch you up."

When Janice had finished putting Kate's makeup on, it was hard to believe that below the layers of cosmetics there were any bruises at all. She watched Janice pack her suitcase. "You don't need much clothing if you're only going for a couple of days. You can't possibly schlepp a heavy bag with your ribs in their present shape." She took some money out of her pocket and put it in Kate's bag. "You'll pay me back when you return. Also, I've put in the medicine and painkillers. It'll make you sleepy, but even towers of strength get sleepy." She smiled. "How old is Belinda?"

"Nearly twelve," Kate said. "I wonder what she looks like," she said dreamily. "God, how time flies."

Janice helped her to the taxi. "You're not going to tell me who you really are," Kate said just before the taxi pulled away from the curb.

"I'm Janice Barker, and I live one floor above you." She smiled coldly. "Call me when you come back, and don't overdo it, Kate. You're really being held together with spit at this point. Remember that."

14

  To Kate's surprise and delight, Belinda was
completely captivating. Her mother and daughter were
waiting for her at the airport and the joy of seeing them
made Kate forget the pain as she hugged and kissed them
both. Belinda had grown taller since Kate had last seen
her and looked more like Elie than ever. She was dressed
in a beautiful sleeveless denim mini-jumper, and her body
had begun to fill out a bit. Her long legs were shapely and
her arms, although thin, were lovely and graceful. There
was almost no semblance of adolescent awkwardness
about her. She is instinctively chic, Kate thought with
satisfaction. For a brief moment she felt a pang of sadness
at the idea that she was not around to see this lovely child
develop into womanhood.

Since Kate did not have a chance to replace the stolen presents, she spent the afternoon shopping for gifts with Belinda. Just before they left the house, Mrs. Johnson said jokingly, "Don't spend too much money, Kate." It was said lightly, but Kate felt an edge of concern in her mother's voice.

"Mother," Belinda said as they were having sodas in the department-store coffee shop, "you won't mind if I go out tonight?" She looked appealingly at Kate. "Grama is furious, but it's a holiday weekend. You understand, don't you?"

Kate was slightly hurt, but she was pleased that her daughter had friends. Besides, she was tired and the pain was returning to her chest and her stomach was aching.

"You run along, baby," she said warmly. "Who're you going out with?"

"Kids from school," Belinda answered simply.

Kate sat with her mother in the kitchen after supper. Belinda was gone and Elie was completely absorbed in a television program in the front parlor. She was in her early twenties but there was something quite childish about her. Although the meningitis had affected only her leg, it now seemed to have affected her emotional development. She was pathetically immature. She looked no older than Belinda and from the little conversation that Kate had witnessed between her sister and her daughter, she could not help but detect an animosity between them. Belinda seemed almost cruel when she talked to Elie. Kate dismissed the thought quickly. She was simply overtired and being too sensitive. More concentrated emotion had gone into the past hours than she had coped with since she left home. She had problems at the magazine but they were concrete and could be solved. Family relationships had not entered her life for quite a while and she marveled at how quickly she had forgotten the tensions that exist in a home atmosphere. Jason, she thought, was right again. It would have been ridiculous to have Belinda in New York.

"Okay, Kate." Her mother's voice brought her back to the present. "How did you get so bruised and what are the pills you keep guzzling down every time you think no one's looking?"

Kate smiled feebly. "Oh, it's nothing, Mom. I tripped and fell in the apartment and chipped some ribs. I'm all taped up and it hurts. I really shouldn't have come but I had to. I won't be home for Thanksgiving or Christmas, so there was no choice. Besides, I really missed you and Belinda." She felt relaxed, sitting in her father's rocking chair, which had been in the kitchen ever since she could remember.

"I bet," her mother said quietly, "and that shiner under your eye is because you walked into a door, and the gash on your cheek is because you forgot to take the spoon out of the cup while drinking."

"I thought the makeup job covered it." Kate smiled at her mother.

"Oh, it's clever, whoever did it, but it's wearing thin after a hot day."

Kate said nothing but her thoughts returned briefly to Janice Barker. Who the hell was she anyway, she wondered again. She was referred to as "doctor" by the Indian intern. Or was she? Kate realized that she'd been pretty foggy in the hospital.

"You're not going to tell me, are you?" her mother said as she came to sit beside Kate and handed her a cup of coffee. "Tell me something else, then. How is it going for you?"

"Great, Mom, really great," she answered, and looked at her mother. The woman looked much older and very tired. "What's wrong?" Kate suddenly asked. "You look tired, and worried."

"Nothing special, Kate. It's Elie, I guess, and Belinda is a handful." She lowered her eyes.

"Is Belinda causing trouble?" Kate was fully alert now. "Is there something you're not telling me about her?"

"No, no," her mother said impatiently. "I'm overexcited, I guess, with you coming home and looking so beat up in spite of your fineries."

"Don't worry about me, Mom, tell me about Belinda."

"There's nothing to tell, Kate. She's growing up too fast, but I think all the kids today are. She's neglecting her schoolwork, and she's running around with kids I don't like, but they're all the same nowadays. She'll outgrow it, I'm sure."

"I can't take her to New York," Kate said defensively. "I just won't have the time to keep an eye on her."

"No need for that," Mrs. Johnson said. "We'll manage." Then, after a silence, "I could use some extra money, though. Everything is so expensive, and Belinda is not like you, frugal and all. She reads your magazine and is convinced that you are a millionaire." She paused for a long minute. "You see, Kate, I can't really do as much sewing as I used to, my eyes aren't so good. Also, I can't take a full-time job because I have to care for Elie as well as Belinda."

Kate could hear the television from the front room. She rarely watched television except when she was being interviewed or when some other person she was interested in was appearing on a talk show. The dialogue that came through loudly was strangely foreign to her. It sounded like some bad B movie.

"What's with Elie, anyway, Mom?" she asked cautiously. "She can obviously get around. Wouldn't it make sense for her to get a job and start seeing people her own age?"

"She won't," her mother said with finality. "She never leaves the house except to go to a movie. She has no friends."

Anger began to well up inside Kate. She certainly did not mind supporting her mother and Belinda, but the idea of having Elie on her hands indefinitely was upsetting. She was about to say something biting when she realized that she was in no position to bring up the subject. Her mother was helping out with Belinda and Elie was simply part of the price she had to pay. The years

125

stretched out into infinity. Belinda would grow up and somehow become an individual who would care for herself. Her mother, for as long as she lived, would be her responsibility, but Elie...She shook her head slightly. She was too tired to think of it now.

"Mom, I'm exhausted. I was going to wait up for Belinda, but I'll see her in the morning."

"Good idea," she said, and Kate detected a hint of relief in her mother's voice.

"As for the money, after the first of the year, God willing, I'll be able to send you more every month."

The sun was streaming through the window when Kate awoke. For a minute she did not remember where she was, then she saw Belinda sleeping peacefully in the other bed in the room and she found herself staring at her lovely daughter. She looked at her watch and realized that it was nearly noon. She took a pill with some water from the glass on the night table and lay back, waiting for the pain to disappear. She had slept well, but something had disturbed the serenity of her sleep.

It was completely dark and she had heard Belinda talking to Elie.

"Don't tell me you didn't get me some," Elie was whispering urgently.

"Oh, fuck off, Elie, I didn't have enough to go around, much less bring you any."

"But you promised." Elie began to whimper.

"Do you know how much you owe me already?" Belinda didn't sound nice.

"I'll pay you, I always do, you know that, you little monster."

"Don't you call me names, you cripple."

"I'll tell your mother," Elie warned.

"That's a laugh."

"What's going on out here?" Kate heard her mother's voice.

"Nothing, Grama, Elie wanted some ice cream and I forgot to buy it." Belinda sounded like herself again.

"Go to bed, both of you," Mrs. Johnson said.

Now, lying in bed with the room bathed in bright sunshine, Kate tried to figure out if she had dreamed the conversation she had heard. She looked again at her daughter. It must have been a dream. All the painkillers she was taking caused her to sleep too soundly and have that strange dream.

Belinda got up around one o'clock and when Kate asked what time she had come in, Belinda smiled charmingly and lowered her eyes. "Oh, Mother, it's a holiday weekend," she said, and Kate never got the answer. Her mother was busily doing the dishes and Kate assumed that she had not heard her question. Kate wanted to ask about the ice cream Elie had wanted during the night but somehow never got around to it.

Sunday went by pleasantly. Belinda was attentive and asked endless questions about *Women Today*, the people her mother met, the celebrities she knew, the restaurants she went to, and finally, with unabashed candor she looked at Kate and asked, "Do you have a divine lover, Mother?"

Kate blushed in confusion and was about to reprimand her daughter when she realized it would be idiotic for her to be home for a day and start disciplining the child. Instead she tried to laugh lightly. "What a grown-up question to ask, Belinda!"

"Well, do you?" the child persisted.

"Belinda, honey, that's a very personal question and I really don't want to pursue the subject."

"Well, then, I'll tell the kids at school that you're simply screwing around with celebrities. That will shut them up." She looked different as she spoke. It made Kate uncomfortable and she swallowed hard.

"You do that if it's what they want to hear." She changed the subject quickly. "But tell me about school. Who are your friends?"

"Oh, I'm going to a dance next month with the most super guy who's graduating next year." The child looked like a little girl again and Kate felt better.

"Aren't you a little young to be going out with high-school boys?"

127

"Mother, I'm twelve and I'll tell you, having you for a mother sure gives me leverage," she said with pride.

Kate felt uneasy, although flattered. "Well, sweets, you know the magazine isn't really meant for your age group, and you mustn't think that the advice in those articles is for little girls. It isn't a confession of your mother's experiences either."

"Oh, yeah? What about your book, before you went to *Women Today*?"

Kate was at a loss for words.

"What's the boy's name?" she countered, but her feelings of discomfort mounted.

"What boy?"

"The boy you're going to the dance with?"

"Jack," Belinda answered.

"Jack what?"

"I don't know." Belinda was obviously bored with the conversation. "Mother, could you send me a sexy dress to wear?"

"Belinda, I hardly think that at your age a sexy dress would be suitable. Wouldn't it make more sense to buy something here in Dayton that you are sure will look good on you?"

"What about that heavenly dress you wore on the Carson show two weeks ago? You know, it was white and had feathers around the neck and around the hem."

Kate knew exactly the dress Belinda was talking about. The gown was made especially for her by Oscar de la Renta and had cost a fortune. It would be ridiculous to send this or any of her formal dresses to Belinda for a teenagers' party.

"Darling, it won't fit you."

"Yes, it will," Belinda said angrily, her face growing red. "I'm as tall as you are and I've got more bosom than you'll ever have."

"Belinda"—Kate found her voice rising in anger— "you stop that immediately. That's a terribly expensive dress and it would be completely out of place for a twelve-year-old child to wear to a high-school dance."

Belinda burst out crying and ran from the room.

"Mom," Kate said in wonder, "what the hell is going on here?"

"She's got a temper, that's for sure," Mrs. Johnson said, wiping her hands. "I try to cope with it but she's high-strung and I just hope she outgrows it."

"Outgrows it, my foot." Kate got up uncertainly. She had forgotten that she was still very sore and the sudden motion brought it back into focus.

She followed Belinda to her room. The child was lying across her bed weeping. "You just don't care, that's all. You just don't care."

"Baby, I do." Kate felt guilty and confused. "I'll be happy to buy you a new dress, Belinda. We'll go buy it tomorrow before I fly back to New York."

"Everything is closed tomorrow and the day after, you won't be here anymore." The child spoke through the sobs.

"Well, you go downtown with Grama and pick any dress you want and I'll pay for it."

"But I want something from New York. Everything they've got here is shitty." She stopped crying and turned around and looked at Kate. "Mommy, can't I come and live with you in New York?"

The word "Mommy" caught Kate's ear and touched her. "Oh, baby, I wish you could. But I'll need a little more time before I can really afford it."

"What's the matter with your face?" Belinda suddenly asked.

For a second Kate couldn't imagine what Belinda was talking about, then she remembered her blackened eye and bruised cheek. "Oh, it's nothing. I tripped in the apartment and bruised myself." She said it lightly but saw that Belinda did not believe her.

"I'd help you if I were there. You wouldn't be alone."

"Soon, baby, soon." Then, to change the subject, she walked over to the clothes closet. "Let's see what pretty clothes you have."

She gasped with surprise when she saw the number of dresses, skirts, blouses, and slacks hanging there.

"Good grief, where did you get so many clothes from?" She recognized some of the clothes that she had sent from New York, but most of the clothes were new.

"Oh, they're all rags. Grama makes me some and when your money comes she forks up a few pennies so I won't look like an orphan."

"Now, cut that out, Belinda," Kate said with anger. "Your grandmother is doing everything she can for you and so am I. As soon as I can, I'll send extra money, and I'll expect you to keep a respectful tongue in your head."

"I'm sorry, Mother," Belinda said, and got up. "I do understand. But could you at least send me some extra pocket money, all my own, so I don't have to constantly ask Grama for my allowance? I know what a hard time she's having and that Elie also costs a fortune with her constantly being sick and everything." She was now standing next to Kate and she put her arms around her mother's neck. "I do miss you so." She sounded sincere and Kate melted with feeling.

"Sure, baby, sure I will."

Sitting in the jumbo jet on her way back to New York, Kate felt troubled. Belinda was manipulating her, of that she was sure, but she did not want to delve too deeply into the matter. The reasons were obvious and justifiable, up to a point. She had abandoned her, in a sense, so it was natural for the child to make extra demands. Belinda's mercurial changes of mood were also disturbing, but then she was at a precarious age and one had to make allowances. Again Kate wondered about that conversation she thought she heard taking place between Elie and Belinda. She was now sorry she had not asked about it. The thought of Elie plunged her into a brooding mood. Something would have to be done about Elie. Just then the captain announced their descent to La Guardia and Kate's heart leaped with joy. She was going home and that thought drove Dayton and its problems out of her thoughts. Jason would be back and she would see him. She couldn't wait to tell him what had happened to her and she would finally have some sympathy. She took out a little mirror and looked at herself. She had covered up the bruises but not as well as Janice had. The thought of Janice somehow made the homecoming all the more exciting. The woman was, after all, a stranger, yet Kate looked upon her as a friend. She mulled the last thought over. She really had no friends in New York or anywhere else, for that matter, except Ben and he was hardly reliable. Janice was different—she was sure of it—and she looked forward to talking to her.

15

When Kate walked into her apartment the horror of what had happened to her there just seventy-two hours before hit her like a thunderbolt.

She put her bag down and dialed Jason's number. He was still away, she was informed, and would not be back until the next day. She left a message that she wanted him to call her the minute he was back. She hung up and was about to call Janice but realized she did not have her number. She looked it up in the directory. There were two J. Barkers in the book, one an MD, the other on West Fifty-seventh Street. As she dialed the latter number she could not help but be puzzled.

"It's Kate Johnson," she said when she heard Janice's voice.

"Hello, Kate." Her voice was pleasant but aloof. "Did you have a nice trip, and how is your little girl?"

"Fine, everything is fine." She paused, not knowing how to continue. She had built Janice in her mind as a warm, friendly person, but the voice at the other end was hardly that of a friend. "Would you..." She stopped. "Janice, can I take you to dinner?" The phrase was strange to her. She had never spent time with anyone in New York who was not essential to her work. This was purely social and she could hardly put it on her expense account as a business dinner.

"I'm on a strict diet, Kate, but it's nice of you to ask."

"Well, how about coming down for a drink?"

"I've got my two boys with me," she answered, and then, sensing Kate's disappointment, she added, "but they'll be leaving in about an hour. As soon as I put them in a cab I'll call you."

Kate showered carefully, trying not to wet the tape around her ribs, but it was impossible. She put on a robe and lay down. She would have to carefully review her trip to Dayton, she decided. There was something wrong in her mother's household, but exactly what it was eluded her. Belinda was a strange child. Too grown up one minute and completely childish the next, and her conception of Kate's job was totally unrealistic. Somehow the child was taking too many wrong things for granted. Her mother was too old-fashioned or maybe too tired to cope with or understand Belinda. Elie was obviously not the best influence on a growing, impressionable child. Again she wondered if the conversation she'd heard between her daughter and Elie were real or part of a grotesque dream. But even a dream had to be motivated by something that was in the air. "Fuck off...you cripple." Those were the words she had attributed to Belinda. Kate knew she would have to make more of an effort to see the child. Moving Belinda to New York was impossible, but as soon as she got her next raise at the magazine, Kate would invite Belinda to New York for a long weekend or vacation. Christmas was out of the question, for there were too many things scheduled for that time of year. Besides, Hank and Jean had invited her for Christmas, and Jason had urged her to go. Hank and Jean knew everybody, and Jason felt it would be a valuable opportunity to be seen in that family situation. As for New Year's Eve, she felt sentimental about it and wanted to spend it with Jason. Thanksgiving came to mind, but it was too hectic and it would not make sense to have Belinda spend it alone with Kate. They would have to eat in a restaurant and that hardly seemed right. At least in Dayton her mother would have a big turkey and invite some of her friends in. Belinda might even spend time with schoolfriends, whereas in New York she knew no one and would be bored. Kate felt that she was rationalizing, but she knew it would actually cost a fortune to bring the child in so soon after her own trip to Dayton and felt she was being sensible.

Her doorbell rang and Kate jumped up. It was Janice.

She had looked forward to seeing her, but now that Janice was in Kate's apartment, Kate felt shy. Janice was cool and aloof, dressed in a magnificently tailored skirt, an equally tailored and well-fitting shirt, a necklace and earrings of matching cultured pearls. She looked different and very distant.

"First," Kate said breathlessly, "I owe you money. You put one hundred dollars in my bag, but I haven't the vaguest idea how much the hospital cost, the taxis, the whole bit."

"I haven't gotten the bill yet, but I'll let you know."

"I thought they didn't let you out of the hospital if you didn't pay immediately."

"It's okay." Janice sounded a bit impatient.

"You have two boys?" Kate asked, trying to make conversation. "Where are they living that you sent them off in a cab?"

"They go to a prep school outside of Philadelphia."

"Are you married?"

"Divorced."

134

"Oh." Kate felt ill at ease. "What do you do for a living?"

"I work in Long Island in a laboratory."

"Are you a doctor?" The question came again.

"It's a cosmetics laboratory," Janice said quietly, obviously not interested in pursuing the conversation. "How are your ribs?" she asked instead.

"They itch terribly under the plaster," she confessed.

"Probably got wet while you were showering. Dr. Farji should have told you about that." She smiled. "Those young interns are good but they often forget all the little details."

"Damn it, Janice." Kate suddenly could not contain herself. "I'm not usually curious about people, but for some reason you really fascinate me. Why don't you simply tell me who you are and what you're all about." She was amazed at herself, but she wanted this woman as a friend. Janice was the first woman, the first person she had met in a long time, that she was drawn to. "There's a Dr. Barker in the phone book somewhere on Park Avenue, and then there is you on West Fifty-seventh Street. What gives?"

Janice looked angry for a minute but then relaxed. "Okay, I'm a doctor but not the doctor on Park Avenue. That's my ex-husband. We met at Duke University when we were both studying medicine and got married while we were still there. We both graduated and specialized in dermatology and opened offices together. We lived in Mamaroneck and have two boys, Stevie and William, who are now fourteen and sixteen." Her face was pale and Kate was sorry she had pushed the question. She had obviously disturbed some serious and painful memories. "We had a dream world together, the four of us. Then John, that's my husband, decided we should open offices in New York. I really didn't want to, but he insisted. It began to go downhill from there. We were divorced a year ago and the dream ended."

"Do you like what you're doing now?" Kate asked. The idea of hiring Janice as a beauty editor began to percolate in her brain. A doctor of dermatology on her staff as a beauty editor! It would be a coup.

"Not particularly," Janice was saying, "but there is no pressure. That's the most important thing for me, there's no pressure."

"What are you earning?" she asked bluntly. Her mind was made up; she wanted Janice on her staff.

"I beg your pardon," Janice said, and her face was now flushed.

"Oh, I'm sorry." Kate was startled for a minute. She had it all figured out but realized that she had not communicated her thoughts. "I really am sorry, Janice," she repeated, "it just seems like a natural that you come and work at *Women Today* as the beauty editor. Your background is super and I must confess, I'm a stickler for honesty when it comes to anything that I put in the magazine. So how much better can I do than have a medical person in charge of the beauty department?"

"You are a pushy little lady," Janice said coldly, her face still red from controlling her rage, "and I suppose that's what makes for success in what you're doing, but I would no more dream of going into that rat race you call a magazine than I'd climb Mount Everest."

"But why on earth not?" Kate was shocked. "I'll top whatever salary you make now and you can have complete autonomy in your department."

"What makes you think I need the money?" Janice sneered. "I earn a fairly good salary, but I also get a very, very fine alimony." She sucked in her breath. I want my husband back, she wanted to say, I want my husband, my home, and my children, not a high salary at some girlie magazine.

Kate became flustered. She had never met anyone who could not be enticed with money. "But you'd have an opportunity to put your experience to use. There are millions of girls out there who are constantly being lied to and cheated by cosmetic firms that will sell them any cream or makeup whether it's good for them or not. You could become a beacon of honesty, someone they could learn to depend on when it came to their makeup."

Janice lowered her eyes. These were exactly her own feelings, the ones she had felt when her marriage was going on the rocks. John, decent, hardworking John, had fallen for the idol of the golden calf. "Who the hell cares?" he shouted at her once when she pointed out that a medication that had not yet been proved safe should not be prescribed by him. "The FDA approved it, didn't they?" he shouted. "And the manufacturer and I have a very good agreement." Although their private practice was growing by leaps and bounds, they had many similar fights in those days, which grew worse, louder, and more abusive. "So you're a better doctor than I am," John shouted one day, "I know it and I bow to your superiority, but you're not going to cheat me of financial success. You and your fine ethics. When a patient is sixty-five and wants to look thirty, what's wrong with my giving her a cream that convinces her that she really does look younger? It won't harm her even if it doesn't do what she thinks it does."

She had graduated way ahead of John scholastically but when they were first married it did not matter. Later, however, it became a bone of contention. When they finally agreed to a divorce, Janice had a nervous breakdown. Her only salvation, according to her analyst, was that she had to take a job that did not put her in a pressure situation. But more than that, Janice herself wanted to be removed from the limelight, allow the dust to settle, be inconspicuous, with the hope that John would come back to her.

"What say, Janice?" Kate's voice came to her. She looked up. In spite of Kate's maddening aggressiveness, Janice liked her. She had guts. Also, the idea of being able to communicate with people rather than laboratory tubes was appealing.

"I'll think about it," Janice said finally, "but I'll tell you right now, there is to be no mention of my medical background and no interference when it comes to a product that I think is harmful." She smiled suddenly.

"You might lose more than you'll gain by having me. I am not overly sympathetic to advertisers who will say anything to sell a product."

"I'll take that chance," Kate said, wondering if she was really doing the right thing. But she had made her decision. She could really make a serious dent with her readers if they came to trust *Women Today* and its beauty editor. Somehow she'd handle the advertisers. "When will you start?" she asked seriously.

"I'll let you know in a day or so. I will have to give notice where I'm working, too."

They looked at each other and smiled.

"Now let's take a look at that tape," Janice said, her voice completely professional.

The phone rang as Janice was retaping Kate's ribs. It was Jason's secretary, who seemed to work seven days a week, twenty-four hours a day.

"Mr. Reid asked me to tell you that he will see you on Friday, as usual," the woman said impersonally.

"Is he back in town?" Kate asked, feeling hurt. She had looked forward to seeing Jason.

"No, he called me from out of town and asked me to give you that message."

Kate hung up and looked at Janice. She was deeply disturbed at Jason's way of relating to her. In all the time that she had known him, he always succeeded in remaining remote from her. He was always warm, helpful, even passionate when they made love, but the cutoff point was when she left his house on Saturday. If she needed him during the week, he was always available to talk to her on the phone. If she had a problem at the magazine, he would spend time helping her out, but except for the hours she spent with him during the weekend, he was inaccessible, as though she were a stranger.

"I'll run along now," Janice said as she repacked the little medical kit she had brought down. Just before she walked out the door, she turned. "I probably will come to work for you." She didn't know why, but at that moment she felt sorry for Kate.

16

Friday came around almost without notice. Kate was frantically busy and energized by the realization that the magazine was really beginning to forge into the big league. Kate had approached several top advertisers directly, with great success. Requests for television interviews, which were hard to come by before the magazine changed its format, now came more frequently than she could grant them. Her book was in its third printing and still selling strongly. People who barely noticed her before were now asking her to dinner parties or dates. Her calendar was filling up with conflicting business appointments and she was thrilled. She had become a known commodity and although being a commodity was hardly flattering, it was what she had aimed for and it was coming true.

She had been too busy to think of the robbery, but while dressing for dinner with Jason, she began to relax and allow some of the pain, both physical and emotional, to surface. She would be seeing Jason and she could finally talk to him about what had happened. She was sure he would understand.

She could not have been more wrong.

"You little fool," Jason said when she was finally in his study.

Kate looked at him with horror. She had rushed over carrying the load of papers in her briefcase, which made the pain in her ribs nearly unbearable. She tried to run up the stairs to his study but found it impossible. When she reached the first-floor landing, she had to stop and wipe her brow. The pain, which she had ignored throughout the week, was now unbelievable. It was as though she had purposely put aside the full intensity of it until she was with Jason and felt she could let down her defenses.

When she finally walked into the study, Jason stood up and took her in his arms. She cried out with pain.

"What's wrong?" he asked as he pushed her away and looked at her.

With tears streaming down her cheeks she poured out the events of the Friday before. Sobbing like a child, she was unable to control the pent-up anguish she had covered so well.

"You are a goddamn fool," Jason repeated furiously. "How many times did I tell you not to live in that awful little tenement?"

She had never seen him that angry before. "Thank God you kept it out of the papers, if nothing else. That's all we need: 'New Editor of *Women Today* Beaten Up in New York.' That would have really established you as a model to our readers."

"Jason, it could happen to anyone." Kate was hurt and bewildered.

"Anyone?" he roared. "You're not anyone. When are you going to begin to understand that?"

"I didn't know you cared," Kate said sarcastically in

spite of her being hurt. This was certainly not the reception she had expected.

"I care to the extent that you work for Reid Publications."

"What a dreadful thing to say, Jason," she said slowly. "Is that all I am, someone who works for Reid Publications?"

"I suggest you move out of that rat's nest as soon as possible into a properly guarded building in a proper neighborhood," he said coldly, ignoring her question.

"I'll move when I want to move," she retorted angrily, but kept her voice down. "As for what happened, let's forget it." She stood up carefully. "Could I have a drink?" she asked. "A nice stiff scotch on the rocks, please." She kept her back to him as she spoke. Her mind was in turmoil. Jason's reaction was totally devoid of any human feeling. She almost laughed when she remembered her lovely fantasy of being taken care of by him, being held, caressed, and receiving his sympathy. His outburst was shocking. To pretend that this was possibly love and hurt for her hidden behind a barrage of angry abuse would have been simplistic, and there was nothing simplistic about Jason.

"Here's your drink, Kate," she heard him say, and she turned around, took the glass and watched him walk over and sit down in his large leather chair.

"Is that the material you want to work on?" he asked, pointing to the briefcase on the floor next to his chair.

She nodded and sat down across from him.

He started sifting through the papers, oblivious of her presence, sometimes grunting with satisfaction, sometimes crossing out a line or rewriting a sentence. She simply sat and stared at him. She finished her drink and got up to pour herself another. He didn't seem to notice. She had had four stiff drinks by the time he finally looked up. For the first time since she had walked in, he looked like the old Jason she had known over the last months.

"Good," he said pleasantly. "Except that I don't like the ideas that Linda is coming up with. Fire her."

The pills and the liquor were taking their toll and Kate's mind was working slowly. She closed her eyes for a minute to clear her head. Then, opening them, she looked directly at Jason.

"I won't fire her, Jason. I think she's damn good, I like her ideas, and she's very bright, alive, and vibrant." She took another gulp from her nearly empty glass. "She communicates something very real. She's living out there in that jungle, and I don't know how she manages, but she has the pulse of this city and the girls in it, along with the naiveté my readers react to. I grant you that it's taking its toll on her, but as long as she's producing what I'm looking for, I won't fire her."

"Well, I'll be damned." Jason laughed almost self-consciously. "Maybe you should get beaten up more often and drink more. I've never seen you quite so aggressive. I've seen you this way with others, but I never thought you'd dare with me."

"Oh, cut it out, Jason," she snapped. "You've been treating me like a child a little too long. With all your worldliness you really see me as the 'weaker sex,' 'the little woman,' the silly little lady from Dayton whom you're guiding along." She caught her breath. Her rage was now full blown. "I am a woman and even if I do go to bed with you I am still independent. You hired me to run the magazine and you know that I'm running it well, very well. Today, beaten up or not, I am a person, and I expect to be treated as a person."

"Well, I'll be a son of a gun." Jason burst out laughing again. "And all this in just one year?"

At that point Kate burst out crying. Jason let her cry and when she finally felt completely drained, he stood up and walked over to her.

"Katie," he said soberly, "I can't help who I am." Leaning over her chair and looking directly at her, he continued. "I will not tolerate weakness. I cannot stand to look at people who are bruised, whether physically or mentally. I've always been like that. I insist that everything that's important to me go my way and when it doesn't, I kick it out, eliminate it, dismiss it as though it never was." He straightened up. "I'm very rigid. I don't bend. I refuse to." He looked around. "You see this room? It's identical to all the rooms I created around the country in offices where I have control. When I don't have control, I either get it or walk away from it." He turned his back to her. "I'm sorry you were hurt by whoever that maniac was." With that statement made he walked over and pressed the buzzer for the butler. "Now I think we'd better have some dinner."

That night, when Kate was in her own apartment, she mulled over the conversation with Jason. She had won a major battle but her whole life in New York would take on a different tone. Jason would not change. He would be as he had been with her since she first arrived and their relationship would be as it had been. She could depend on him in many ways, but he was clearly unapproachable as a human being. He had succeeded for so long in eluding attachments that could cause him any hurt that it would be futile for her to try to foster one. She felt a sense of great loss, although what was lost she didn't know. A foolish, girlish dream based on no foundation whatsoever? He wanted nothing from her except a successfully run magazine and Friday night and Saturday companionship. She was his editor in chief of *Women Today* and as long as she did her job well, she would be just that.

17

The December issue was in preparation and Kate marveled at how time had flown. The Christmas issue never ceased to send a special thrill of excitement through her, and this would be the fifth one since she had come to *Women Today*. The magazine was now completely hers, in concept, in content, in appearance. Her meetings with the board of directors were reduced to once every two or three months, and then she was feted and complimented and buoyed along as the most creative and successful editor in the country. Sales were going up constantly, advertising was literally pouring in.

She felt secure enough to share her success with the editors who worked with her. She was also aware of their needs and made sure these needs were met. Janice, with her dread of outside pressures, functioned best when left alone. She was still in love with her husband and had no interest in meeting or dating men who might threaten her attempts to get him back. Linda required little encouragement or flattery. A smile of appreciation from Kate, a note of thanks, were all that was needed. If anything, Kate suspected that more and more the job was becoming the focus of Linda's life. Usually first in the office in the morning, Linda often stayed late as well, and on her way out Kate would see her poring over an article or having a meeting with a writer. Carol now participated fully in all staff meetings as Linda's assistant, offering suggestions for future articles that were always fresh, well thought out, and unusual. Kate often wondered if her ideas came from personal experience or from fantasy, but Linda was always able to translate everything she said into real-life terms. Kate knew she would soon have to promote Carol to the status of junior editor but kept putting it off. Linda and Carol worked together too well, and she rationalized that a promotion might interfere with the relationship. Kate was extremely grateful for the friendship between the two women, for it helped relieve her own feelings of guilt for not socializing with Linda outside the office. Maggie was a nine-to-five person but took a great deal of her work home. She was loyal and devoted to the magazine, but her family came first. Time off for a sick child, a graduation party, an anniversary, for any of the many occasions that required her attention at the expense of being at the office, was given by Kate without resentment. Dee Dee was involved with a new young photographer, whose work did not impress Kate but who was constantly hired by Dee Dee without Kate's interfering. Dee Dee had gone through several traumas since Kate had come to New York. Her fanatic women's-liberation stand was seriously impaired and had come under attack when it was discovered that after several years of being divorced from her now famous Hollywood-director husband, she was suing him for alimony. Her public statements justifying her actions were simple and beyond reproach—she had helped him achieve his success and she felt the alimony was her due. It was not an unreasonable point of view and many women agreed with her. Her detractors, however, were loud and abusive. Kate knew that Dee Dee was also in deep financial trouble and assumed it had to do with Dee Dee's unbelievable extravagance on clothes, jewelry and makeup.

"It means too much to her," Janice explained one day when Kate brought it up. She rarely discussed the staff with anyone, but Janice understood Dee Dee better than anyone and liked her as well. Kate did not mention the money problem, but rather the incredible emphasis which Dee Dee placed on appearances. "You can't begin to imagine what it must be like for someone who justifies her whole existence by her beauty, who sees it vanishing before her eyes."

"But she's still exquisite. Her posture, her manner, her flair, they're all there," Kate exclaimed.

"You see it, I see it, but she's too close to herself to see it objectively." She smiled a sad smile. "That's why most models marry men who are not great Adonises, but rather men who look up to them and spend their time adulating their looks. They need men like that around who will go on worshipping them. Dee Dee, poor soul, is alone. She would have been better off if her ex-husband had not become the success that he is but still needed her. He would remember her as she was when they first met, were first married. An intellectual woman brings many other factors to a relationship. Dee Dee brought her looks."

"But this new man is exactly like her husband. She's building another mediocrity to the point where he'll leave her the minute he makes it."

"And don't you dare stop her," Janice warned.

Well, Kate wasn't stopping her. On the contrary, she allowed Dee Dee to go off on location shootings just so that she could be with her young man.

The intercom buzzer sounded and Kate picked up the phone. It was the bank manager. She held her breath.

"Miss Johnson, that check for five hundred dollars

you stopped payment on was cashed several days ago."

"Has it been endorsed?"

"Yes, by Mrs. Johnson, just as all the others were in the past."

"Thank you," Kate said quietly, and hung up.

She knew exactly what had happened. Belinda had forged her grandmother's signature. Mrs. Johnson had called frantically a few days earlier to complain about not getting her monthly check. Kate was surprised. The accounting department sent out the checks promptly. Assuming it was lost, Kate had put a stop-payment on it. Now that the mystery was cleared up, Kate felt faint.

The situation with Belinda had grown progressively worse. For a month during the past summer the girl stayed with Kate in New York. It was a disastrous vacation. Belinda sulked almost constantly. She was uninterested in most of what New York had to offer. The theater was a bore, museums were for squares, sightseeing was for tourists. The teenager never picked up a book to read and was totally incapable of entertaining herself. Television and movies were her only interests and since Kate was at the office most of the day, Belinda obviously spent her time going from one movie to the next. Her need for money was never-ending, and Kate never knew how she spent the money. Belinda would say she had been shopping or having lunch out and going to a movie. When Kate finally took her to visit Maggie Pearson, Belinda was almost rude to the family, who were going out of their way to be nice to their mother's boss and her daughter.

It was with a sense of relief that she saw Belinda off to Dayton after the four-week visit.

Now the forebodings of disaster Kate had put aside since Belinda left had been realized. Belinda had stolen the money.

She picked up the phone to call her mother but hung up immediately. She had to think the matter out. The money was important but there was something far more serious that had to be considered. Belinda was behind her grade level in school, and was unmanageable at home. The girl could no longer stay in Dayton to be cared for by an old woman and a cripple. The last word ripped through her as though she'd been struck. Elie, sweet beautiful Elie, whom she had envied so as a child, who had taken her father's love away from her, was now just "a cripple." She forced herself to concentrate on Belinda. If only she could call Jason and ask him what to do. It would be wrong from every point of view. Janice? No, it was too personal. Maggie? It occurred to her that Maggie was probably the best person to consult, but she felt embarrassed. What Belinda had done was criminal. She could not expose her own daughter. Linda. Yes, Linda would be the most understanding and sympathetic. She had worked with children in the convent. Underprivileged children, children who were troubled, children who needed help.

She was about to pick up the phone again when Dee Dee stormed into the office.

"I warned you," she said in a high-pitched, hysterical voice that was totally out of keeping with her usual manner. "I told you that rotten bitch would get us all into trouble and she did!"

"What in heaven's name are you talking about?" Kate tried to bring herself back to the present. "What trouble?"

"Kate"—Dee Dee tried to lower her voice—"I had a whole Christmas concept of lovely, droopy, chiffony clothes, comfortable, easy, long, and dreamy. The model was to be wispy, faded, hazy, cool, elegant. But the clothes were not to be transparent. I didn't need nipples showing through the tops. I didn't want suggestions of pubic hair or suggestive poses."

"So?" Kate snapped, although she didn't mean to. It was the same theme almost every month even though the wardrobes and concepts changed constantly. By now Dee Dee should know that Betsy always withdrew at the last and did what had to be done. "We've been through this before."

"Not quite," Dee Dee answered. "Not quite. This time the model complained and her agency just called and refused to allow us to use the pictures. We did not get a release from the model, and furthermore, while the lady at the agency had me on the phone she announced, and with great satisfaction, mind you, that her models are not going to be available to us anymore."

"The hell with her. Call another agency and I'll talk to Betsy."

"I already did, and word has gone out. No agency is going to give us their girls."

"Okay," Kate said slowly, "we'll find them on the street. I will personally go out and find them. Shop girls and secretaries are just as lovely as some of those insipid idiot girls who are models and their fees are going to be a hell of a lot cheaper." She paused for a minute. "As a matter of fact, I think that's a great gimmick. We'll mention that the Christmas issue is exactly what we've been talking about. The real, honest, hardworking single girl is going to be featured as proof of what we've been writing about."

Dee Dee was staring at Kate with amazement and admiration. "By God, you're a cool one, aren't you." She relaxed and sat down. Taking out a cigarette, she lit it and inhaled deeply. "What I don't understand about Betsy is why she has to degrade these girls," Dee Dee said. "It just doesn't make any sense."

"I suppose she doesn't really see it as degrading and I'm surprised you do. What's so degrading about showing a woman's bosom or backside or pubic hair, anyway? You're all for letting everything hang out, aren't you? Equality, men and women, it's all the same?"

"Well, you don't see male models being photographed nude, except of course in the trash magazines." There was silence in the room for a minute. "Of course the nude females in *Esquire* and *Playboy* are there because those magazines feel that men are turned on by these girls, and we object to the fact that women are used like that," Dee Dee said.

"Well, I'll be a son of a gun." Kate's voice was suddenly filled with excitement. "A nude-male centerfold. Of course." She was nearly beside herself with excitement. "Naked women in the centerfold turn on men—why not a male nude? Equality, great. Let it all hang out," she said, and blushed. The obvious pun, which she did not intend, struck her. Kate was still uncomfortable with anything that was in any way crudely suggestive.

"Boy, Kate"—Dee Dee burst out laughing—"you've finally made a good pun and you're red as a beet."

Kate giggled self-consciously, then became serious. "All right, now down to business. We're set for the November issue and what we're missing is the fashion pictures for Christmas. Tomorrow at the meeting we'll get everyone out to look for girls to pose for you. With all of us looking, we'll find the right ones. Do you need two or three?"

"Two will do," Dee Dee said. "No need to burden us too heavily. But what happens for January? Those bitches who run the modeling agencies are tough."

"I'll work something out," she said with assurance. This was a problem she could discuss with Jason. He'd help her find a solution.

Dee Dee stood up. "Are you serious about the male nude?"

"Of course I am. I think it's a sensational idea, don't you?"

Dee Dee shrugged. "You're the boss." There was no sarcasm in her voice as she walked out of the office.

As the door closed, Kate's mind drifted back to Belinda. She dialed Linda's number and asked her to come in.

Linda didn't look well. Kate noticed it the minute the young woman walked in. Her hair was disheveled, there were huge dark rings under her eyes, and the clean, spotless look that Kate always associated with Linda was gone. The warm smile she flashed as she sat down, however, dispelled Kate's concern.

"You look worried," Linda said, and Kate relaxed. Linda was truly one of the sweetest, warmest people she had ever met. Briefly she wondered why she never associated with her outside of work. She had so little time, the answer came quickly.

"We have a problem with the modeling agencies. They won't give us any of their models because they feel we are exploiting them by showing too much of them."

"What will you do?"

"Oh, we'll find some good-looking girls in department stores or in some offices; we'll work it out."

Linda was silent, knowing that Kate would soon tell her what was really troubling her. Linda's affection for Kate had grown in the years they had worked together. She also felt sorry for her, although she did not know why. But despite her compassion for the people she worked with, especially Kate, she had little time to think of them. Her own life had taken a bad turn. She wanted so to share her warmth, her love, her deep feelings with someone that she now found she was throwing herself at men who were unkind, unfeeling. Her affairs were brief and usually ended badly.

"Linda"—Kate interrupted her thoughts—"Linda, I have a serious problem with Belinda."

"Oh, I'm sorry," she said. "What's happened?"

Quickly Kate related the story to Linda, who listened attentively.

"Poor baby," Linda said after Kate finished talking. "She must be tortured out of her mind to have done something like this."

"What do I do?"

"How old is she now?"

"Nearly sixteen."

"She still has at least two years of high school then, doesn't she?"

"She's not really interested in her schoolwork," Kate said sadly. "She's way behind in several of her classes."

"Why don't you send her to a good parochial school? There are some excellent ones around. I can check them out for you easily. There is a superb one in Connecticut called Windham. I know the mother superior there and I'll gladly talk to her."

"But that won't solve the problem," Kate said with

anguish. "She's stolen money from me, from my mother, from my sister. It's not the money, it's what she is inside, that caused her to do it."

"Send her to a parochial school, Kate. They'll understand and cope with what's troubling her. I promise you. These are bad times for kids. You're away from her. . . ."

"It's my fault, isn't it?" Kate became defensive.

"Placing blame is not going to help anyone. You did what you thought was right and Belinda is young enough to be helped. Your mother is two generations away from her. Your sister is ill. Don't punish yourself."

"Will you call for me?"

"Certainly," Linda said gently. "It'll all work out, you wait and see."

As Linda stood up to leave, Kate looked at her gratefully. "Are you all right?" Kate asked, focusing her attention for the moment on Linda. "How's the apartment?"

"I'm fine," Linda said, smiling, "and I adore the apartment," she added enthusiastically. "You were an angel to give it to me. Do you like where you're living now?"

Kate had finally moved to an East Side apartment and with Jason's guidance had it furnished by a well-known decorator, and she had to admit that she loved it. She, of course, paid him for the furniture at cost, and got him to do several issues with his by-line on the decorating pages. "It's heaven," she said, feeling better for the first time since she got the news about Belinda and the money. "Did you get any new furniture?" she asked Linda.

"Didn't really need anything. What you left was just fine."

When Linda left, Kate sat back and wondered about her. When Kate vacated the apartment, she had left the bare minimum—a bed, a worn-out dresser, a broken armchair, and a couple of other unpainted pieces of furniture. And Linda said that she hadn't really needed anything else. Kate felt a chill go through her. Linda was still a nun at heart. She was a superb editor for *Women Today* but Kate suspected that her efforts to produce fresh ideas for and unlimited twists to each article were exacting a price. Linda was pushing herself out of her milieu, was forcing herself to live a life contrary to her basic feelings and beliefs. Kate felt a terrible sorrow for her and for a brief moment found herself totally immersed in thoughts about someone other than herself and the magazine.

She shook her head to clear away this unpleasant insight. She couldn't cope with this now. She excused herself with the thought, there's never enough time, and automatically picked up the phone to call Jason. She would have to attend to the modeling agencies even though she had already decided to let them stew for a while.

18

The autumn sun threw off little warmth as Kate rushed toward the waiting car, It was nearly noon and she had an appointment with the headmistress of the school in Connecticut. Settling back in the seat, she felt chilled and nervous. She picked up the woolen blanket lying neatly folded next to her and covered her knees.

"We'll stop first on Eighth Avenue and Fifty-seventh Street to pick up Miss Wilson," she said to the driver. "Then we'll go on to Connecticut."

So much had happened since the day the bank informed her of the missing check Belinda had cashed, which still stood out like a monument of disaster. Concern for her daughter, followed by Dee Dee's problem with Betsy, the magazine's problems with the

modeling agencies, and Kate's apprehensions about
Linda were disturbing enough. But she was most annoyed
by a dreadful confrontation with Betsy the day Dee Dee
had informed her of the modeling agencies' decision.

The conversation started off badly. Betsy had come
in and thrown herself on the sofa.

"What's the big fuss?" she said in her foreign accent,
always more pronounced when she was annoyed.

"Betsy"—Kate tried to be pleasant—"why do you
do these things? I give you a free hand to do anything you
want when it comes to layouts, concepts, drawings, but
I've had so much trouble with the models you photograph, and now they won't work for me. *Women Today* is
my magazine, and although I delegate—"

"*Your* magazine?" Betsy sat up and looked
strangely menacing. "You must be mad to think that this
is your magazine."

"I beg your pardon?" Kate could not believe her
ears. "Of course it belongs to Reid Publications, but
everything that it is today is what I've brought to it."

Betsy's laugh was like the hiss of a rattlesnake. "My
dear Kate," she said in a low voice, "*I* have created this
magazine." She waited for her words to sink in. "I have
given it the look it has today, you must admit that."

Kate bit her lip, stifling the reply racing through her
mind. Betsy was the perfect art director for *Women
Today*. She was also an incredibly limited, vain, and
egotistical person. Arguing with her was as fruitless as
arguing with a three-year-old child. Was it worth losing
her at this crucial point, or should she simply give in and
wait? Kate turned her back to Betsy, striving desperately
for full control, then she turned around and smiled.

"Yes," she said, "in a way you're right, Betsy. You've
been an unbelievable factor in the style of *Women Today*,
and without doubt you've contributed to the success we
have. I think you know we're all grateful to you. But,
Betsy, it is my responsibility to put this book on the stand
every month, and you're making it more difficult with
your attitude toward the models." She walked over to the
girl, who now looked very pleased. "Please, Betsy, try to
cooperate with Dee Dee."

"I do like your idea of using girls other than models for the Christmas issue," Betsy said condescendingly, ignoring Kate's plea. "As a matter of fact, we really don't have to go very far. We can use Carol and Marrianne."

Kate nearly burst out laughing but restrained herself. Carol's loathing for Betsy was thinly disguised. Whenever the two women were in the same room together, Carol actively avoided Betsy. Kate had once asked Carol about it, and the girl, in her cool, almost distant manner, grimaced with disgust.

"She reminds me of an evil little worm," she said with more emotion than Kate had ever seen her exhibit. "She's not only evil, she's stupid and she lies. A dreadful combination, don't you agree?" Kate had to admit that young as she was, Carol had summed up Betsy brilliantly.

Now Betsy's voice came back to Kate. "What do you think, Kate?" Kate turned around to look at the woman. She seemed to have forgotten her vicious mood of only moments earlier.

"Talk to Dee Dee about your idea and see what she says," Kate said confidently. Dee Dee would know exactly how to cope with the situation to everyone's satisfaction.

Kate avoided telling Jason about any of the personal interactions at the magazine until she felt she had them under control. Last night, feeling that most of her problems were temporarily solved, she had related to him the whole scene with Betsy. Jason listened in silence. When she finished he looked up at her.

"You know, Kate," he said quietly, "for a bright lady you can be very dense when it comes to evaluating people."

"What's that supposed to mean?" she asked, her voice rising slightly. Criticism always put her on the defensive.

"She hates you," he said simply. "I've seen it from the start. For some unknown reason she wants to ruin you."

Kate lowered her head. She knew he was right.

"She must be fired," she heard Jason saying, and looked up.

"I won't fire her now, Jason, not yet," Kate answered quietly. "Betsy is still very important to me. I must get our image more firmly established before I can look for someone else."

"You mean you're going to keep her after this mess?" He paused for a minute, too stunned to go on, then, in a louder voice, he continued. "Kate, how self-destructive can you be? You must be aware that by using nonmodels for the Christmas issue you are further antagonizing the agencies. They'll never forgive you—don't you understand that?"

"They'll forgive me," Kate answered firmly. "We have a successful book, we use many models, we pay the going rates, and if need be I'll even raise the rates for special jobs. These girls and their agents are in business to make money and the more they are seen, the more work they get."

"You're really that sure of yourself?" Jason's voice softened.

"Yes," Kate said, although her feelings of confidence were nowhere near what they seemed. "Yes, I'm that sure of *Women Today*."

Jason was unusually warm and uncharacteristically considerate that evening. He suggested that they change their plans and stay home for dinner. They ate a delicious meal prepared by his cook, and when he made love to her that night, she knew he was aware of her as he had not been in quite a while. She felt it and was grateful for it. Her evenings with Jason had deteriorated. He was still a good lover, but she no longer enjoyed it as she had when she first went to bed with him. Now she would try desperately to respond to him, but only by conjuring up complex erotic fantasies in which Jason played no part could she actually derive any pleasure from the lovemaking. If he knew it, he did not let on. She strongly suspected that he, too, felt as she did, that their lovemaking had become a habit, but they weren't prepared to admit that they had become physically bored with each other. Also, they were bound by their love for *Women Today* and the determination to make it a success. It was this rarely exhibited concern for her that probably prompted him not to wake her up for breakfast. When she awoke and realized the hour, she asked Jason if she could borrow his car for the trip to Connecticut. She had never asked him for it before and he agreed without question.

"Miss Johnson." The driver had stopped the car and Kate looked around. She saw Linda standing on the corner.

"That's her," Kate said, indicating Linda to the driver, and he jumped out and led her to the car. Watching Linda come closer, Kate noticed again that she looked pale and drawn. She had a scarf around her head so that none of her hair showed and for a minute Linda looked like a nun.

"Hi, Kate," Linda said cheerfully. "It's cold, isn't it?"

"You're not dressed warmly enough," Kate said seriously. Linda was wearing a thin black coat, Loafers, and no stockings.

"Oh, I'm all right. And it's nice and warm in the car," she said, and her smile was bright. "You do fuss, don't you?"

Linda was right. Kate always felt a concern for Linda.

"Now, tell me, how did Belinda take to the idea of going to a boarding school?" Linda asked, changing the subject.

"Not very well," Kate said soberly. "But when I told her that she would spend every Sunday in New York with me she calmed down."

"But that's great," Linda said, noting Kate's unhappy tone.

"Yes, except that my sister, Elie, took it very badly." Kate paused for a minute. "I don't quite know why, but she burst out crying, ran from the room, and refused to come out to say good-bye to me when I left."

"What did your mother say?" Linda asked, curious.

"Oh, my mother was hurt at first. She felt she had failed me and that I was taking Belinda away because she hadn't done a good job with the child."

"Well, in a way it's true, isn't it?" Linda said gently.

"Yes and no. My mother is not a young woman anymore. Elie is a handful for any mother and Belinda is not an easy teenager. Remember, she feels that I've deserted her for a job, which in a way is true—"

"Oh, stop that right this minute," Linda interrupted. "You did what you thought best. What would your lives have been like if you'd stayed in Dayton working at a job that didn't challenge you? Over the years you would have become a dried-up, frustrated woman. As it is, you've made a success of your life both financially and intellectually. You love your work, you help thousands of women who benefit from what you do, you thrive on it and are sharing whatever you have with your family. One doesn't have to be on top of people to love them and help them. You don't love Belinda less just because you're not home every evening at five-thirty. And you know your mother and sister are much happier in Dayton with their friends and neighbors than they ever could be in New York."

Kate wanted to believe what Linda was saying, but the facts weighed heavily against it. "But Belinda is in trouble, deep trouble."

"It's silly to worry now about what would have happened if you'd stayed in Dayton. Are you really sure that she wouldn't have been in an equally difficult situation with an unhappy mother sitting around, subconsciously feeling that her child has kept her down?"

"Well, be that as it may," Kate said, and the two women fell silent. Elie's tearstained face came to Kate's mind. "I hate you, Kate," Elie had screamed as she hobbled from the room when she was told that Belinda would be leaving Dayton. "You've always taken everything away from me. You with your fancy airs and expensive clothes."

Kate closed her eyes. Her thoughts were too muddled. Her usually disciplined mind was suddenly exhausted. Belinda was her first priority. She would put her in a proper atmosphere and try to get her back into some sort of mold. Kate's work was now more important to her than ever. She enjoyed the success, the power, the adulation—and the money. She was earning a good salary now and would be earning more every year. The royalties from her book were properly invested and they alone would be sufficient to support her mother and Elie. Her new contract with Reid Publications called for increases every year and she could afford to spend whatever it took to help her daughter overcome the problems that were disturbing her. She felt her body relax. *Women Today.* How she loved her magazine! The thought of it gave her a feeling of serenity in spite of the turmoil raging inside. The Christmas issue was exquisite. The stories, the articles, the editorial pages, fashion, food, decorating, were shaping up for the following months. Furthermore, she had succeeded in attracting several prominent writers to do articles for her and advertising agencies were asking to be included in her forthcoming issues. Sales were now reaching into the ninetieth percentile and she was seriously thinking of the nude-male centerfold. She was keeping it as an ace up her sleeve for the right moment. Linda, Dee Dee, Janice, Allyson, Carol, and Betsy all agreed that it was an extraordinarily novel idea. Hank was the only one who laughed when he heard it, assuring her that there was not a man who would agree to pose. She decided to ignore his comments and instead she and her staff embarked on finding a known personality who would consider doing it.

Contentment began to steal over her like a warm and loving flame. Her mind moved on to the forthcoming anniversary luncheon she was giving on December 31. It was her fifth anniversary at the magazine. Vaguely she knew it was an inconvenient date for the staff, but she had asked them at one of their weekly meetings if they minded and they all seemed sincerely anxious to come. She was looking forward to this lunch with greater pleasure than ever before, since she had broken her rule and bought each one of the editors a gift. It was above and beyond the bonus Reid Publications always gave at Christmas. She had discussed it with Jason and he suggested a smart briefcase from Louis Vuitton. She had priced them and found them exorbitant. Instead she called one of the luggage places that advertised in *Women Today*. She chose a pale blue case, had the name of *Women Today* stamped on each in gold letters and the name of the editor in the lower right-hand corner. She thought the gift extremely smart and was proud of her choice.

"Here we are." Linda's voice woke Kate up. She shook her head. It was unlike her to doze off.

She looked around. They had left the main highway and were driving along a narrow, tree-lined curving lane. The trees were so thickly intertwined overhead that for a brief moment Kate thought night had fallen. Suddenly they came out of the tree tunnel and a magnificent Spanish-style ranch house lay before them.

"This is a school?" Kate gasped with surprise.

"It's one of the best," Linda assured her.

Kate's fear that the teachers and headmistress would be nuns was unfounded. Miss Winston, the headmistress, turned out to be a charming, intelligent, and perceptive woman. She put Kate at ease immediately and within minutes Kate poured out all of her concerns about Belinda, her behavior problems, her disdain for school. She even told her about the check incident. There was a brief silence after Kate's final confession.

"Is Belinda involved with drugs?" Miss Winston asked.

"Drugs?" Kate felt faint. She had never once considered drugs as a possibility. The memory of that dreadful, whispered conversation she thought she had heard or dreamed about between Elie and Belinda long ago in Dayton exploded in her brain like a grenade. Of course, she thought, that would explain the bizarre scene. Looking at Miss Winston, Kate felt like crying. "Oh, my God," she whispered, "drugs! I never once thought of that and I should have, I suppose."

"No reason that you should have, and for all you

know, Belinda doesn't have a drug problem."

"Are you going to accept her anyway?" Kate asked haltingly.

"I'll accept her, Miss Johnson, for the second semester. If it is a situation that can be coped with, we'll handle it." She smiled warmly and reassuringly. "And you must not jump to conclusions. If nothing else, after she's been with us for a while we'll be in a better position to evaluate what is best for her."

They walked out to Kate's car. Linda was nowhere around.

"She's probably in the chapel," Miss Winston said.

They found her kneeling in prayer and Kate felt a pang of pity for the young woman. I must invite her home, she thought. Linda is too fragile to be alone in the city.

19

Janice Barker was dressed and ready to leave for work. She was deeply depressed, as always, during the holiday season. The boys had gone off skiing with John in Aspen, Colorado, and although they were going to spend a couple of days with her when they returned, her holiday was ruined. It was December 31 and had it not been for the luncheon Kate gave for the senior staff members, Janice would have gone to visit her family in Massachusetts. The luncheon meant a great deal to Kate, since this year it marked her fifth anniversary at the magazine. It was a tradition by now, and somehow Kate seemed oblivious to the fact that it spoiled everyone's holiday plans. This baffled Janice. She did not particularly like Kate but respected her incredible capacity for work and appreciated her unbelievable intuition, which over-shadowed her blatant, unpalatable self-centeredness. Janice suspected that if Kate had the gall, she would have asked specifically for extravagant gifts this year. Janice never ceased to be fascinated by the number of gold bracelets and chains on Kate's wrists and around her neck. At times she reminded Janice of the pawnbroker in *Crime and Punishment.* She would not have been surprised to find all of Kate's fortune hoarded in the huge handbag she carried with her always. Janice, who did not have to worry about money, finally went to Cartier and picked up an expensive and heavy charm to add to Kate's collection, but she could not help wondering how the others managed. For a moment her feelings of dislike for Kate deepened into hate. She shook her head as though to clear it of this unpleasant thought. It was unlike her, but she was so unhappy that her feelings of compassion were at a low ebb.

As she waited for the elevator she thought of knocking on Linda's door and inviting her to share a cab to work. Poor Linda. Since she'd moved into Kate's old apartment, Janice had been invited down just once. The place was much as Kate had left it. She remembered thinking that the room lacked any personal touch, not a picture, not a vase, nothing other than a tiny painting on wood of the Christ Child, which hung over her bed. After that first visit, which was awkward, Linda being totally at a loss as to how to entertain anyone, never invited her again. Often after that Janice saw Linda coming into the house accompanied by strange men. She never noticed Janice or else pretended that she did not see her. Soon Janice made a conscious effort not to make her presence known if Linda happened to be in the lobby when she came in and avoided getting into the elevator if Linda was there with anyone. The first few times, it took Janice several minutes to realize the woman she was looking at was in fact Linda. She seemed to be a completely different person from the girl she worked with. At one point the superintendent of the building approached Janice and wanted to talk to her about the strange lady who had taken Miss Johnson's apartment.

"Don't you work at the same office?" he asked, bewildered at her reticence about discussing it.

"Miss Wilson and I do work at the same office and we have a very cordial relationship. I should hate to have her discuss me with you and I really feel it is wrong for me to discuss her." She smiled pleasantly.

He persisted. "She's heading for trouble. . . ."

"Please," she almost pleaded, "I really don't wish to be involved." Her tone had a finality about it that made the man realize it would be fruitless to pursue the subject.

Janice felt guilty about this. She hated people who never wanted to be involved with their fellow humans, but she was holding on for dear life herself, right now, and felt her precarious emotions wouldn't be able to handle someone else's troubles.

After that conversation she'd watched Linda more closely at the office. Linda grew sloppier by the day. Either her hem was down or she had a run in her stockings whenever she wore them. Her shoes were always worn down at the heels and her fingernails, although clean, looked dirty. Yet the smile, the graciousness, the warmth, and the razor-sharp brain were always operating. Janice had put the conversation with the superintendent out of her mind. This morning, however, she found herself worrying about Linda. She took a step toward Linda's door, then turned away and walked briskly down the stairs.

Had she tried to reach Linda, Janice would not have found her in. Linda awoke, as was her habit, at five A.M. She did not need a watch to tell her the time. She looked around and realized she was not in her own apartment. The only light in the room was from a television set; the station had gone off the air sometime during the night and had at that early hour not yet started its broadcasting day. Frightened, she reached out and turned on the lamp on the night table and looked around. Her clothes were on the floor and she noticed that her underpants were ripped. Not daring to move, she glanced at the rest of the room and finally her eyes came to rest on a matchbox lying near the bed. She was in a Ramada Inn motel. She got out of bed slowly and a pain shot through her head. She knew the pain well. It was a hangover from too much wine. She looked for her purse but could not find it. She usually carried aspirin with her for these mornings. She continued to search for the bag but knew she wouldn't find it. Whoever she had come to the motel with had simply taken it or she had given it to him. She had done this before. Somehow she always gave things away when she got drunk. Walking into the little bathroom, she turned on the light and looked at herself. She looked ghastly. Tears began to roll down her cheeks. Why do I do it? she asked the image in the mirror. Why did she always pick a man up, spend money on him, and end up in bed with him? Fear of being alone was always the answer. But she refused to accept it. Something deeper was causing her to act in this way but what it was eluded her. The endless resolves to stop this hateful pattern were forgotten almost as soon as the pledges were made. She splashed cold water over her face and drank some to quench the dreadful thirst burning her throat. Then, walking over to the window, she pushed the heavy drapes aside. It was still dark out and she saw nothing but the walls of the next building facing her. Her head was aching and she crawled back into the bed. Before she fell asleep again she tried to remember the man she had spent the night with. She had gone out again after having dinner with Carol and her young man. She had met someone at a bar. But no face appeared. Her mind went blank and she was asleep.

When she next woke, she sat up with a start. It was December 31 and she had to be at Kate's luncheon. She dialed the operator and asked for the time. It was nine A.M. and the operator informed her coldly that checking-out time was ten A.M. and they wanted the room cleared by then.

She dressed quickly and suddenly she remembered that she had not bought Kate a gift. Simultaneously she remembered that her bag was gone, that all her bonus money had been in it, and that the money was meant for an expensive gift for Kate. She wanted to give her something of value. Expensive gifts, things, objects, were all-important to Kate. Now she had no money and all the pain she felt for herself was wiped away as this thought crystallized.

When she reached her apartment she called the office to say that she would be going directly to the luncheon. As she showered and dressed, her mind busily raced through the possibilities of how she could get a gift for Kate. She had nothing of value that she could hock or sell. She had no money and would not have any until the next payday. The stolen bonus money was meant to carry her through the week as well as buy the gift. She looked at the small icon of the Christ Child as she removed it from the wall, and the tears started to flow again. Kate was not religious, but she would surely know how much this meant to her and would appreciate it as such. Kate was her friend.

Dee Dee was furious with herself. Something basic had changed in her and she did not like it. She had put off thinking it out, knowing she was not yet ready to face it. This morning, however, when she awoke and remembered that she was expected at Kate's luncheon, a fury ripped through her. It had to be an idiotic, childish, embarrassing affair. The fact that she would be going to it deepened her rage. She poured herself a cup of coffee and nearly scalded her mouth as she gulped it down. She felt like a caged animal as she began pacing her bedroom. She had awakened earlier than usual. She hated the early hours of the morning but she was unable to fall asleep again, so she got up, lit a fire, threw herself into the wing chair beside the fireplace, and watched the fire as it leaped up ferociously and then settled down to a pleasant, flickering flame. She tried to absorb herself in the sight but her mind was driving her in a direction she desperately tried to avoid. Finally, unable to suppress the need, she got up and walked stiffly into her bathroom, took a vial of pills out of the cabinet, and gulped one down. Closing the small bottle, she looked at the prescription. The medication had no name, only the doctor's signature was clearly visible—Dr. Mark Schmidt. She replaced the bottle in the medicine cabinet and walked back to the bedroom. She lit another cigarette, resettled herself, this time in the chaise longue, which stood in the far corner of the room, closed her eyes, and waited for the pills to take effect. She was defeated and she knew she would call Dr. Schmidt later in the day to make an appointment. The thought upset her. She had not seen him in several weeks and was trying to shake off the need she had for him.

The room was completely silent except for the crackling of the wood in the fireplace. Usually this sound was soothing, this morning it was not. Lighting another cigarette from the one she had just finished, she looked around. It was a room she had decorated with love. The theme of beige, white, and rust ran throughout the apartment. The curtains, bedspread, upholstered antique chairs contrasted brilliantly with the highly waxed dark parquet floors. Little Kirman rugs, seemingly carelessly thrown around, were actually placed with careful thought. Every lamp, every ashtray, every accessory down to the original Ming vase containing fresh yellow roses, had been chosen with great care.

It was a far cry from the squalor of her childhood in the Williamsburg section of Brooklyn, daughter of an auto mechanic and a housemaid. She rarely thought about her family. Both her parents were dead, and her sisters, twins, whom she had helped support through high school, were now married and living somewhere out west. She heard from them from time to time but was completely indifferent to their existence.

She had quit school when she finished eighth grade and gone to work as a cashier in a restaurant in Flatbush. She was fourteen years old but looked older. It was there that a man had suggested she go the Conover Model Agency. They accepted her even before she had pictures to show them. She stayed on with her family until the twins graduated from high school and then she simply moved away, and except for an occasional call from her mother, she never really saw them again. When both her parents were killed in a car accident she attended their funeral. They had never been a close-knit family, and she remembered feeling little sense of loss or sorrow. Later, when she received notifications of her sisters' marriages, she sent them each a check. Through the years she would occasionally get a note from one or the other announcing the birth of a child. She always sent an expensive gift for the new baby, adding a brief, pleasant note of congratulations.

The ringing of the phone clamored for attention, but she made no move to answer it. At that early hour it was probably someone from the office wondering if she was coming in. She would call them in a while and tell them she would be going directly to the luncheon. The thought of the lunch made her remember her anger. Now, however, the feelings were dulled. The pills had done their work and she could face some of her anger. Normally she would not have minded Kate's luncheon. Although she had never really grown to like Kate, Dee Dee enjoyed her work, enjoyed working for a successful magazine, and could not help but admire Kate for bringing *Women Today* from near bankruptcy to the lucrative business it now was. She even succeeded in drowning her resentment of Kate for taking Jason away from her. There again, she was not emotionally involved and only missed the lovely, expensive gifts that Jason had occasionally given her. The job also allowed her time for the women's-liberation work, and she knew she was an excellent example of what a woman could achieve on her own with determination and hard work.

Things began to fall apart for her when she met Toby Jackson. He had done a photography job for her and although she knew he was not really a good fashion photographer, she kept using him whenever possible. Toby was a clean-cut boy of Norwegian descent, tall and blond and completely sincere. He was twelve years younger than she, although he was unaware of it. He moved in with her and she found him to be a pleasant companion, considerate, bright, and head over heels in love with her. For the first time in her life, emotions she had ignored for too many years bubbled forth. She was actually in love with the boy. When he asked her to marry him, she tried to laugh it off.

"Dee," he said seriously, "I want to live out my life with you, have children..."

She did not hear the rest of the sentence. He wanted children! Suddenly she knew that she wanted them, too, and that it was too late. Quickly she left the room and walked into her dressing room and stared at herself in the full-length mirror. Her figure was still young and firm, although her thighs had developed a slight slack and the little telltale bumps were clearly visible. She peered at her face. Shamelessly she placed her hands against her cheeks and pulled her skin taut over the cheekbones, which immediately erased the grooves that had begun to dig deep around each side of her thin, aquiline nose. Letting go of her face, she watched the tapestry of fine, almost invisible lines reappear on the surface of her skin.

Everything changed after that day. She could think of little but her longing for her own youth, which she now felt she had squandered. Doubts about the women's-liberation movement grew. There was an enormous difference, she decided, between the male role in life and the female role. Men of her age could father children, men older than she were considered young, whereas at forty-five she was simply a frustrated, aging, barren woman. She began to question the motives of many of the women she encountered in the movement. A few were satisfied with their achievements, but many were also beginning to find that their life's priorities were after all their homes and their children. The movement had done some good, but it had also caused pain and harm to the many adherents who were in reality looking for the security of marriage or something more binding than the rat race of trying to survive alone. Yes, she could now walk into a bar and have a drink without an escort, she could now pick up the dinner check for a male companion with nonchalance, she could now demand a salary commensurate with her abilities, but she was alone.

Toby's youth, which she had at first enjoyed, was now a mirror screaming the contrast between them. That, more than anything else, drove her to Dr. Schmidt. She had heard a great deal about him. He was considered a charlatan, a Satan, a menace by some; a miracle worker, a genius, a giant in medicine by others. Fully aware of the controversy raging around him, she made an appointment and was immediately drawn into his web. His charm, his brilliance, his medical acumen, were phenomenal. She followed his instructions to the letter, taking the pills, receiving the weekly injections, and soon she began to feel better than she had in years. As she fell deeper and deeper into dependence on him she was blinded to the fact that he was draining her financially. Before she met Dr. Schmidt, money was of little consequence to her. She earned it easily and spent it without thought. Suddenly she found herself overdrawn at the bank, with bills piling up that she could not pay. Not since she'd started modeling had she felt as insecure as she did now. In a frantic housecleaning she asked Toby to move out and canceled her standing appointment with the doctor. She even had to sell most of the lovely jewelry she had accumulated over the years.

The phone rang again and this time Dee Dee picked it up.

"It's Murray." The voice came through faintly.

"Where the hell are you calling from?"

"St. John, the Virgin Islands. I'm on the ship and we're docked a few miles offshore."

"Murray, you're a fool." She laughed in spite of herself. "Why are you calling?"

"When can you fly down?" The voice was still faint.

"Really want me to come?"

"Honey, I'll charter the plane if it will bring you down sooner."

"That's sweet, Murray," Dee Dee answered, and could not hide the pleasure she felt. "But I'll take a commercial airline and be there sometime tomorrow."

"Just call when you're leaving and I'll meet you at the airport," he assured her, and then, after a short pause, "I'm looking forward to it, Dee Dee." She knew he meant it.

When she hung up the phone she walked into the bathroom and opened the medicine cabinet again. She wanted to remove the pills, the injection syringe, the thin rubber hose, and throw them away. But she didn't. Murray Simon was a nice man, a rich man, a good man, and she had known him for years. But would she really want to spend her life with a successful clothes manufacturer traveling around on his yacht?

Murray looked and sounded like most of the other men she met on Seventh Avenue. The only difference was that he was married and never played around. When he finally asked her out to dinner, she discovered that his wife had died sometime back, and only now was he ready to take a woman out. She had seen a great deal of him since that first date. He never asked her to move in with him and when she finally went to bed with him she discovered that the simplicity of his lovemaking, his warmth and thoughtfulness, his total adulation of her, erased much of the confusion and pain she had lived with for so long.

Dee Dee sighed deeply. Could she really marry someone like Murray? She seated herself in front of her dressing table and turned on the radio. Pleasant music flooded the room. She felt relaxed and almost allowed herself to be happy. The announcement by the disc jockey that it was eleven-thirty reminded her to start applying her makeup. Kate's luncheon was at twelve-thirty. As she was dressing she remembered that she had not yet bought a gift for Kate. It had to be expensive, of that she was sure. Kate could have millions in the bank and she would still look and sound poor. How pathetic, Dee Dee thought, as she started rummaging through her now depleted jewelry box and picked up a Gucci chain with a huge, gaudy, colorful cross. Someone had given it to her and she never wore it. Kate, she was sure, would adore it. She grimaced to herself. Even Kate, she thought, knew who Gucci was.

As she rode to the luncheon she was preoccupied with what she would take with her on her trip. She did not know where her relationship with Murray would lead, but he was a friend, a dear, thoughtful friend. She had never known a man who was also a friend.

20

Although it was barely noon, 21 was crowded. Allyson walked in, aware that she was early, but Cliff was finally asleep after a restless night and she simply had to get out. He was making a serious effort to stop drinking but the results were having strange effects and the hallucinations that he was now subject to were depleting them both.

"How do you do, Mrs. Fenster." The maître d' approached her and extended his hand. "You're early for Miss Johnson's luncheon, but if you'd care to go upstairs I'll have someone take you up."

"No thanks," she answered pleasantly, hiding the feelings of annoyance she felt at being there in the first place. "I'll have some coffee down here while I wait."

Settling herself in one of the small armchairs in the downstairs lounge, she took out a cigarette and forgot to light it. Cliff was going to die, she thought impersonally. Her Cliff, whom she had nursed and coddled for so many years, was going to leave her finally by giving up and dying. The doctor had warned them both that unless he gave up alcohol completely he would not live. She would be left alone, working for Kate Johnson, whom she despised, because she was nearly sixty and could not possibly get another job with as much prestige or earn the salary that Jason was willing to give her. It all seemed so unfair. When she and Cliff were first married they both worked for Reid Publications. He was a top executive and she was an up-and-coming junior editor. Her potential was obvious to everyone and Cliff encouraged her and guided her. As she began to climb the ladder leading toward editor in chief of one of the Reid publications, Cliff started his descent. At first she was unaware of what was happening, being too absorbed in her own career. She had no idea that he was unhappy with their life together. At that time his drinking was simply a social function and he was the life of any party. They were invited everywhere, and even though Allyson suspected that the invitations were actually directed at Cliff, she did not object. They had wanted children but it turned out that she could not have any. Cliff took it in good grace, never letting on till many years later how seriously disappointed he was. They had been married some fifteen years when Cliff announced that he wanted a divorce. It came out of the blue. Even now that scene pained her. He had been gone for a week to what she assumed was an advertising convention in Arizona. Waiting for him that evening, she prepared dinner and invited several guests to come in for drinks afterward.

She was in the kitchen when Cliff walked in. He was sober—she could see that immediately—and she was relieved. As she turned to kiss him he turned his head away.

"I rinse my mouth twice a day," she said lightly, hiding her hurt.

174

"Allyson," he said quietly, "I want a divorce."

"Divorce?" She mouthed the word as though she were speaking a foreign language. "But why? Why would you want a divorce?"

"Is it really important why?" he asked, obviously trying to avoid answering.

"Of course it's important." She spoke slowly, trying desperately not to stutter. "We've been married for fifteen years. We've had what everyone considers a good marriage."

Cliff walked over to the kitchen cabinet where they had some liquor, poured himself a stiff scotch, and gulped it down.

"I could rest my case on that phrase alone," he said, his back to her as he poured himself another drink, "what *everyone* considers a good marriage." Then, turning to her, he smiled wanly. "Do *you* consider this a good marriage? Do *I*?" he asked. "Think of it, Allyson, do we really have a good marriage?"

"You're fencing with me now," Allyson answered, trying hard to keep herself from sounding like a scolding mother. "Yes, I think we have a good marriage. I thought you felt we had a good marriage. So why do you want a divorce?"

"I have a child." The words thundered out in the large, immaculate kitchen. "I have a seven-year-old boy whom I adore. I've known his mother for many years, knew her before I met you. After you and I got married I stopped seeing her. Then one day I bumped into her." He paused for a minute. "Oh, it must have been some ten years ago. We started the relationship again and she got pregnant. She didn't want to abort the child, and I certainly didn't encourage it."

"And I couldn't conceive." Allyson completed the thought. She felt a knot form in her chest. "Oh, Cliff, we could have adopted a child, if only I'd known it was so important."

"No, we couldn't have done that, Allyson," he said sadly. "You were, are, for that matter, too intent on making a success of your life outside the home."

There was a long silence as Cliff poured himself still another drink. Allyson watched him and saw the slightly glazed look that always came into his eyes when he drank too much too quickly. She made no effort to stop him.

"So now you want to leave me and go live with the other woman and the child," she said, breaking the silence. "Is that it?"

"I don't really want to leave you," Cliff said, and his voice grew hoarse, "but the boy means a great deal to me."

"Can we adopt him?" she said without thinking.

"You must be kidding, Allyson. Women don't normally give up their children. His mother loves him. She doesn't even know that I'm here talking about a divorce."

Allyson bit her lip. It was foolish of her to have said that, but she hadn't had time to think out this new situation. She knew that she would never give Cliff up. The question was simply how to hold on to him.

"Cliff, darling," she said, suddenly changing the somber mood, "I've got the Drakes and the Connors coming in for drinks after dinner. It's late and I'd hate for them to come in while we're eating. We'll talk about it after they leave." She walked over to him and caressed his cheek. "I won't give you up easily, darling. I'll fight for you, you must know that." She smiled. "I love you so very much." He took her hand in his and held it tightly.

Cliff got very drunk that night and was still asleep when she was ready to go to work. She decided to stay home. Her work was important but she did not want Cliff to wake up to an empty house. As she waited her thoughts raced ahead. She had to find out who the competition was. She could not give Cliff a child, but she could point out the disagreeable facts of leaving her when she knew more about the woman who had a hold on him. He had little money of his own. That was her first thought. With all his love for the child, life with a growing boy for someone who was used to comfort and peaceful, gracious living, would be burdensome. Besides, Cliff was a social animal, loved people, entertaining and being entertained. Looking for baby-sitters at his age was hardly a pastime he would relish. All these thoughts had merit if the woman was not wealthy. Intuitively, Allyson felt that the other woman could not offer Cliff the things she had to offer.

It was not difficult to find out what she wanted to know. Cliff told her everything. The child's mother had a little boutique in the Village. She lived over the shop, which was hardly lucrative. She had been a dancer, but after the boy's birth she gave it up. She could not travel with the child. Besides, she was in her mid-thirties when she gave birth and the hopes of a successful career as a dancer had long been laid to rest.

Allyson listened quietly as Cliff related these facts to her. When he finished talking he looked at her pleadingly. "What should I do, Allyson?" he asked.

"Let's live with this new situation for a while, darling," she said as she leaned over to kiss his cheek. "Together we'll come up with something that will make the whole thing easier for everyone."

A few days later Allyson went down to the shop in the Village. She bought a hideously ugly skirt to justify lingering to get a better view of the woman who was her competitor. Olivia Dawson, if she knew who Allyson was, did not let on. Allyson had purposely come into the shop in the late afternoon, figuring that the child would probably be around just before closing time. Soon after she arrived a little boy came down a circular stairway that was hidden behind a screen. Allyson was stunned. The boy looked exactly like Cliff and she felt a tug of nausea at the pit of her stomach.

"Mommy," the child said, and although he was very young, the timbre of his voice was similar to Cliff's. "Can I go have a hamburger at McDonald's?"

"Okay, honey." His mother leaned over and hugged him. "This is my son," she said to Allyson with pride. "Oliver Fenster, man of the family." She took some money from her pocket and gave it to the child. "Mind when you cross the avenue," she called after him as he rushed out the door.

So Cliff had given the child his name. Allyson was shocked.

"Is it all right for someone that small to go alone?"

she asked with concern. Her heart was beating furiously. This tiny creature could have been hers.

"Sure," the woman answered. "When you grow up in this neighborhood you develop a sense of survival. Oliver is strong and sure of himself. He's only seven but his soul is years older."

Allyson paid for her purchase and escaped as quickly she could before the tears she was holding back appeared.

That night, as they finished dinner, Allyson suggested to Cliff that he go see Oliver.

"Oliver?" Cliff asked with amazement.

"I met him today," she said quietly. "He's beautiful and bright and charming. So's his mother."

"Did she know you?"

"I didn't give her my name."

There was a heavy silence for a few minutes while Cliff took another drink. It was his fifth, Allyson noted, but she made no effort to stop him.

"Why do you want me to go?" Cliff finally asked.

"I don't want you separated from him. I want to make it possible for you to have a relationship with him without guilt because I want you to stay with me."

Cliff put down his drink and walked over to her. Picking her up, he nuzzled his face against her neck. "I do love you so, Allyson," he whispered.

"And I love you, darling. And that's why I'm glad you told me about the boy." She moved away gently. "How you must have suffered all these years." She smiled. "Now it's over. You and I have our life together and you and Oliver have a life as well. I shan't interfere with it and I know you won't let it interfere with us."

It was a risk, she knew, but she was also aware that Olivia Dawson was hardly someone who could lure Cliff away from her. She had so much more to offer Cliff.

Their life together after that took on a fairy-tale quality for a while. Cliff was grateful for her understanding, totally unaware of her trepidation. She was positive that Olivia and Cliff were no longer lovers and that their time together was spent with Oliver.

When Oliver was sixteen Allyson insisted that the

boy go to a good prep school. "My contribution toward the education of the son I never had," she announced. She had not seen him again except for an occasional photograph that Cliff would bring home. Each time the tug of uncontrollable jealousy would clutch her heart, but she learned to cover it up. Nine years had gone by and the strain had abated. Cliff was drinking more heavily and the heartbreak she felt for him grew. Sending the boy away was a step toward relieving them both of the unbearable situation.

There was another reason why Allyson wanted the boy to leave. She was working as substitute editor in chief for *Women Today* while Jason was looking for a permanent editor. She wanted the job desperately and needed all the powers of concentration she could muster with the hope that she would land the job, after all.

"Want a light, Mrs. Fenster?" The maître d' was standing beside her and Allyson looked dazed for a minute trying to bring herself back to the present.

"Oh, yes." She smiled self-consciously as she put the cigarette to her lips. She looked at her watch. It was now twelve-thirty. In a minute Kate would arrive and soon everyone else would be there. She took a sip of her coffee. It was cold and bitter but it relieved the dreadful dryness in her mouth.

She inhaled deeply. Well, she did not get the job and Oliver was away. Instead Kate was her boss. A limited, self-centered bitch who by sheer willpower had succeeded in making *Women Today* a success even though everyone in the business laughed at Kate's lack of sophistication. If only she could have found another job, she thought for the hundredth time, if only, if only, if only....

"Allyson, you're here already." Kate was standing beside her. "How sweet of you to be so punctual."

"It's an important date and I wouldn't think of missing a minute of it," Allyson said in a sweet, syrupy voice.

Carol slid out of the taxi and waved at the redheaded, bearded young man who stayed behind.

"Pick you up at ten," he called after her.

"Make it nine," Carol called back. "I don't want to be late getting to Dad's place."

"Okay," he answered and the taxi moved away, leaving her looking at the disappearing car and feeling strangely confused. Then she turned around and pulled open the heavy glass door of Cartier and rushed into the store.

"Good morning, Miss Butler." The store manager walked over the minute he recognized her.

"Good morning, Mr. Jenkins," Carol replied, and smiled broadly. She'd known the man since she was quite young, having shopped at Cartier with her mother and grandmother.

"How's your mother?" he asked as he fell into step with her.

"Mother's fine. She's in Palm Beach for the holidays," she said automatically as she scanned the various counters they were passing. "Father has not been well and she felt they'd be better off there."

"Father" was reserved for Duncan Brentwood, her mother's second husband, and "Dad" was for her real father. It amused her that she never got them confused. Mr. Jenkins continued to inquire about her two brothers and Carol made perfunctory replies but she was no longer listening to him. It was almost noon and she had to be at 21 before twelve-thirty.

"What is it you're looking for?" the store manager asked, sensing her disquiet.

"I don't really know," Carol replied. "A gift for my boss, Miss Johnson."

"I've seen her on television," Mr. Jenkins said politely, "but I can't really tell what her preferences would be."

Hang her preferences, Carol thought as she caught sight of a tray of delicate gold chains.

"They're lovely," she said, walking toward the counter.

"I'll send someone to help you," the manager said, and walked away.

Carol made herself comfortable in one of the small

armchairs and continued staring at the chains. They were hair-thin and beautiful. Some had a tiny dangling pearl, others had a small, glittering stone, like a teardrop. They'd be lost in the shuffle of Kate's gold chains, Carol thought mirthlessly, but decided to buy one, anyway. She'd be damned if she was going to give in to Kate's tastelessness.

"Will you be charging this, Miss Butler?" the salesman asked when she had chosen one with a pearl.

"Yes, of course, but to my account, not my mother's," she said, and then on impulse picked up another one, with a teardrop stone, and asked him to wrap it separately. Somehow the little ornament reminded her of Linda and although she knew Linda hated being given gifts, she found she could not resist the temptation.

The man bowed slightly and walked away and Carol felt a sigh escape from deep within her. She looked around at the lovely objects in the display cases and a feeling of restlessness enveloped her. The luxury of the store, the deep, lush carpets, the pleasant lighting, the tranquillity of the expensive shop, so reminiscent of the atmosphere she had grown up in, were suddenly, again, unpleasant to her. She felt embarrassed at being so privileged and knew that it was Jim who evoked these feelings.

She had not seen him since the day she was carried on a stretcher to a private plane in Nairobi. She had contracted a severe case of hepatitis and her mother and Duncan had chartered the plane to bring her back to New York. She was nineteen and Jim was twenty-six. She met him the day she arrived in Africa with a Peace Corps group; he was the instructor who was to take charge of them. He had flaming-red hair, long and in disarray. She fell in love with him on sight. They spent a glorious year together working with children in godforsaken villages, and Carol, who had dropped out of college because she couldn't stand her pampered schoolmates, the senseless classes, the irrelevance of her studies, felt that she had finally found something that would compensate her for her one true frustration—her desire to be a writer worthy of her father's pride. Jim Krasna, a graduate of the University of Chicago Law School, had decided to work for the Peace Corps before settling down to practice law. He, too, was restless and wanted to see another side of the world. When he met Carol and they fell in love, it all made a great deal of sense. He was the first person she ever confided in about her father, Donald Butler, a writer who had been blacklisted during the fifties and had fled to England with her mother before Carol was born. While she was growing up she never dared mention the notorious case to her friends, certain they would not have been sympathetic. Jim was deeply affected by her story. She told him about her desire to be a writer and about her attempt to win praise from her father, whom she had not seen since her mother divorced him when Carol was three years old. When she was fifteen, having heard that her father was teaching literature at Harvard, she had sent him several of her short stories, anonymously, asking for his comments. Choking back the tears, she showed Jim the letter she had received in reply. It was a devastating letter in which the man coldly suggested that the writer forget about writing and devote his or her time to doing something constructive.

As intimate as they were, she never spoke to Jim about her mother or stepfather or her two older stepbrothers. They were her family but she was in rebellion and was embarrassed by their wealth.

Carol was sick for a long time and it was the love and care her mother and Duncan bestowed on her that made the nightmare of her convalescence bearable. Aside from the discomfort of being ill, she missed Jim desperately and was deeply hurt by his silence. When she recovered a bit she wrote him but received no reply. As the months went by with no word from him she stopped thinking about him. Instead she settled back into accepting the life her family offered. After leaving the hospital, she returned to the town house in the East-Eighties where she had grown up. Her year in Africa, her illness, the long hours of being alone while recovering, plus hours with a fine therapist, matured her. Even her two stepbrothers, Frank and Duncan, Jr., who never paid much attention to her as she was growing up, were suddenly attentive and anxious to please. Frank, who was still unmarried, made a point of taking her out and introducing her to his friends with pride. She was always popular and she melted easily into the wealthy singles crowd of Palm Beach, East Hampton, and New York. Jim became a vague and pleasant memory.

It was at a fashion show at the Plaza, two years after returning from Africa, that Carol heard about the job opening at *Women Today*. Someone mentioned that the new editor was looking for a secretary. Having taken a course in typing and shorthand, she decided to apply for a job. She was having great difficulty with her writing and thought the experience of working with people who wrote would be worthwhile. She did not want to write for *Women Today*. She had grown too insecure about showing her work to anyone. The idea was simply to be around creative, productive people. She was not at all sure of herself when she walked into Kate Johnson's suite at the Regency but when she saw Kate sitting behind her desk in the huge living room, looking small and nervous, her confidence suddenly returned. She knew the interview went well and the only time she faltered was when Kate asked her if she could write.

The job proved to be interesting and turned into something exciting when Linda Wilson was hired. It was Linda who insisted on having Carol at the editorial meetings, just as it was Linda who urged her to start putting her thoughts down on paper, and it was Linda who pored over every one of Carol's presentations, correcting and improving them. But most important, it was Linda who urged her to seek out her father.

When she finally met Donald Butler again, a new dimension was added to her life. Her father was an extremely attractive man, charming and bohemian in manner and outlook. She found him living on Long Island in a huge, rambling, rather rundown house inhabited by several cats and two loving dogs. She understood her mother's attraction for him and also realized why her mother had found it impossible to live with him. His total disregard for money was amusing but must have been a hardship on a woman who was used to luxuries and the easy life. Also, he was a dreadful flirt and Carol never ceased to be amazed at the number of women who doted on him. It was he who urged her to move out of her mother's house, saying it was time to start living her own life; start depending on herself, cultivating her own taste and personality, and stop hiding behind the life-style that, although pleasant, was bound to be stultifying.

Moving into her own flat on Sutton Place was exhilarating. Her job at *Women Today* was growing into something special. Her social life was thriving and she discovered facets to her personality that opened up thoughts about the future and led her to start setting goals. She was enjoying her life to the hilt, she was in no rush. Time was on her side.

And then, last night, while waiting for Linda at the Sign of the Dove restaurant, she saw a redheaded man leaning against the bar talking to a pretty young woman. His hair was cropped and he had grown a beard, yet she recognized him immediately. Her feelings were in turmoil, and she felt herself grow cold. She continued to stare at him. Finally, as though aware of her gaze, he turned and looked at her and a broad smile of recognition appeared on his face. Within minutes he excused himself from the lady he was talking to and came over. The years melted away. He seated himself beside her and, leaning close, kissed her cheek.

"You've grown up, Carol," he said gently as he picked up her hand and held it, "and it suits you."

She could not find her voice and was relieved when at that moment Linda walked in.

"Jim Krasna," she said hoarsely as she tore her eyes away from him, "this is my friend Linda Wilson."

They had a drink and Jim invited them both to dinner. Carol was pleased when Linda accepted.

Still stunned at seeing Jim again after all these years, she felt nervous and awkward, and feared her own emotions would betray her, but dinner went smoothly. Linda carried on a brilliant conversation that masked Carol's discomfort. Jim was opening a branch office in New York and Linda listened attentively to his description of some legal brief he was handling. Her comments were perceptive and Carol could tell Jim was impressed. They moved on to other subjects and Linda held her own while Carol sat back and listened. She was too emotionally overwhelmed to participate fully and was grateful that Linda was able to continue the conversation so gracefully.

"She's as bright as a whip," Jim said when they dropped Linda off on the corner of Eighth Avenue and Fifty-seventh Street, "but she's going to have a dreadful hangover in the morning."

Carol was taken aback. In all the time she'd known Linda she had never seen her drink to excess.

"Are you sure?" Carol asked, feeling nervous for no special reason.

"I suppose it depends on what her capacity is," he answered. "She looks like she's used to heavy drinking."

The taxi driver interrupted the conversation. "Where to now?"

Automatically Carol gave her home address.

When they reached Sutton Place, she invited Jim up to her apartment. She was lost in her own thoughts and Jim in his. They had been completely out of touch for seven years. Carol wondered if he had thought about her as intensely as she had about him after she was sent home ill from her Peace Corps assignment.

She opened the door to her apartment and walked in. Although the room was sparsely furnished in a Japanese motif, every piece in it was precious and expensive. The double-height ceiling and the circular stairway in the middle of the living room added to its dramatic look. The long windows facing the river were bare and the lights of the bridges flickering in the distance gave one the feeling of being on a ship. The collection of African wood carvings was excellent, all bought on Madison Avenue or at auction.

Carol was removing her coat when she realized Jim was still in the doorway.

"Come in," she said lightly.

He walked in slowly and moved around the room, looking at the paintings and statues. When he came to stand at the grand piano, which stood beneath the stairway, he picked up a photograph of her father and stared at it.

"Is he the one that's keeping you in this grand style?" he finally asked, looking hurt.

"No, as a matter of fact the man in that picture on the sideboard is." Carol pointed to a picture of Duncan on his yacht.

"Well"—Jim cleared his throat—"I guess that explains why you never wrote me after you got out of the hospital. Obviously this is what you were after and it sure is a far cry from Africa."

Carol was too amused to be upset. "Oh, stop it, Jim," she said as she walked toward him. "The man in the picture you're holding is my father and the man on the yacht is my stepfather and in truth, neither is supporting me. I'm supporting myself and I have an income from a trust fund my grandmother left me."

The look of relief on his face moved her, and in a minute she was in his arms and the passion they had felt for each other when they first met returned.

The ringing of the phone woke Carol. It was her mother.

"Darling, you never called after leaving here on Christmas Day," Margaret Brentwood chided good-naturedly.

"Oh, Mother," Carol said, laughing as she looked around for Jim. The thought that he might have left frightened her. When she heard the shower running she relaxed. "You know you would have heard about any plane crash or if anything happened to me."

"I know, sweetie," her mother said, "but I do miss you, and Duncan and I were wondering if you couldn't possibly come down this afternoon and spend the evening with us."

"Mother, it would be insane, since I have to be at work the day after tomorrow. You don't seem to realize we don't get time off when the weather grows bad."

Jim came out of the bathroom at that moment and, hearing her remark, burst out laughing.

"Who's that?" Carol heard her mother ask.

"Mother, I had a friend stay overnight," Carol said candidly.

"Oh" was all Mrs. Brentwood could muster, and the conversation ended almost immediately. She had never come to terms with her daughter's life-style.

"Why did you say that?" Jim asked when she replaced the phone.

"Say what?" Carol asked as she got out of bed and pulled on her robe.

"Tell your mother you had someone staying over."

"Why not? It's the truth, isn't it?"

"Do many men stay over?" Jim asked as he started dressing.

"Many?" Carol raised her eyebrows. "What do you call many?"

She knew she was being arbitrary, knew she did not mean what she was saying, but somehow Jim's question lent a sour note to the dreamlike quality of their reunion. A great deal had happened to her since she had seen him. She was a grown, sophisticated young woman, a working girl in New York. She was her own person. All these thoughts flashed through her mind but she also knew that none of them was the cause of her anger. The truth was that she was testing him. It was totally out of character. She had long since stopped playing games with the men she dated.

"Sorry I asked," Jim said as he knotted his tie in front of her dressing-table mirror. Their eyes met and Carol felt confused.

"Why don't you go into the dining room and have some coffee. I'll shower and be right out."

Jim had suddenly become a threat. He was not just another man to have an affair with. He could make demands that she was not ready to face.

Dressed in a silver-gray wool mini-jumper, a white turtleneck sweater, and knee-high gray leather boots, Carol walked into the dining room, feeling more secure and in control. Jim was having coffee and reading a copy of *Women Today*. He looked up appreciatively. "Where you heading?"

"I've got to be at a luncheon my boss is giving."

"Today, on New Year's Eve?"

"Yes, I know it's strange, but then she's a strange lady."

"You'd think she'd want to spend it with her family rather than with her employees."

"Oh, she is spending it with her family. We're it."

"I get the feeling you don't like her."

"As a matter of fact, I do," she answered, and then after a moment's thought continued. "Maybe 'like' is the wrong word. I respect her, admire her concentration, am fascinated by her ambition. In fact, when you consider who she is, where she comes from, what she had going for her when she took over this bankrupt magazine, you must admire her. Here she is, a nobody who came from nowhere, no money, no background, no education, no looks, yet she's succeeded in getting thousands— hundreds of thousands—of women of all ages to listen to her, follow her advice, wait to hear what her opinions are. It's unbelievable."

"Why are you working for *Women Today*?" Jim seemed not to have heard any of what she had said.

"It's a good job," Carol answered almost defensively, "it's considered a coup to be working there. Besides, I adore Linda and you'd be surprised at what we do together that is of value."

He leafed through the magazine. "Yes, I would be surprised," he said. Then, putting it down on the table, he lit a cigarette and poured himself another cup of coffee. "Can I see you tonight?" he asked without looking up at her.

"Only if you're willing to spend it with my father and me on Long Island."

His face brightened. "You see your father? That mean old man who made fun of your writing?"

"He doesn't know I write," Carol said. "He doesn't know I wrote those stories years ago, and you mustn't tell him." Her voice took on a pleading tone. "Jim, you must promise never to mention it to him or to anyone else, for that matter."

"Have you given up?" he asked quietly.

"No, I haven't given up, but it's so hard." She occupied herself with pouring some coffee into a mug. The endless rejection slips from publishers loomed before her eyes. She never spoke about her own writing to anyone, not even to Linda, but she never stopped trying to get her stories published. She felt exposed, vulnerable, now that she had told Jim. "I keep trying," she said quietly, "but somehow the most I can come up with is some article for *Women Today*."

She heard Jim get up from his seat and in a minute she was in his arms and he was kissing her face, her mouth, her eyes, murmuring words of reassurance. Finally, pushing her away to arm's length, he looked at her.

"You finally look and sound like the little girl I first met in Nairobi. I was sure she was there somewhere, but you have done a pretty good job of hiding her."

She did not want to hear what he was saying. "That little girl has long since departed." Her manner reverted to the Carol Butler she had cultivated, nurtured, and was actually pleased with. "Jim, darling, I do have to run along. It's late and I haven't even gotten a gift for the lady."

"You really should quit that job," Jim said, ignoring what she'd said, "and concentrate on your writing."

"Oh, no." Carol swung around. "Never. I'm staying right on. It's more than just a job. Someday I can make *Women Today* better, more sophisticated, more literate. I won't give up writing, but I won't give up my job."

As soon as the words were out of her mouth she

regretted them. It was the first time she had ever put into words her ambitions where the magazine was concerned. She had never even admitted them to herself.

"Your packages, Miss Butler." Carol's thoughts were interrupted by the salesman. "And if you'd just sign this slip, please."

She signed for the purchases and rushed out of the store. It was twelve-twenty-five and she was grateful the restaurant was just one block away.

As she made her way through the crowded street she wondered about her relationship with Jim. He had told Linda he was moving to New York and it occurred to her that that was all she really knew about him. They had been so emotionally involved with each other that none of the pedestrian questions were asked. Did he have a girlfriend? A wife? Would he give either up for her? Would she ask him to? Would he accept her life-style? Would she want him to live with her? Was she ready to settle down? She was glad they were spending the evening with her father. They would see the old year out and greet the new year together. It was a good omen and all the trepidation she had felt while at Cartier disappeared.

People were milling about in the lobby of 21. Carol greeted several people she knew as she scanned the room for Kate or any of the other editors from the magazine. When she spotted Allyson and Kate, she edged over to them. Within minutes Dee Dee, Maggie, and Janice appeared, followed by Marrianne Tyler and Stephanie Banks. Carol looked around anxiously for Linda. When she saw her walking toward them, a sigh of relief escaped her. Jim had been right, Carol thought. Linda looked hung over. Her face was unusually pale and the poorly applied rouge further emphasized her sickly pallor. Carol walked over and put her arm through Linda's. Together they headed for the small elevator that took everyone up to the private dining room where luncheon was being served.

"Shall we wait for Betsy?" Kate asked.

"No, let's go up," Dee Dee said quickly. She knew

Betsy had decided to ignore the luncheon but didn't want to be the one to break the news to Kate. "She knows where we'll be."

21

The private dining room was magnificently decorated. Fresh bouquets of flowers were in every corner. The heavy drapes were drawn and only the small crystal sconces with tiny bulbs shed a glow over the room. An old-fashioned tea cart was set up as the bar, stocked with liquor and a vintage champagne in silver ice buckets. Two waiters were serving huge, translucent shrimps and pâté de foie gras. The table was set with a gleaming white damask tablecloth and tall candles in majestic silver holders. Dee Dee caught Allyson's eye and they both smiled, knowing full well that Jason was to be credited for the elegance. Kate would never have allowed such lavish entertaining.

Kate was bubbling with joy. She was the hostess, she

was the boss, she was in charge. She would have been stunned if she had had any inkling of the feelings of her luncheon guests.

Dee Dee watched her carefully. In the years since she arrived in New York, Kate had taken her wardrobe into her own hands and the results were dreadful. On this special occasion she had put on a Pucci print, which could be elegant on a tall, slender woman but looked cheap and tacky on Kate. Dee Dee knew that Kate took the latest fashion fads as the law of the land, especially if the label was of a known designer. The miniskirted look was completely wrong for someone as small as Kate. Her spindly legs were hardly long enough to carry it and the Charles Jourdan shoes were much too heavy for her anatomy. Without looking, one could tell what part of the room she was in. The jangling bracelets were noisier and heavier than ever, the endless chains looked as though they would make her keel over. To add to all the other aesthetic insults, she had put on numerous thin rings, which she displayed constantly as her hands fluttered around emphasizing some non sequitur.

"Kate, your hair looks heavenly," Allyson was saying, and Dee Dee turned away to hide her smile. "Who's doing it for you these days?" Allyson continued, and everyone but Kate seemed to hear the mockery.

"Ben," Kate answered seriously. "I simply adore his work. And he comes up to the apartment when I want it done in a hurry."

Janice interrupted the conversation. "I personally think it's too long." It bothered her that Allyson should be making fun of Kate on this special occasion. Normally Kate could fend for herself but she was too excited to think that anyone would want to hurt her on this day.

"Do you really?" Kate looked at Janice anxiously.

"Janice is right, Kate," Dee Dee said. She, too, felt guilty that Allyson was mocking Kate so blatantly.

"I think you look lovely," Linda said, clutching her champagne glass. The sincerity was unmistakable. "May I propose a toast?"

Everyone turned to look at her. Linda was deathly pale, her skin almost transparent in the dimly lit room. Her eyes were darker than usual and serious. All lifted their glasses.

"To one of the most understanding and humane ladies I know." She drank quickly and everyone followed suit. An awkward silence followed.

Suddenly the door opened and Jason came in. Quickly he walked over to Kate and kissed her cheek. His affection and respect for her shone from his eyes. "I know I've not been invited, but I really wanted to be here today." He picked up a glass and toasted Kate silently.

The meal was superb and the chatter around the table was pleasant. Whatever trepidation each had had before coming dissipated gradually. Kate was upset that Betsy had not come but put it out of her mind for now.

"I think I'd like to make a little speech," Jason said as they were drinking their coffee. Everyone looked up with relief. In years past each had been called on to say something complimentary about Kate.

"Here's to one of the bravest and gutsiest women I've ever met. A woman after my heart," Jason said as he looked directly at Kate. She felt a hot, embarrassed flush rise to her cheeks. It was the closest Jason had ever come to saying he loved her. She looked at him for a long moment and wondered if he were really making a public declaration to her.

Everyone was up and milling around finishing their after-dinner liqueur, and Kate's eyes followed Jason. She watched him smile warmly at everyone, say a few words to Dee Dee and then to Allyson. Finally he stood next to Carol Butler. Her heart skipped a beat. There was an intimacy in his manner with the young woman that she hadn't noticed before. Picking up a glass of champagne, Kate watched them closely. Carol was a stunning girl. She was also bright, lively, alert, and a fine editor with a good mind and a nose for what was real and today. Suddenly she knew that if she had to choose to be someone other than herself, she would have liked to be Carol Butler. Jason pressed Carol's shoulder and moved toward Kate.

"Come a little earlier tonight," Jason whispered in her ear. "I have a surprise for you." He leaned over and kissed her cheek. The dreadful moment of blind jealousy disappeared. She smiled broadly at him.

"Will six be early enough?"

"Perfect." Then he was gone.

Within minutes all the others left as well, each thanking her profusely for the leather briefcase. "I hope you like it," she said sincerely. Gift giving was strange to her and she felt awkward but childishly pleased with herself.

The room was suddenly quiet. The last waiter had cleared the table and only the bartender stood by.

"You can go, too," she said to the waiting man. "I'd like to be alone for a few minutes. Just pour me another glass of champagne if you would."

Left alone, she started opening the gifts. Greedily she opened first the ones with the most expensive-looking wrappings. The richness of the present inside gave her a warm glow. The last two were obviously home-wrapped and not so exciting. Therefore she was surprised to feel a lump in her throat when she opened the present from Maggie to find a beautiful handmade afghan. When she saw the icon from Linda the tears came, and she sat there helplessly, unable to stop crying and unable to figure out what was making her cry.

22

Jason had showered and was sitting in his study, dressed for the evening except for his tie and jacket. Instead he had on a new cashmere robe that Dee Dee had sent him for Christmas. Rare old brandy was in the decanter, an heirloom that he had picked up years back in his travels, and a humidor with the cigars Hank and Jeannie had sent him was nearby. It was his sixty-second birthday but no one except Hank knew it, and Jason was not sure if even he remembered. At any rate, Hank was tactful enough not to let on, if he did.

Jason looked around indifferently. The room, like all the others he had furnished around the country, was comfortable, masculine, and very much his. He had no feelings for any of the objects around, except that they served him. He was a man of habit and little sentiment. Success, power, wealth, and what the last could afford were all he really cared about.

It was four in the afternoon. The draperies had been drawn, the fire was burning pleasantly, the silence complete, and for the first time in many years Jason felt a restlessness that disturbed him. Usually this feeling came to him before making a serious decision in a multilateral business deal. Then the disquiet was constructive, exciting, almost thrilling. Then his mind would grow razor sharp as he did his mental manipulations, like a chess player working out the final moves leading to a resounding checkmate. Now, however, nothing was important enough to warrant these strange and disturbing feelings.

He tried to concentrate on the papers lying on the table beside him but soon gave up the attempt.

Instead he poured himself a drink and leaned back in the huge leather wing chair. Finally the thoughts he was trying to escape caught up with him and he knew what was troubling him. For the first time in his life he felt old. The feelings had been creeping up on him for a long time but he'd been busy and succeeded in drowning them in the hectic schedule he insisted on. Now, in the quiet, darkened room, he allowed himself to face the truths he he had tried to evade.

The first crack in the facade he had built came when Tar called him. He had not heard from his brother, Tarquin, for twenty-two years. He'd been home alone on Christmas Eve when the phone rang. He had hated the holiday since his mother passed away on Christmas Eve. His entire house staff was out and no one knew he was home. He was tempted not to answer, then picked up the receiver cautiously.

"Jason?"

He recognized the voice immediately and was speechless.

"Jason? Is that you? It's Tar."

"Yes," he answered slowly as painful memories

returned too quickly. "Yes," he repeated. "How are you, Tar? Where are you?"

"I'm in New York for a week seeing Robert. He's just come in from London and wants to see the city." There was a pause. "Would you have supper with us?"

"I hate going out on Christmas Eve. Why don't you come here and bring Robert with you." He was surprised at what he was saying but the invitation was extended and he could not take it back.

"We can't make dinner, we're going to a show, but we'll come in afterward for a drink if you'd like."

"Sure," Jason answered stiffly. "Around eleven, then?"

He hung up, shaken. Not only would he see Tar after all these years but he would see Robert, Tar and Rozanne's son. The boy would be at least twenty by now. The last time Jason saw him he was barely three years old. He had accidentally bumped into Rozanne and the child at the Savoy Hotel in London.

Tarquin was twelve years younger than Jason. At first Jason resented his brother's birth, since he had enjoyed the privileges of an only child. His mother had doted on him and his father took special pride in his achievements. He grew to hate Tarquin when it became clear that their mother would never recover from Tar's birth. She was ill for several months, in and out of hospitals, and finally died of a hemorrhage that the doctors could not account for but blamed on her advanced age when she'd given birth to Tarquin.

Jason was sent off to Choate, the exclusive prep school, and then to Yale, and except for brief vacations at their estate in Long Island, the brothers had little contact over the years. Because of the age difference they spent little time together and Jason knew nothing about his brother. Tar was reared in Boston by Aunt Mary, an unmarried sister of his mother, and months, even years, went by without the two meeting. When their father passed away, Jason took over the business and it was understood that Jason would be the executor of the estate, including Tar's share in it. At the funeral they stood side by side and Jason was surprised to see his brother a grown man of eighteen, almost as tall as he was and handsome, with a shock of black hair and dark brown intense, serious, almost brooding eyes. Jason felt little brotherly love for the boy but took his responsibility as guardian seriously. He was relieved to learn that Tarquin had no interest in business.

"I trust you, Jason," Tar had said when they came back to Jason's house after the funeral. "I have no mind for business, hate it, as a matter of fact."

"What are you doing these days?" Jason had asked, simply to have the facts rather than out of interest.

"I've been accepted at Harvard and I want to major in history and philosophy. I'm glad it's Harvard, since I can keep an eye on Aunt Mary. She's getting on in years, you know, and let's face it, she really devoted her life to me."

"That's great," Jason said, and wondered about this soft, strange, unambitious young man. "Dad left her something in his will, so she will be cared for financially."

After that meeting they saw each other occasionally when Jason found himself in the Boston area or when Tar came down to New York on the rare weekend.

Jason was too absorbed in his work and making a success to worry or think about Tar. He was also emotionally involved with a woman for the first and only time in his life. Rozanne Kleet was a newspaperwoman who worked for one of his papers in New York. She was bright, ambitious, strong and passionate, and excellent at what she did. She was not a beautiful woman, but she exuded a sense of excitement and love of life. She moved in with Jason soon after they met and except for the marriage certificate they lived as man and wife.

Jason could not really recall the day when Tar first met Rozanne. The memory always eluded him. The Second World War had ended. Europe was in turmoil and Rozanne took an assignment in England. Jason did not want her to go but did not tell her, feeling that it was wrong to impose his will on another.

"You don't mind, do you, Jason?" Rozanne asked

as she was packing her bags. "I won't be gone for long."

"It's your decision," he remembered saying, knowing that what he really wanted was to plead with her not to leave him.

"I know," she answered as she came close to him and laid her head on his chest. "It's my decision."

He missed her terribly but never mentioned it to her. He tried to get over to Europe as often as possible and it was during one of those visits that he introduced Tar to Rozanne. Tar had graduated from Harvard, then spent a year in the army in England as an intelligence officer, and was now working on his doctorate at Oxford.

The shock of getting the telegram announcing Tar and Rozanne's marriage was horrendous. His first reaction was to fly over to England. The idea was preposterous. Rozanne was his; he needed her and he wanted her. Also, she was eight years older than Tar, she was a career woman, and she wanted so much out of life. Surely Tar could never give her the things she wanted. The marriage, he was sure, would never last.

He looked at the telegram again: GOT MARRIED YESTERDAY STOP ARRIVING FLIGHT 112 BOAC STOP REGARDS ROZANNE AND TAR.

He sent his car to get them and suggested they stay with him before leaving for Amherst, Massachusetts, for Tar was going there to lecture at the college.

Rozanne was gay and charming and seemed extremely happy. Jason tried to avoid spending time alone with her. He did not trust himself and was afraid he would say something that would give away his true feelings. But the encounter was unavoidable. It was the day before they left and Jason was in his study working when Rozanne walked in and sat down. He did not hear her come in but felt her presence.

"You don't give a damn, do you?" she asked bluntly.

"Give a damn about what?" Jason asked as he looked up at her. She was everything he wanted in a woman. Say it, a voice inside screamed, say that you want her, need her, love her. Instead he simply stared at her blankly.

"That I married Tar."

"If that's your decision, far be it from me to interfere."

"I really thought you loved me," she said sadly. "I honestly thought I'd succeeded in penetrating that shell, that turtle's hump you hide under."

"Rozanne," he said slowly, "what do you want? You lived here with me. I gave you everything I had. Above all, I shared my life with you. I thought you wanted the things I wanted. I believed your ambition was mine, your dreams were mine, that we would achieve them together. No woman had ever lived in this house but you, and I doubt that any woman ever will." He stopped to control the impulse to plead, to beg, which was greater now. "What is it you wanted?"

"You never asked me to marry you," she said slowly.

"No, I never did. I didn't know you wanted marriage."

"Yes, I wanted marriage and I want children."

"Well, you strike out on both scores. I want neither," he said coldly.

She stood up and so did he.

"Are you in love with Tar?"

"Very much," she answered. "In many ways he's like you except that there is a kindness and a gentleness which you don't have and probably never will have."

She moved toward him and he was drawn to her. In a minute she was in his arms and he was kissing her with a passion he was never to have for a woman again.

It was at that moment that Tar walked in.

Jason saw him before Rozanne did. He let go of her abruptly and she turned around and looked at Tar.

"I think we'd better leave," Tar said quietly. Rozanne walked over to him and put her hand in his.

"He knows about us, Jason," Rozanne said, breaking the dreadful silence.

And they were gone. Jason had not seen Tarquin since. That was twenty-two years ago.

He made no effort to follow their lives but he did know that they had a baby boy, whose name was Robert.

He also heard that the marriage had broken up and that Rozanne had taken the baby and moved to London, gone back to work, and finally married a titled man and was now a popular figure among the elite of London society.

"Mr. Reid." The butler had come in quietly and Jason was relieved of the painful memories. "It's almost five-thirty and you said you were expecting Miss Johnson at six."

"Thank you, Lee." Jason got up and walked to his bedroom.

Kate would be arriving in half an hour and Jason wondered if he could actually go through with his plans. He was going to ask Kate to move in with him. In a strange way she reminded him of Rozanne. They had the same drive, the same ambitions, much the same intensity for work. The difference between the two women was that Kate did not want the things Rozanne did. Kate did not want marriage or children. She had a daughter but never spoke of her. She had a capacity for work similar to his and was totally involved in it. She would be a good companion and he enjoyed having her around. But more than that, her presence, he hoped, would stop him from searching for the elusive something he was now tired of looking for. She might fill his life enough so that he would not feel the need for someone like Carol Butler, who was too young for him and too different from the women he had known throughout his life. Jason had taken Carol out several times and found her bright and charming, amusing and witty. Yet he often felt she was laughing at him. There was a youthful lack of inhibition in her manner, a jargon he found too hard to follow. She was heading for the top and was willing to accept a helping hand, but her terms of reference were different from his. She was the present and future, and he felt that somehow, while he was not looking, he had become the past.

He had felt it even more strongly when Tar arrived with Robert on Christmas Eve. Tar had grown older but was still the gentle man he had always been. He was pleased to see Jason and would have hugged his brother if he could have done it gracefully. Robert was the surprise.

202

He looked like Rozanne but was tall and slender. He spoke with a clipped British accent and his manners were impeccable. But soon after they arrived Jason noticed that the boy was one of the new breed of youngsters. His politics, his outlook, his opinions, his way of wording his thoughts, were refreshing, bright, stimulating, but different. He and Carol were of the generation that was making its mark. Robert was on his way back to Stanford University, in California, where he was majoring in journalism. When Jason offered to help, Robert thanked him, much as Carol had when he'd made a similar offer, but the conditions were clear: Stay out of my life—no strings, no promises, no vows.

Jason heard the doorbell ring and knew it was Kate. He smiled. Her punctuality was something he admired. With new resolve he decided to offer Kate a share in his home and his life.

23

Kate arrived at her apartment at three-thirty, after the New Year's Eve luncheon, determined to have a short nap before dressing for Jason's party. The elation she had felt at lunch had disappeared, to be replaced by an unexplained feeling of loss. She had examined her gifts again. They were beautiful and expensive. She envied people who could spend their money easily. Her frugality was so much a part of her that she never considered the possibility of change. The good buy, the sale item, these were the things she prized. She adored her apartment because it had been furnished at the smallest possible cost. Removing her shoes, she threw her coat on the hall table and walked into the living room. Although it was only a one-bedroom apartment, the living room was unusually large, with a row of windows facing the East River. The dining area was cleverly cut off from the living room by a magnificent Chinese screen. The navy-blue satin intermingled with soft peach velvet decided on by her decorator was lush and soothing. She went into her bedroom. This was her room, her achievement. Here she prevailed and got the paisley fabrics she loved. The walls were covered with it, and the bedspread, the skirt on the box spring, and the drapes were all of paisley, too. She had a king-size bed, the one extravagance she allowed herself. She walked to the bedroom window, also facing the river, and looked down at the water. It had begun to rain and she saw the drops splash furiously into the river and disappear. It did not excite any thought other than that her hair would be ruined. Annoyed, she turned away from the window and started to undress.

The room was dark now and as she hugged her naked body she knew that what she wanted was to be loved. Jason did not love her. She had misread his compliments at lunch out of a need that had been growing in her for too long. No one loved her and she actually loved no one. She thought of Belinda. It would be a lie to pretend that her feelings for her daughter were feelings of love. She had been separated from her too long. Belinda was an obligation. Her mother? Elie? No, they, too, were simply an obligation. For the first time in years she thought of Mike. Had she loved Mike? It was so long ago that she could not even remember what he looked like. Had he loved her?

She felt chilled and, pulling back the heavy quilted bedspread, got into bed. It was a foolish extravagance, after all, she thought as she looked at the empty space beside her. Suddenly she wanted Ben. He did not love her and she did not love him but he gave her, if only for a little while, the warmth of his body, the gentle caresses. He made her feel less lonely.

Quickly she dialed his number. She was sure he would be home. His boyfriend, Greg, was in the chorus line of a Broadway musical and there was a special performance that afternoon. Ben had been furious, since they were giving a New Year's Eve party and he had to prepare for it alone.

"I know you're up to your ears in work, but please come over," she said when he answered the phone.

"Oh, for Christ's sake, Kate, what's up?" He sounded annoyed. "I know you don't need your hair done. You just want to get laid, don't you?"

"Ben..." she started to protest.

"It's okay to want to get laid, Kate. But say it, I won't think less of you for it."

"Okay, I want to get laid," she whispered, and felt herself grow hot with embarrassment. "Will you come over?"

"Sure." He laughed for the first time. "I'm up to my ass in cocktail dips and frankly it'll be a relief to get out."

"I'll tell the doorman to let you up and I'll leave the door open."

"Boy, you're really horny, aren't you?" He laughed again and hung up.

When Ben made love to her the fantasies she had to conjure up when she was in bed with Jason were superfluous. Ben verbalized the fantasy. As he kissed her mouth, her breasts, her thighs and vagina, he would excite her further by telling her about his love affairs with the men and women he knew. "And someday, Katie, we'll make it a threesome or a foursome. Would you like that? I'll find you a nice girl and she'll be doing it instead of me and I'll be watching, then we'll switch." Or he'd talk about instruments that would make the lovemaking more erotic and exciting. "I'll get some and bring them over. Would you like that?"

She never answered but simply enjoyed feeling his whole body giving her pleasure, serving her needs.

Ben never ejaculated when making love to her. At first she asked him to, sometimes even pleadingly. "I want you to enjoy it, too," she would whisper, but he ignored her and spurred her on to another orgasm.

"I'm enjoying it," he would sometimes answer, "so why don't you just relax. You've got to admit it's better than Jason, who goes in, does his little trick, spurts it inside, and zip, it's all over."

She resented his describing Jason this way but she never bothered to defend him.

The grandfather clock in the front hall struck the hour and Kate realized that it was five o'clock. She and Ben had been together for an hour and now she had to dress. She hated to stop. It was always exciting to have Ben inside her, but today, for some reason, he was more passionate than ever before.

"Ben," she said quietly, "Ben, I've got to go."

He did not answer, but his lovemaking became more aggressive and suddenly she felt him come. It exploded inside her and instinctively she knew that never again would she feel the thrill she felt at that moment. He continued to push himself farther and farther into her and she felt a dull but pleasurable pain. She also felt a sadness.

His movements stopped suddenly and he lay on top of her, limp and wet, and she heard him moan quietly.

She pushed his face away from hers and looked at him. He stared at her as though in anger and with a quick motion he got up and rushed into the bathroom.

When he came out he was the old Ben again. He smiled warmly at her. "You'd better shower and then I'll do your hair. It's a mess."

As Ben stood over her, fiddling with her hair, she reached up and touched his hand. He pressed hers with affection. They both knew that it was over. They would still be friends but never again lovers.

She put on a long red velvet skirt and a pink St. Laurent silk shirt she had bought for the evening. Ben was in the living room having a drink when she came out.

"How do I look?" she asked casually.

"I think you look great, Katie," he said lightly.

"Will you escort me down?" she asked, and remembered that this scene had been played five years before when she had gone to Jason's New Year's Eve party.

"It will be my pleasure, Miss Johnson," Ben answered as he put her arm through his. "My pleasure."

She knew that he, too, remembered.

24

Jason was standing in the doorway of the study when Kate came up the stairs. He kissed her on the cheek and she felt his lips linger for a fraction longer than usual. She responded quickly by turning her face to him and kissing him on the mouth.

"I'm expecting everyone to come around seven and I did want some time alone with you," he said as he poured her a drink. He did not ask her what she wanted, she thought pleasantly, he knew. Pouring himself one, he turned and toasted her with his eyes.

"You look lovely tonight, Katie," he said warmly, and for some reason that she couldn't understand she felt uncomfortable. This was not like Jason.

"Thank you, Jason," she said, and wanting to break

the strangeness of his mood, she continued. "It was a lovely luncheon, wasn't it? And I really appreciated your coming. It was thoughtful and a marvelous present, not to mention the fabulous lunch you ordered. It must have cost a fortune." She knew she was rambling but could not stop. "I wonder why Betsy didn't show up," she added, unable to control herself. "She's really an awful little bitch, you know. As a matter of fact, you were right—she does hate me and wants to see me fall on my face. But I'm stronger than she is, and let's face it, she's still working for me, not I for her, and she'll go on working for me for as long as I want her to. I'll be calling the shots, you can be sure of that." She stopped to catch her breath and downed her drink.

Jason watched her and did not interrupt. When he saw her empty glass he simply walked over, took it out of her hand, and refilled it.

"Incidentally, Jason, did you know that we're up three points this month over last Christmas in sales and eight points over last month?" She smiled self-consciously. Why was she going on so?

"Katie, I do believe you're nervous for some reason," he said when she grew silent.

"I am," she answered candidly, "and I'm damned if I know why."

"No matter, it's been an exciting day and you've worked hard for a long time without a vacation. It's really very understandable."

"Come to think of it, Jason," she said suddenly, "I haven't been away since the day I came to *Women Today* except, of course, for going to Dayton, and that was hardly a vacation." She paused briefly. "Jason, do you think I could go away for a couple of weeks?" Belinda was coming to New York on New Year's Day and Kate had planned to drive her back to school on the third. It would work out well if she could go on from there for a ten-day vacation. "I've never had a vacation." She smiled, almost to herself. "I've been working from the time I was seventeen and not once did it occur to me that I could actually go away and rest." She looked at him for a long moment. "How the hell does one take a vacation, anyway?"

He laughed good-naturedly. "Frankly, I don't know either." He finished his drink and poured himself another.

They were both behaving strangely, Kate thought, but was fearful of what would happen if they stopped chatting.

"I suppose I could look up one of the summer issues of *Women Today* where they give advice to their readers about vacations."

"Hey, that's a thought," Jason countered. "A damn fine magazine, that one," he said with mock seriousness.

"Actually, I think one calls a travel agent, who gives you advice according to what you're looking for and how much you want to spend." Kate now became serious. "I really could use some time off. I'm exhausted. The question is, do I want a warm or a cold climate?"

"Why not go to Mexico," Jason suggested. "I have a lovely house in Acapulco. It's fully staffed, it has a pool, a tennis court, and a stable."

"Sounds great, except I don't ride or swim or play tennis. As for a staff, I'd be a nervous wreck by the time I got back simply from wondering how to deal with them."

They both laughed. "Okay, would you like to go to Aspen? I have a magnificent lodge there with no help, and don't tell me you don't ski. It won't matter."

"Could I really, Jason?" she said seriously. Being alone in a lodge sounded lovely. She might even meet some nice people there. "How much is the plane fare to Aspen?"

"If you go there, I'll have my plane take you and bring you back. You really deserve a vacation." He was now serious, too. "As a matter of fact, if you go to Aspen, I've got a perfect gift for you." He got up and left the room. He was back in a minute with a huge box in Christmas wrapping and an enormous silver ribbon around it.

"Merry Christmas and happy New Year, Katie," he said as he handed the present to her.

She unwrapped the box and opened it. A magnificent fur peeked out from under the mounds of tissue paper. Taking it out, Kate felt faint. It was by far the most magnificent fur coat she had ever seen.

"It's exquisite. It's mink?" she asked shyly as she put it on. The fit was perfect.

"It's sable," Jason said quietly. "Everyone has a mink and you're too special to be dressed like everyone else." He took her in his arms. "You're very special," he whispered.

She threw her arms around his neck and kissed him. He was holding her tightly in his arms and suddenly she heard him speak quietly into her ear.

"Kate, why don't you come here and live with me?"

She moved away and stared up at him. It was not a proposal of marriage. Jason was asking her to move in to be his companion.

"Jason, are you serious?" she asked in dismay.

"More serious than I've ever been about anything in my life," he answered, moving away, as though embarrassed, and made them both another drink.

Kate took hers and sipped it slowly. She was not a big drinker and neither was Jason. But tonight they were both nervous.

"I'm flattered," Kate began slowly, then amended her words. "No, that's corny. I've thought of it a hundred times, wanted it desperately at moments, but now, somehow, it all seems wrong." She contemplated what she was saying. "Wrong is not the word. It's sudden and I can't quite see why you want me here."

"We've got so much in common. I love your company, I know you enjoy mine. We think alike, we have the same interests and drives. You love your work and it's so closely intertwined with mine. I have a great deal to offer you and you have a great deal to offer me." He stopped for a brief moment. "I'm lonely, Kate." The last phrase seemed to have been wrenched out of his gut. It was a dreadful admission for someone like him.

Marriage, Kate was thinking. It's marriage I want. To live with Jason would end the dream of romance not only with him but with anyone else. She still yearned and longed for the love that somehow had eluded her all her life, and she was still young enough to have a passionate romance with someone.

She placed her drink carefully on a coaster on the highly polished coffee table. Leaning her head against Jason's chest, she felt his arms encircle her and hold her close. At least say that you love me, she pleaded silently. It would tip the scale, make the difference. She clung to him. Jason said nothing. The room was completely silent.

"Think about it, Katie," Jason said finally. "Go on your vacation and think about it. There's no rush." He pushed her away gently and raised her face to his. "My offer stands and for whatever it's worth, you can be sure there is no competition for the position I offer you in my life."

They heard the chimes of the front door and somehow they were both relieved. Jason kissed her gently on the lips. "I'd better go and greet the guests," he said, and was gone.

Kate took off the coat and stared at it for a long time. It was the most luxurious thing she had ever owned. She pressed the soft fur against her face. She could have it all if she moved in with Jason.

Jason's New Year's Eve party was traditionally a gracious and elegant affair. Kate knew everyone and although she had become accustomed to their chitchat and small talk, she never really enjoyed it. She drank a little more than usual, which helped ease the discomfort. The dinner was superb, and after they had finished the dessert, Jason announced that he had a new film, not yet released, that he would show in the living room. Everyone was standing around chatting, nursing their after-dinner drinks, when Kate became conscious that someone she had never seen before had come into the room. At first glance she thought it was Jason, then realized it was someone who looked like Jason but was considerably younger.

"My brother, Tarquin." Kate heard Jason introduce the man to some people who were near the entrance to the room. When they reached Kate, Jason introduced them, and she felt the man's powerful handshake and could barely find her voice to say the expected pleasantries.

"I didn't know you had a brother, Jason," Kate finally said when she could trust herself to speak. She looked at the younger man. "Tarquin? That's quite a name."

Jason laughed. "We call him Tar and I'm sure you can, too." They moved away. Kate tried to concentrate on what someone was saying to her but her mind was filled with the image of the man she had just met.

All through the screening in the darkened living room, Kate felt Tar's eyes on her. He was sitting in back of her and she felt as though his eyes were boring holes through her head. Several times she had to squash the impulse to turn around and look at him.

The movie was over just before midnight. When the magic hour struck, everyone kissed the person standing closest and then proceeded to peck the cheeks of closer and dearer friends and relatives. Jason came over to Kate and kissed her lightly. She turned around and knew she was looking for Tar. He was standing beside her. Leaning down, he kissed her on the cheek. "Happy New Year, Kate," he said, and his smile was warm. He looked like Jason but now, as she looked at him, she saw the difference. Tar's eyes were gentle and brooding. Neither quality could be attributed to Jason's.

"Happy New Year, Tar," she answered, and did not look away.

"May I see you again?" he asked.

She nodded. "Please call me. Please do." She gave him her number, and he jotted it down.

Kate knew that Jason expected her to spend the night with him and for the first time she was embarrassed. The idea of Tar's being a witness to her relationship with his brother bothered her. She had several more drinks and was upset that she was not really feeling any effect. The guests began to leave and to her great relief she noticed that Tar was leaving, too. Before he walked out, he came over and shook her hand. "I'll call you tomorrow."

"Just as long as it's not too early." She smiled.

"Around noon?"

"I'm picking my daughter up from the airport around one in the afternoon. Try me around five."

"Will do," he said, and left.

She stared after him for a minute. Was he the romance she was waiting for, she wondered. How ironic, she mused, to fall in love with someone who looked like Jason but who had the qualities she sorely missed in him. Or did she? Did she truly want Jason to be different? The thought was too complex and she erased it from her mind. She looked around for Jason and was relieved that she was in his house, that she was his girl, that she could have all that he offered if she consented to move in with him. Suddenly she could not wait to be alone with him. Tonight, she would make love to Jason and please him as never before.

25

Kate picked up Belinda at the airport. Mother and daughter hugged each other warmly. However, as soon as they were in the taxi heading for the city, Belinda announced that she would not be going to school after all.

"I hate school," she said angrily. "I'm a lousy student and I'm failing some of my classes. Besides, whatever I want to know I can find out for myself."

Kate tried to reason with her but to no avail. Finally, in desperation, she announced that if Belinda did not go to Windham she would have to go back to Dayton because there was no way for Kate to keep her in the city.

"I don't need you," Belinda said belligerently. "I can earn a living very easily."

"Really?" Kate asked as they left the cab in front of her house. "How, if I may ask?"

"I could be a model. A photographer's model," she answered with assurance.

Kate looked at her daughter. There was truth in what she was saying. Now, sixteen, she was tall and wiry, her blond hair long and straight, her slanted eyes a greenish blue, her mouth full and sensuous. Yes, Kate thought, she could probably make it as a model. They were just entering Kate's apartment and suddenly Belinda gasped. Kate's heart sank.

"What happened?" she asked quickly.

"Is this where you live?" Belinda asked as she looked around her mother's living room.

Kate let out a sigh of relief. "Yes, honey, this is where I live and you can spend every weekend here while you're at school."

"Mom, I'm not going and you can't force me." Belinda's sullenness had returned.

"Belinda, I can force you even though I'd rather not have to."

The argument continued for most of the afternoon. Kate was tired and confused. She prepared lunch and was annoyed at having to do this simple chore. It had been too long since she had to cope with kitchens and young people.

Around four o'clock, with Belinda ensconced by the large color television set in the living room, Kate decided to take a nap. The ringing of the phone woke her.

"It's Tar here." She heard his voice and the memory of the man she met briefly the night before came back to her. "Did I wake you?" he asked with concern. "You did say around five."

"Oh, it's all right, Tar." She cleared her throat. "My daughter arrived and we've been having a time of it, so I thought I'd escape into the never-never land of sleep."

"Would you have dinner with me?"

"I don't think I can. I really should spend time with Belinda. She's off to school at Windham in Connecticut if I can ever get her to go." She was surprised at herself. Linda was the only person with whom she had ever discussed her problems with Belinda. She laughed

216

self-consciously. "I'm sorry to bother you with all this domesticity. I really never talk about these things."

"I don't mind it," he answered, and she was sure he meant it. "How old is she?"

"Sixteen."

"Well, why don't I take you both to dinner, then."

"Would you really?" Kate was excited at the thought.

"I'll pick you up around seven."

She gave him the address and hung up. She got out of bed and realized that the house was very quiet. Pulling on her robe, she ran into the living room. Belinda was nowhere in sight. She ran into the kitchen, looked in the small powder room. Belinda was gone. Kate was in complete panic. The child had no money, as far as she knew, and no friends in the city. She thought of calling the police, but since Belinda had been missing for less than an hour, there was nothing to report. Kate tried to compose herself and think rationally. Belinda may just have gone out for a walk. That thought frightened her even more. East End Avenue in the Eighties was a pleasant area, but the side streets were not exactly safe, especially for someone unaware of the dangers of New York.

She dressed quickly, made herself some coffee, and sat down to wait. She tried to read some of the articles she was working on but found, for the first time in her life, that even work could not distract her. Suddenly she remembered that Tar was picking her up at seven. It was now past six. She had no idea where to reach him and knew that she could not call Jason and ask him his brother's whereabouts.

At seven sharp the doorman rang her apartment and announced Tar's arrival.

The minute he walked in she blurted out her problem. She felt like a fool but somehow Tar understood.

"Okay, let's work this out quietly and rationally," he said as he walked into the apartment. "You fell asleep around four and woke up at five. It's now seven. You say she probably has no money with her, is that right?"

She nodded, feeling numb.

"What does she usually like to do?" he asked.

"I don't really know," she answered, and felt embarrassed. "I haven't lived with her for so long," she said helplessly.

"Has she ever spent time in New York before?"

"Yes. She spent a month with me once."

"What did she do while you were at work?"

"Went shopping or to the movies."

"Well, the shops are closed, so that leaves the movies." He thought for a minute. "Let's get a paper and see what's playing around here."

They discovered a double feature playing on Eighty-sixth Street around Lexington Avenue.

"Assuming she went to the movies, she'd be out by eight or eight-thirty," Tar said. "Let's wait and see and worry if she's not here by nine." He smiled reassuringly at her. "She'll be back, I promise. Even big girls get frightened when it gets dark. I promise you that when she walks out of that movie house and sees that it's dark outside, she'll rush back here like a rabbit being chased by a fox."

His reassuring tone calmed her. They sat in silence and it did not really bother either of them. A delicious intimacy developed. She made some more coffee for both of them. It was during those hours that she found out about Rozanne and Jason, about Robert, and the story of how the marriage ended.

"She was ambitious and wanted the world," Tar said quietly, and there was no bitterness in his voice. "I'll say one thing, though, she did try to adjust to the campus atmosphere, but the pull toward that world she loved more than me was too great. She simply could not give it up." He was silent for a minute. "We thought we could work it out. I was young and I was sure that she could have her career and her marriage." He smiled briefly. "It just didn't work out."

"Is she happy now?" Kate asked cautiously.

"Very happy." He thought for a minute. "At least I think she's happy. I see her whenever I go to London, and we have a grand time together. She's remarried and somehow keeps both her marriage and her career going. She's even been a good mother to Robert. So I guess it was me. I couldn't take the competition." He fell silent and a brooding look came into his eyes.

"Are you still in love with her?" Kate asked, and felt a twinge of envy.

"No," he said slowly. "No, I simply regret the hurt I caused Jason and the fact that I didn't really have the opportunity to enjoy Robert through the years when he was growing up."

At that moment the house phone rang. Kate rushed to answer it. Belinda, the doorman announced, was on her way up.

"She's here," Kate called to Tar as she went to open the door.

"Don't get angry before she tells you where she went. Give her the benefit of the doubt," Tar called back.

Belinda walked in and the look on her face indicated that she was expecting a fight. When she saw her mother and realized that no reprimand was in the offing, the wind was taken out of her sails.

"I went to a movie," she said as she walked past Kate into the living room.

"I wish you'd left me a note, honey." Kate followed Tar's instructions. "I was worried."

"Couldn't find a pencil or paper," Belinda said as she sat down on the couch, pulling her legs under her in a seductive manner.

Kate's eyes went to the desk in front of the windows. Yellow pads of paper and a container holding sharpened pencils were in full view. She was about to point this out when she felt Tar's hand on her elbow.

"I'm Tarquin Reid," he said as he walked over to Belinda. "What movie did you see?" He sat down on the couch next to her.

"Hi," she said, smiling up at Tar, and Kate could not help but notice the loveliness of her daughter. She also realized that Belinda was flirting with him. "I saw the most god-awful double bill. I really didn't think they'd

219

show such shit in New York. I thought they only played that stuff for the yokels in Dayton."

Kate gasped silently at Belinda's language.

"We have an awful lot of yokels in New York, too," Tar answered.

"Where did you get the money to go to the movies?" Kate suddenly remembered to ask.

"I took ten dollars from your purse," Belinda said, but for the first time she looked like a little girl who had done something wrong. "You see, Mom, you were asleep and I didn't want to wake you." She looked anxiously at her mother. "You don't mind, do you?" Quickly she put her hand in her jacket pocket. "Here's the change. I took a taxi to the movie, since I didn't know how far it was. Then when I came out knew I could walk here easily, but I was scared. It was so dark and spooky."

"Well," Tar broke in, "I'm starved, and since I've invited you both to dinner, I would like to suggest we get going."

Over dinner the subject of school came up again. Belinda repeated her sentiments and Kate felt the rage rise in her.

"Mom," she said patiently, "I'm a lousy student, don't you understand? I hate school, always did. You'd be throwing your money away, sending me there."

"You know something, Kate," Tar said slowly, "if you'll forgive my butting in, Belinda does have a point."

Kate was dismayed.

"Not everybody is meant for school," he continued. "As a matter of fact, I'm appalled at the number of students up at Amherst who really shouldn't be there at all. They'd be happier and better off if they were out in the world learning to earn a living rather than taking up space in a classroom." As he spoke he pressed Kate's arm affectionately but she also knew that he was telling her not to say anything.

"But let me tell you something else, Belinda. At sixteen you're a bit young to go out into the real world and fight for survival. You were frightened by the jungle you

saw when you walked out of the movie, you said so
yourself. So why don't you make a deal with your mother
and continue until you graduate high school. You'll make
up the classes you failed. How does that sound? Besides,
you may just find out that you've been going to the wrong
school, had the wrong teachers. Windham might prove to
be a totally new experience."

"How did you know the name of the school?"
Belinda asked in surprise.

"I'm a teacher, remember? I know the names of
most of the schools on the eastern seaboard."

"Is it a nice place?" Belinda asked, impressed.

"It's one of the loveliest places around," Tar assured
her. "Incidentally, do you ride? They've got a great stable
nearby and they're big on tennis."

By the time dinner was over, Belinda had agreed to
go off to Windham for a year, and all the frayed nerves
were calmed.

Kate went to the office the day after New Year's and
decided she would take the vacation she and Jason had
discussed. She didn't know where she would go but she
knew that both Aspen and Acapulco were out of the
question. She wanted to plan an independent vacation.
For the moment she did not want to take anything more
from Jason. When she spoke to him, she did not mention
that she'd seen Tar.

"Will you let me know where you are?"

She smiled to herself. That was usually *her* line. "I
won't be gone that long," she said.

"I'll miss you." There was a pause. "Have a good
time, Kate." He hung up.

She saw Tar that evening for dinner, dropping
Belinda off at Radio City Music Hall. Kate was amused to
find that Tar knew little about New York or any of its "in"
places. They ate at Le Vert-Galant, on West Forty-sixth
Street, since they were to pick Belinda up after the movie.
It was an intimate dinner, with little conversation. For the
first time in her life Kate enjoyed sitting with someone and
not having to be aware of who was around. Office

221

problems were put aside. Belinda was all right, and Kate was about to go on vacation.

It was over coffee that Tar suggested she come up to his place in Amherst.

26

The sound of a howling wind woke her. Kate didn't open her eyes, but listened to the eerie sound, which was oddly comforting. She even felt safe and warm as she nested under the heavy down quilt and felt Tar's strong arms around her, holding her, protecting her.

"Happy?" he asked quietly.

"Yes." She opened her eyes and looked at him. She took her arm out from under the blanket and caressed his face with her fingertips. "I didn't know such happiness existed," she whispered as she pressed her naked body to his.

She had been in Amherst for a week, and lying beside Tar, she found the thought that she would be leaving there in a couple of days unbearable.

"What are you thinking about?" Tar asked.

"That the vacation is coming to an end," she said, and felt sad.

"Did you enjoy it?"

"Only because I was here. I think I would have died if I'd had to be alone somewhere resting." She smiled. "I really don't think I know how to rest. It would probably exhaust me."

"Did you miss the office?"

She thought for a long time and knew that in spite of the pleasant, nonpressured hours spent with Tar, the office, the staff who worked for her, Jason, the rat race, the compulsion to increase the sales of each issue, none was very far from the surface of her mind.

"Yes," she said finally, "I did."

She felt him stiffen and knew she was hurting him.

"I could pretend I didn't," she said quietly as she pressed herself closer to him. "Oh, Tar," she cried desperately, "it's as though there are demons chasing me. I don't know where they came from but they're there all the time."

"Demons are part of the fairy tales we grow up with, but they don't really exist."

"They do, though," Kate protested, "they do. I've lived with them too long and know them too well."

"When you recognize them you can ask them to leave. You can have an open discussion with them. They're yours and would fully understand if you asked them to go away."

She closed her eyes. Yes, the demons were hers and she was used to them. But more important, she liked them. They were the ones who had propelled her to get to where she was. She shuddered and Tar held her closer. It occurred to her that she had never, under similar circumstances, been in bed with a man who would not at that moment begin the game of making love. Yet there was more passion in his holding her than there had ever been between her and any other man. She wished she could stop thinking. She wished Tar *would* start making love to her and erase, blot out, the confusion she was feeling. But the silence, the warmth of his body, the feelings of being safe and cared for, only deepened the conflict.

Tar was not an exciting man, but he was brilliant, witty, perceptive, and kind. He was only a fair lover. Certainly in no way did he compare with Jason and she could not even think of her escapades with Ben. Yet she desired Tar as he desired her and when they made love she felt truly happy and an almost unbearable contentment came over her when they were both satiated. There was no playacting or fantasizing as there had been every time she'd slept with a man in the past. She knew she made Tar happy and he knew he had satisfied her. She was being made love to sincerely, almost naively, a process of giving and taking, of sharing. In a way it was like the first few months with Mike. The last thought frightened her. She was a child then. Now she was a woman, an experienced woman. The conclusion was pressing forward. She was in love with Tar! The admission was painful. It simply did not fit into the scheme of her life. Frantically she looked for her demons. She was not ready to let go of them. She needed them, she wanted them. They were her allies.

Tar leaned over and kissed her on the mouth. It was a simple kiss, full of love and tenderness.

"What do you want?" she asked almost harshly.

He moved away quickly and raised himself into a sitting position. She saw a look of bewildered sadness come into his eyes. She threw herself into his arms, her head resting against his bare chest, and burst out crying. She felt his arms encircle her and hold her.

"I don't want anything, Kate, other than what we've had since you've been here," he said quietly.

For a minute he sounded like Jason. He, too, pretended that he was making no demands. They were brothers in the sense that neither was going to force his wishes on anyone close to him. But they each wanted something. She knew how Jason went about getting his way, and she wondered how Tar would. She had established her independence from Jason. Would she succeed with Tar, too?

"But you must have wishes, desires, dreams. Everyone does," she persisted.

"I've come to a point in my life where I only want the things I know I can get," he said quietly.

She looked up at him. Say it, she wanted to cry out, say it so that I can turn you down and clear the air.

He smiled and patted her shoulder. "Kate, my dearest, I think I'll go light the fire downstairs so the house will be warm when you're ready for breakfast." He kissed her lightly on the head and got out of bed.

The next two days were more frantic. Kate could not stand to be away from Tar. She had to touch him, be near him. They spoke little and yet more was said in a gesture or a look than in any worded declarations.

When he took her to the train, still no questions were asked, no demands made.

"When will I see you, Tar?" she asked as they waited on the platform in the railroad station.

"The school semester is just beginning and it's rough until the new kids get established." He held her close. "I'll call you when I know I'm coming into New York."

She leaned against him, saying nothing.

"You can come up here whenever you like, Kate. You know that, don't you?"

She heard the train coming and still she did not move.

"I love you, Kate," he said soberly. "I love you too much to ask you the obvious."

Only then did she lift her head and look at him. He smiled a slow, sad smile. "I know," he said, looking directly at her, "the demons are out in full regalia, daggers pointed, horns pushed forward, ready for the lunge, the kill. I won't torment you by fighting them."

He leaned down and kissed her and then, picking up her suitcase, he led her to the train door.

27

Kate arrived at her office earlier than usual. She picked up the mail from her secretary's desk and began to sift through it but found it impossible to focus on what she was reading. Putting it aside, she leaned back on the sofa and tried to figure out the reason for her discontent. On the surface all was going well. Belinda had been with Miss Winston for well over a year, and though there had been no blatant drug problem, the girl had at first been extremely moody and often ill-tempered. She suffered terrible insecurities about her appearance and her identity. Analysis was Miss Winston's recommendation and Kate, hating the idea, agreed. It made a huge dent in her earnings, but it did help. Belinda was much happier, her schoolwork had improved tremendously, and she would soon be a senior and hoping to graduate. In a sense, though, Kate was running three households and although she was making a great deal of money, she found that she was not saving enough to ward off any sudden disaster should one occur. Worry about money always depressed her, but she knew it was not the cause of her unhappiness this morning.

Her thoughts shifted to the magazine. There again, everything was running smoothly. The sales were going up each month and she now had a completely free hand in all decisions. Jason's attitude toward her was better than it had ever been. Never once during these past months had he repeated his proposal that she move in with him, but she knew the offer was still a standing one. There was no urgency, no pressure. She did miss Linda, who had been away for ten days visiting her friends in Canada and was due back today. For a moment the thought of Linda succeeded in stirring a murmur of emotion in her. But as quickly as the feelings for Linda rose, they disappeared, to be replaced again by the feelings of utter desolation.

She sighed deeply, painfully allowing a truth to surface. She had met Tar, spent time with him, and left without any commitments to him. Except for their brief times together during the past year and a half, her life was emotionally empty. It always had been really, but Tar had partially filled the void. Having tasted this deep emotion, however briefly, made her more aware of the emptiness. The heartthrobbing excitement she had once felt with Jason was gone. The momentary physical satisfaction she had with Ben was no more. Even Belinda, whom she used to look forward to seeing, could not fill the emotional void. In desperation she had begun to date various men, and as much as she hated casual affairs, she even went to bed with one or another of these men. They were all dull, colorless. None was a man she could really be involved with, nor would she have dreamed of introducing any of them to Belinda or anyone else, for that matter. Like the affairs in Dayton, they were somehow shoddy. She missed Tar, or the feelings that he inspired. They spoke often, warm and pleasant conversations. She knew she simply had to say the word and he would accept her into his life as his wife and companion. Belinda adored him and spent time in Amherst with him even when Kate was too busy to go. Tar became the father Belinda had never had. But Kate's demons were in full control. Tar kept telling her that she could control them, but the fact was they never let go and she was powerless. Would they be her only companions in the end? The prospect was grim. She found herself trying desperately to escape from further truths when the door opened and Betsy walked in.

"Well, aren't we the early birds," Kate said, unable to hide the sarcasm in her voice.

"I've just come from a mad, mad, wild party," Betsy chirped, ignoring Kate's tone. "The wildest, and I should know what they are. And you'll never guess, but I found a male nude for us."

"Really?" Kate was immediately interested. She had almost forgotten about it. The board members, when they got wind of the idea, called her in and made their objections clear. Kate took note of their feelings but filed the project away as a possibility for the future. Also, she had run into greater difficulties than she'd anticipated in turning up a known personality who was secure enough to go along with her idea. "Who is it?"

"Chuck Delany," Betsy said as she began sifting through her portfolio.

"You take your portfolio to parties?" Kate asked, again feeling the hostility she was having a hard time hiding these days.

"That is silly," Betsy said as she emptied the contents of her portfolio of drawings and pictures and scattered them all over the rug.

"Who the hell is Chuck Delany, anyway?"

"Oh, you are truly a square lady, Kate," Betsy said with disdain as she proudly held up a photograph and handed it to Kate.

Kate felt her stomach contract as she stared at the face of a man who, although not handsome in the conventional way, had, without doubt, the most exciting face she had ever seen. He was staring directly into the camera and Kate had the feeling that she was being undressed by the eyes in the photograph. His hair was dark and straight, his nose seemed broken, his mouth sensuous, although the lips were thin and the smile was cruel. He was wearing an open-necked white shirt that contrasted with the olive tone of his skin.

"Chuck Delany is the up-and-coming young star of television, stage, and screen." Betsy's voice penetrated Kate's dazed mind.

"I've never heard of him," Kate said, putting the picture down and trying to control feelings she could not understand.

"That is because you are old-fashioned, Kate," Betsy said impatiently. "You work, screw Jason Reid once a week, and have little bitty affairs every so often which make you feel that you are a woman of the world, but you really do not know what is happening in this city, much less the country."

Kate winced and Betsy went on. "You have fantasies that you are a liberated woman, but you are not. If life had been kind to you, you would be married and bringing up several children." There was no malice in Betsy's voice. She was simply stating a fact as she saw it.

Kate wanted to slap her. Instead she swallowed hard and picked up the photo again.

"And he's willing to pose nude?" Kate asked. Her mouth felt dry.

"He loves the idea."

"Is he in New York for any length of time?"

"He just finished two films in Hollywood, and is now going into a play which will open soon."

"Okay, arrange for him to come up and see me," Kate said trying to keep the excitement out of her voice.

"He will not come up to see you, Kate, I can guarantee that. I think you will have to call him personally and go see him."

Again Kate felt her anger rise, but she checked it. "All right, where do I find him?"

"He is at the Plaza for now, since the studio is

paying him for his stay there while he is promoting his films. He has an apartment somewhere in the Village."

"I'll call him." She picked up the mail and sifted through it, ignoring Betsy and hoping she would leave.

"I will be happy to make the date for you," Betsy said, taking the photograph, which Kate had put on the coffee table, and repacking her portfolio.

"I'll make the appointment, thank you." Kate looked up. "I have to see what my schedule is like."

"I'm seeing him tonight, I can arrange it all. Maybe you would like to join us?" Betsy persisted.

"No, thank you, Betsy," Kate said again, more forcefully. "I don't intend to make this a social affair. It's business and I would rather keep it that way." Then a thought struck her. "How much will he want?"

"With me it is all social," Betsy said bitchily, "and I never, but *never,* discuss money with friends." With that she swept up her portfolio and left the room.

Kate looked at the clock on her desk. It was not quite nine A.M. She wanted to rush to the phone and ring up the Plaza but controlled her impulse. Betsy had said she had just come from a party, and if he had been there he would probably just be going to sleep. She decided she would wait until ten. That seemed like a decent hour. After all, she did not have to know that he had been to an all-night party with Betsy. Instead she picked up the phone and called Ben.

"Sorry, Ben dear," she said when she heard his drowsy voice. "I did wake you, didn't I?"

"It's all right, Kate," Ben said, and cleared his throat. "I came in late. But it's good you woke me. I've got an appointment at nine-thirty. What's up?"

"Ben, who's Chuck Delany?"

"Oh, oh"—Ben laughed lightly—"you're getting into the groove, aren't you?"

"Groove or not," Kate snapped, "who the hell is he?"

"He's going to be the hottest thing since the pill." Ben became serious. "He's young, in his early twenties. I don't know how talented he is, but he does have that special something they claim everyone wants, although heaven knows what that is."

"He's willing to pose for the nude-male centerfold. What would you say he looks like in the nude?"

"Why, Kate Johnson, such intimacy at this hour of the morning?" Ben laughed good-naturedly.

"Oh, for Christ's sake." Kate was furious now. "Is he tall, muscular, thin, short? You know what I mean."

"Kate, I know damn well what you mean, and none of the mentioned features are of any interest to you, really. What you want to know is how his prick looks and that I'm afraid I have not yet investigated."

Kate blushed and was glad Ben was not in the room with her. And simultaneously the thought flashed through her mind, Is he gay? But she dared not ask.

"Okay, Ben"—Kate made her voice light—"I'll just have to check it out for myself." As Ben began to laugh, Kate realized the double meaning of her remark. "Oh, Ben, you know what I mean." She, too, began to laugh. "How about coming around to do my hair this morning?"

"At the office?"

"Why not? I washed it last night, and it looks a mess."

"I can be there around eleven."

When Kate hung up she wondered why she had asked Ben to do her hair. She could easily have waited. There were no pressing engagements and she was not seeing Jason until Friday night.

She tried to concentrate on her work; she dictated letters into the recorder, attended to several editorial corrections in the forthcoming issue, and made several business calls. She found it hard to keep her mind on what she was doing. Her mind was filled with the extraordinary face of Chuck Delany.

Kate looked at her watch. It was only nine-thirty-five but she could not contain herself any longer. Quickly she picked up the phone and dialed the Plaza. The operator asked who was calling and Kate gave her name. It seemed an unusually long time before she was put through. The voice that answered was low and guttural.

"It's Kate Johnson," she said forcefully. She was hardly able to control her excitement.

"Ah, the titless wonder from *Women Today*." He laughed softly. "The hungry one who wants a male nude."

"For the centerfold of the magazine," Kate said quickly, and forced a laugh.

"But of course," Chuck Delany answered, and the tone changed. "What can I do for you?"

"I'd like to meet you, if possible, and talk to you about what we're looking for."

"When?"

"How about lunch today?" Kate suggested, and knew that she had planned to meet with him that day and that was the reason she wanted Ben to do her hair.

"Let me see," he said thoughtfully. "It's Thursday," then, after a moment, "Oak Room at one o'clock?"

"I'll reserve a table," she said.

"See you," he said, and hung up.

Kate put the receiver down slowly. Thursday was the staff meeting day. But that was at four. She would surely be back by then. She pressed her hands together. Her palms were wet and she felt nervous.

It was one-twenty and Kate was beginning to get angry. The Oak Room was crowded and she knew several people there, who greeted her warmly, and a few had asked her to join their table. She had refused, but she was feeling foolish now, sitting alone nursing a drink she did not want. She gave herself ten more minutes. If Chuck Delany was not there by one-thirty, she decided, she would leave. She glanced at the headlines of the afternoon paper she had picked up before coming into the restaurant. They referred to a grisly murder of a young woman in Queens. Kate shuddered. The memory she had long since put aside of the robbery in her apartment returned briefly. That thought was followed by thoughts of Linda. Kate had put strong bars on the windows after that dreadful incident, which made the apartment considerably safer. Still her mind lingered for a moment on Linda. She hadn't yet come into the office when Kate left for lunch. Kate knew that she had no right to be annoyed at Linda's absence. In all the years Linda worked for *Women Today* she had never gone away on vacation. Instead she would stay in New York, calling in every couple of days to check to see that all was running smoothly. She would even take work home with her while ostensibly resting. Therefore, if Linda had decided to stay away longer, no one could fault her. Still, Kate was annoyed. They had discussed this before Linda went off and Kate had specifically asked Linda to come back for the Thursday staff meeting. It was an important one. Kate's annoyance suddenly began to turn into concern. She decided she would check up on the matter as soon as she got back to the office. She looked at her watch again. It was one-thirty. She picked up her bag.

"Boy, you sure sink into yourself when you think, don't you?" Chuck Delany was standing at her table and Kate looked up into the eyes in the photograph that had so captured her. They were even more compelling in person.

He was quite tall and was wearing a white shirt open to the waist, and several gold chains and a medallion gleamed against his nearly hairless bare chest. The wide leather belt emphasized the smallness of his waist and his narrow hips, which seemed smaller still because of his broad shoulders. The shirt sleeves were rolled up and Kate noticed his hands. The fingers were long and almost delicate, although there was a powerful masculinity about them. His hair was longer than in the photograph and seemed darker. His eyes were deep brown pools and the whites around them were blinding.

"How do you do," she said, and the breathlessness in her voice bothered her. "Do sit down."

"That's Chuck Delany with Kate Johnson," Kate heard someone say from a nearby table. As always, recognition pleased her.

"You're a helluva lot better-looking in person than you are on television," he said as he continued to

234

scrutinize her in an unabashed manner, "you know, without all that shit they put on you, the hairpieces and lashes and stuff. You're also a lot smaller than I thought."

"Will you have a drink?" Kate asked, deciding to ignore the back-handed compliment. She could not quell the fluttering in her stomach.

"Yeah," he said finally, and turned to call for a waiter. "I'll have a double martini, very dry," he said as the waiter came over, then, turning back to her, he leaned over and took her hand. "I do the ordering, okay?"

Kate lowered her eyes. Her hand resting in his embarrassed her. She bit her lip and wondered what she should say next.

The silence became awkward, since Chuck was obviously not going to be helpful. Even when the waiter brought his drink he did not let go of her hand. She watched him take a gulp and purse his lips. "It's as good a chaser for a hangover as any." He smiled. "What about you? Wanna eat?"

"I'm not particularly hungry, but I suppose we'd better order something." She was about to mention that she had been there since one o'clock but decided against it. It made little difference now that she was sitting across from him.

"How 'bout a chef's salad?" he asked, and without waiting for an answer, he grabbed hold of a passing waiter and ordered a chef's salad for her and another drink for himself.

She was tempted to make a remark about the second strong drink but stopped herself. He certainly looked as if he could take care of himself.

"You know," she said haltingly, "I'm embarrassed to admit it, but I've never seen you perform."

"Well, maybe we can remedy that."

"I mean on s-s-stage or screen," Kate stuttered.

"Well, as the saying goes, ya can't win 'em all, can you?"

"When is your next picture coming out?" She tried again.

"If I tell you will you go?"

"Of course I will." She tried to smile but her lips felt stiff.

"There's a preview tonight at Rizzoli's projection room. Would you like to come?"

"I'd love to," she answered too quickly. "What time?"

"Around nine."

"Just give me the address and I'll meet you there."

"No way. I'll pick you up."

"I'll still be at the office."

"I'll pick you up there."

Vaguely Kate remembered that Betsy had said she was seeing Chuck that night. She certainly did not want to be the third party to their date and was wondering how to word it or get out of her commitment.

"You're sure it's no trouble? I mean, if you have another engagement and are just being polite..."

"Do I really look like someone who would be that polite?" He laughed loudly, yet it was not a vulgar or unpleasant laugh. "I'll just shift a couple of things around and I'll come by for you."

At that moment her food arrived and Chuck let go of her hand. She started to nibble on her salad but found it impossible to swallow. The whole situation was preposterous. She was sitting in the Oak Room of the Plaza with a complete stranger years younger than herself and she felt like a sixteen-year-old virgin out with a superstar.

"No wonder you're so skinny," he said, breaking into her thoughts, "you don't eat."

She looked at him again and knew that all she really wanted was to go to bed with him. Somehow she was sure he felt the same. "You're really not going to eat that, are you?"

She shook her head.

"Would you like some coffee, or a drink, maybe?"

She shook her head again. This is insane, she kept saying to herself. After taking a deep breath, she cleared her throat.

"The truth is I never eat lunch and I'm not much of a

drinker." She felt better, more like herself. "The reason I was so anxious to meet you is that from what everyone says"—and she tried to smile—"you're *it*, and if you're really willing to be the first male nude for our magazine, I hope to be able to set it up as quickly as possible."

He looked at her seriously for a minute, then the smile, which she realized never really reached his eyes, returned. "That's a lot of bull, and you know it." He was silent for a minute. "You simply wanted to meet me, didn't you? Admit it. There's nothing wrong with that."

She was completely flustered, since it was true.

Finally, knowing that she had to say something, she straightened up, wiped her mouth with her napkin, folded it carefully, and looked directly at him.

"Yes, I did want to meet you."

It seemed an eternity before she lowered her eyes and was able to continue.

"How much do you want for posing for us?" she asked, and then felt foolish.

"Money?" His laughter broke out again. "You couldn't afford to pay me."

"You mean you'll do it for nothing?" She was flabbergasted.

"Have your lawyers draw up the release."

"When will you pose?"

"I'll set the date with Betsy."

Betsy's name jarred her. She did not want him to see Betsy. She did not want him to see anyone but her.

"Better still," he continued, "have the papers drawn up by this evening and I'll sign them when I see you." He paused. "Okay?"

He has the instincts of an animal, Kate thought.

"Why don't we go up to my suite and have coffee," he suggested casually.

Kate glanced at her watch. It was three o'clock. She had to get back to the office by three-forty-five at the latest to prepare for the staff meeting. The thought of Linda flashed through her mind. Of course Linda could run the meeting if Kate were not there. But it was possible that Linda would not come in.

"I'll have to make a call, though."

"You can call from my room."

He waved for a check and Kate reached out for it when the waiter came over.

"Don't ever do that again," Chuck said quietly, and for the first time she saw the cruelty she had seen in the picture. His lips grew thinner and a whiteness formed around them.

Kate was relieved that they were alone in the elevator. As soon as the door closed he took her in his arms and kissed her. She responded and found herself clutching at his back.

Once in his room Kate clung to him and he kept kissing her face, her neck, running his hand down her back, and pulling her closer to him. His body began to gyrate and she responded. He unbuttoned her blouse and she felt the cold metal of the chains against her bare skin.

"This is why you wanted to meet me," he whispered, and the passion in his voice matched hers.

She mumbled her agreement and felt his teeth biting her lower lip. It hurt but she did not cry out. Now I'm behaving like an animal, she thought. We're both behaving like untamed animals. It did not matter.

"The bedroom is over there," he whispered, "unless you want to make it right here," he added as he started to lead her toward the bedroom door, unzipping her skirt as they walked. Suddenly the phone rang shrilly and they both froze.

"Fuck whoever that is," Chuck said in anger.

Kate could never decide what made her push him away. "No, answer it, it may be for me."

"For you?" he gasped. "What do you do, leave messages with your office when you go out with a man?"

"Sue, my secretary, knows I'm having lunch with you and she probably tried to have me paged."

The ringing seemed more urgent now. "Please, Chuck, answer it."

It was Sue. It was nearly staff-meeting time and everyone was wondering if there would be a meeting.

"I'll be there," Kate said, blushing in spite of herself. "Let Linda start the meeting."

Linda, Sue told her, had not come in.

"All right," Kate said, and the feelings of unease she felt when she was reading the paper in the Oak Room came back. "I'll be there within a quarter of an hour." Before hanging up, she asked Sue to call Linda at home.

"You're really going to walk out on me?" Chuck asked.

Buttoning up her blouse, she walked over to him and put her arms around his neck. "Not because I want to." She tried to sound light but, touching him, she felt the desire for him that had been put aside for the minutes she was on the phone. "Oh, Chuck, I do want to stay, but I've got to go. It's my job." She picked up her bag, which had fallen on the floor. She looked at him. "Will I see you tonight?"

"Yeah," he said absently. "Sure, I'll see you later."

He did not see her to the door. Instead he turned his back to her and was lighting a cigarette as she picked up her coat and walked out.

28

The meeting went badly. Kate was unable to concentrate on what was being said. She had always enjoyed, actually reveled in the material her staff worked on and read to her on these occasions. Always she took in every word and would immediately file each idea into a category for future use. Layouts, pictures, type quality, colors, would form in her mind and she would be thrilled and would feel invigorated. This afternoon she sat and tried to listen but found her mind wandering. She accepted the individual papers on which the ideas were typed, trying to smile her appreciation, knowing that everyone was aware of her distraction. The fact that Linda was not there made it even worse. But even her concern for Linda was overshadowed by the recollection of being in Chuck's suite. Every time the thought surfaced, she lowered her eyes, afraid the desire she felt for him would show.

After everyone else left, Betsy remained to discuss a particular layout. Kate tried to concentrate on what Betsy was saying but for the first time since coming to New York, she did not care about *Women Today*.

"It's fine, Betsy," she kept saying, knowing it was not like her to go along that quickly with what Betsy wanted. She could not wait for her to leave. She wanted to be alone. She wanted to call Chuck.

As Betsy was leaving, she turned to Kate. "You met Chuck Delany, didn't you?" she asked, and it sounded like an accusation.

"Yes, I had lunch with him," Kate said quietly as she turned to her typewriter and started putting a sheet of paper into it.

"Attractive, isn't he?"

"Yes, very." Kate started typing.

"Is he going to pose?" Betsy persisted even though Kate pretended she was too busy to talk.

"I'm having a release drawn up by the legal department."

"When do you want me to photograph him?"

"Soon, I guess," Kate answered and stopped typing. "Why don't you set the date for early next week." Kate turned to look at Betsy.

"I could do it over the weekend," Betsy said coyly.

"If you'd like, by all means." Kate kept her voice even. "Are you sure he's free?"

"Oh, I do believe I can persuade him to be free." Betsy mocked her openly now.

"Then by all means, do it over the weekend before he changes his mind."

"Why should he?" Betsy asked.

"I don't know that he would." Kate tried to keep the irritation out of her voice. "He seems like a reasonable person. He indicated that he would do it and I believe him."

"Did he make a pass at you?" Betsy asked suddenly.

"Betsy, why don't you get off my back?" Kate felt her voice rise. "I don't interfere with your personal life and I would appreciate your staying out of mine."

"Oh, ho," Betsy exclaimed in triumph, "he did make a pass, eh?" She began to laugh and pushed the door open. Kate could hear the laughter even as Betsy walked away from her office.

"You filthy little bitch," she whispered. "You dirty, filthy bitch."

Angrily she turned back to her typewriter. "Now is the time for all good men to come to the aid of their country" was typed several times. She furiously ripped the page out of the typewriter. She had never behaved so foolishly in all her life. Clenching her teeth, she rang Sue and asked her to call Linda again. Putting a fresh piece of paper into the typewriter, she stared at the white sheet. She did not know what it was she was going to type; all she knew was she had to do something. She glanced at the clock. It was not quite six P.M. Chuck would be coming by at nine. She made a mental note to leave word with the elevator man that she was expecting a visitor. She thought of calling him at the Plaza but decided against it. She clasped her hands tightly, as though to restrain them from doing anything foolish.

The intercom buzzed. Linda was not home. She hung up and tried to concentrate her thoughts on Linda. What was the name of the convent she had gone to? Kate was sure that Linda had gone up to Canada to see the mother superior. Linda was very unhappy and lonely. Kate had never followed up her intention to befriend Linda outside the office. She knew now this was wrong. Linda needed friends. Or was it she who needed Linda? This thought upset her. Of course she needed friends. But if she had Linda as a friend, would she discuss Chuck Delany and the insane madness she felt for him with her or anyone else?

She buzzed Sue again and asked to be put through to Richard Roth, head of the legal department. She waited on the line. She wanted the release to be ready for signature before she and Chuck went out that night. There was something unreal about the situation and she knew that business had to be attended to before things got out of hand. Suddenly she wanted to call Betsy and make sure that the pictures were taken as soon as possible. She knew she would not agree to have him photographed naked after he made love to her. She would not be willing to have him exposed to the eyes of a million strangers. But would she want Betsy to photograph him? It would have to be Betsy. Was Betsy sleeping with him? The thought made her ill. It could not be. Betsy is a lesbian, she thought, trying to reassure herself. Or was she? Ben would tell her. She was about to pick up the phone to call Ben when Sue announced that Mr. Roth was on the phone.

She swallowed hard before she spoke, then she realized she could not even discuss the wording of the release.

"Hello?" she heard Richard Roth say. "Kate, is that you?"

"Yes, Richard." She found her voice. "Sweetie, I need some legal papers drawn up. A release."

"But you have the standard release in your office. Won't that do?"

"Well," she said, "come to think of it, we could probably work around it. But if I have any problems, can I ring you back? How long will you still be there?"

"I'll be here until six-thirty. So don't hesitate." Before hanging up, he asked, "What's it for, anyway?"

"I'll call you back." She ignored the last question.

She rang Hank and asked him to come in.

She explained the problem briefly. "Will the regular release we use for models do for Delany?" she asked finally.

"I don't see why not," he said thoughtfully. "Why, are you anticipating problems?"

"Not offhand, but it's a first and someone might raise some objections and I'd like us to be protected."

"Have you spoken to Richard?"

"Yes."

"And?"

She felt herself blush. "Could you do it for me?" she blurted out.

"Oh, Christ, Kate, you are too much. You get

yourself a male nude, and God knows you've been talking about it long enough, and now that you've actually trapped one, look at you. You're blushing like an elementary-school girl." He walked over to her. "You never cease to baffle me." He patted her on the shoulder. "Sure, I'll speak to him first thing in the morning."

"No, now," she said urgently.

"Why the rush?"

"I want him to sign the paper tonight before he changes his mind," she said quickly.

"You're seeing him tonight, I gather."

She nodded. "Going to see a preview of his last picture. I've never seen him on the screen. As a matter of fact, I've never even heard of him until today."

"That's what I like about you. An ostrich to the end. You parade around as though you were George Sand leading a bunch of liberated women to the battlefront when in fact you probably haven't had a proper lover in . . ." He stopped, realizing what he was saying. He knew she was sleeping with Jason, as did everyone. "Oh, hell," he said. "Give me a release and I'll call Richard from my office and have it typed up if there are any changes he thinks are needed."

"Be discreet with Richard. I don't want the board on my back just now," she called after him.

He was back within fifteen minutes, a retyped release in triplicate in hand. "This should do it," he said, handing the papers to her. "How about a drink?" he asked, and there was concern in his voice.

"I'd love one."

"I'll get it from my office. Scotch, isn't it?"

They drank in silence and Kate felt less tense. She wondered if she could talk to Hank about Chuck. She decided against it. Hank was Jason's friend. It would be tactless.

"Hank"—she broke the silence—"do you and Jean really have an open marriage?"

"It's closing up a bit." He smiled wanly at her. "We're not getting any younger and I'm practically over my 'menopause' and Jeannie, bless her soul, probably never really saw us as an open-marriage couple. Just played along with it."

"Was she ever unfaithful to you?"

"If she was I never knew about it, never wanted to know about it, and would have been damned annoyed had she told me about it." He sipped his drink. "Why do you ask?"

"I wonder if you'd mind her writing an article for us about open marriages."

"I'd break her neck if she did, and I'd break yours first for asking." He said it without anger but he meant what he said.

She lifted her glass to him. "Oh, for liberated men and women!" she said, getting back at him for what he'd said to her earlier.

They had several more drinks and chatted amicably about the magazine and people they knew in common. Kate was grateful for his company. Nine o'clock seemed a long time off and she dreaded being alone.

Hank left at eight-thirty. The office was empty. The building was probably empty. Kate got up and walked through the office cubicles of the people who worked for her. Looking around her little empire gave her strength. She was the boss of this organization. She ran it, she controlled it; she made it live. She was passing Linda's office and went in. It was bare except for a little picture of Jesus Christ and a small cross lying on the metal desk. She picked it up and held it close. Linda had her God. She wondered if she could call on God to help her now. She felt very lost, very confused, and very lonely. Something awful was about to happen and she could not guess what it would be. Replacing the cross on the desk, she walked out quickly. She felt like an intruder.

It was almost nine. The minutes ticked by and she itched to do something that would make time go by more quickly. She decided to try Linda once more. She had made no real effort to find out Linda's whereabouts. Quickly she pressed the button for her private line and called Janice.

"Sorry to bother you at this late hour," she said

when Janice came on the line, "but if you have a chance either this evening or tomorrow morning, would you check and see if Linda came back from Canada?"

"When did she go to Canada?" Janice asked in surprise.

"Well, as far as I know, she left ten days ago and was scheduled to come back today."

"I could have sworn I saw her a couple of days ago," Janice said.

"Well, all the more reason to check on her. She could have come back sooner and as I said, she was not due back until today."

"Sure, I'll go down later. I have a dinner guest but when we finish dinner, I'll run down. Do you want me to call you?"

"No," Kate answered, "I don't really know that it's that urgent. It's just . . ." She knew that she had no reason or right to worry. "I'll be out for the evening. If I don't get in too late, I might ring you. Or else I'll see you in the morning." She hung up.

The clock said nine and Kate started getting ready to leave, placing her coat on the chair. She filled her briefcase with papers she was taking home. She combed her hair for the tenth time, smoothed out her skirt, and put extra rouge on her cheeks. Looking closely at herself in the mirror, she put more mascara on her eyelashes and darkened the eyeliner on her upper lid.

The minutes ticked by and she picked up a magazine and began to skim through it.

At nine-thirty she rang up the Plaza and asked for Chuck Delany. They rang his room after inquiring who was calling. She asked for him to be paged. He did not answer the page.

She wanted to leave the office but dared not move. At ten o'clock, feeling completely miserable, she rang the hotel again. Still no answer in his room or to the paging.

Before leaving, she went into Hank's office and poured herself another drink.

It was a pleasant evening and Kate decided to walk. When she reached the Plaza, which was on her way, she went in on impulse. She called Chuck on the phone. There was no answer. She was relieved that he was out. What could she have said if he *had* answered?

Quickly she walked to the front desk and asked for paper and an envelope. Stuffing one of the releases that Hank had given her into the envelope, she scribbled a short note.

> Chuck, sorry I didn't get a chance to see the preview of your movie. I guess I'll have to pay at the box office when it's released. My bad luck. Please sign the enclosed and if you'll let us know when it's ready, I'll send a messenger along for it. Betsy will be in touch with you about a date for photographing.
>
> Kate J.

Handing the envelope to the desk clerk, she almost ran out of the hotel.

It had been the most devastating day of her life.

29

The ringing of the phone woke Kate. It sounded ominous and she made no effort to answer it. The ringing continued and still she did not move. She felt sick. Her head was aching. She raised herself from the pillow and looked around the darkened room. She was in her bedroom, and in a flash it all came back to her. When she walked into her apartment after delivering the note to the Plaza, she went directly to the bar at the far end of the room and poured herself a drink, and another and another. She wanted to get drunk, wanted to obliterate everything from her mind. It was the first time in her life that she had deliberately set out to lose her sense of being.

The phone stopped ringing. She turned on the nightstand light. It was just past midnight. It was less than two hours since she'd arrived home.

Laboriously she got out of bed and as soon as she stood up the room began to whirl and she felt she was going to throw up. She ran into the bathroom. She had not eaten all day and the retching did little to relieve the feeling of nausea. She pressed her head against the cool tiles and waited for the dizziness to disappear. Switching on the light, she saw herself in the small bathroom mirror. She looked awful. Her mascara formed black patches under her eyes, her makeup was streaked, and saliva had dried at the corners of her mouth. She poured cold water over her face and drank thirstily from the tap.

She was walking back into her bedroom, smearing cold cream over her face, when the phone started ringing again. She walked past it and got into bed. She wanted to sleep. Even tortured, dream-ridden sleep was better than lying awake listening to the telephone. Vaguely she wondered who it could be. Belinda was safe at school, Jason was away, and her mother wouldn't call at this late hour. Chuck? It wasn't possible. She hadn't given him her number and she was not listed in the phone book.

When the room grew silent again, she lay back on her pillow and closed her eyes.

The phone rang again and this time Kate jumped out of bed and with great force pulled the cord from the wall. A ripple of plaster fell to the floor and Kate stared, horrified, at the torn cord in her hand. It was so unlike her. She had a temper, a bad one, but she had always prided herself on her ability to keep it in check. She was not given to physical violence. It frightened her in others, it was devastating in herself. Pulling a cord from the wall was a violent act and she was terrified.

She rushed to the house phone.

"I tripped in the dark," she said to the doorman when he finally answered, "and I've pulled the phone cord from the wall." She paused, wondering why she was bothering him.

"Can I do something for you?" he asked, and she could hear his puzzled tone. "Do you need something urgently?"

"Well, no," Kate said slowly. "Well, yes, as a matter

of fact, could you call the phone company..." She stopped. She was being a hysterical woman. "No, there's no emergency, but if anyone should try to reach me and can't get through they might call the house number. Would you explain to them that my phone is out of order?"

"I'm sure the operator will explain that, Miss Johnson," he said politely, "but if someone does call, I'll let you know."

As she entered her bedroom she avoided looking at the torn telephone cord and crawled back into bed.

Her head was still aching but the nausea had abated. Now she allowed herself to review the events leading to these feelings of devastation.

Nothing extraordinary had really happened. She'd met a good-looking man and was attracted to him. He was going to spend the evening with her. He's stood her up. Was that any reason to feel so shattered? She had to admit she'd behaved equally badly when she walked out on him at the Plaza. They were on their way to bed when a phone call from the office made her scurry away like a fool. So for all she knew, he might have been deeply hurt at the rejection and was getting even with her. What, then, had caused this dreadful collapse of her strength and assurance? The answer came slowly. Because of Chuck she had abandoned her love for *Women Today*. For a brief moment that day she had actually let go of her most precious possession—her total commitment to her magazine. That a man, any man, could do that to her was horrifying. She certainly was not in love with Chuck Delany. He was too obvious, too narcissistic, much too young.

She compared her feelings for Tar with those Chuck evoked in her, realized there was no comparison. Tar was thoughtful and experienced, a man of substance. Everything about him was based on concrete achievement. She loved Tar but knew she was not willing to abandon her loyalty, her devotion, her passion for *Women Today*. She never even considered it. She wondered if her feelings for Jason, when they first met, would have withstood the test. It was a farfetched idea, for Jason, *Women Today*, and she were one. Actually, Jason was the most appropriate man for her to spend her life with. But he represented stability, an end to her dream of romance. And she knew that Chuck *was* that dream. He was romance!

As her thoughts came round full circle, she wanted Chuck even more. She had to see him again. She wanted him to make love to her, wanted to make love to him. She would resolve her problem with the magazine. Now that she knew her role at *Women Today* was in jeopardy because of him, she would be able to cope with it and win. The scene of them in the suite came back in a flash. She felt her whole body tremble with excitement at the thought of lying in bed with him, holding him, being held by him. . . . She felt herself blush even though she was alone in her room.

The house-phone buzzer catapulted her back to the present. She was suddenly alert, every dulled sense coming into focus. Automatically she looked at the clock. Only fifteen minutes had gone by since she'd torn the phone cord out of the wall. She ran to the front hall and picked up the earphone.

"Sorry to bother you, Miss Johnson, but there's a Miss Barker on the phone and she said it's urgent. What should I tell her?"

"Tell her I'll be right down."

She threw on a robe and ran to the elevator. It seemed an eternity before it arrived. When she reached the lobby, she ran to the house phone.

"What happened?" Kate realized she was shouting. "Sorry, Janice." She lowered her voice. "What happened?" she repeated.

"I think you'd better come over here, Kate. It's Linda."

"What about Linda?" Kate persisted.

"Just get over here, Kate," Janice said with authority, "now." She hung up.

As Kate was dressing she knew she did not want to go. Whatever it was, she was not prepared to cope with it.

Linda had done something foolish, gotten into trouble. It would be ugly and messy and Kate did not want to be a witness to it. Nor did she feel in any way that it was her responsibility. Linda was probably lonely and looking for sympathy. The recollection of herself waiting for comfort from Jason after her own robbery came back to her. "I will not tolerate weakness," Jason had said. "I cannot stand to look at people who are bruised, whether physically or mentally. I've always been like that. I insist that everything that's important to me go my way and when it doesn't, I kick it out, eliminate it, dismiss it as though it never was.... When I don't have control, I either get it or walk away from it."

Well, she thought stubbornly, I'm like that, too. It may not be nice, but that's who I am. She felt a strong affinity for Jason as she got into a cab and gave the driver Janice's address. Jason certainly got what he wanted out of life. She wanted much the same things. That was probably what he'd seen in her the first time they met. That strength, that determination, that overpowering need to survive, with only one goal in mind—to get to the top. That was the most important thing in the world—being on top.

"Here you are, miss." The driver stopped the taxi in front of her old building. It looked shoddy.

As she entered the lobby Janice was waiting for her. Wordlessly they got into the elevator.

"What happened?"

"There's been an accident."

"Another robber?" Kate asked haltingly as the horror of her own experience returned.

Janice preceded Kate into Linda's apartment.

The sight that greeted them was more dreadful than anything Kate had anticipated.

The room was flooded with a harsh light coming from a bare bulb dangling from the ceiling on a thin wire. The window shades were drawn and Kate looked around furtively. There were numerous empty wine bottles everywhere. Some were broken and the shattered glass was strewn all over the floor. Slowly Kate looked toward the bed. Linda, covered with a worn, filthy sheet, was lying on a bare mattress. Her head was completely bandaged and she was deathly pale. Kate moved toward the motionless figure. Linda's eyes were closed and the expression of serenity on her face made Kate think of her as she must have looked when dressed in a nun's habit.

"Is she dead?" Kate whispered as she looked up. For the first time since entering the apartment she noticed a man standing in the far corner of the room and smoking a pipe.

"No," he answered as he removed the pipe from his mouth. "But I doubt if she'll last the night." He came closer. "And frankly, I think we should get an ambulance and get her to the hospital before she does die."

"It was an accident," Janice said quickly. "Apparently Linda had been drinking very heavily for the last few days. She never went to Canada. The super told me she'd been locked in here for the past ten days, going out only to buy wine. She must have fallen and hit her head against one of the broken bottles." She caught her breath. "Kate, we've got to get her to a hospital. She's lost an awful lot of blood."

Kate looked at Janice and then at the man.

Janice caught Kate's bewildered look. "This is John Barker, my ex-husband. We were having dinner at my place when you called."

Kate continued to stare at him. He was tall and good-looking. His hair was gray and curly, cut in a modified Afro style. His eyes were blue and he had a mustache. He looked like a prosperous doctor and Kate wondered how Janice could have left him. They looked like man and wife, well suited to each other.

"Anyway, when we finished dinner, I went down to check on Linda," Janice continued. "I couldn't get in, there was no answer, and somehow I got nervous. I got the key from the super and the three of us came in here to find..." She didn't have to finish the sentence. "Anyway, John bandaged her up and stopped the bleeding. Now we've got to get her to the hospital." She paused briefly. "But I felt that you should know what was going on."

Hospital, ambulance, publicity, newspaper headlines. The thoughts raced through Kate's mind.

"If she needs hospitalization, why the hell didn't you call an ambulance?" Kate asked coldly. "Why did you need me?"

"There will be an awful lot of explaining to do, for starters," Janice said firmly, but Kate noticed her defensiveness. "She has no relatives that I know of, and I thought there should be someone around..." She stopped and suddenly her face grew white with rage. "Oh, for Christ sake," she said, losing her temper, "I thought you cared about her and would want to do everything possible for her. Besides, I was thinking of the publicity."

"Well, bringing me in certainly will make her more of a news item, wouldn't you say?" Kate snapped.

"Okay, ladies." John broke into the hostile dialogue. "You fight it out on your own time. Right now I'm going to call the hospital and get them to send an ambulance over." He walked toward the phone. "And then I'll have to call the police."

"The police?" Kate froze at the thought.

"It's an accident, there's no doubt of that, but it's a strange scene and the police get very sticky when something like this goes unreported."

"Before you call anyone, I'm going to call Hank Storm." Kate walked quickly to the phone and dialed Hank in Greenwich.

"Do you know what time it is?" Janice asked quietly.

"Late," Kate replied coldly. The phone rang several times before she heard Hank's sleepy voice.

Quickly she told him what had happened and mentioned that the police would have to be called.

"Oh, Jason will love that." Hank sounded more awake. "Give me the number and address and I'll call you back in a minute. And for God's sake, don't do anything until I call."

"Will five minutes make a difference?" Kate asked as she hung up.

"No," John said, and he sounded tired. "It really

won't matter whether she's DOA or if she's in this state when she gets there."

It took less than five minutes for Hank to call back. "Richard Roth will be over in a few minutes. Let him call the police. He'll know whom to contact. As for you, Kate, get your ass out of there," Hank said. Then, after a brief pause, "I'm sorry, Kate. I know how fond you are of her." And he hung up.

Kate related the message to John and Janice. "I'll leave now, and naturally, Dr. Barker, *Women Today* will undertake all expenses."

Walking over to the bed, she looked down at Linda. She was a nun and had always been a nun. All the time she worked for *Women Today* she was forcing herself into an unfamiliar world. She had gone against her nature, her needs, against who she really was. She, too, had demons driving her, and with time she lost control over them and they had pushed her over the edge.

As Kate was leaving she turned to Janice. "I'm sorry I sounded so heartless. I do appreciate all you've done."

Waiting for the elevator, she saw John walk over to Janice and put his hand on her shoulder. It was a protective touch and Kate envied her.

Dawn was breaking as Kate hailed a cab. It sped through the empty streets and Kate leaned back, allowing exhaustion to overtake her. As the cab stopped for a red light next to the Plaza Hotel, she was tempted to get out and go up to Chuck's room. Would he be alone, she wondered. The thought that he might not be restrained her. The cab moved on.

East End Avenue was deserted. Kate rushed to the entrance of her building and rang the night bell. As she waited she looked around and saw a white sports car parked across the street. Someone was sitting at the wheel, head thrown back. It made her nervous and she rang the night bell again. She saw a light go on in the lobby and within a minute the door was opened. Simultaneously the door of the sports car opened and Kate saw a man come running toward her. It took her a second to realize it was Chuck. They entered the lobby together.

"I've been waiting for you for a long time," he said, breathing heavily, and she could smell the liquor on his breath.

"I waited for you earlier this evening," she answered evenly, although her heart was pounding with excitement.

"I got all tangled up after you left the hotel," he said as they waited for the elevator to arrive, "and by the time I looked around it was eleven, and there was no way to reach you."

Standing beside him as the elevator shot up, she knew he was lying but it did not matter. He was there, drunk and unsteady, but he was there.

"How did you find out where I lived?" she asked.

"Well, let me tell you that was no easy matter. I finally got my agent to call someone from Celebrity Service and they gave him the address."

She did not answer. It made sense, but again she was sure he was not telling the truth. More likely than not, he'd got her address from Betsy.

As soon as they entered her apartment Chuck took her in his arms and kissed her urgently. "God, I've missed you," he whispered.

All her rage, all her unhappiness, all the pent-up misery suffered during the endlessly long night, evaporated. She found herself clinging to him.

"The phone won't ring again, will it?" he asked as he buried his head in her hair.

She burst out laughing hysterically as she pushed him away. "Not a chance," she said when she caught her breath. "Not a chance."

She walked into the living room, trying to compose herself.

"Would you like a drink?" she asked, then regretted the question.

"Just point me in the right direction and I'll make it myself."

She watched him walk toward the bar. He was like a slick alley cat, dressed in black Daks and a black

256

turtleneck sweater. His physical beauty was dazzling. Unable to restrain herself, she followed him and put her head on his back and circled his waist with her arms.

"I want you," she whispered, and her voice sounded strange to her.

He turned slowly, glass in hand, and kissed her lightly on the lips. Then, disengaging himself, he finished the drink in one gulp.

She moved away and went into the bedroom. She was behaving stupidly, but it made no difference. She undressed and put on a long robe over her nakedness. When she came back into the living room, Chuck had settled himself on the sofa, another drink in hand.

"Come here, babe," he said hoarsely, "I want you."

She slipped down beside him and within seconds he had her robe off and was kissing her. She lay back and felt his hands moving over her body, touching her breasts, her stomach, and finally her vagina. She closed her eyes and now his lips were searching her body, sucking briefly at her breast, her stomach, and slowly reaching her inner thighs. She caught his head between them and his tongue penetrated deep inside her. Reaching down, she pressed him closer. She heard herself gurgling with pleasure. She did not want him to stop. Chuck was playing out her fantasies. Her mind went blank except for the keen awareness of her body and the pleasure Chuck was giving her. Then something in her rebelled. She was thinking only of herself when she really wanted to give him pleasure, too. She began to mumble, almost pleading. Still he did not stop. Time ceased to exist when suddenly Chuck lifted himself up and she felt his fingers pressing his soft penis into her. His body movements were now frantic and within seconds he ejaculated. A small cry escaped from him as he rolled over and lay beside her, his head resting on her shoulder. They were both bathed in perspiration and except for the panting sounds coming from Chuck, the room was silent.

Kate could not reach her feelings. She felt numb. She had been made love to in this manner before, but always it was followed by a complete act of lovemaking.

The idea that Chuck was less than a perfect lover caused her physical pain and she wanted to cry out in frustration. She squirmed silently. Was it possible that this beautiful creature, this sex symbol, was not really capable of having a complete erection?

"God, I'm drunk," Chuck said, and his speech was slurred.

That's it, Kate decided with relief. Chuck was simply too drunk to make love to her properly.

Slowly her arms encircled him and held him tight.

"It's all right, my love," she whispered reassuringly. "It's all right."

He stayed in her arms, nestling like a child. "I love you, Kate," he said, and he sounded sleepy.

When Kate woke up she was still lying on the couch with Chuck sleeping peacefully next to her. Sunlight was streaming through the windows and she disengaged herself from him carefully so as not to wake him.

30

Linda was dead! Kate knew it the minute she stepped out of the elevator. There was a hushed silence in the offices of *Women Today*, although it was nearly nine-thirty and everyone was in. There was the usual bustle in the corridors, but it was subdued.

Sue followed Kate into the office and placed a sealed memo on her desk.

"It's from Richard Roth," she said, and Kate noticed that her eyes were red.

"Who told you?" Kate asked as she ripped open the envelope.

"There is a notice on the bulletin board."

It was probably Janice who had put it there, Kate decided. Well, it had to be done and it seemed like the most sensible way to go about it.

"Oh, Miss Johnson, it's too terrible," she heard Sue say, but she was absorbed in Richard's note.

> We've attended to everything. If anyone from the press contacts you or anyone else in the office there is to be no statement made and they are to be referred to me. The funeral will take place in Canada. We've contacted the mother superior of her convent and she is sending for the remains. Sorry about all this.

It was signed Richard Roth, Legal Department, Reid Publications.

"Sue," Kate said, looking at the girl, who was still standing by her desk with a forlorn look on her face, "it is tragic, but that's it. Now, would you get everyone, and I mean everyone, into my office as soon as possible. I don't care what they're doing, I want them to stop and come in here. It's important."

She glanced at the interoffice memo again. "The remains" were the words that struck her. All that was left of Linda and her aspirations was "remains" that would be shipped off to Canada to be buried in a nuns' cemetery under a name Kate could not remember. She sat back in her swivel chair and tried to conjure up Linda's face. Already it was blurred. She searched deep inside to feel if there was a sense of loss at Linda's death. There was none. Linda had played out of her league and failed.

The office filled up quickly and Kate gave specific instructions as requested by Richard.

"There will be a short statement to the press by the legal department and I think it is for the best," she said firmly as she looked at the sea of faces around her. Everyone looked sad and listless. Carol was grief-stricken and quite pale. The only pair of eyes that were staring at her with anger were Janice's. Kate lowered her own. She could not understand what Janice expected of her. "It was a tragic accident and I believe it would do no good to speculate to the press as to what brought it about. Linda was a devout Catholic and will be buried in Canada. I think we can serve her memory best by saying nothing more about it."

She said her words with finality and everyone got up to leave.

"Janice," Kate called out, "could you stay a minute?"

When the office emptied out, Kate looked inquiringly at the woman.

"Don't tell me you're interested," Janice said unpleasantly.

"Oh, come on, Janice," Kate replied quickly. "You know I'm interested. When did she die? Did she ever come out of the coma? Did she say anything?"

A small smile appeared on Janice's lips. "No, she never woke up again. She simply drifted off into death."

"Well, what happens now?"

"Happens?"

"Where do I find someone to replace her?" Kate asked, and immediately wished she hadn't said it.

"You're a monster, Kate," Janice said without feeling. "That's really all you can think about at this moment, isn't it?"

"Would you prefer my lying and pretending?" Kate was getting angry.

"I really thought you cared about Linda," Janice answered.

"Yes, I cared about her and if I have any feelings today about it all, it's that I blinded myself to thinking she was managing her life outside the office as competently as she did in the office. But I couldn't really help her. No one could. You lived in the same building with her—could you have prevented what happened?"

Janice lowered her eyes. She thought of all the times she'd wanted to see Linda, planned on stopping in to talk to her, then had avoided her because she did not want to get involved. In this respect Kate was actually right.

"I'm sorry. It's just that I must be exhausted," Janice said, and turned to go. Then, turning back, she said, "Carol is talking about a memorial service for her or something like that."

"I probably won't attend," Kate responded automatically, "but if Carol thinks she'd like to organize it, it's fine with me."

"Well, I'll let you know if we're going to have one. You can decide then whether you'll come or not." She paused awhile. "I think you should."

"We'll see," Kate answered, and wished Janice would leave. There were things to be done and the conversation about Linda was interfering with her thoughts. She would think of Linda on her own time and then she would figure out her feelings.

Story editor. That was her main problem at this moment. She could do Linda's job for a while without difficulty, but it would take up too much of her time. Time was suddenly precious. Having free time to spend with Chuck was imperative. She pulled her mind away from thinking of him. It was too distracting. She picked up the various story ideas Sue had placed on her desk and tried to concentrate.

Story editor. The thought came back. The obvious choice was, of course, Carol Butler. She was the only one who could fill Linda's place. But she rejected the idea as soon as it came to her. Carol was a threat and Kate was not going to stand for that. With new vigor she attacked the papers on her desk and the morning flew by.

When Sue walked in and announced that she was going to lunch, Kate was shocked to see that it was nearly two.

"I'll be back in half an hour," she announced quietly. "But I'd like to leave around four."

"Four?" Kate raised her brows.

"Carol organized a small memorial service for Linda at the church around the corner. It's at four-fifteen and since it's Friday, I thought you wouldn't mind."

Janice had not invited her and Kate felt offended even though she had indicated that she would not go. She detected a certain disdain in Sue's voice and understood it but resented it nevertheless.

"Will you be coming back after the service?" Kate asked, trying to avoid showing any emotion.

"No, if it's all the same to you," Sue answered slowly. She loved her job and had always respected Kate, but at that moment she hated her and was having a hard time hiding her feelings.

"It's okay," Kate said finally. "See you on Monday and try to have a nice weekend."

The buzzer on her desk sounded a few minutes after Sue left and Kate picked up the phone. "Yes," she snapped.

"Oh, boy, don't you sound friendly." It was Jason. She was pleased and displeased almost simultaneously. He had been away, and would expect her to spend the evening and the night with him on his return. Now he was back. She wanted to see him desperately but was not willing to give up her time with Chuck.

"Jason," she said, her voice softening, "what brought you back so soon?" Then she added quickly, "Although I must admit I'm glad you're here. You've heard about Linda?"

"That's why I'm back," he answered soberly. "It's a mess and I'm glad you kept a cool head and consulted Hank about it. It could make for bad, bad publicity." There was a pause. "I hear they're holding a memorial service for her."

He knew everything and Kate wondered about that.

"I've spoken to Hank," he continued, as though reading her thoughts. "I hope you're not fool enough to go." He wasn't asking, he was stating a fact. "All we need is for the press to get wind of it, and have you there with photographers taking pictures. It would blow the whole thing wide open and I wouldn't like that."

"I'm not going," Kate answered quietly. She had not planned on going but not for the reasons he was giving. She simply wanted to close a bad chapter. Suddenly she remembered that Jason had asked her to fire Linda long ago, and she had refused. He knew all along there would be problems with Linda.

"But I must confess," she continued, "it's been a shocking experience, Jason, and I didn't sleep at all last night." She had to get out of seeing him that evening.

"Yes, I heard," he answered almost sympathetically. "Go on home and rest up. I'll ring you in the morning."

At three-forty-five the door to Kate's office opened and Maggie Pearson came in.

"Kate," she said, and her voice sounded unusually

harsh, "I hear you're not coming to the memorial service."

"No, Maggie," Kate said, and felt guilty for the first time since she left Linda's apartment the night before. "No," she repeated more defiantly.

"Kate, I respect you, actually admire you, and in a way I love you, but I'm angry at you now." She came over to the desk. "Linda loved you more than anyone else in this office. She worshipped you. It seems little to ask to spend a miserable half hour in memory of her."

Kate stared at Maggie with astonishment. She knew the older woman was probably her most faithful friend and champion in the office. Now it was uncomfortable to see her so angry.

"Maggie, hold it," Kate answered defensively. She reiterated Jason's sentiments as though they were her own.

"You really think you're that important?" Maggie said sneeringly. "Do you actually believe that in this enormous city reporters have nothing better to do than come over to a crummy little church on the West Side in the afternoon to take pictures of the editor in chief of *Women Today* at a memorial service for one of her friends?" She was speaking quietly, but her anger was obvious.

Kate was stunned at what Maggie was saying. "I'm sorry you feel this way, Maggie," she said softly. Normally she would not have tolerated anyone talking to her in this manner, but she had to respect Maggie's sincerity and deep emotions. Also, she was concerned that Maggie might walk out, and she had troubles enough without that. She stood up and walked around the desk. "Let me mourn Linda my way," she continued, hoping her words would pacify Maggie.

Maggie burst out crying and Kate put her arm around her. "Oh, Kate, it's so sad, so terribly sad and wasteful."

Kate breathed a small sigh of relief. "Yes, it is wasteful, but Linda was too tortured to go on with her life here. It's a dreadful thing to say, but I suspect that with her enormous faith, she is happier now." She moved away. The scene she was playing was unlike her and she could not sustain it. "Forgive me for not going. It's for the best. We each have our own way of expressing our sorrow. I don't need a priest to stand up and tell me about Linda. He didn't know her and would just be mouthing words which would upset me. You see, I knew her better than most."

Maggie pulled herself together. "I suppose you're right, Kate." She wiped her nose with a handkerchief. "I'm sorry I was so harsh."

When she left, Kate returned to her desk and for the first time that day wondered why she had not heard from Chuck. She also realized that she had not called the phone company about repairing her telephone. Quickly she dialed the business office and asked if someone could come over to her apartment later in the day. It could not be done before noon the next day. She panicked for a minute, then reconsidered. Jason would not be able to reach her in the morning. She would have those extra hours with Chuck. She went back to her work and again became immersed in what she was doing. There were no interruptions, since everyone but a skeleton phone crew was gone. When she next looked at her watch it was nearly five o'clock. Again she wondered why she had not heard from Chuck. She called the Plaza, only to discover that he was not in and the front desk did not know where he was. He had not picked up his messages or his mail. She wondered if he were still asleep in her apartment. Now the fact that her phone was not working upset her. She was about to dial the doorman of her building but realized the day man would not know about Chuck. The night porter didn't come on until much later. She rose from her seat and went out to the front office. She hadn't received any calls since Sue left and she wondered if there was anyone at all around. The receptionist was reading a popular paperback and was oblivious to Kate's presence. There was a huge florist's box on her desk. Kate walked over and looked at the envelope. It was addressed to her.

She ripped the envelope from the box and tore it open. "With all my love, babe. See you." The card was signed Chuck.

"When did these arrive?" Kate asked, trying to control herself.

"Oh, Miss Johnson." The girl looked up. "I ... I ..." she stammered, "they arrived two hours ago."

"Well, what the hell were you doing out here?" Her voice was shrill with hysteria. "You little idiot, you fool, you ... you ..." She wanted to hit her, push her off the chair, grab her hair. "You're fired—do you hear me?—you're fired as of this minute." She was acting like a madwoman, but she couldn't help it. "Get out," she screamed, "just get out, now." With her rage still not in check, she picked up the box of flowers and rushed into her office. Once there, she ripped the top off and saw magnificent long-stemmed red roses. There were at least two dozen of them and they were breathtaking. She picked them up and felt hot tears running down her cheeks. At that moment she noticed an envelope nestled in between the leaves. She took it out, pricking her fingers as she disentangled it from the leaves, and tore it open. It was Chuck's signed release. Her soft whimpering turned to uncontrollable sobs.

31

A heavy snow was falling. It was the worst storm the city had suffered in many years and everything seemed to have come to a standstill.

Kate stood at the entrance of the Regency Hotel waiting for the doorman to find her a taxi. She clutched the heavy plaque wrapped in festive paper that she had just received at the cocktail party given in her honor in the grand ballroom of the hotel. A feeling of unabashed pride surged through her as she relived the sight of herself standing in front of the roomful of celebrities, all connected with the publishing world, who had come to applaud and congratulate her on her success as editor of *Women Today*. Jason had been there, and the pride in his eyes when the master of ceremonies gave her the award of

Editor of the Year made tears spring to her eyes again. Memories of her first days in the city flooded her mind. She had been so young and so naive. She recalled standing on the terrace of the hotel, looking down at the rushing mass of humanity, being frightened. Then she was determined to conquer the city at any price. Well, she had conquered it but now she wondered if the price she'd paid was too high. Somehow standing alone in the snowstorm on her way to an empty apartment made her wonder if the success was truly worth it.

"I have your taxi, Miss Johnson." The doorman touched her arm as he started to lead her toward the waiting cab.

"Hi, babe." She heard the voice and recognized it immediately. Her heart sank. Standing before her was Chuck Delany. He was drunk, a foolish smile on his face, a vacant, glazed look in his eyes.

She had not heard from him since the day he'd sent her the flowers. That was more than eight months ago. She felt paralyzed. All the scenes she'd rehearsed for just such an encounter flashed through her mind. She was unable to verbalize any of them as she looked at him now.

"Hey, babe, howya been?"

"Miss Johnson, your taxi," the doorman urged.

"She doesn't want it," Chuck answered for her as he began leading her back into the hotel. Her first impulse was to pull away and run toward the waiting car. She looked back briefly and saw that it was already taken. She felt numb as she reentered the lobby with Chuck.

"It's been ages, hasn't it?" Chuck went right on talking as he steered her toward the bar. "I've just been on one merry-go-round," he continued, "and every time I wanted to call you, something came up." He smiled sheepishly. "You know how it is?"

They were now in the dimly lit bar, sitting close to each other, and Chuck was ordering drinks.

"You do drink martinis, babe, don't you?" He turned to her after placing the order.

"You son of a bitch." She'd found her voice and now hissed the words through clenched teeth. "You filthy bastard"—her anger and humiliation took over—"you're too drunk to even know who I am." She stood up. "I don't drink martinis, Mr. Delany, thank you, and when you sober up, if you want to see me, call my secretary and she'll give you an appointment."

Turning away before the tears came, she ran out of the bar. She did not stop when she reached the street. She continued running up Park Avenue, feeling the tears streaming down her face, cutting icy grooves into her cheeks as the snow hit against them. Finally, exhausted, she stopped and looked around. She was on Park Avenue and Sixty-fifth Street. An empty cab driving slowly because of the icy roads came toward her and she stopped him, got in, and gave him her home address. It was Friday and she was expected at Jason's for dinner but at that moment she could not bear to face anyone. She would call him, she decided, and say she was ill. It was, of course, an idiotic thought. He wouldn't believe her.

"Driver, I've changed my mind. Take me to Thirty-eighth Street between Park and Lexington."

He grumbled for a moment but changed his course and headed downtown.

In all the time since she had spent the night with Chuck, not a day went by when she did not think of him. At first she jumped every time the phone rang, but he never called. As weeks passed she began reading stories about him in magazines and in gossip columns. He had walked out of the play he was to do on Broadway when he was offered a fabulous deal to do a movie in Hollywood. There had been a legal hassle in which he'd lied blantantly, insulted and threatened, until finally the lawsuit was dropped and he was let off the hook. He was the *enfant terrible* of the motion-picture colony and everyone quickly forgave him. He was named bachelor of the year or of the century, depending on which column you read. His pictures were everywhere. Each of his escapades was related in great detail. At the opening of his latest film he was mobbed and the police had to be called in to protect him. The opening was in New York and Kate had itched to ask Betsy if she had seen him, but she'd restrained herself.

The worst of it, however, was that her work was

suffering. In the past, work would soothe her, help her forget the hurts encountered in her day-to-day existence. Now even *Women Today* could not smooth out the feelings of desolation that plagued her. Receiving the award at this time was ironic. Sales had not yet started to go down, but she was sure that her neglect would eventually catch up with her. She dreaded the day but somehow was unable to pull herself together.

The cab came to a stop in front of Jason's house. After paying the driver, she rushed up the steps of the town house and rang the bell. Lee greeted her warmly as he took her coat and briefcase.

"Mr. Reid is not home yet, Miss Kate," the butler said, "but I've got a fire in the study and I'll bring up some hot tea."

"I'll have a hot bath first," Kate said absently as she started up the stairs.

Sitting in the study, dressed in one of Jason's robes, Kate stared blindly at the fire. She had several of her own garments in the house, but somehow she wanted to wear something of Jason's. She felt safer, more secure dressed in one of his robes. She breathed deeply and enjoyed the aroma of his tobacco clinging to the garment. As Lee served the tea she tried to eliminate the feelings that Chuck had rekindled in her.

"Mr. Reid called," Lee was saying. "He said he would be quite late and suggested you have dinner if you are hungry."

Kate was surprised and slightly hurt. This was unlike Jason.

"I'm not hungry, Lee." She was suddenly very tired. "I think I'll just turn in. I feel chilled and I'm exhausted."

As she walked into Jason's bedroom and got into the enormous four-poster bed she knew she could hold out no longer. Picking up the phone, she called the Plaza. Mr. Delany was not registered there. She called the Regency. He was not there either. She recalled Betsy's saying he lived in the Village. She called information, and was told there was no listing for Chuck Delany in the city. She thought of calling Celebrity Service, but it was after nine on a Friday night. There was no way to reach anyone there. She fell asleep, feeling hopelessly alone. She could not decide which disappointment was greater—meeting Chuck and not being recognized by him or having Jason let her down by not coming home on time.

When she awoke, it was daylight and Jason was sleeping peacefully beside her. She hadn't heard him come in and he hadn't awakened her. She moved closer to him and automatically he took her in his arms.

"Jason, please hold me close," she whispered. He did as she asked but did not wake up. She felt safe and protected, and knew that this was what life could be if she came to live with him. Habit, affection, respect, comfort, and complete appreciation of her work on her beloved magazine. It was not a bad bargain, yet she wanted to cry.

When Kate arrived back at her apartment she knew she would have to make a decision about her future. Having put water on the stove, she was waiting for it to boil when the doorbell rang. It was unusual for the doorman to let anyone up unannounced. She went to the door and looked through the peephole. It was Chuck.

"Please leave me alone, Chuck," Kate called out imploringly.

He rang the bell again, keeping his finger on the button so that the racket became deafening. Finally she let him in.

"Where the hell have you been?" he asked furiously as he walked in. "I've been calling and calling. I was up here till the wee hours of the morning. I nearly froze my ass off waiting outside this fucking house. I came back this morning and you were still not here." He stopped for a minute and looked at her. "Thank God the guy downstairs is a fan of mine and he let me come up."

Kate burst out laughing hysterically. "Where the hell have *I* been?"

He stormed past her. "You don't know who I am," he said, mimicking her voice of the evening before at the bar. "What bullshit, what utter crap!" He continued his rampage.

Kate followed him into the living room. He was sober and he really looked angry.

"Chuck, it's been a long time since I saw you last,"

271

she said quietly. "What did you expect me to do, fall into your arms and pretend nothing happened?"

He looked around at her. "Yes." He sounded like a little boy. "Yeah, as a matter of fact, that's what I expected. Although now that you mention it, you're probably right." He came over to her and put his arms on her shoulders. "I've missed you terribly, Kate." He seemed sincere and Kate became flustered.

"Chuck," she said firmly, pushing him away, "I'm not quite sure I understand what game you're playing. You spent one night here with me. You leave without a word. You've been in town several times since and you've never bothered to call or made any effort to see me. What was I supposed to think?"

"You're right," he said sheepishly. "You're absolutely right." He pulled her toward him gently. "I've behaved badly, and for some ungodly reason I thought you'd understand." He was looking directly at her and she felt her determination fade. She even began to feel guilty for not being more understanding. As he began to kiss her she knew he made no sense, knew she had nothing to feel guilty about, but she didn't really care. When he fell to his knees and was hugging her body against his face, all rational thinking left her.

Belinda unlocked the door to her mother's apartment and walked in. The place was unusually quiet and she decided her mother was still asleep. It was strange, since Kate was usually up and had hot croissants and coffee waiting for her when she came in on Sunday to spend the day. It had become a pleasant routine that both mother and daughter looked forward to. Placing her small overnight case on the hall table, she walked into the living room. The sight of an ashtray filled with cigarettes caught her eye. Next to it stood two half-empty cups of coffee. Kate never entertained anyone, as far she knew. In fact, one of the major turning points in her attitude toward her mother came when she began to realize how lonely Kate really was in spite of her so-called glamorous life.

With slight trepidation she turned toward the tiny hall that led to the bedroom. Her mother's clothes were carelessly strewn all over the floor and a man's trousers and shirt were lying nearby. A fur-lined coat was draped on the armchair near the entrance to the small hallway. Belinda was embarrassed and didn't know what she should do. Her hand reached out to touch the coat. It was of soft camel's hair and cashmere and it felt expensive.

Suddenly she heard a soft murmur coming from the bedroom, followed by laughter. In a flash Belinda rushed to the hall, grabbed her bag, and was out the door, closing it quietly behind her.

Sitting in a small coffee shop off East End Avenue, Belinda could see the building her mother lived in. She stared at it and tried to squash her feeling of rejection. It had taken a long time for her to come to terms with who her mother was and what her feelings were toward her. It was a confused and twisted road she had traveled with Dr. Sheckley, her therapist, trying to reconstruct a mother-daughter relationship that had been so abused since Kate abandoned her and went to New York. It was no simple matter to overcome the feelings of being rejected, unloved, passed over for a career. She grew jealous of the life she assumed her mother was living and tried grotesquely to be like her. For a brief period her friends in Dayton envied her, but then they began to make fun of that "sex-crazed Kate Johnson." Confused and having no one to talk to, she stole money from her grandmother, hoping to get a reaction. None was forthcoming. When she was introduced to marijuana, she discovered a friend in Elie. They grew closer, then Belinda found herself dominating Elie, and with that came a loathing and an end to the closeness. When she arrived at Windham, she tried again to emulate her mother. She wanted an identity more than ever. Although enrolled as Belinda Cameron, she immediately announced she was Kate Johnson's daughter. Here the reaction was different from that in Dayton. The young women at the school were simply disdainful. Although they borrowed and read Belinda's copies of *Women Today* sent to her from Kate's office, they always made fun of it and were merciless toward Kate. It was this disdain that stirred almost-forgotten emotions in her. A flood of memories rushed forth. Kate hugging her when she was a child, holding her, kissing her. A mother's pride and happiness for her child. A mother who read to her, slept with her, and soothed her. That mother of long ago loved her. Slowly her own feelings of distrust disappeared and the need to love her mother came back. With this emotion came the desire to protect her. In spite of her success, Kate was alone and Belinda knew it. After a while Belinda began to show some of that love and when she realized it would not be spurned, the healing process began.

Belinda felt better. She was on safer ground. She now turned her thoughts to the sight that had greeted her when she entered her mother's apartment. Her mother was obviously in bed with someone. Belinda knew very well that her mother was having an affair with Tar, although they were always discreet. Whenever they were up at his house, each had her own room and full privacy. But it was obvious that Tar and Kate were very attached to each other, and the love he felt for her mother was both touching and reassuring. Belinda never felt like an intruder but, rather, a member of an emotionally united family. What she saw in her mother's apartment was in poor taste and showed disregard for Belinda. That hurt, but not unbearably.

Reassured, Belinda walked over to the public phone and dialed Kate's number. It rang several times before her mother answered.

"Mom, I'll be over in a little while. I was driven in and I'm all the way downtown. I'll be there in about half an hour." And she hung up.

Kate hung up the phone and turned back to Chuck. She resettled herself close to him.

"My daughter will be here in a few minutes, darling."

He began to kiss her face, ignoring her statement. She returned his kisses and for a brief moment forgot what she was saying. She could not get close enough to

274

him. She wanted to melt into him, become part of him. She wanted to go on being petted, caressed, and mauled by this beautiful man who could not perform a simple act of fornication. It did not matter. He knew how to give a woman pleasure. He used every other part of his body to compensate for his deficiency. She was so absorbed in accepting his lovemaking that it was a while before she felt the guilt of accepting without reciprocating. He would not permit it. Several times during the night he tried to push himself into her. Sometimes he succeeded and actually reached a climax, but mostly he would mumble pathetically, making feeble excuses for his momentary inadequacy. Each time it happened she would lie passively, praying silently that somehow he would grow inside her, feel full manhood, achieve what most men did so easily and naturally. These thoughts were completely selfless. She was satisfied simply by being with him. She wanted it for him. There had to be some deep-seated fear and hurt that robbed him of his masculinity. Each muffled apology stabbed at her gut.

Reluctantly Kate pushed Chuck away and got up.

"Darling," she said hoarsely, standing next to the bed, "please get dressed."

He looked up at her, smiled, and reached out for her. "Come back, Kate. Come back, I miss you."

She had to control the impulse to lean down and kiss him.

"You've got to get going, Chuck. Belinda will be here and Sunday is her day with me." She was grateful that Belinda was late in arriving. She realized she had completely forgotten about her daughter and felt ashamed.

Quickly she went into the bathroom and showered. She was dressed in a house robe and had put on a bit of makeup when she came back into the bedroom.

Chuck was dressed and lying on the bed, smoking a cigarette.

"Do you really want me to leave?"

"No, I don't really want you to leave. But I'm afraid that like it or not, I'd rather you were not here when she comes." She did not know why she felt that way, but suspected that her obvious passion for Chuck would be too difficult to hide in front of Belinda. "You'll meet her another time."

While she was making up her bed the events of the night before came back to her vividly and she knew she was blushing.

"I'll call you later," Chuck said from the doorway.

"Oh, my God, yes." Kate was suddenly frantic. "Oh, Chuck, you will call." She rushed over to him and put her hand on his cheek, kissing him lightly on the mouth.

"Later, I promise." He blew her a kiss and was gone.

Kate and Belinda were having lunch and the atmosphere was pleasant. When her daughter first walked in, Kate thought she seemed strained, but her concern was quickly dispelled as Belinda plunged into stories about school, school friends, studies, and plans for the future. The girl's school work had picked up remarkably since she entered Windham.

"Tar thinks I can get into Smith," Belinda said enthusiastically.

"What does Miss Winston say?" Kate asked happily. Things had worked themselves out after all. Belinda was becoming her own person. She was lovely and bright, and planning a proper, productive future.

"She's all for it," the girl answered. "Did you know that Tar is really a very well-known professor in his field? Miss Winston says that he carries a great deal of clout and if he recommends..."

Kate busied herself pouring more coffee. Tar had given Belinda a home, a father's concern, a protective shield, an identity. The last thoughts made her pause. What had she given the child? The instinctive competiveness, so much a part of her, took over.

"Are you sure you want to go to Smith, though?" Kate asked seriously. "It's an all-girls school. I should think you'd want to try a coed establishment." She waited a minute. "What about Columbia or NYU, right here in New York?" It was a foolish suggestion, Kate knew, but she could not resist making it. "You've always wanted to live in the city." She did not mean what she was saying. She did not want Belinda in New York. That would interfere with her own life.

At that moment the doorman rang up on the house phone.

"I can't imagine who it could be," Kate said as she started clearing the table. "See who it is, sweetheart?"

"It's Chuck Delany," Belinda called out, and she sounded in shock. "Is it *the* Chuck Delany?" She ran into the kitchen excitedly. "Oh, Mom, do you really know him?"

Kate nearly dropped the cup she was holding and was grateful she had her back to Belinda.

The doorbell rang and mother and daughter nearly collided as they walked toward the door.

He had shaved and changed into fresh clothing. His dark hair was slightly wet from the dampness outside, his suntanned skin glistened from the cold. He was wearing his furlined camel's-hair coat over his shoulders. In his arms he carried an enormous bouquet of flowers. When he smiled, Kate felt her knees grow weak.

"May I come in?" he asked pleasantly as he looked at the two women staring at him.

"Of course, Chuck," Kate said as lightly as she could. "What brings you out so early in the day?" He was looking appreciatively at Belinda. Pride and jealousy briefly struggled within Kate. "Chuck, this is my daughter, Belinda," she said as she took his coat and handed the flowers to Belinda. "Sweetheart, put these lovely flowers into a vase. There's one in the kitchen."

The minute the girl was out of sight, Chuck leaned over and kissed Kate on the cheek.

"What are you doing here?" She was upset at the intrusion.

"I missed you," he answered, and ambled into the living room.

Belinda came back holding the heavy vase with flowers and Chuck leaped up to help her, placing them on one of the side tables. She had seen him in several films and on television. He was the idol of all the girls at school, yet looking at him in her mother's living room, knowing he had been to bed with her earlier in the day, made him repulsive. But it was not only that thought that made him abhorrent. He was a threat to Tar. Belinda loved Tar and secretly hoped that someday her mother and Tar would marry. She would then have a home and a real father. But Tar could never compete with someone like Chuck Delany. Her initial feelings of dislike deepened. There was something unhealthy about Chuck, she decided. He was downright revolting to her. She had a hard time controlling the impulse to ask to be excused. Instead she joined her mother and Chuck around the living-room coffee table. The strain was great, but Chuck seemed oblivious to it and spent the time telling them about Hollywood. Around four in the afternoon Chuck suggested they go ice skating. Kate laughed nervously. The years when most children learned to ice-skate she'd been busy struggling to survive.

"I haven't been on skates in God knows how long," she lied, and was surprised at herself.

"It's like bicycle riding," Chuck chided her. "Once you've done it you never forget it."

"Would you like to go?" Kate looked at Belinda.

"I don't really think we have time. I've got to catch the five-thirty train to school."

"Take a later train," Chuck suggested nonchalantly.

Kate caught the pretended nonchalance. "No, if Belinda does that she gets in too late and the school's car won't be there."

"Call the school and tell them to send one later," Chuck persisted.

Both mother and daughter objected and Belinda went to Kate's room to pack her belongings.

"Chuck, I'll take Belinda down to the train," Kate said as she stood up, "so if you'll forgive me, I have to get ready, too." She felt old.

"I'll wait for you here."

"I don't want Belinda to know about us."

"Are you ashamed of me?" Chuck asked mockingly.

278

"Oh, damn it, Chuck. You're making it very difficult."

He laughed softly as he got up, too, and took her in his arms and kissed her on the mouth.

"Sir, are your intentions toward my mother honorable?" Belinda asked lightly, and Kate pulled herself away from Chuck, blushing.

"Are you ready, darling?" she asked quickly.

"Sure thing, Mom." Her voice was soft and warm. Embarrassed as she was for herself, she felt unbearably sorry for her mother. This old woman with the young, boyish movie star. It was painfully grotesque.

Kate did not catch Belinda's pity. She smiled at her daughter. "I won't be a minute." She left the room reluctantly, aware that she was leaving Chuck and Belinda alone.

When she came back into the living room they were sitting opposite each other. Chuck was smoking a cigarette, Belinda was leafing through the latest issue of *Women Today*. They looked bored.

32

The first few months after Chuck came back were the happiest ones in Kate's life, although she soon learned that he had returned to her to escape from a scandal. Within days of his appearance the headlines exploded in every newspaper and magazine around the country. Chuck was being sued on a morals charge, having been caught in a drug and sex raid instigated by the mother of an underaged girl who had participated in the orgy. The producers of Chuck's new film could have coped with the scandal except that the girl turned out to be pregnant and she swore Chuck was the father. Kate was fully aware of how ludicrous this was. Chuck would hardly be able to impregnate anyone, but it was not likely he would use his impotence as a defense. Although the film was completed, the producers decided to withhold distribution while the lawyers tried to work out a deal with the girl. They figured the scandal would die down and the whole affair would soon be forgotten, but for the moment Chuck was advised to get out of Hollywood and stay out of trouble and out of sight for a few months.

The day the news broke, Kate came home from work to find Chuck sitting in a darkened room, newspapers strewn all over the floor.

"You had no doubt I'd take you in, did you?" she said quietly, trying to hide her deep hurt.

"I knew I could come to you, yes," he answered. It was the most forthright statement he had ever made to her.

Kate walked over to the couch where he was sitting and touched his hair. "Why me?" she asked in a subdued voice.

He took her hand in his and looked up at her. Even in the dim light his eyes seemed to sparkle. "I knew you'd understand because you're sensitive and bright, because you're your own person. You're strong and independent."

Kate held her breath. He was saying nice things but not what she wanted to hear.

"And I love making love to you, feeling you, being with you," he went on, and Kate felt herself melting inside. When he pulled her gently down beside him all rational thoughts were eliminated. He needed her and wanted her. That was all that mattered.

Kate's life from that point centered around Chuck. Knowing that he was waiting for her at home made her work at *Women Today* all the more exciting. She felt she was better able to understand her readers because of her feelings for Chuck. Occasionally she thought of Tar and tried to compare her feelings for him with her feelings for Chuck.

There was no comparison. Chuck was her fantasy. He played out every dream she'd ever had, asleep or awake. His physical beauty, his grace, his movements, his youth, never ceased to thrill her. She learned what pleased him and grew to enjoy the softness of his genitals, his silky pubic hair against her face when he allowed her to make love to him. On the rare occasion he would get a semblance of an erection and she would want to cry for this beautiful man who had been cheated of his masculinity. They never discussed it but she never stopped hoping that someday, miraculously, she would succeed in erasing the blocks that caused his impotence. Tar, on the other hand, receded in her thoughts and feelings. He continued to call and invite her to come and spend time with him. She knew Belinda went there often and had spent some of her vacations with him. Although it bothered her that her daughter was finding comfort in Tar's home rather than in hers, she was helpless in the face of her need for Chuck.

But she continued to spend her Fridays with Jason. It was inevitable that Kate's first fights with Chuck would be over those weekends she spent with Jason.

"Going off to fuck the boss?" He'd stand in the doorway to the bathroom as she tried to put on her makeup and dress for the evening. She did not know how Chuck spent his time during the week when she was at work, but she came home to be with him every evening. Fridays he was alone, and he hated being alone.

"Honey, believe it or not, we do have work to go over." She tried to laugh it off.

"I bet," Chuck would answer sarcastically, taking her in his arms almost viciously to try to delay her departure. It took every bit of willpower and discipline on her part to tear herself away and she was always late getting to Jason's. She knew Jason was annoyed at her tardiness, but her mood was euphoric and their evenings, after the first strained minutes, would be pleasant and productive.

But as time went by and Chuck became more restless their fights became more violent and abusive.

"Can he still get it up at his age?" Chuck would taunt her, and though she never answered, she was amazed that he would even refer to another man's sexual capabilities. She began to suspect that he had actually succeeded in denying his impotence to himself. It had first occurred to her when the news about the pregnant girl came to light. Chuck had seemed almost pleased. At the time she had dismissed the thought. Now she wondered.

"What will you do this evening?" she asked, ignoring his ugly remark.

"I think I'll go out and get laid," he answered nonchalantly, and Kate suddenly wondered if he actually saw other women during the day when she was at work. It even dawned on her that perhaps he couldn't make love to her because he was exhausted. It was an insane thought, but her jealousy created these feelings of paranoia.

To her surprise, Kate realized that since resuming her relationship with Chuck, she had begun to enjoy being with Jason more than she had in a long time. As much as she craved Chuck, she missed normal lovemaking, was no longer bored with her physical relationship with Jason. She was again receptive to him and reciprocated his every gesture, holding him inside her long after they had both been satisfied. If Jason suspected she was having an affair, he never indicated it. He certainly did not expect fidelity from her and she did not expect it from him. He seemed rejuvenated by their newly discovered pleasure as lovers and was warmer than ever.

Saturday afternoon she would rush home, anxious to see Chuck. Vaguely he began to remind her of Mike. Then, one Saturday, Chuck was gone. She waited all afternoon and evening for him to call or come home. On Sunday, when Belinda came, Kate was visibly distracted. Although they did not quarrel, Belinda left earlier than usual and a few days later called to say she would not be coming in for several weeks because she would be studying for exams. Kate, upset about Chuck, accepted the excuse. He showed up several days later as though nothing had happened and glowered at Kate when she tried to reprimand him. Fearing that he would leave again, she accepted him back without further comment. But their fights became worse.

One night she was late coming home from a live

television interview. She was exhausted and was looking forward to having a pleasant nightcap with Chuck before going to bed.

"Did you see the show?" she asked as she began to undress.

"Yeah, sure did," he answered, and Kate stiffened at his tone.

"What did you think?"

"You looked like a drowned cat." He sounded like a spiteful child. "Whoever makes you up must hate you, because you looked dreadful. As for your voice..." He started to mimic her and she ran from the bedroom and threw herself on the living-room sofa, shaking with embarrassment. She still felt insecure when appearing on camera but never dared ask anyone for an opinion. The comment from Chuck was shattering. He followed her into the living room. "And that outfit... God, where the hell did you get it, a thrift shop on Third Avenue?"

"It was made specially for me by Scassi," she protested in spite of herself. He was obviously jealous of her but was succeeding in hurting her deeply.

"Well, it sure doesn't look like anything on you."

She started crying helplessly and he continued the tirade awhile longer. Upset as she was, she knew he enjoyed torturing her. But from that day on, she stopped accepting television interviews.

One night shortly afterward, over a pleasant dinner in the country, Chuck suggested she run a feature story on him in *Women Today*. Kate didn't know what to say. The magazine had been running a monthly article titled "The Under-Thirty Bachelor of the Month." They were mostly eligible, successful, clean-cut business executives with solid backgrounds, university graduates, more often than not with prestigious social pedigrees. Chuck Delany hardly fit into any of those categories. That plus the unwholesome publicity still around made it impossible to use him.

"You won't, will you?" he asked when she didn't answer.

"Well, honey," she said, "fact is, we're really sticking to the business world . . ." Her voice faltered.

"I don't believe my ears," he said quietly, and his eyes became glazed with anger, the small, thin-lipped smile playing precariously at the edges of his mouth.

"You'd run me as a male nude, though, wouldn't you?" He could barely be heard.

"Oh, Chuck, I wouldn't do that now. I couldn't."

"The only reason you wouldn't is that you don't have a nude photograph of me." He continued now in an almost conversational tone. "But I bet you wouldn't hesitate if you had one and thought it would benefit your little magazine."

"Chuck, I wouldn't do it, no matter what." She was shaking.

Suddenly he burst out laughing. "Oh, I can see it," he said. "I've been behaving like an angel and if for some ungodly reason I had really posed for you and you printed it, it would ruin me all over again."

"Chuck, stop it," Kate said indignantly. "I wouldn't do anything to hurt you in any way and you know it. I'm in love with you. Don't you understand?" She meant every word she said and was surprised at herself. She had never before told anyone that she loved him.

"But by the same token you wouldn't help me either," he said soberly, "and you know it would help me no end if you did do a good, solid, clean story about me."

"I'll take it up with the board the next time we meet." She lowered her eyes as she spoke. It was a pathetic lie but there was nothing else she could do.

The final blowup came when he asked her to dinner at 21. For months they had been going to out-of-the-way restaurants to avoid the gossip columnists. But now time had done its work and Chuck was anxious to appear in public again. She noticed that he was taking better care of himself. He'd cut down on the drinking and started going to his barber again, and a sunlamp was doing its work as his face tanned and the sickly pallor disappeared.

"I hate Twenty-one," Kate lied.

"Well, we could go to Elaine's, El Morocco, Côte Basque—you name it."

She objected to each one with a feeble excuse.

"You won't be seen with me, will you?" he finally asked.

She protested but his anger exploded and he slammed out of the apartment.

After two weeks Kate began to suspect that he was not coming back. He had never stayed away that long before.

She tried to concentrate on her work, occupied herself with the endless details that went into running the magazine, but the idea of not seeing him again, not being with him, not touching him, was inconceivable. As discreetly as possible she tried to find him, but to no avail. When she read that his movie was about to be premiered in New York, she called his studio in Hollywood. They were polite but gave no information as to his whereabouts.

Her loneliness became unbearable. Coming home at night to an empty apartment was a nightmare. Chuck had become a part of her and she did not see how she could go on without him. She thought of calling Tar but rejected the idea. Ben was away working on a movie set. She even canceled her Friday dates with Jason. Finally she called Belinda. As she waited for her daughter to come to the phone she remembered holding Belinda the night Mike had walked out on her. The child had been her shield from loneliness then, now she was reaching out to her again.

"Hi, Mom." Belinda's lilting voice came through.

"It's been ages since you've been home, honey," she said, hating herself for doing it. "Why not try for this weekend?"

"Mom, I'm in the middle of exams." Belinda sounded sincerely upset. "I'm dying to see you, too, but it will have to wait until I'm through."

"When will that be?"

"In a couple of weeks." She paused briefly. "Are you all right?" she asked with concern.

"Sure thing, baby," Kate answered, trying to sound cheerful. "But you will come home then, won't you?"

"I'll come home before graduation and stay with you if you'd like."

Kate hung up the phone and looked around her living room. It was a lovely room but it lacked warmth. It did not look lived in.

33

The staff meeting of the first Thursday in June was over and as everyone was leaving the room Kate asked Hank to stay. She was nervous and upset. These meetings, once such a pleasure, were now a burden. In the past she'd started each meeting with an announcement about how well the magazine was selling. In recent months the news was hardly cheerful, and as Kate looked at the women sitting around her she wondered if their expressions hid a spiteful pleasure at her recent setback. She had to talk to someone, and Hank was the only one in the office she could trust to understand and maybe even help.

Hank took out his pipe and became absorbed in cleaning and lighting it. He felt uncomfortable at being asked to stay. Kate's behavior had become erratic and he did not want to be her confidant. Seemingly preoccupied with his pipe, he watched her through lowered eyes as she paced up and down the room, her fingers intertwined in a desperate grasp, her knuckles white. Everyone knew that she was having an affair with someone. Rumor had it that it was Chuck Delany. Hank was aware that she knew Delany from the time she had asked him to take care of the release for the centerfold nude. But that was months ago and the subject never came up again. He knew she was still seeing Jason, although sporadically. He and Jean had had dinner with them several times in the last few weeks. Kate always seemed completely relaxed and even amusing. He'd confided in Jean and asked her opinion.

"She's not the type who could carry two affairs at one time," Jean assured him from her perch of secure domesticity. "And it would certainly not be someone like Delany. He's a dreadful type and he's years younger than she is and let's face it, Hank, she's a prude of the first order."

Hank smiled at his wife's thought process. He almost agreed with her analysis. The rumors, however, persisted and as the days and weeks went by and Kate's state of mind deteriorated, he wondered if she really was juggling two affairs and finding that difficult to cope with.

"How about a drink?" Hank asked, unable to stand the stillness or Kate's frantic movements. "I'll get a bottle from my office." He stood up, wanting to escape.

"I've got some liquor in the cabinet by the window," Kate said absently. "And make mine very light." Then, looking at Hank, she smiled at his expression of surprise. "No, I haven't become an alcoholic, I just decided to leave some of the liquor we get from advertisers in the office."

Hank was relieved that he could busy himself with the drinks. Kate was not a drinker, he knew that, but he also knew that she had been drinking more than she could take. Too often when she came into the office in the morning, she would have a hungover look. The bottle of aspirin on the desk was constantly being replenished and the electric coffee maker was used to excess.

"What's happening?" she asked when he finally

turned around and handed her the drink. She was now sitting behind her desk.

"Happening where?" he asked, knowing full well she was talking about the drop in sales of *Women Today.*

"It's the third drop in three months," she whispered, and her voice trembled.

"Kate, honey, there are cycles in everything. We've been going gung-ho for so long—"

"That's the line for the board of directors, Hank," she said, her voice now tinged with hysteria. "Has Jason spoken to you about it?"

"J.C. wouldn't discuss it with me without discussing it with you first and you know that, Kate."

At that moment the phone rang. It was her private line and her heart began to pound furiously. It had to be Chuck, since only he and Jason ever called on that number and in recent weeks Jason had been avoiding her just as she was avoiding him. She was tempted not to answer. She looked at Hank and knew he would misunderstand her not taking the call even more than the conversation that would follow.

She picked up the phone slowly.

"Babe"—Chuck's voice came through and Kate pressed the receiver close to her ear, hoping the voice would not reach Hank—"when you comin' home?"

He was drunk and she wanted to cry with frustration, anger, and relief.

"I'm rather busy now," she said stiffly. "If you'll tell me where you are I'll ring you back."

"Who you got there?" He became indignant.

"I've just finished a staff meeting and there are several things I've got to attend to." She tried to keep her voice steady.

"It's not that motherfucker Reid, is it?" He became garrulous.

"I'll call in about fifteen minutes." She tried to smile.

"Don't you dare hang up, d'ya hear me?"

She hung up and Hank got up quickly.

"I'll run along, Kate," he said tactfully.

"But I've got to talk to you, Hank," she pleaded.

The phone rang again and she looked at it and then at Hank.

"Why don't you come to my office in a little while and we'll talk there." He nearly ran out of the office.

"Don't do that." Kate spoke through clenched teeth when she picked up the phone again. "I've got work to do, Chuck."

"I miss you, babe." He sounded sincere.

"Well, where the hell have you been for the last two weeks?" She hated herself for asking, aware that she would only antagonize him.

"You do miss me then, don't you?"

"Chuck, you've been drinking, haven't you?"

"You sound like my mother," he said angrily.

She bit her lip. She knew if she went on like this he might disappear again and she ached to see him.

"I'll just finish a couple of things and be home shortly." She changed her tone. "Yes, I do miss you, honey, dreadfully."

"I've got great news for you, babe," he said, forgetting his anger. "They're releasing my picture next week. I'm clean, kosher, and rarin' to go." He sounded like a child and Kate couldn't help but smile. "It'll be a big opening-night bash and I want you to be my date."

When she hung up, fear crept into her face. He had completely forgotten that their last fight was precisely about his wanting to go out and be seen with her and her not wanting to.

She sipped her drink and tried to pull herself together. Suddenly she remembered Hank and she got up quickly and rushed down the hall.

"Sorry I've kept you waiting," she said as she entered his office. He was leaning back in his swivel chair, deep in thought.

"It's okay," he answered, and sat up. "Everything straightened out?"

"Hank"—she plunged right into her problems—"what's happened?"

Hank looked at her for a long time. "All right, Kate," he said finally, clearing his throat, "I'll give it to you straight. You've been neglectful, forgetful, and let's face it, your heart's not in *Women Today* anymore."

She winced as though she'd been struck. "How can you say that?" she whispered. She felt a frantic gnawing in her gut as she dropped slowly into the large wing chair opposite Hank's desk.

"I hate to be the one to say it, I can assure you. But, Katie, look at the facts. Since Linda died, which was a long time ago, you've hired and fired four story editors. You try to do the editing yourself and you're good, but it takes time away from the things you should be doing as editor in chief." He paused for a minute. "Think of it, when did you last do a television interview or give a lecture or see the advertising people? You hardly have time to do the editing of what comes in from the various departments. You had a knack of bringing it all together. There was a style which was all yours and it was great. There's a sloppiness to the magazine now you would never have stood for before you got involved..." He didn't finish the sentence and Kate wondered if he knew about Chuck.

"Is it too late?"

"Nonsense," Hank said with assurance as he got up to pour himself another drink. The conversation was difficult. Kate looked like a beaten stray dog. "Just get yourself into shape and start doing the things you did before this slump." He looked around. "Everyone gets into a rut on occasion. But it's not too late. You're talented and you just have to pull yourself together."

He returned to his seat. "And for God's sake, get yourself a story editor."

"It's not that easy," Kate said defensively.

"Come on, Kate, you know damn well that Carol Butler could do it with her hands tied behind her back."

Kate swallowed hard. Jason had mentioned it once. She had objected to his interference and it had never been brought up again. Now Hank was saying it and she knew he was right. She also knew she would not take the suggestion. She simply could not afford to have someone like Carol in a position that threatening to her, especially at this point in her life.

"She got married," Kate said lamely.

"So?"

"She wouldn't have the time—"

"Crap," Hank interrupted. "She married Jim Krasna, who's a fine young man, and neither of them interferes with the other's career."

"What happens when she gets pregnant?" Kate fought on.

"Kate—stop it. Carol has been married for over a year and you know goddamned well she hasn't missed a day of work, hasn't rushed out without finishing a job. This is a different generation. They work things out differently."

Kate was silent, knowing Hank was right.

"Remember, Kate," Hank went on, "that's a cruel and hungry crowd of readers out there and we've grown stale."

She caught the plural reference and smiled feebly. "*I've* grown stale, you mean," she corrected him.

The intercom on Hank's desk buzzed. Kate's private phone had been ringing and Sue wanted to know if she should answer it.

Kate got up and walked over to Hank. He stood up and put his arm around her shoulder, hugging her warmly as he led her to the door. "You can do it, Katie. Remember, you pulled this magazine from the bottom to the top and it's still up there. With just a little more of your intuitive antenna working we'll be number one again in no time."

As she entered her office the phone was ringing and she rushed to it.

"I'm on my way, Chuck," she said coldly.

"You mad at me, Kate?"

"Oh, God, Chuck, we'll talk about it when I get home."

As she left the office building she resolved to put an end to her relationship with Chuck. It was sick and destructive. Chuck was a phase, whereas *Women Today* was her life. Somehow she had to find the strength to remove him permanently from her life.

34

"Will you be alone?" Ben asked when Kate called him to come and do her hair.

"I don't understand the question," Kate said, perplexed.

"Just a question," he answered evasively. "But *will* there be anyone else there?"

"Of course not. I'm alone," she answered. "I'm going out later to Chuck Delany's opening and I really look like the wrath of God and it would help if you came over."

When she hung up the phone, Ben's question bothered her. It occurred to her that in the last few months he had been doing her hair at the office. Then he had been away for a while. She herself was so preoccupied with Chuck that she had lost track of many things, and was not very observant when it came to anything other than her own personal problems. It had been a long time since Ben had come to her apartment. She decided she would ask him what it all meant.

She undressed, poured herself a drink, and ran her bath. Her nerves were raw. She did not want to go to the opening but she feared that if she refused, Chuck would simply walk away and never return. She wished again that she had the strength to split up with Chuck once and for all, but knew that she needed him, was hungry for his attention. He had been accepted back by the motion-picture industry and was staying at the Plaza at the studio's expense. The press, however, was not so quick to forgive and from all she read about him in the columns, they had not forgotten the scandal that had disgraced him. It did explain to Kate the reason he wanted her to be his date for the evening. The producers were obviously taking a risk with the hope the multimillion-dollar picture would be a success. They believed Chuck Delany was a valuable property and that his name would draw the crowds.

Kate was trying on clothes when Ben arrived.

"You planning an auction?" Ben asked as he stared at her bed, which was strewn with every dress she owned.

"Ben, I don't know what to wear," she wailed. "I want to look..." She did not know how to continue.

"You want to look great," Ben said, understanding her dilemma.

Quickly he began to sift through the mound of dresses on the bed. Kate wanted to look young, he knew that. He also knew her frilly dresses never really succeeded in achieving the look she wanted.

"It's a black-tie affair, isn't it?" Ben asked as he picked up one garment after the other, trying to hide his feelings of pity. Kate actually did not look bad for her age. Her skin, except around her mouth and upper lip, which was lined, was quite smooth. Her eyes were clear, her hair, now streaked ash blond to hide the strands of gray that had begun to appear, looked natural. Even her figure had not really changed since he met her. She was still quite thin except for her hips and a slight thickening around her waist.

"Here," he said finally as he picked up a silver silk man-tailored shirt and a long A-line skirt in a slightly darker gray moire.

"It's not dressy enough," Kate said, and sounded like a pouting child.

"It's a good look," Ben said firmly as he walked over to the open closet and started choosing a belt. He found a beautiful heavy Dior silver chain and extricated it from the others. "Where did you get this magnificent thing?" he asked in amazement.

"Dee Dee gave it to me years ago," Kate answered, and from her tone he could tell she had never worn it.

"Well, this is perfect," he said with authority.

She looked unhappy and Ben smiled. "Trust me, Kate. I want you to look smashing, too, believe me." He handed her the outfit he had chosen. "Now get dressed, then I'll do your hair."

"What made you ask if I'd be alone?" Kate asked as she started putting on the shirt.

"I didn't want to run into Delany," he answered simply, settling himself in the small armchair next to a skirted dressing table.

"You've known about him all along, then." She tried to cover her shock.

"I know the crowd he runs around with." He sounded uncomfortable.

Obviously Chuck had not been as discreet as she was. All through the time she spent with Chuck she'd never dared mention his name to anyone.

"Have you ever met him?" she asked, curious. It occurred to her that she should have talked to Ben. It would have helped.

"Once or twice." He did not seem to want to continue the conversation.

"You don't sound impressed."

"Kate, let's skip it. I don't like him. He's not nice people."

She wondered, as she had before, if Chuck was a bisexual. She was about to ask but, seeing Ben's expression, she decided to drop the subject.

She was now fully dressed and she stepped into her silver sandals.

"How do I look?" she asked tentatively as she stared at herself in the full-length mirror inside the closet door.

"Terrific," Ben said as she sat down, and he started doing her hair. He was concentrating on what he was doing, knowing that she was actually asking if she looked young enough to be Chuck Delany's date. "I know I'd be flattered to be seen with you." He smiled warmly at her.

Before Ben left, he hugged her as she waited at her door for the elevator to come.

"Kate," he said soberly, "it's none of my business, except you know how I feel about you. After tonight keep away from him if you can. Believe me, I know what I'm saying."

The elevator arrived at that moment and he stepped in and was gone before she could answer.

At eight-thirty sharp the doorman announced that Mr. Delany was downstairs waiting. Kate put on the gray moire cape, trimmed with light gray feathers, that went with the skirt. It was extremely flattering close to her face. She looked at herself for a brief moment. She looked well, she was sure of it, but she knew she could not compete with the starlets and young women who were bound to be at the opening. With a heavy heart she went down to meet Chuck.

In the huge black chauffeur-driven limousine Chuck was sitting in the corner of the car dressed in an exquisitely tailored tuxedo. The dress shirt was pleated and was in a bright pink that suited him and emphasized his tan. No one but Chuck could get away with it. His physical beauty was so breathtaking that Kate had to avert her eyes.

She settled herself at the far end of the seat and tried to pretend a nonchalance she did not feel.

"Come over here, babe," he said, pulling her toward

298

him. She didn't resist and moved over, nestling in the crook of his arm. "You really look nice, Kate," he whispered into her hair, "and I'm glad you've come. It means a great deal to me."

Kate knew he was being honest, still she was sorry she had come. Instinctively she knew it would end badly.

As the car pulled up to the Palace Theatre the crowd, realizing Chuck was the passenger, rushed toward the door and it took several policemen to push them away so that Kate and Chuck could get out. Microphones were shoved at Chuck and the flashbulbs were blinding. Kate wanted to run and hide. Instead she stood by the star of the evening and smiled feebly. When they were finally allowed to move into the theater, Kate was relieved. It was a star-studded audience along with the regular opening-night social crowd. Everyone looked glamorous and Kate felt dowdy by comparison. It never failed. No matter how lovely she looked to herself in her own home, the minute she was surrounded by people she felt out of place and wanted to escape. Suddenly she caught sight of Jason, standing with Carol Butler and several other people. Jason saw her and smiled pleasantly but made no move toward her. Carol Butler did not see her. She was involved in a conversation with a couple of men, who were laughing gaily at what she was saying. Neither of them was her husband. Kate had never met him, but she had been told he was a redhead. Upset as she was, Kate wondered if Carol had really succeeded in having a work life and a home life. She looked so poised, so confident, so... happy! More than ever, Kate envied the girl.

Kate remembered little of the movie. Later, at the opening-night party at the Starlight Room, she stayed only because she did not have the strength or the courage to leave. People kept coming up and congratulating Chuck. She knew some of them. They all knew her. She was too uncomfortable to appreciate this fact.

It was four A.M. when the driver delivered them to Kate's apartment house. Chuck did not get out of the car.

"I'm exhausted, Kate," he said drowsily. He was

drunk but not in a mean way. "I'll call you in the morning." He kissed her carelessly. He was already leaving her and she knew it. The thought frightened her.

When she left for the office the next morning, she picked up the morning papers. Pictures of herself and Chuck were on the front page. She read the reviews in the taxi. They were not very good and Chuck was attacked viciously. Several reviewers included references to his affair with the pregnant girl. Kate could not decide if she was pleased or not. She knew he would stay with her as long as there was still a smattering of scandal around him. To be used so blatantly was dreadful. To know that she would permit herself to be used made it even worse.

When she arrived at the office there was an urgent message from Jason. He wanted to talk to her. She put off calling him. It was bound to be a difficult conversation. He was obviously going to discuss the falling sales and bring up Carol Butler's name as story editor. Kate was out of arguments as to why she did not want Carol and knew she would have to give in. She buzzed Sue and asked her to have Carol come in. She decided to jump the gun and promote her before the talk with Jason. It was a defeat but she could do nothing about it.

She was waiting for Carol when Betsy walked in. Kate was annoyed at the intrusion but there was something about Betsy's expression that made her stop what she was doing and lean back in her chair.

"I've got something wonderful for you, Kate," Betsy said pleasantly. But the tone belied the statement. She took a large manila envelope from behind her back and handed it to Kate.

Slowly Kate opened the flap and took out a batch of glossy photographs. They were all of Chuck and two young women. All three were naked and were performing various unnatural sexual acts. Kate wanted to throw the pictures at Betsy. Instead she went from one picture to the next as though propelled by some outside force. The women in the photographs were young and very pretty. Their arms were thin, their necks long, their breasts youthful and firm. In each photograph Chuck's genitals were hidden either by a hand, a face, or a body. In several photographs Chuck was the onlooker while the girls were involved with each other, and the expression on his face was of supreme exhilaration. Kate had to make an effort not to show the jealousy, revulsion, excitement and overwhelming desire for him raging inside her. Finally she forced herself to look up at Betsy, who was standing quietly staring at Kate. Her eyes were unusually green and venomous. With superhuman effort Kate controlled her trembling hands as she placed the pictures on the desk and prayed her efforts at appearing calm would be rewarded when she spoke.

"What do you want me to do with these?" Her voice obeyed her. It lacked inflection but was quiet and distinct.

"Remember the centerfold nude?"

"We certainly can't use any of these for the centerfold."

"I know that," Betsy said. "This is the one I thought we could use." She handed Kate another photograph.

Kate reached out and took it from her. It was a magnificent color shot of Chuck alone, looking handsomer than ever, his eyes clear and the expression on his face enchanting and sexy. Here again he was posed in a way that did not expose his sexual organs, although he was completely naked. Kate was sure every reader of *Women Today* would react to him as she did. She swallowed hard.

"Yes, we could use this one," she said.

Betsy reached down to pick it up, but Kate put her hand firmly over it. "You can take the others," she said. "I don't need them. I'll just hang on to this one."

The two women looked at each other and the loathing between them was like a live wire. Finally Betsy smiled.

"Okay, Kate." Picking up the rest of the photographs, she put them back in the envelope and marched out of the room.

Kate didn't know how long she sat and stared at the picture on her desk. The desire, the passion she thought she could control, erupted and she felt herself trembling.

She lowered her head to the desk and waited for the feelings to pass.

She remembered little after that. Carol came in and Kate offered her the job as story editor. The girl accepted it coolly. She wanted to discuss salary and other benefits, but Kate suggested she talk to Hank. When Jason called she informed him of her decision and he, too, seemed cold and aloof.

"I think we'd better meet on Friday, Kate," he said. As in the past, he was commanding, not asking.

She agreed without any feelings of resentment. In a short space of time she had been reduced to the inexperienced girl from Dayton, Ohio, who stood in a room at the Regency, alone, feeling lost and frightened. After all the years in New York, knowing so many people, she actually had no one to talk to who would understand or care, and she had no strength left to fight.

Walking over to the liquor cabinet, she took a stiff drink. For the first time since taking over *Women Today*, Kate left the office at two P.M. She was feeling sick.

35

As Kate walked into the street the harsh June sun was beating down on the pavement. She started walking furiously and soon felt warm. It had looked like rain when she left the house in the morning and she had worn a raincoat. Without slowing her pace, she took it off. For a brief moment she felt as though she had lost or forgotten something. Then she realized that for the first time in many years she had no briefcase with her, no manila envelope stuffed with papers to work on at home. Her impulse was to turn around and rush back to the office, but her legs kept racing furiously ahead as though independent of her brain and its directions.

People kept rushing by her as though she were in a speeding car. Faces loomed up and disappeared. Car horns seemed loud and the noise made her head spin. She felt nauseated and looked around for a coffee shop. She had to drink something cold. Her throat felt as though something were lodged there and she was unable to swallow it. The coffee shop she entered was filled with the remnants of the lunchtime crowd and she could not bear so many people. She left quickly and rushed on, searching for a quieter place.

When she next looked up she realized she was on Third Avenue and Seventy-fifth Street. The restaurant on the corner was open. She had eaten dinner there once and remembered it as a pleasant place. She went in. There were only two people sitting at the bar. She sat down at a corner table and ordered a Bloody Mary on the rocks. Sipping the drink slowly, she felt exhausted and for the first time since looking at the pictures of Chuck, she let her mind face the pain they had caused her.

Several questions occurred to her. When were the pictures taken? Why had they been taken? Did Chuck know Betsy would show them to her? Had they planned it to hurt her and, if not, why had Betsy shown them to her and why today? The answer to the last question came immediately. Betsy was jealous of her for having gone with Chuck to the opening of his film. A long-forgotten scene—Betsy coming into her office with Chuck's picture, announcing that she had found a male nude for the centerfold—came back to her. Now that she thought of it, there had been something possessive about Betsy's manner when she spoke of Chuck. Chuck had stood Kate up that night and now she recalled that Betsy had indicated that she was seeing Chuck later. Kate had never asked Chuck about that evening. As a matter of fact, she never asked any questions. Her hysterical infatuation blinded her to too many things. Suddenly she remembered that Ben had said he ran around with people who knew Chuck. It was Ben who'd introduced her to Betsy... but Betsy was a lesbian and Ben was a bisexual. Kate's mind began to spin, and she closed her eyes. Minutes later she opened them and looked around the dimly lit room and saw a woman staring at her. The woman was strangely familiar. She was middle-aged, haggard, unkempt, and unattractive. With panic Kate realized it was her own reflection in the smoky mirror lining the opposite wall of the restaurant. She gasped with horror. Is that what she really looked like? A middle-aged lady? She looked at the check, counted out the change, and walked out of the restaurant in a daze. Hailing a passing cab, she got in and gave him her home address. She would call Ben, she decided, the minute she got home and make him tell her about Chuck, Betsy, himself, the people they went with. Chuck and Betsy were obviously laughing at her behind her back. Now she wondered if Ben were, too. But Ben was her friend. Ben was actually the only friend she had in New York.

The taxi pulled up in front of her house. She pressed a couple of bills in the driver's hand and ran into the building. The doorman called something after her but the elevator door closed and she did not hear what he said. As she was looking through her purse for her key it occurred to her that Chuck had a set of keys and might be there. For a moment she hesitated. She had been so overwrought she had not taken it into consideration. She realized she did not want to see him. Suddenly he revolted her. She took a deep breath and put the key in the lock. As the door opened she heard a woman's voice and Chuck's gurgling laugh. Haltingly she walked into the apartment. The living-room drapes were drawn and Kate made out the image of Chuck standing in the middle of the room wearing a short bathrobe she had given him. A woman was standing in the doorway leading to the kitchen. Kate flicked the light switch, flooding the room with light, and she realized the woman was Belinda. Chuck and Belinda! Her mind snapped.

"You little tramp," she shrieked as she rushed toward her daughter. "You filthy, conniving, rotten brat." Her voice sounded strange in her ears. "Get out—do you hear me?—just get out, get out, get out..." She could not stop the rage, the hysteria.

"Mom." Belinda stared at her. "Mom, stop it."

Kate heard Belinda's voice but could not make out

what she was saying. Then, with a force she did not know she possessed, she hit the girl across the face. Angry as she was, she caught a look of bewilderment on Belinda's face, which changed into an expression of deep pain, and the girl rushed out of the apartment, slamming the door behind her.

Kate looked around. The silence was deafening. She saw Chuck light a cigarette and walk slowly toward the bedroom. She moved to block his way and felt as though she were moving in slow motion. She lifted her arm to strike him. It felt heavy. He grabbed her hand and held it in midair until it hurt and she cried out in pain as he pushed her away, continuing his way into the bedroom. Frantically she followed him, lunged at his back, and began tearing at his robe, ripping it until her fingernails dug into his naked back.

He turned abruptly and hit her with the back of his hand, catching her across the eyes. For a moment she was blinded. Thrown back against the doorframe, she needed every bit of strength she had not to fall. She felt faint but held on.

"You're evil," she whispered hoarsely when she finally caught her breath, "completely and thoroughly rotten." The room came into focus again. "How could you?" she went on. "With Belinda? She's only a kid."

"She's no kid," Chuck said mockingly as he started dressing quickly. "And God almighty, having to make it with you all these months, a dried-up, frustrated, middle-aged hag." He grinned. "I deserve a young cunt for a change."

"And what the hell could you do with a young cunt?" she asked, and felt the laughter rising in her throat.

She saw him stop dressing and turn toward her. She stopped laughing and went on deliberately. "You with that pathetic limp dead thing between your legs. You're not a man, you're a eunuch, or as close to being one as you can get without being castrated." She caught her breath for a second, then continued, her voice now almost in control. "You're right, though, it had to be an aged, frustrated hag who could take that endless sucking or perverts like Betsy and her little dikes who could excite the sexless sex symbol of the world."

"You're really crazy." His laughter was ugly and Kate wanted to cover her ears. "You really think you can put yourself in the same category with Betsy or any of the others." He sneered. "Let me tell you there is more woman in any one of them than there ever was in you. You'd give your eyeteeth to be in the place of those girls. You'd crawl to have one of them want you, touch you, make love to you. . . . As for having an affair with a man, in your little puritanical brain you could never begin to imagine what it's like to have an affair with anyone." He stopped but Kate caught an uncertainty in his voice, and she pounced on it.

"Maybe you're right," she said coolly, fully in control now. "But I'll tell you something. Remember when you made fun of Jason Reid? Can he still get it up, wasn't that your question? Even I, the middle-aged, frustrated hag, needed to feel a man inside me. I reached a point where I gladly went there on the weekends, just so I could have a man. You need fantasies with little girls and boys, I wanted a man."

Chuck was fully dressed and Kate saw his face take on a strange look. She had succeeded in hurting him and she was frightened.

"Just because I couldn't make it with you doesn't mean I couldn't make it with anyone else." The smile, the thin smile she remembered from the past when his anger surfaced, appeared. "Well, I've served my prison term." He walked past her, grimacing with disgust as he avoided touching her. "It's been a nightmare, I assure you. As for my being revolting, you enjoyed every minute of it and if nothing else, we all had a good laugh at your pathetic infatuation."

He was gone and Kate could not move. They *had* all laughed at her. Chuck, Betsy, Ben, and God knew who else. All the time she was involved with Chuck they had simply used her as a butt of their jokes.

Vaguely she heard a whistle and it took her a minute to realize it was the teakettle. It had been whistling for quite a while. She walked into the kitchen. Belinda had put the kettle on and the water was now boiling furiously. Turning down the fire, she walked back into the living room. It was as she had left it in the morning. Suddenly she felt very calm. She put out the lights and walked to the door and double-locked it. Returning to the bedroom, she picked up Chuck's torn robe and folded it. She undressed slowly, carefully smoothed out the sheets and fluffed the pillows, and got into bed. She felt as though she were watching herself do these things, her mind reciting her actions: "Now I'm straightening the bed, now I'm getting into it. . . ." She wanted to sleep. Whatever had to be thought about or attended to would wait. Now she had to sleep.

Belinda rushed out of her mother's house and only after sitting in the park outside Gracie Mansion for a long time was she able to bring herself to think rationally of what had happened.

It was all so obscene and frightening.

She had come home hoping to surprise her mother. Her exams were over and her grades were excellent. She had decided to spend the week before graduation in New York with Kate, knowing it would please her. The visit would also give her an opportunity to tell her mother about Robert Reid. She had met him one weekend when she was visiting Tar and she did not know if she was in love, but they were taken with each other and she was planning on spending her summer vacation with Tar and him in London. Tar was pleased and Belinda was sure her mother would be, too.

When she entered the apartment, the sunlight was streaming through the living-room windows and her heart was bursting with happiness. She had bought flowers and was putting them in a vase when she realized someone was standing at the kitchen doorway. For a minute she was frightened, then she saw it was Chuck. All her feelings of cheer evaporated.

"It's been ages since you've been in town," he said pleasantly. "Wasn't because you were trying to avoid me, was it?"

She walked past him into the living room.

"I didn't know you were still around," she said coldly.

"Oh, your mother is quite smitten with me, little girl, or didn't you know?"

"Are you living here?" she asked, ignoring his remark.

"On and off," he answered as he sauntered behind her into the living room.

"Well, is this the on time and how long does it last?" she asked as she went back into the kitchen. The man was completely repulsive to her and she could not stand to be in the same room with him. She was sorry she had come. It was a mistake to try to surprise her mother. Somehow she had blocked him out of her thoughts. She had read the story about the pregnant girl and assumed that Kate had long since gotten rid of him. The whole affair had been totally out of character for her mother, anyway.

"It depends," Chuck said, having followed her again.

"What depends?" she asked, forgetting her question.

"If I'm living here or not."

"Okay," she snapped, "I don't really feel like playing games with you, Mr. Delany. If you're living here, I'll leave and no one will be the wiser."

"You can stay, little girl," he said sweetly. "I'm through. I've paid my debt to society and I can now go back to the land of the free."

"Does my mother know that?" she asked, suddenly concerned. Chuck Delany was a cruel man and instinctively she knew he was capable of hurting Kate deeply.

"I don't really give a damn," he answered.

"How about a cup of coffee?" she asked, changing her tone. Obviously he meant a great deal to Kate, and Belinda did not want to cause her mother unhappiness. She didn't want to be the cause of his leaving.

"Well, that's more like it," Chuck said, and smiled. Walking over to the windows, he pulled the blinds shut. "The sunlight is killing my eyes. Do you mind?"

Belinda hesitated briefly. "No, not at all."

She filled the kettle and lit the fire. Standing in the doorway, she looked at him. He was dressed in a short bathrobe; his muscular legs were exposed and were extremely well shaped. The belt tied tightly around his waist showed the extraordinary contours of his body. Now, in the darkened room, Belinda was frightened.

"You're a very beautiful girl," Chuck said in a husky voice as he stood staring at her.

"Thank you, Mr. Delany," Belinda answered, trying to decide what she should do to break the tension.

"You don't like me, do you?" He continued to stare at her.

"I haven't given it any thought," she answered.

"Yes, you have," he said, his voice rising. "You goddamned well have given it thought. That's why you haven't been around for so long."

"I've had exams," she answered defensively, and was annoyed at her discomfort.

"One of the reasons I stuck around your mother was that I kept hoping you'd show up."

"That's an ugly thing to say." Belinda got angry.

"You don't think I came around for your mother, do you?"

"I really don't want to go on with this conversation," Belinda said, turning away.

"Look, I can have any broad around, and most of 'em would give their eyeballs to go to bed with me."

He's stupid, too, Belinda thought bitterly. She felt even sorrier for Kate.

"I'm sure you're wanted by any number of women, Mr. Delany, but you're not my type," she said condescendingly. She resented what he'd said about her mother. She was uncomfortable, knowing her mother was having an affair with this fool, and she resented the way he spoke about Kate. "As a matter of fact, Mr. Delany," she said coldly, "if you must know the truth, I find you quite repulsive. And you're right, I stayed away because being in the same room with you makes me feel sick."

He burst out laughing and started toward her when the door opened and Kate came in.

Sitting on the bench, Belinda instinctively raised her hand to her face as the memory of her mother's slap came back to her. Yet in spite of her own unhappiness she knew her mother was in a worse state. She considered going back to the apartment to explain that nothing had gone on between herself and Chuck, but decided against it. Kate would be too upset to listen, and Belinda wanted to avoid the possibility of a further confrontation with Chuck.

She looked around and saw children playing in the sand box while others were being pushed along on the swings. They were laughing and enjoying the warm, pleasant weather of early summer.

"Higher, Mommy, higher," a little blond boy was calling, and a young woman, laughing gaily, pushed the swing and the child squealed with joy. A blurred picture of herself as a child came back to her, but she could not remember her mother ever taking her to a park. Kate was always too busy. It was Elie or her grandmother who went with her. She had not seen them since she'd left Dayton and for a brief moment she felt guilty. She wrote to them often and they answered her letters. Her most recent letter to them was an invitation to come to her graduation. She had meant to talk to her mother about that, too. Tears started streaming down her cheeks. After all this time she felt removed from them. Tar and Robert, they were her family now. The thought of them eased her feelings of loneliness. Suddenly she wanted to see Tar. He'd understand. He would help her.

She got up and walked back to her mother's building. The doorman lent her five dollars and she took a subway down to Grand Central Station. While waiting for the train to Amherst she called Tar and asked him if she could come up.

He was immediately concerned, aware that she had planned on spending time with Kate.

"Is she all right?" he kept asking.

"Tar, I'll tell you all about it when I get there."

"Should I call her?"

Belinda hesitated. She loved Tar and knew he had

311

been hurt the last few months when Kate said she was too busy to come up to visit. "Tar," she said tentatively, "it can wait till I get there."

Sitting on the train heading for Amherst, Belinda watched the scenery rush by and tried to rehearse what to say to Tar that wouldn't cause him further pain yet would tell him enough to find a clue to her own actions and feelings. Every child, she thought, had a right to expect things from a mother. Yet here she was behaving as though she were the mother and Kate the child.

36

Kate opened her eyes and looked around her bedroom. The pleasant morning light was coming through the thick curtains swaying gently in the cool river breeze. I am very calm, she thought, why am I so calm? These feelings were usually reserved for Sunday, when her schedule was fluid. It was not Sunday, yet she didn't have the frantic feelings of having to rush and get things done. She looked at the clock and saw that it was six A.M. She had been asleep for over twelve hours. She had gotten into bed yesterday afternoon. With a jolt, the events of the day before flooded back into her mind and she started to shake. She put her hands to her eyes as though to shut out thoughts. Then, with a purposeful movement, she flung the blanket off and stood up. The room whirled and she sat down quickly. She felt warm and damp. Her breath came in short gasps. She lay back on her pillow. For a minute the room spun around her. Finally the sensation stopped and she felt weak and depleted.

When she next woke up the phone was ringing. As she reached over to answer it she noticed that it was now nine-thirty A.M.

"Are you all right, Miss Johnson?" It was Sue.

"I don't feel too well," Kate confessed, and her throat ached as she spoke. She tried to sit up but felt too weak. "Is anything the matter?" She tried to speak naturally.

"I was simply worried about you, Miss Johnson," Sue was saying. "Should I call the doctor?"

"No," Kate said quickly. She hated doctors. "I'll get up and have some tea and call you in a little while." She hung up, feeling exhausted. She barely made it to the kitchen and realized she could not possibly cope with making tea or doing anything at all. She crawled back into bed and knew she would have to give in and see a doctor.

"It's nothing serious," Dr. Simon said as he finished his examination and put the stethoscope away. "You're exhausted, run down, and quite hysterical."

The words made no sense. She had never felt calmer in her life. She was about to protest but felt too tired.

"I'll have the pharmacy send up some medication and some tranquilizers. You're to take both as prescribed," he ordered.

"I hate taking pills," Kate protested.

"I know," he answered gently, but maintaining the stern, authoritative manner to hide his concern. There was actually little wrong with her physically but her psychological state was precarious. She was suffering from an emotional state close to a nervous breakdown. He dared not say it and even regretted mentioning the hysteria. He did not know her well, but over the years he'd seen her on occasion either in his office or at parties in Jason's house. The way she drove herself always amazed him. There were times when he wanted to say something to Jason about it but knew it wasn't ethical. Now he was worried. "And you're to stay in bed for the rest of the week. Do you understand?"

Tears began to slide down her face. She had never been ill and had no idea how to cope with sickness. The thought that there was no one to take care of her made more tears come.

"Do you have a maid?" Dr. Simon asked, knowing instinctively her concern.

"Letty comes in twice a week," she answered, sniffling like a child. "Tuesdays and Fridays."

"Good," the doctor said with satisfaction. "It's Tuesday and you simply tell her to come every day this week until you are well enough to get up and do things for yourself again."

He was packing his bag when Letty walked in. Letty had been with Kate for several years, although Kate rarely saw her, leaving for work before the woman came and arriving home long after she was gone. Still, over the years, a bond had formed between them. Letty was a fifty-year-old black woman who admired Kate Johnson and was always leaving little fan letters for her employer whenever Kate appeared on television or there was a photograph of her in the newspaper. Letty was a celebrity in her neighborhood because she worked for the lady who ran *Women Today*.

Letty and the doctor walked out of the bedroom, leaving Kate to doze off from a shot the doctor had given her.

Briefly the doctor explained to the older woman what had to be done and Letty swore to take care of everything.

"She can have up to eight tranquilizers a day," he whispered, not wanting Kate to hear him. "I want her doped up as much as possible for a few days. Sleep will be the best cure. And for Christ sake, unplug her phone and keep daily problems away from her. I'll speak to her office and tell them to lay off for now."

Letty sat in the living room when she finished her daily chores and slept on the living-room couch, guarding the phone so it never rang more than once. She had worked for other people all her life and knew without being told what had transpired in Kate's household since Chuck Delany came into her life. She had hated the man from the first and knew it would end badly. She felt it was over now, and she was pleased.

Kate slept most of the time. Even the disturbing dreams vanished as she fell into the deeper sleep induced by medication.

"What day is it?" Kate asked one evening as she sipped some tea Letty had brought her.

"Thursday, Miss Johnson." Letty was relieved to see some color back in her employer's face. Kate was sitting up and her eyes were clear for the first time since she'd fallen ill.

"Good God." Concern rose in her but did not bloom into full panic. "You mean I've been in this state since Tuesday morning? Have there been any calls? Has anything happened that I should know about?" The unfamiliar calm returned.

"Your office called several times and your secretary told me to assure you that everything was under control. A Mr. Tar called and said to take good care of you. Mr. Reid called and sent beautiful flowers. Ben came by and sat with me one afternoon." Letty smiled happily. "He's a nice young man, Miss Johnson. And Miss Belinda said she will see you at her graduation and that you better be well by then."

Everything was in order. Her office, Tar, Jason, Ben, Belinda, they were all there waiting for her to reenter their lives. All except Chuck. She mulled the name over in her mind, and for a minute she felt a dull pain. Quickly she pushed him into the back crevices of her brain. She could not cope with him, yet.

On Friday Kate called Jason.

"Can a convalescent come and visit you this evening?" she asked almost coyly.

"I was expecting you, Kate." He sounded as he always did. "We had a date, remember?" He cleared his throat and Kate knew he was pleased to hear from her.

"Besides, we have a great deal to talk about, you know."

"Yes, we do," she agreed. Her mind was clear and alert. She was feeling well and strong. *Women Today* was in trouble and she was expected to bring it back to life.

Dinner was over and Kate sat in Jason's library, looking at material sent over by Sue.

"It's amazing how behind one can get in just a few days," she mused as she started sorting out articles and photographs for future issues.

Jason grunted and continued sifting through his papers.

"I've asked Sue to arrange some television interviews," Kate continued, "and I'm going to work on setting up appearances in various women's clubs and schools that want me to give lectures."

"Don't overdo it, Kate, just yet," Jason said offhandedly. "You were sick, you know."

"Sicker than you know," Kate answered slowly. "But let's face it, Jason, I've got to get in there and pitch. We're in pretty bad shape."

"It is bad," Jason agreed without rancor, but Kate felt embarrassed. It was shameful the way she had neglected *Women Today*.

"You'll also have to find a new art director," Jason said quietly, and Kate felt herself go numb.

"A new art director? What happened to Betsy?"

"She quit," Jason said, not looking up at her, seemingly absorbed in something he was reading.

Kate put down the paper she was holding and clasped her hands in her lap. Her mouth felt dry.

"Betsy quit?" Her voice was hollow.

"She eloped with Chuck Delany." Jason now looked up at her.

Kate felt a small throbbing in her neck. She put her hand to her throat, hoping to stop the tremor.

"Betsy and Chuck...married?" She tried to smile.

"Yes," Jason said quietly, "the press had a field day with it." He continued, "I'm afraid Delany is not their favorite star."

317

Kate took a deep breath. "Well, I'm glad we have Carol. It would have been a mess to have to look for a story editor *and* an art director."

"Never thought of that," Jason said, and he sounded relieved, although looking at him, Kate could not decide if he actually was aware of what she was thinking or feeling.

Kate did not stay late that evening. She was still weak from her days in bed and she was amazed at how solicitous Jason was when it got to be ten o'clock. "No reason to overdo it the first night out," he said as he kissed her on the forehead while they waited for the car to come around.

"Jason"—Kate leaned against him briefly—"I will be able to get the magazine back on its feet, won't I?"

"I think so," he said soberly, "but it will take doing." He was very serious and it frightened her. She looked up at him. "Katie, I've never lied to you and I don't intend to start now. When you first started, it was from scratch and in a way it was easier. Now there are rumblings of competition all over the place. You've set a pace which others are trying to emulate. We're still out front, but you'll have to put everything you've got into it to make up for lost time."

She wanted to protest. It hadn't been that long.

The car came and Lee jumped out to open the door for her.

"I'll make it." She looked directly at Jason before stepping into the waiting car. "I'll think of something."

Jason smiled warmly. "I'm sure you will, Katie."

Kate got into the limousine, sank back into the upholstery, and with no warning, her mind exploded with anger and thoughts of vengeance. Betsy and Chuck married, and *Women Today* dying. Chuck caused her to let her magazine go. *Betsy and Chuck married.* Her mind ground out the phrase. Forcing total acknowledgment . . . Betsy quitting, Chuck and Betsy laughing at her. "It's not your magazine." Betsy's voice came back to her as though the woman were sitting in the car next to Kate. Jason had once told her Betsy hated her. Kate knew it but ignored it. The idea of breaking up the staff was unthinkable. She had a winning team and was afraid to make any changes. "It will take doing," Jason had said. Kate threw her head back and stared up at the darkened sky through the back window of the car. It was all because of Chuck, and Betsy was party to it. They had set out to ruin her and they'd nearly succeeded. Suddenly she began to laugh, oblivious to Lee sitting up front and looking at her through the mirror. They wouldn't ruin her, *she* would destroy them first. Betsy had given her the weapon. The nude photograph of Chuck was in her safe at the office. Running a naked picture of Chuck in the centerfold would end his career. The board of directors had been against the use of a male-nude centerfold, but she would get around it.

As Kate was undressing she looked at the bottle of tranquilizers sitting on her nightstand. She picked up the bottle and put it away in the bathroom medicine chest. She didn't need them. She couldn't afford to dull her senses in any way. A centerfold of a nude Chuck Delany was the next project and she needed all her faculties to push it through.

37

When Kate returned to the office she threw herself into her work as she had not done since Chuck had come into her life. To everyone's amazement she started a staggeringly large series of television and radio appearances. No show was too small and no appearance too demeaning. She gave interviews to many reporters, from the largest newspapers to student papers. She even agreed to go on a college tour. In the past the mere suggestion would have sent her into a state of depression. She had not gone to college and was too insecure to face young, brash coeds. Now the tour was being arranged and she was all set to embark on it in February. Still sales did not go up. The summer issues were weak as a result of her previous neglect. Persuading advertisers to hang in was the most difficult chore. They had no sentiment. Proof of rising sales would have to come first before they would commit their advertising budget to *Women Today*. It was a vicious circle but Kate forged ahead, goaded by only one thought—her overwhelming need to destroy Chuck.

It was at a weekly staff meeting that Kate decided the nude would be in the Christmas issue.

"I think we have it all now," Carol said after everyone had presented his thoughts for the December issue, "except the 'Special Christmas Surprise Gift' pages."

The minute Carol mentioned the annual centerfold feature, which Kate had introduced when she'd first come to the magazine, she knew what those pages would contain. She put her hand to her face to hide her elation.

"Any suggestions?" she asked when she felt she could control her feelings and simulate interest.

"How about a wedding spread?" Maggie asked and everyone laughed. Maggie's oldest daughter was getting married and Maggie was completely involved in planning the wedding. "You know what I mean," she went on good-naturedly, "pictures of the bride, the clothes, the setting, the food, and you've got to believe the food will be exquisite."

"It could be very pretty," Janice said thoughtfully, "and since we don't have text on those pages, the effects can be lovely."

Janice looked sad, Kate thought as she looked at her. She was the most respected beauty editor in the business and Kate felt fortunate to have her.

"Or we could do a winter ski-resort affair in a remote lodge in Utah," Dee Dee suggested. "The clothes this year are sensational for that sort of thing. We could do a whole spread of what is needed to make it romantic even though rustic—fireplaces, candlelight, and how to rough it elegantly."

Everybody nodded except Allyson, who was noncommittal. She had grown less aggressive since Cliff had his last stroke, and seemed almost fearful of voicing an opinion. Kate wondered if she still harbored the loathing for her that she felt when Kate first took over the magazine. She was sure Allyson would still jump at a chance to take over but was doing nothing to further her wish, as she had at the beginning.

"I don't know," Carol said thoughtfully. "I wish we could do something more daring, more hip, more avant-garde, something no one else ever did. Make it a *real* surprise gift for the readers."

It was when Carol spoke that Kate suddenly realized the centerfold nude would not only serve her purpose as far as Chuck was concerned but would also benefit *Women Today*. It would be a first for any magazine and would get them back into that uncontested place at the top of the selling list. And since there was no text involved, the board of directors would never know about it until the magazine was out. They had come to trust her completely and although text was still sent over for their approval, Kate doubted that they even looked at it.

"Why don't you think about it, Carol," Kate said, and looked at the beautiful young girl and wondered if she would ever have the imagination to think up a male-nude centerfold. Carol was very good at what she did. Jason had been right to suggest her for the job of story editor, but Kate was no longer worried about being pushed out by her. With all her brightness, her awareness, and being part of the Ivy League crowd filling the chic bars of New York, she did not have something Kate had. She did not really know the audience of *Women Today*. She never would, because she had a basic disdain for the women from places like Muncie, Indiana, or Biloxi, Mississippi. Carol was a valuable story editor but only as long as she worked for someone like Kate, who had done her homework and never forgot what she learned.

By the time the list of articles was in for December, Kate had approved the wedding scenes for the centerfold. It was an expensive layout but Kate consoled herself with the thought of being able to use it another time.

August was drawing to a close when Dee Dee came

into Kate's office and announced the layout was ready. "It's all there, Kate, and I think it's really the most beautiful issue we've ever put out."

Dee Dee had mellowed over the years. She was now living in the lap of luxury with a retired clothing manufacturer and was still extraordinary-looking, but Kate no longer felt in awe of Dee Dee. Kate also knew that Dee Dee had lost interest in taking over *Women Today*, which made for a more relaxed relationship.

"So if you'll look it over, I'll be off," Dee Dee said, and smiled happily.

Kate was aware of Dee Dee's vacation plan for the end of August and had been depending on it.

"How long will you be gone?" she asked with interest, and was pleased at her ability to be so cool in the face of what she was about to do.

"I'll be back toward the end of September."

"Great." Kate smiled, too. "Why don't you run along. I'm sure it's all perfect. I'll look at it before I leave the office."

When everyone had left for the day, Kate went to the art department. Tony was the only one around.

She glanced at Dee Dee's layout. It was truly beautiful.

"Off to the printer's in the morning," Tony said, wiping his hands and preparing to pack up for the day.

"Almost," Kate said quietly as she sat down on one of the high stools.

Tony was putting on his jacket and Kate's tone made him look at her.

"What do you mean, almost?"

"I want a different centerfold."

He looked uncomprehendingly at her.

Slowly Kate took out Chuck's picture from the envelope. She had it all planned except for this confrontation with Tony. He would be the one she had to trust. She was aware of his complete loyalty to her, knew his admiration for what she had done for *Women Today*. She also knew him to be a conservative, almost prudish man.

Tony stared down at the nude photograph and gasped audibly.

"And, Tony, I don't want anyone to know about it until the issue comes out," she said, trying not to sound nervous.

"Kate," Tony whispered, "Kate, you can't mean it."

"Oh, I mean it, all right." She laughed softly.

"They'll hang you for it."

"I doubt it," she answered pleasantly, almost conversationally. She didn't want him to worry. "As you know, Tony, we're not doing as well as we were and it's up to me to come up with something different. We did it once, remember? When I first came, you were shocked at my ideas but I was right. We made it then. We were up there, right on top for an awfully long time. Well, we're sliding down and unless we can shake them up again, we'll go right down to the bottom." She waited for a minute until her words sank in. "This will do it, I promise you."

"Kate, are you sure this is right?"

"More sure than I've ever been of anything in my life."

He looked down at the picture again.

"Have it statted for the spread first thing in the morning and just send it all off to the printer." She was now the editor in chief again and she was no longer asking, she was giving orders. "And, Tony, this is between us."

When he left, Kate continued to sit deep in thought. She was jeopardizing Tony's job and they both knew it. She would manage, since she had a contract, but would Tony? She could not think of that now. She would face it when the time came.

38

It was Monday before Thanksgiving and Kate had the December issue on her desk when the phone rang and she was ordered to the meeting room of the board of directors.

All seven board members were seated around the table with Jason at the head. The magazine was on the table and they were all staring at her.

"I can't imagine what got into you, Miss Johnson," Thomas Grand said almost before she sat down, his face white with anger. "Especially since we specifically said a male-nude centerfold was out of the question."

Kate looked at him and remembered the first time she'd sat in front of the board of directors and Thomas Grand had been angry at her ideas. He looked older, she thought, and wondered if she, too, had aged as blatantly. She glanced over at Jason and, as in the past, knew he would not say a word in her defense. She had no idea what he was thinking. At that first meeting he was fully aware of her plans beforehand and had encouraged her ideas. This time she had fooled everyone and she was sure he didn't relish the idea that she had put something as serious as a male-nude centerfold in the Christmas issue without consulting him.

"I believe it will give an enormous boost to the sagging sales," she said simply as she looked back at Grand.

"It's obscene," John Davon said. "I'll bet you every advertiser we have will cancel and frankly, I won't blame them."

"Why don't we wait and see," Kate suggested politely. She was feeling light-headed and strangely removed from the angry mood of the meeting. "The magazine will be out on the stands on November twenty-fifth. It's still three days away. I believe you'll be pleasantly surprised."

"We're not waiting any three days, Miss Johnson," someone said, and Kate didn't bother to look at the speaker. She had worked too hard, concentrated every bit of energy she had since June for just this moment, and her feeling of triumph seemed to insulate her from the angry faces around the table.

"We've decided to disperse with your services as of right now," the voice went on.

She heard the words and they made no sense. She turned to look at Jason. She could not tell what he was thinking.

"I don't think you can really do that," she said quietly, now directing her attention to the men sitting around the massive table. "I do have a contract, you know, and it has four more years to go."

"There's a morals clause in it," someone said.

For a minute her poise was ruffled. "There's nothing immoral in that photograph," she said, controlling her increasing dismay. She had thought about it at the time she plotted this act, but somehow she never believed it would come to this. She looked at Jason again. A small smile was playing on his lips as his eyes met hers.

"We think there is," Davon said angrily. "All of us are convinced this picture is obscene and as far as I'm concerned, this meeting is over. Personally I'm pleased to be in a position to stop scum from appearing in magazines like *Women Today.*"

"This meeting, Mr. Davon, may be over but not my employment with *Women Today.* There are courts in this country and I intend to take this matter all the way to the Supreme Court if necessary. A nude of a prominent male star, done in good taste, as this photograph is, is not obscene except in the eye of the beholder." She was furious and allowed it to show. "May I suggest that it is you who are seeing obscenity where none exists."

Everyone stood up at once and within seconds the room was empty except for Jason and Kate, sitting at opposite ends of the highly polished mahogany table.

"Bravo," Jason said quietly. "That was quite a speech."

"And would you believe it was unrehearsed, since I didn't think it would come to this," she said wanly.

"You should have known it would," he said without malice.

"Well, you certainly didn't do anything to stop it."

"You didn't expect me to, did you?"

She looked at him for a long time. "Yes, I did," she said slowly. "As a matter of fact, I really thought you would."

"Why?"

"Because you know I'm right and it's a sensational gimmick and will do the trick."

"It might," he said thoughtfully.

"It will!" Kate became defiant. "You know it will."

Looking at her now, he was reminded of the first time he'd seen her, plotting out the promotion for her book with her agent. She was as insecure now as she had been then, pretending an air of assurance that was hard for her to maintain. He cleared his throat, putting the memory aside.

"Well, it won't be long before we know," he said, looking away from her.

Suddenly Kate was angry. "You really are quite a dreadful man, Jason," she said deliberately, "you have no loyalties, no feelings, no gratitude or respect for anyone, do you?"

"I don't like your tone, Kate." He was getting angry, too. "What you've never understood is that I am first and foremost a businessman. I never allow feelings to cloud my judgments. I loathe people who do. Furthermore I don't like to be outsmarted in business." He emphasized the last word and Kate felt uncomfortable but he continued before she could figure out what he was trying to say. "Had you presented me with this project, had you consulted me, it would have been a different matter. As it is, I like to keep my options open." He paused briefly. "Will it work? Are you right? Only time will tell."

"Would you have approved of it?" She felt contrite. She should have realized that by presenting the idea for the male nude as a boon to the magazine, she probably could have convinced Jason.

"I don't see any reason to speculate at this late stage."

"Well, I'm going to fight the board's decision."

"I think you should."

They both stood up. She was thinner than ever, her face pinched with worry and uncertainty. She looked at him briefly and he saw the dreadful need in her eyes. Jason was tempted to take her in his arms and console her, but he was not going to give in. He was a master at covering his emotions. They walked to the elevator and Jason pressed the button.

"Are you all right?" he asked softly.

"I don't know," she answered honestly.

"Where are you going?"

"I don't know."

"My car is downstairs if you'd like Lee to drive you."

"No, thanks," she answered, and at that moment the elevator arrived and she stepped in.

As Kate walked out into the cold, clear November day she stood for a long time wondering what she should do. People rushed past her and now, alone on the street, the full impact of having been fired hit her. For the first time since coming to New York she had no job, no office to go to, no meetings, no deadlines, no plans. To all intents and purposes, she had no future.

She started walking uptown slowly. It occurred to her that in all the years she had been in the city, she had never once taken a leisurely walk through Central Park. She entered the park at Columbus Circle. She was amazed at its beauty and marveled at the loveliness of the ponds, the placement of rocks, the curving paths and the little bridges. There were few people sitting around, since it was quite cold. The silence was soothing and for a while her mind felt rested.

A couple huddled in a passionate embrace made her pause. The girl had flowing blond hair and the young man was tall and dark. Chuck and Betsy came to mind immediately, and the thought of them jolted her. Briefly she tried to rekindle the feelings of triumph she had felt all the months when she had thought of their reactions to the Christmas issue of *Women Today*. She was sure it would destroy Chuck. His reputation could not withstand another scandal. But now, as she quickened her pace, a feeling of uncertainty overtook her. She was suddenly not sure the centerfold would really reverse the downward trend of *Women Today*.

She looked around for an exit. She wanted to get home. She had to do something about hiring a lawyer to counter the board's decision about her employment. Ed Smilow would be the choice, she decided. She had known him since her first days at *Women Today*. He had been a staff lawyer for Reid Publications. Then he joined a prestigious law firm and had risen rapidly and was now one of the top corporate lawyers in the city. She had consulted him on occasion about private matters and he had negotiated her last contract with the magazine. He knew the inner machinations of the Reid empire and could tackle it on its own level.

"It's Kate Johnson," she said with authority when his secretary answered the phone. "Is Mr. Smilow in?"

"Oh, Miss Johnson." The girl obviously knew who she was and Kate gained confidence from the recognition. "He's away for the Thanksgiving holiday."

"Where did he go?" Kate's voice faltered. "Can you reach him? It's very urgent."

"He's in Switzerland skiing."

"Can you get a message to him that I want to talk to him? It can't wait."

"I'll try and I'll call you back."

Kate gave the girl her home number. "Call back in any event, would you?"

When she hung up the phone her hand was shaking and her palm was wet. She began to undress but she could barely unbutton her blouse. I have to get hold of myself, she kept thinking. Going to pieces at this point would be the worst thing I could do. Suddenly she remembered the tranquilizers prescribed by Dr. Simon. She took the bottle out of the bathroom cabinet. There were only six pills left. She took two and swallowed them quickly.

Dressed in a long bathrobe, she went into the living room and started pacing furiously up and down the room. She had to get out of town for a few days. Tar had invited her up for Thanksgiving dinner, expecting her in Massachusetts later in the week. Now she decided she would call and tell him she would arrive earlier. Belinda and Robert were coming from London, where Belinda had been attending the London School of Economics and Robert had a job with one of Jason's magazines.

For a minute she felt better. Being with Tar, Belinda, and Robert would be nice. She had met Robert at Belinda's graduation and was enormously impressed with him. Tar had behaved well, even though Kate suspected that Belinda had told him some of what had happened when she was last in New York. But, typically, Tar asked no questions, made no recriminations. He was the same warm, friendly, trustworthy man he always was. They resumed their relationship, although there was a difference. They had to try harder to be natural with each other. He still made no demands and no declarations but Kate felt that time was running out and she knew she would have to make a decision about her feelings for Tar. The similarities between Jason and Tar never ceased to amaze her, although each used a totally different approach. With both men, the unspoken was louder than any words.

Kate looked at her watch. Only a few minutes had gone by since she'd called Ed's office. As much as she wanted to talk to Tar, she was afraid to use the phone for fear of missing the call from Ed's secretary. She was also acutely aware that no one from her office had called her. By now they all must have heard about her being fired. She felt deeply hurt and wondered if they were gloating. Allyson, she decided, would probably be made temporary editor in chief, and Carol would be moved up to a senior position. The thought distressed her.

The pills were not having any effect and Kate decided to take two more. She swallowed them and then took the remaining two, hoping to speed up the process.

She was dozing on the living-room couch when the phone rang.

The young woman from Ed's office informed her that she had reached the hotel where Ed was staying but he was out for the evening and was not expected back till very late. "But I did leave a message that you wanted to speak to him and I gave him the number where he could reach you."

When she hung up Kate's mind began to race furiously. She had to find another lawyer. She simply could not wait. Mentally she ran down the list of lawyers she knew but all the likely ones were connected with Jason Reid or Reid Publications. She thought again of calling Tar but felt too tired. She thought of Ben. He probably couldn't suggest a lawyer but it would be good talking to him. He'd surely understand.

She poured herself a scotch and gulped it down. Refilling the glass, she lay down on the couch again and dialed Ben's number.

"Kate." Ben's voice sounded as if it were coming from a distance.

She wanted to ask him to speak up when she heard him call her name again. It was now clearer.

Suddenly she felt herself being pulled up and she opened her eyes. Ben was holding her up and wiping her face with a cold, damp cloth.

"What are you doing?" she asked, and realized her words were slurred. Her mouth felt dry, her tongue heavy.

"You idiot," Ben said angrily as he sat her up on the sofa, propping pillows behind her.

She looked around and the room seemed to be whirling and it took several seconds before her eyes cleared and the spinning sensation stopped.

"What happened?" she asked again. This time she spoke more naturally.

"Well, I'd say you're a sore loser," he quipped, and Kate could see he was relieved.

She had called Ben, she now remembered, and she had heard him answer the phone. After that it all went blank.

"I must have fainted," she said incredulously. "I don't ever remember passing out in all my life."

"Honey, you didn't faint, you took an overdose of pills and stupidly drank some liquor and that will do it every time."

"Ben." Kate's voice rose in indignation. "You don't really think I'd try to commit . . ." She couldn't even finish the sentence.

"Well, Katie, to the untrained eye of a friend, seeing an empty bottle of pills in the bathroom and smelling liquor on your breath would lead me to say that you tried to end it all just because you lost your job."

"I feel sick," Kate said, ignoring his last remark as she got up. Ben caught her before she fell and helped her to the bathroom.

332

When she reentered her bedroom, she saw that Ben had pulled down the covers and she got into bed, grateful for his thoughtfulness.

"Would you like some strong tea?"

She nodded and closed her eyes. Had she subconsciously tried to kill herself because she had been fired? The thought upset her. She wasn't a quitter. It had all been a freakish accident.

"How did you get here?" she asked when Ben came back with her tea.

"You called me, remember? Well, I answered the phone, heard your voice, and then there was a silence and I heard the phone fall. I ran out of the apartment and as I was waiting for a cab I saw the headlines of the afternoon papers about your being fired. It all clicked. That driver must have thought I was a nut."

"Headlines?" Kate said with awe.

"Every afternoon paper has it in big bold black letters. 'Wonder Woman Kate Johnson of *Women Today* Fired by Reid Publications.'" He shrugged. "But you shouldn't have done it, Kate."

"Ben, I didn't do anything. There were only six pills in the bottle and I had one, maybe two drinks, and I didn't have even those with any thought of killing myself. I just couldn't relax."

"If you say so." Ben willingly dropped the subject. "Wanna tell me what happened at work?"

"Not really," she said, feeling exhausted. "All I know is that for the first time since I was seventeen, I don't have a job." Putting the thought into words suddenly made it a reality and she felt a terror she had never known before. "Ben," she whispered frantically, "Ben, what do I do now? Oh, my God, Ben, what happens now?"

"You drink your tea and rest for a while," he said with authority. "I'll sit in the living room and when you get up we'll talk about it. Although, offhand, I'd say you pick yourself up and leave the city for a few days." He got up and Kate grabbed his arm.

"Please don't leave me alone," she pleaded, "stay and talk to me."

He pulled up a small armchair and sank into it, lighting a cigarette.

They sat in silence.

"Ben," Kate said after a while, "tell me about Chuck and Betsy."

"What's to tell?"

"What kind of people are they?"

"He's the lowest form of humanity, totally evil, completely amoral. Betsy is simply a sick girl who isn't very bright, power hungry, a lesbian who's also a namefucker. She hates men, couldn't begin to have a relationship with one, and Chuck, who couldn't get it up for anyone, is a perfect match for her."

Kate's face grew red with embarrassment. "You mean he's really impotent?"

"Oh, Katie, you're really unbelievable. You screw around with a guy for months and . . ." He began to laugh but stopped when he saw her expression. "I'm sorry," he said quickly. "That was ugly."

Everyone knew about her and Chuck and everyone knew how sick her relationship with him was. Kate closed her eyes, feeling utterly humiliated.

"You all must have had a great time at my expense." She turned her head away, unable to look at Ben.

"Katie," Ben said gently, "I never laughed at you. I did hurt for you but I couldn't very well say anything. As for the people who run around with the Betsys and Chuck Delanys of the world, believe me, they never laugh at anyone. They're too sick to know anyone else exists and are convinced that their way of life is the norm. They spend their lives pretending the rest of the world is crazy and that's how they survive." He walked over to the bed, lay down beside her, and putting his arm underneath her shoulder, he hugged her. "Try to sleep, Katie. We'll talk again when you get up."

She nestled close to him. "You won't go away, will you?"

She felt drained of all emotions as she drifted into sleep. Her last thought before going under was that she would go up to visit Tar, spend time with Belinda and

Robert, and try to remake her life with them. The thought made her want to cry. That's not what she wanted. She wanted *Women Today*, she wanted to be back at her office as editor in chief—that's all she really cared about.

39

The Thanksgiving dinner was over and everyone was laughing and talking, obviously enjoying one another's company.

Kate sat in a large comfortable wing chair next to the fireplace in Tar's living room and looked at the animated faces of Belinda, Robert, and the eight students whom Tar had invited to his holiday feast. Tar was sitting on the floor, his students around him, and Kate felt like an outsider.

When the guests first arrived and were introduced to her, Kate saw their expressions of interest in who she was. As the evening progressed, however, the conversation took a philosophical turn that she could not follow and that actually bored her. She closed her mind off from what they were saying and concentrated on the young women, including her own daughter. They were completely different from the girls she knew, the girls she spoke to through *Women Today*, the girls who bought her magazine. They were all quite pretty, but there was a carelessness in their dress and confident manner. She looked at Belinda. She was more beautiful than ever and Kate wondered what Belinda thought of *Women Today*. She knew she'd never ask her, knew she wouldn't want to hear her answer. She looked over at Tar. He was talking to the group and they were all listening intently, their intelligent faces filled with admiration. Again Kate tried to listen to what he was saying. He was discussing the merit of truth as a prerequisite to survival. She wanted to get up and leave the room but knew they would misunderstand. She put her head back and tried to look as though she were listening. The thoughts of *Women Today* came back to her immediately. She wondered if Allyson had taken the job of editor in chief and if Jason were again embarked on finding someone else to replace her. Would he possibly give the job to Carol Butler? She was very young, Kate thought indifferently, and was amazed at the lack of emotion these thoughts evoked in her. She felt neither jealousy nor anger.

Since getting on the train to come to Amherst, she felt drained of emotion, as though everything that made her act or react had been wiped away. She was simply a shell devoid of feelings.

"Mom?" Belinda shook Kate lightly and Kate realized she had dozed off. She looked around. The room was now empty except for Tar and Robert, who were clearing the table and putting the room in order.

"I'm sorry, honey," Kate said quickly. "I'm still exhausted." She tried to smile.

"Belinda," Tar said, coming into the living room, "you should have let her sleep." He was truly concerned. "But now that you're awake, how about a brandy or, better still, why don't we open a bottle of champagne and drink to Robert and Belinda?"

"That'll be nice," Kate said, trying to simulate pleasure she did not feel.

"You will come to London for the wedding, won't

337

you, Mom?" Belinda said as she sipped her champagne.

Kate was about to say something about her schedule at work and realized the absurdity of the thought. "Of course I will."

"Tar is giving me a present by bringing Grama and Elie to London," Belinda said happily. "I hope Grama is well enough to travel by then."

Mother and Elie, Kate thought, and felt a twinge of guilt. They had been unable to come to Belinda's graduation because her mother was not well. She thought of them so rarely. But Belinda remembered. Belinda cared and she didn't. Belinda was a complete person and she wasn't. That was the simple fact. Everyone seemed to care about something or somebody. She didn't. For a long time she cared about *Women Today*. Now it had been taken away from her.

"You look all in, Kate," Robert said with concern. "Are you feeling all right?"

Kate looked over at the young man who would soon be her daughter's husband. He was handsome, wealthy, bright, and he loved Belinda. They had a future. They would have children, they would love them, play with them, worry about them, and build a family unit. Would she have wanted that for herself?

"Okay, kids," Tar said as he stood up. "Let's call it a night, shall we?"

When the two of them were alone, Tar came over and sat on a small stool next to Kate's chair.

"Want to tell me about it?"

"There's nothing much to tell," Kate answered. "I worked for *Women Today* for a long time. I built it into one of the most successful magazines. Then it started going down. I did something I thought would revive it. The board didn't agree with me, so they fired me. It's as simple as that."

"What did Jason say?"

"He'll wait for the public's verdict before he'll say anything. Jason believes in always being right, so he won't commit himself," she said without malice. She was simply stating a fact.

"Aren't you angry?"

338

She thought for a minute. "No," she answered, and they both knew she meant it.

Tar watched her closely. By the time she arrived in Amherst, he had already heard the news about her being fired and he was greatly concerned when he drove to the station to meet her. She looked older than he'd remembered, which saddened him. What concerned him more was her lack of emotion, her complete indifference to everything. He had long since given up the thought of their ever having a life together, but his feelings of affection for her were still strong and he hated to see her state of apathy. Something in her seemed to be dead. Now that the magazine had been taken away from her she didn't seem to care about anything. He marveled at his brother's ability to behave as he had. Both Jason and Kate were actually crippled in their own way. They were successful, powerful, envied, and respected by all who did not know them. To Tar they were hollow shells who were emotionally cut off and who would always be. He loved them but, more than that, he pitied them.

"Go on up to bed, Kate," he said gently, standing up. "We'll talk again in the morning."

She stood up obediently and he kissed her warmly. "I'll always be around, you know," he said, and smiled down at her. "For whatever it's worth."

She pressed his hand gratefully. She had loved Tar and now it was over. She wanted to feel a sense of loss, but there was none.

"May I stay for a few days?" She looked up at him questioningly.

"For as long as you like, Kate, you know that."

The weekend passed pleasantly. On the Monday following Thanksgiving, Kate left for New York. Tar, Belinda, and Robert begged her to stay but she felt restless. There was nothing waiting for her in the city, but being away from it was worse. She had to pull herself together, she kept saying to herself. She could not go on living in a vacuum.

Once in the city, Kate called several publishers who had tried to lure her away from *Women Today*. Two of them were away until after the first of the year. The third one did not call her back. She spoke to Ed Smilow and he also suggested they meet after New Year's.

She never left the apartment. She slept a great deal and spent her waking hours looking through back issues of *Women Today*. She fingered each page with care and found herself marveling at the numerous innovations she had made. The hours spent leafing through the magazines were the only ones in which she felt alive; awareness of her accomplishments made it possible for her to get through the day.

Except for Ben, she saw no one. Letty came in every day and Kate asked her to answer the phone and say she was out. There were pitifully few calls.

On Wednesday, while Kate was dozing, she heard Letty answer the phone and a few minutes later the woman came in and said a Mr. Grand had called. Kate felt faint. She wanted to rush to call him back but succeeded in controlling the impulse. Instead she put a call through to Ed Smilow.

He came to the phone immediately.

"Ed, can you check out something for me?" she asked with uncertainty. It was unlike her, but her insecurities were riding high. "Can you find out how *Women Today* is doing, saleswise?"

"You've got to be kidding, Kate." He roared with laughter. "You mean you haven't heard?"

Her heart began to pound. "Heard what?" she asked cautiously.

"You can't find a copy anywhere in the city, or, as far as I understand, in the country. It's a smashing success, the public is clamoring for it, and J.C. is hopping mad at everybody."

"I just had a call from Thomas Grand," Kate said, controlling her excitement. "What do I do?" The question was asked simply but the tone, the texture of her voice changed. "They won't get me back that easily."

"I should hope to tell you," he agreed readily. "You can ask for the sky and they'll give it to you."

"No, I don't think I'll do that." She knew exactly

what she would ask for. "I'll call you later," she said quickly, and hung up.

She didn't want to talk to Thomas Grand. She wanted to talk to Jason. And she wanted Jason to call her. That would be her price. Finally, after all those years, she was truly her own person and she would make Jason admit it. She felt alive again. All the feelings of emptiness, loneliness, not belonging to anyone or anything, were gone. She had *Women Today* again and that was all that mattered.

When Thomas Grand called again, Kate took his call. He hemmed and hawed and finally asked her to come back. "We will obviously take into consideration the mental anguish you suffered the last few days, Kate." He was being humble and she loved it.

"I'll think about it, Mr. Grand, and I'll let you know after the first of the year." She hung up, smiling. Now she only had to wait for Jason to call. He would not have the patience to wait four weeks. She was in her own ball park again, she was calling the shots, and she knew her opponent.

The day went by and there was no call from Jason. Thursday came and went and still he did not call. Her confidence did not falter. When he called she'd make him sweat. She rehearsed the conversation, going through several scenes. Each verbal confrontation had her the winner. She could not lose.

On Friday Jason called. Letty had answered the phone.

"Yes, Jason," Kate said, not hiding her pleasure at hearing his voice.

"You're coming over tonight, aren't you, Kate?" He said it simply and, as always, it was not a question, it was a command. "And don't be late, we've got an awful lot of work to do."

She was too stunned to answer.

"Kate, are you there?" he asked after a minute of silence.

"Yes, Jason, I'm here."

"Good, I'll see you around six." He hung up.

341

The evening started off as all their other evenings had since she'd first come to New York. Kate arrived punctually and Jason greeted her in his study. He was pleased to see her and hugged her warmly.

"You look well, but much too thin," he said as he held her at arm's length. Then he smiled. "I missed you, and I'm glad you're back."

Dinner was pleasant, and Kate was quiet. In her moment of triumph there was no joy. Somehow she had again been reduced to the girl she had been the first time she went to his office at the top of the Dayton *Chronicle* building.

In his study, while drinking coffee, Jason handed her a batch of papers and settled himself in his usual armchair and started sifting through his own documents.

She made no move to look at what he handed her. She simply sat looking at him. Finally, becoming aware of her stare, Jason looked up.

"You're awfully quiet, Katie," he said. "Is anything the matter?"

"Jason, something terrible has happened." She spoke slowly. "I was put into the most dreadful position possible, I was thrown to the dogs by your board of directors while you stood by, and now I'm back and you're behaving as though nothing at all took place."

"What is it you want me to do?" he asked, genuinely astonished. "I told you I'm glad you're back. I really missed you. *Women Today* needs you. I need you. What more do you want?"

"Don't I deserve an apology?" she asked, feeling petty and childish, but she was somehow defensive and could not imagine why.

"For what? You did an unforgivable thing. You betrayed a confidence, a trust. But the worst part of it is you did it for personal revenge. *Women Today* and any benefit it might get from your action was an afterthought."

Kate froze.

"And it was also stupid. You probably gave Delany the biggest boost in a waning career. He was going nowhere fast and now he's a hero."

Kate blanched. "You knew," she whispered.

"Of course I knew," he said offhandedly.

"And you didn't care?" It was all too painful.

"Katie, I'm an old man. Those petty emotions men are supposed to have have been dead a long time." He paused for a moment. "As a matter of fact, my dear, the last time I did feel an emotion resembling jealousy was when I first realized you were having an affair with Tar."

"Oh, Jason." Kate felt she would begin to cry and she could not imagine why. She lowered her eyes, biting her lip, for fear it would start trembling.

Jason looked at her and again remembered the first time she'd sat in his office in Dayton. She still looked fragile but he knew her strength and it was that that never ceased to amaze him and always drew him to her.

He stood up and walked over to her. Raising her, he took her into his arms and held her tight. She clung to him.

"Trust me, Kate," he said, and his voice was low and compelling. "I told you when we first met that I knew more about you than you know about yourself, and I was right. For people like us there are only three things that really count. Work. Success. Power. I have it and I've taught you how to get it. You love it, it's the only thing you really love."

The tears trickled down her cheeks. He was right and she knew it. She could have had love and marriage with Tar and she had thrown it away. She'd had a wild, hysterical romance with Chuck and it had been sick and painful. And she'd had a cool affair with Jason, who was sophisticated and worldly. All three were over except her relationship with Jason, which could go on without luster, without passion, and almost without desire. It was not that Jason did not care for her or that she did not care for him. In a strange way they felt deeply for each other, but their feelings were not those that men and women usually have for each other. It dawned on her now that Tar, subconsciously, loved her because she was an extension of Jason. Chuck had gotten involved with her because she was the successful editor of a powerful magazine and he could use her. Jason cared for her because she'd made *Women Today* the success he wanted it to be. No one had loved her simply as a woman. The thought upset her, yet she knew she would go on with her life as editor in chief of *Women Today* and would continue her relationship with Jason. They would never live with each other, instead they would live next to each other, their lives running in parallel lines and never really meeting except in their insatiable ambitions. He would never be there when she truly needed him, just as she would not be available to him if he ever needed her.

Standing close to Jason, being held by him, she faced the dreadful fact that she was incapable of honest, deep feelings for any man because something in her had died along the way to the top or perhaps had never been there. She also knew that Jason was equally empty inside. They had both sacrificed the basic human feelings most people were endowed with. They were crippled and were using each other as crutches.

But then it struck her that she felt great contentment standing in the circle of his arms. She felt safe and peaceful... and she always felt this way with Jason. It may not be "love," she thought, but it's all I want. She even accepted the fact that it was all the involvement she was capable of accepting from anyone. She also realized that in this they were alike, since this was all *he* was able to give or accept.

Removing herself from Jason's embrace, Kate turned slowly and walked to her seat in the far corner of the room. Automatically she started sifting through the papers Jason had given her when she suddenly remembered his remark about Chuck.

"Did I really help Chuck's career?" she asked.

Jason looked up and smiled. "I'm afraid you did, Katie, but don't worry about it, you'll come up with something that will kill him yet. I have faith in you."

She returned his smile and they looked at each other for a long moment. For the first time, Kate saw that Jason was an old man and for a brief instant she felt sorry for him, but it passed quickly and she settled herself into her seat and began going through material for the next issue of *Women Today*.

ABOUT THE AUTHOR

Coming from an international background, AVIVA HELLMAN was educated in Jerusalem, New York and London. Formerly a model, she was also the first publicity director at *Cosmopolitan* magazine. She worked as a literary agent in television and movie departments, and is currently living in New York and writing novels. She is the author of an earlier novel, *Agency*.

A Special Preview of
the entertaining opening pages of
the provocative new novel by
the author of ASPEN

WHY NOT EVERYTHING
by
Burt Hirschfeld

"Hirschfeld's romp of a book is funny, sad, pointed, crazy in the happiest sense."

Publishers Weekly

Happy endings are out of style.

So says Walter and Walter knows about such meaningful matters. Walter, my husband, is a man of sober single-mindedness, a trait I greatly admired when first we met.

Walter is a committed literary person. That is to say, he reads a great deal, informing his brain with large chunks of knowledge, common and extraordinary. Walter reads history, biography, novels, whodunits, Screw magazine, memoirs, Commentary; whatever comes his way. Walter belongs to seven book clubs, subscribes to twenty-seven periodicals, including the Times Literary Supplement, The New York Review of Books, even Rolling Stone; and Walter loathes rock music. If those big-money quiz shows were still on TV, Walter could win a fortune. And, boy oh boy, could we use the cash.

Personally I prefer movies. Especially the kind they don't make anymore. Old-fashioned pictures with fadeouts, dissolves, halos of light around the faces of the leading women. I like my movie stars to look like movie stars, special, that is. Larger than life, an aristocracy of beauty and talent. What I enjoy most on movies is plenty of kissing, poetic declarations of love and eternal fealty. Also fireworks going off instead of naked men and women fooling around with each other.

Blue movies put lots of strange and unsettling ideas into my head. That makes me nervous. It becomes hard for me to concentrate, harder still to get to sleep at night. Besides, those old pictures always had happy endings, and that's what the world needs more of these days.

Which brings us back to Walter. Walter is a

practical man. He insists sad endings are inevitable and realistic, even if painful. True to life is the way Walter likes his movies, plays and books. "Most people never get what they want," he is fond of saying. I say, "Why shouldn't people get what they want?" Why shouldn't I? Living happily ever after strikes me as a pretty good idea.

Here I am, reasonably pretty. Attractive, at least. Well, I used to be. What I've got is an okay face. My eyes are exotic, sort of. Not exactly Chinese, but heading in that direction. My skin is on the pale side and I have to be careful in the sun and about the kind of makeup I wear. Not that I've been using it often lately. As for my mouth, it doesn't amount to much. Too wide, too much lip. I've always admired girls with thin lips, cool and neat. The kind of mouth Cici Willigan has, a perfect mouth. And then there's my hair, kind of wiry and rebellious. There are times when I let my hair go its own way much of the time. As for my figure, it's good enough. Not what you'd call petite, except in the chest area, but slender, and with a shape. Men used to look at me a lot. Not as much as they looked at Cici, of course, but they looked. Some of them. Some of the time.

I perceived myself as an incomplete puzzle, parts scattered all around. Put them all together and—voilà! key elements still were missing

Give me back my parts! . . .

For too many years I had labored in an arid garden of self-pity that gave up weeds of discouragement in return. A West Side zombie was what I'd become, jailed by bars of my own making. A rising tide of unfocused anger left me flushed, trembling, more and more out of touch with myself and the real world. I wanted desperately to take charge of my life. Change it at least. To get a firm hold on one small segment that would belong only to me. Was that so unreasonable? Was it wrong to do what I wanted to do?

I gave it a great deal of thought and came up with a solution, which I presented to Walter. "I think we should leave the city," I told him one evening.

"Leave the city." Walter had a tendency to repeat what I said.

"Yes. It's awful, living here."

"Where would you like to live?"

"In the suburbs. Long Island, maybe. Or Connecticut. We could buy a house," I ended with an anxious rush.

"Have you forgotten," Walter replied slowly, "I'm out of work?"

I gave that one up and thought about the problem some more. And discovered another answer to my unsettled state and presented it to Walter the following week.

"What would you say if I told you I want to have another baby?" I didn't really mean it. I was all for zero population growth, at least in my own case.

He put aside the book he was reading, assessed me gravely. He frowned. In horror, I assumed. I noticed Walter was showing more gray at the temples. If anything, he had become better looking as he grew older. Not that Walter was old, far from it. Just sliding without protest into middle age.

"Another baby?" he said. "You don't mean it."

"Stevie is almost five years old. Wouldn't it be nice . . . ?"

He shook his head regretfully. "I'm out of work, remember."

Walter's logic was sturdy and unshakable. I needed another, a much sounder plan. It took nearly three weeks of hard thinking before I came up with one.

It was a marvelous idea. Exciting, stimulating, and scared me half to death. I began to quiver and was unable to get warm.

I would get a job. Go to work. Make a career. What an awful idea. I was jumpy, suspicious, exceedingly afraid of the Demanding Demons that I was about to unleash. It was a personalized fear, like the fear of being punished, a night fear trodding heavily into my consciousness. This beast could destroy me.

I found Walter behind the *Collected Poems* of James Wright. I stood erect and cleared my throat, waited for him to pay attention.

"Yes?" he said eventually.

"Suppose I told you I wanted to go back to work?"

"Go back to work."

"Get a job."

"Get a job—you?"

A convulsive shock broke over me. I really meant it. Really wanted to find a job, purposeful and productive work, create a special place for myself in this world. I braced myself for Walter's response, afraid he might mock me, even laugh out loud. Not Walter, that wasn't his way. His eyes glinted and his jaw seemed to square itself, like some terrific TV hero.

"Soon," he said evenly, "I'll be back at work."

No matter what I suggested, it seemed to turn Walter's thoughts back to his own employment situation. Obviously, in his mind, we were inexorably linked up so that any movement at one end of the chain gave off a sour clunking at the other.

Walter had been out of work for nearly a year. We lived off unemployment insurance, food stamps, and had used up almost all of our savings. Not to mention my meager emotional reserves.

"One day runs into another," I said. "It's as if I exist in a fog. What happened to the Libby I once was? I want to do something with my life."

"After six years of marriage, of not working, one does not simply go into the marketplace and announce one's availability. Times change. Skills once in demand no longer are. A new generation of workers is on the scene."

"It can't hurt if I try."

"Who will take care of our son?"

"A housekeeper."

"A good housekeeper will cost more than you're likely to earn."

That sent a chill through me. "There's always day care."

"Not for my son."

"Lots of working mothers . . ."

"I don't think so."

"We could put Steven back in nursery school. Next fall he'll enter kindergarten and—"

"The afternoons. That leaves the afternoons."

"I'll arrange it, Walter."

"I must be frank, I believe you'd be wasting your time."

Had he given his assent? My hopes rose. "Oh, I really need to go to work, to accomplish something, something that's mine alone." I began to weep.

Walter changed his position. Any overt display of emotion made him uneasy. He assumed a wise expression and delivered his all-purpose explanation for my loss of control. "You must be premenstrual."

I gagged on my resentment. "That's not it."

"Check your calendar."

"I already did."

"Then you must be coming down with something."

You bet. A bad case of depression and defeat. "I'm fine," I lied.

"Take two aspirin."

"I'll be all right."

"People don't cry when they're all right."

He brought me two aspirin, one Valium, and a glass of water. The water had a sickly gray cast to it.

"Would you like me to take your temperature?"

"No, thank you."

He kept insisting until I agreed to a trade-off;

I'd get into bed and he'd bring me a cup of hot tea. He sat on the foot of the bed, not wanting to contract my disease, and read to me out of James Wright. Poetry couldn't fix what ailed me. I was tripping along a narrow line searching for dignity, self-respect, tilting crazily toward disaster, at the same time picking at the bare bones of my thoughts. What would it be like to have a job again? To do good work again? To know that somebody depended on me and was willing to pay for what I did, believing that what I contributed was mine alone and special. That made me feel good. Although I knew damn well nobody in his right mind was going to hire me. That's when the shivering started all over again.

The next morning Stevie woke me, yelling that his bed was wet. Stevie, beautiful fruit of my womb, my hope for the future, a four-year-old nag. A raucous reminder of my maternal shortcomings. Okay, kid, you peed in your bed, you can lie in it and suck your thumb. Oh, the guilt . . .

Stevie's relationship with his thumb played havoc with Walter's emotional stability. Walter gave no credence to the sucking instinct or other forms of oral gratification.

"You know what it means?" Walter couldn't bear to give the sucking a name.

"What?" I replied with assumed innocence. There was in me, you see, a niggling quality of character which I detested. Oh, I understood Walter's attitude very well. He perceived the pernicious traces of faggotry in every suck in the same way Tailgunner Joe McCarthy used to see Bolsheviks in every federal closet.

"What's wrong with you?" Walter said it mildly, in complete control of his emotions.

Only two things, I almost answered. My fears and my anxieties. Otherwise mark me down as being in tip-top condition. That comes from the eminent Dr. Xavier D. C. Kiernan, M.D., Ph.D. Former seminarian, former authority on urban affairs, former instructor in Latin at Fordham University. Kiernan, one of the world's foremost dispensers of advice, fancies himself as a laureate among shrinks when what he really is is greatly full of shit. It took many, many painful and expensive sessions for me, to discover that Xavier D. C. Kiernan knows very little about human people.

Question: If I'm so smart, why do I feel so bad?

Next to me, Walter stirred grumpily. Why grumpily, you wonder. When it comes to body language, Walter is a linguist. When it comes to verbal communication, however, Walter suffers from emotional lockjaw. All Walter's feelings have been deposited in a well-guarded cerebral vault. Safety first, and very little interest paid.

"Steven is crying."

"I know."

"You should do something about it."

You do something about it, I wanted to say. Just one morning, you get up first. You make the coffee. You squeeze those damned oranges. You go to Stevie, peel off those clammy, smelly pajamas. Instead I said, "I'll take care of it." Which was kind of funny since I didn't feel capable of taking care of anything. But why let on?

I opened the drapes and sneaked a look outside. The bright sunlight made all the pollutants in the air dance and sparkle, and in the distance the skyline seemed to shimmer. On such a fine morning, a right-minded wife and mother should wake up feeling good. Full of the old get-up-and-go. Instead I felt like a lost and lonely little girl. I doubted I could make it all the way through my life and was terrified by the awful possibility that I might.

"Ah." Walter had the covers up to his chin and his eyes were closed. "What a nice day."

I put on an old flannel robe but it didn't help at all. I was still cold.

"A good day to take Steven to the playground."

Playgrounds and playpens. I'm troubled by anything with bars. "I'll see." I went into the bathroom.

Walter opened his eyes when I came back into the bedroom. "You're old enough to shut the door," he said, right on schedule. Walter believes in lofty principles by which to live, beauty in all things, and privacy in the john. The splash of my pee sets Walter on edge, relatively speaking, that is.

"Next time." I gave him my most conciliatory smile and pulled on my old lavender sweater with the big C.C.N.Y. on it. There were holes in the elbows and the cuffs were frayed, but it was strung with good memories and kept me warm. A really nice sweater.

"You didn't flush."

If it weren't for Walter, how could I get along? I went back into the john and flushed. When I reappeared, Walter nodded his approval.

"You really should take Steven to the park."

"I have a very low opinion of Central Park."

"It's becoming a phobia."

"You may be right."

"Of course, I'm right. You're afraid."

"Afraid, yes. I admit it."

"There's nothing to be afraid of."

"Just muggers, purse-snatchers, rapists . . ."

"Don't exaggerate. It's safe enough during the day."

"That's how much you know."

Walter sat up and tugged· at his T-shirt, which had gathered under his armpits. "What are you trying to say?"

"Last time out some weirdo flashed his pride-and-joy at me."

"His *what?*"

"His ding-dong."

"His penis?"

"That's the word, Walter."

"Is that your idea of a joke?"

"Aired it out and played rub-a-dub-dub . . ."

"In Central Park?"

"In broad daylight so nobody could miss anything."

"In the playground?"

"That was his game."

"What did you do?"

"Do! I didn't do anything. Did you expect me to lend a hand?"

"You could have left."

"I couldn't move. I was paralyzed with fright. The sonofabitch watched me every minute."

"Watched you?"

"Watched me watching him."

"You watched him do it?"

"There was a certain fascination."

"I don't understand you."

"A thing like that can ruin all your fantasies."

"Fantasies. Are you saying you fantasize about things like that?"

"Well, not exactly like that."

"I don't understand you."

"That's what Dr. Kiernan says."

End of discussion. Walter, the great reader, didn't read Freud. He didn't believe in psychiatry. I wasn't sure I did, either. But what else was there?

It required a massive effort on my part not to respond to Stevie's continuing howls, but I managed it. In the kitchen, I made coffee. It was flavored with mother's guilt. Or was it that I simply made lousy coffee?

I was halfway through that first cup when Walter appeared in the doorway. He wore only his underwear and a look of disapproval.

Walter walked into the kitchen, his Fruit of the Loom ass clenched and hardly moving. There was a time when I believed Walter had the most beautiful ass in the world. Either his ass had changed a lot or I had. . . .

Picture me. Huddled up in the lower playground envying Stevie the sand, and shivering. Asking the same old question—What Is Going to Become of Me?

Take a peek at my past glories. Most Likely to Succeed in my class at the Bronx High School of Science; you have to be pretty bright just to get into that place. Magna Cum Laude at City College; a major in math, a minor in psych. Plus courses here and courses there, taken out of sincere intellectual interest or to fill in empty spots in my social life, which were many.

Beginning in my second year in high school, I held a variety of jobs. At night, on weekends, on holidays, summers, piling up a wide and somewhat disconnected experience. There must have been a hundred jobs. Some paid well and seemed to promise an unlimited future. Others were ordinary and offered nothing beyond a small paycheck.

Taken in total, it all looked good. Even now it looks good. A background that must inevitably lead to Success. Status. Riches, even. Except it didn't work that way. From High Potential, I had slipped steeply down to Emotional Loser, your everyday West Side schlepp. What happened? Who did it to me? Where did I go wrong?

Why?

Please, God, show me the road back.

A job was the answer. Plunge into some rewarding work. At least a job that paid well. After all, Walter was still without gainful employment and showed no signs of altering the situation. Walter, who had the hots for the printed word like nobody I'd ever known. Not to mention an M.A. from Columbia and a Ph.D. from the University of Chicago, no less. Walter, who had been without a job for the full gestation period, was overdue.

All that was getting born was my disgust and dismay. Walter was getting on my nerves. Do you think I should have left him? Just split with Stevie?

If I really had the nerve, I'd've left them both. Together. That would certainly have made a serious dent in Walter's reading time. Instead, I hung around and took it.

Unemployment insurance, our savings, food stamps; that's what we lived on. Also an occasional loan from Walter's brother, Roger, a completely and utterly despicable, but rich, human being. We also borrowed on Walter's life insurance. Not much; Walter owned only enough insurance to get him a decent burial. Then there were Sybil's CARE packages, which helped in an odd way. Sybil Markson was my mother, but more of Sybil later.

"Libby Pepper!"

I jumped up. Like a sybaritic schoolgirl caught in the midst of some shameful act. Afraid I'd come under attack, I took up a vaguely defensive stance, ready to fight or run. Preferably run.

"Libby, it's been so long!"

Accusation; I was ashamed, anxious to make amends, wishing I had acted in a more considerate fashion. I squinted through the polluted air at the woman who confronted me. The Manhattan vapors cleared long enough for me to make out her features. That *face*. That glorious, unforgettable, perfect face. Carole Cynthia Willigan.

"Cici!" I took an uncertain step in her direction.

She smiled indulgently. "Dear Libby."

Through grade school, high school, even unto that Gothic enclave on Convent Avenue, Cici Willigan had been my dearest, closest, most intimate friend. My only friend, come to think of it. In concert, we had plotted grand strategies meant to carry us to victory over our enemies, as well as other dramatic and rare accomplishments. We had reveled in anticipatory joy over the superb love affairs that would come our way with handsome and tireless sexual adventurers. Not to mention marriages to shamefully rich merchant princes.

"Cici!" I flung myself at her.

"Libby!" She clasped me to her bosom.

She felt great. She smelled great. She let go of me before I was ready to let go of her.

"Four years, Libby. For shame."

"You're right." Boy, did she look terrific.

"You could have phoned, Libby. . . ."

"You're right." A telephone works both ways. Why hadn't she called me? I didn't dare ask.

"I thought about you often, Libby. Wondered what happened to you."

"The usual stuff."

"There was nothing *usual* about the Libby I knew. I'll bet you have your own business by now, rich and incredibly successful. I've been published, you know."

I knew, I knew. All those articles in *Cosmo* and *New York* magazine. "You are a beautiful writer, Cici."

"What kind of work are you doing, Libby? I've got a piece coming up in the Sunday *Times* magazine next week."

"That's fantastic. I—"

"All this time, and you never called even once."

I apologized.

"I understand," she said. "Life fills up. It can become overwhelming. There are just so many hours in a day, days in a week. . . . Good friends should not be apart so much. It isn't right."

"Not right at all."

She sure looked good. She'd always looked good, of course. But not this good. By some magic trick she'd acquired the face of a *Vogue* model and the body of a Hollywood sex kitten. She looked good enough to eat. At once I felt perverted, grotesque, depressed by the dirtiness of my mind. It occurred to me that I had forgotten to comb my hair.

"Still not wearing makeup," Cici said.

"You're not wearing a bra." I blushed and

took in those tight pink hot pants, thigh-high French leather boots, and a lot of flashy rings on her lovely, tapered fingers. Oh, how I envied her those fingers.

"The natural look," she said. "That was always Libby's way."

I felt frumpier than usual.

"The twins," Cici said, with a gesture.

I peered around her. There stood a pair of neat and beautiful miniatures of Cici, watchful, silent, polite. The twins.

"Scottie and Brucie."

One after the other, they offered clean hands in a manly handshake. How Nice to Meet You, each of them said. Mother's Told Us All about You, they said. Compared to the twins, Stevie looked like a savage. "Nice boys," I said, and maneuvered to screen off Stevie from view.

"I," Cici was saying, "am ticketed for lunch with Bella. Do you know Bella? Of course you do. At Tavern on the Green. A series of interviews is what I'm up to. With women who count. The out-front women, breaking new ground for us all, if you know what I mean."

I didn't know what she was talking about, but I wasn't going to say so.

"*Good Housekeeping* is interested," Cici said. "None of your common women's crap shit, these are to be straight-from-the-shoulder pieces. Tell it like it is. Hit 'em where they live. Next week it's Betty, the week after, Gloria. Maybe I can do a story about your career, Libby. From Grand Concourse to Grande Dame. That has a certain ring, don't you think? We must talk about it. The Movement, the Movement, my true passion. What are we if not sisters in blood, tears and oppression?"

I felt as if I were a couple of paragraphs behind, on a cerebral treadmill with no chance to catch up. I didn't have a career. . . .

"Cici . . ."

"Poor Hedda," Cici said.

"Hedda?"

"Hedda is my housekeeper, Hedda Svenson. Beautiful woman but not reliable. Without a sense of time. Do keep an eye on the twins for me, Libby, until Hedda shows. Won't be more than a few minutes. Is that your son over there? Looks a great deal like you, Libby. Darling, you and—what's his name?—your husband, must come to dinner. One night next week, I insist. Let's say seven-thirty on Wednesday. No, that will never do. Next week is a bitch of a week. The week after. Tuesdays are out, all those gallery openings. You must make the rounds with me sometime, all those painters . . . Oh, damn, damn, the week after is a drag, all filled up. Anytime after will do. Tell you what, you call me, sweet? We'll arrange it. You will call? Bye-bye, now . . ."

She swept out of the lower playground and it was as if the sun had suddenly gone out leaving me in a world bare, gray and lifeless. I began to shiver again.

Seeing Cici again brought back all the old hungers, all the thwarted fantasies. The worlds left for others to conquer, the peaks I never attempted to scale. Not trying, that's the Original Sin. Anger and cowardice existed side by side in me, and weirdnesses and shortcomings; giving birth to passivity and inaction. Libby Pepper, a half-person, crippled and incomplete, dealing out duplicity with every breath. . . .

All the old lines of thought, past dreams of glory and achievement came rushing at me. All the victories that were supposed to come my way. None of it had happened.

I had surrendered all my dreams when Walter, the man in my head, became the man in my bed. He had given me what I wanted—a husband, a home of my own, a son. Conflicting inner forces rose up, gave me trouble. Part of me wanted to blame Walter for what had happened to me—or didn't happen. For allowing me to let go of what once I had been, slipping into the soft coma of indecision and inaction. If only Walter were to blame, I could hate him and that might make it easier.

Or was it my mother? Did she encourage me too much to became a wife and a mother, to steer me away from any other kind of life?

Or was it the dream itself that was at fault? Should I have recognized it as empty and false from the start?

Cici had stirred everything up. One look at her said it all loud and clear for me. Cici had all the parts of her life in perfect working order. Husband, children, home, job. She was beautiful. Smart. She had figured life out. She must have all the answers. I would ask for her assistance, sit at her knee and absorb her wisdom. There was only one thing wrong; I didn't even know the questions.

As for me, just a sweet little job would satisfy me. Paying a modest little salary. Nothing pretentious, nothing grand. Some remote corner of the universe where I could lie low and function without much pressure in mild and quiet competence. Something that belonged exclusively to me.

Was that too much to ask for?

I made up my mind to give it a try. When I grow up, I said to myself, I want to be exactly like Cici Willigan.

Fat chance.

Libby decides to go for the brass ring . . . a job, a lover, success and her erotic fantasies fulfilled. She unexpectedly discovers that getting the prize may be less important than winning the battle.

(Read the complete Bantam Book, available July 1st, wherever paperbacks are sold.)